"A fun and witty paranormal romance . . . an entertaining and engrossing read . . . engaging and memorable. Also, the fact that it is a paranormal romance with lots of immortal characters but no undead ones makes it refreshing and unique." —BookLoons

"Book three in this delightful series pours on the romance big-time and adds complications galore. Aisling's never-say-die attitude is mixed with a snarky humor that gives this magical saga extra zing. MacAlister's comic genius really shines through!" —*Romantic Times*

Fire Me Up

"[A] wickedly witty, wildly inventive, and fiendishly fun adventure in the paranormal world." —*Booklist*

"Who knows where she will take us next! . . . [A] fascinating and fun writer." —The Best Reviews

"Fresh, funny, and fabulous . . . *Fire Me Up* will crack you up. With so many intriguing, intelligently drawn, distinctive characters, it is no wonder [Katie MacAlister] is soaring to the top." —A Romance Review

"MacAlister's ability to combine adventure, thrills, passion, and outlandish humor is fast making her a superstar. Unstoppable fun!" —*Romantic Times BOOKclub*

You Slay Me

"Smart, sexy, and laugh-out-loud funny!" —Christine Feehan

"Amusing romantic fantasy. . . . Fans will appreciate this warm, humorous tale that slays readers with laughter." —The Best Reviews *continued . . .*

Katie MacAlister

Playing
with Fire

A Novel of the Silver Dragons

A SIGNET BOOK

SIGNET
Published by New American Library, a division of
Penguin Group (USA) Inc., 375 Hudson Street,
New York, New York 10014, USA
Penguin Group (Canada), 90 Eglinton Avenue East, Suite 700, Toronto,
Ontario M4P 2Y3, Canada (a division of Pearson Penguin Canada Inc.)
Penguin Books Ltd., 80 Strand, London WC2R 0RL, England
Penguin Ireland, 25 St. Stephen's Green, Dublin 2,
Ireland (a division of Penguin Books Ltd.)
Penguin Group (Australia), 250 Camberwell Road, Camberwell, Victoria 3124,
Australia (a division of Pearson Australia Group Pty. Ltd.)
Penguin Books India Pvt. Ltd., 11 Community Centre, Panchsheel Park,
New Delhi - 110 017, India
Penguin Group (NZ), 67 Apollo Drive, Rosedale, North Shore 0632,
New Zealand (a division of Pearson New Zealand Ltd.)
Penguin Books (South Africa) (Pty.) Ltd., 24 Sturdee Avenue,
Rosebank, Johannesburg 2196, South Africa

Penguin Books Ltd., Registered Offices:
80 Strand, London WC2R 0RL, England

First published by Signet, an imprint of New American Library,
a division of Penguin Group (USA) Inc.

ISBN-13: 978-0-7394-9666-4

PUBLISHER'S NOTE
This is a work of fiction. Names, characters, places, and incidents either are
the product of the author's imagination or are used fictitiously, and any resemblance to actual persons, living or dead, business establishments, events, or
locales is entirely coincidental.

The publisher does not have any control over and does not assume any
responsibility for author or third-party Web sites or their content.

I am profoundly grateful to all the readers who have taken the time to let me know how much they've enjoyed visiting my Otherworld, and I am especially appreciative of those people who've pleaded for books featuring the silver dragons. This first silver dragon novel is dedicated to all those dragon fans, with the hope that they enjoy seeing Gabriel through a new pair of eyes.

Chapter One

"Good twin calling evil twin. The weasel crows at midnight. How copy?"

"Oh, for mercy's sake . . . I'm busy! Stop sending me silly messages in code! If you have something to say, just say it; otherwise, radio silence, remember?"

"You're no fun anymore. You used to be fun, but lately, I've noticed a change in you. Is it menopause, May?"

Cyrene's question took me aback so strongly, I stopped creeping down the darkened hallway and blinked in dumbfounded surprise at the mirror that hung on the wall opposite.

No reflected figure blinked back at me.

"Are you still having your period? Do you experience hot flashes at night? Are you now growing, or have you at any time in the recent past grown, a mustache?"

"Goddess help me," I murmured to no one in particular, and tried my best to ignore the perky little voice that chirped so happily in my ear as I continued to make my way down to the dark and deserted room. I thought for a moment of just turning off the miniature radio that allowed Cyrene to contact me, but knowledge born of long experience with my twin reminded me of the folly of such an idea.

"Boy, you really are in a grumpy mood if you won't rise to the bait of menopause," she said in a mildly disgruntled voice.

I stopped briefly to admire a beautiful dull–sea green vase that sat in a glass-fronted display case before slipping silently across the room to the door opposite. "That's because it was completely ridiculous. You're older than me, which means you'll be menopausal before me."

"I'm barely older than you. Just a few years, really. A thousand at the most. What are you doing now?"

Trying to keep from going mad, I wanted to say, but I knew better than to do that, too. Cyrene being helpful was survivable. . . . Cyrene hurt, depressed, or unhappy could have dire repercussions that I truly didn't want to contemplate. "I'm in the library, approaching the office. Which could well have extra security, so radio silence from here on out, OK?"

"You said I could help you." The petulance in her voice was potent enough to make my lips tighten.

"You're helping me by guarding the front of the house." I sidled up to the door and gave it a good long look. There were no wards that I could see. I held up my hand, lightly placing my fingers on the wood. Nothing triggered my sensitive danger alarm.

"I'm on the *other* side of the street!"

The doorknob turned easily, the door opening with the slightest whisper, which bespoke attentive care by the house staff. "Gives you a better view."

"In a tree!"

"Height gives you an advantage. Hmm." Across the small room, another lovely antique display case stood, this one lit from within, the yellow light spilling out of the case and casting a pool on the thick carpet beneath it. There were a couple of pieces of object

d'art in the case, but it was the slender glass vial that
sat alone on the center shelf that held my attention.

"Hmm what? I think I'm getting bugs. There are
definitely bugs in this tree. What hmm? Did you find
the thingie?"

"The Liquor Hepatis? Yes. Now, hush. I have to
figure out how this case is protected."

"This is so exciting," Cyrene whispered. "I've never
been a part of one of your jobs before. Although this
watching business is a bit boring, and I don't see that
it's necessary if you said this mage is in England somewhere. I mean, after all, it's a mage!"

The disdain in her voice was evident even over the
tinny radio.

"I never did understand what you have against
mages. They're just people like everyone else," I murmured as I eyeballed the mundane electronic alarm.

"Oh, they think they're so high and mighty with
their arcane magic and deep, dark secrets of the uni-
verse. Bah. Give me a nice simple elemental spell any
day. Mages are very overrated. I don't see why you
don't just go in and get the thingie."

"Overrated or not, Magoth said this particular mage
was gone, but his staff is here, and not even a mage
would leave something as valuable as an arcanum of
the soul unguarded," I answered, disabling the alarm.
Mages, as a rule, dislike modern security measures,
usually preferring to rely on their own arcane resources, and the owner of the case before me was
no different.

I smiled at the spells woven into the wood itself,
intended to keep intruders out. They had no effect on
me, however, so once I tossed a small, aluminum-
coated piece of cloth over the minute security camera
bolted high in the corner of the room—it wouldn't do

to have images of me recorded for all posterity—I simply opened up the case and reached for the vial.

Something glimmered for a fraction of a second to the left of the Liquor Hepatis. I jerked my hand back, narrowing my eyes at it.

"Did you remember to cover the camera?" Cyrene asked suddenly. "You don't want them seeing you when you decloak."

"I'm not a Klingon bird of prey, Cy," I said absently, scanning the shelf holding the glass vial. There was nothing else visible. Had I seen just a reflection from the vial, perhaps? A bit of light creating a prism from the glass? Or perhaps the mage had done something to the vial that was beyond my experience?

"No, but you can be seen when you do anything requiring concentration. Or so you say—I couldn't see you when you juggled at the party we gave in Marrakech."

"The discussion about you using me as a party trick is going to have to wait for another time," I murmured, shaking my head at my foolish thoughts. The owner of this house might be a mage, but he had a misplaced confidence in his ability to keep his Liquor Hepatis safe. I reached for it again, catching another momentary glimpse of something tantalizingly just out of the range of my vision. *"Agathos daimon!"*

"What?"

"Agathos daimon. It means—"

"Good spirit, yes, I know. I've heard you mutter it often enough. Why you can't swear like any normal person is beyond me. What are you *agathos*ing about, anyway?"

I turned my head to the side, my peripheral vision catching the sight of a small lavender stone box sitting behind the vial. The second I tried to focus on the object, it vanished.

"There's something else here. Something . . . important."

"Important how? Can I come down out of this tree yet? I'm getting eaten alive here."

"No. Stay there until I'm out of the house." I removed the vial, securing it in an inner pocket of my leather bodice as I gave the case another look, but nothing was there. I turned my head again, my fingers groping blindly along the slick glass of the shelf. They closed on a small, cold square just as the lights in the room burst on.

"Agamemnon's tears!" Cyrene squawked in my ear. "Someone's there! There's a car out front and lights just went on in three different rooms—"

"Thanks for the warning," I whispered through my teeth. Voices outside the room heralded someone's imminent approach. I glanced quickly around the room, desperately hunting for a dark corner where I might hide, but the room was far too bright for that.

"I'm sorry! I was picking bugs off my arm and didn't see the car pull up. What's going on? Why are all the lights in the house on? Oh, no—I think one of the men is a mage. He's . . . yes, he's a mage! He's probably the owner! Mayling, you have to get out of there!"

She wasn't telling me anything I didn't know. I leaped to my feet as the doorknob started to turn, jamming a chair underneath it to keep the door from opening.

"Mayling!" Cyrene yelled in my ear, in her excitement using her nickname for me once again.

I ran for the window, praying I could make it outside into the darkness before the door opened. The door burst into a thousand pieces, turned to ash, and drifted slowly to the ground as I jumped onto the table next to the glass.

"Mayling!" Cyrene's bellow was loud enough to

hurt. A man's shape appeared in the doorway, pausing for a moment as he evidently heard my twin.

"Mei Ling!" he cried, running forward, obviously hearing Cyrene but misinterpreting my nickname for a proper name. It wouldn't be the first time that had happened. "It's the thief Mei Ling!"

Instinctively, I shadowed when I heard the men's voices, but the room was too bright to remain hidden. Just as soon as he looked toward the window, the man would see me. I had no choice but to go through the window.

"Agathos daimon," I repeated softly to myself as I put my hands over my head and flung myself through the glass.

"There!" the man cried as pain burst into being all over my body. "She's there! I heard someone say her name! It's the thief Mei Ling on the ledge outside!"

The blessed warm darkness of a late March Greek evening embraced me, making me all but invisible to watchful eyes as I raced down the narrow ledge, shinnying down a pipe to the ground.

"Where are you? Are you all right? *Mayling!*"

"I'm fine. I'm outside the house, but stop yelling or the mage's people will find you," I hissed into the microphone. "Can you get out of the tree without being seen?"

"Oh, thank the gods you're all right. I just about had a heart attack! Yes, I think I can get down. There's a handy branch right . . . oomph!"

Across the street from the elegant villa located in Nea Makri, a small resort town outside of Athens, a black, vaguely human shape fell to the ground. I hurried around the edges of the square, avoiding pools of light from the houses until I reached my twin.

Her face, lit dimly from the lights at the nearest

house, looked up at me as I stopped next to her. "I fell."

"I saw. You all right?"

She nodded, peering at the house as I quickly pulled her to her feet. "What are they yelling? I can't make out the words."

"It's probably nothing but a lot of swearing. Oh, and my nickname. Well, not my nickname—the other name."

"What other name?" she asked as I hurried her away from the house and down the dark side street where we'd left the rental car. "Oh, you mean that Asian thing that someone made up?"

"They made it up because they heard you yelling my nickname in Dresden when I helped the naiad sisterhood get back the icon that was stolen. Fortunately, they were looking for an Asian person and paid no attention to little old me."

A guilty look flitted across her face. "I didn't know that people would think that was your real name. Besides, that was at least ten years ago. Surely they've forgotten that by now?"

"Hardly. The fame of Mei Ling lives on. . . ."

We stopped in front of the car. I was about to pull out the car key but realized with some surprise that I was holding something.

"What's wrong?" she asked as I stared at my hand. "Goddess! You're bleeding! You went through the window?"

"Yes." I unfurled my fingers and stared at . . . nothing.

"We'd better go," she said, taking the key and unlocking the door. "I'll drive. You can slump down so you're less obvious. I know no one can see you when you do your cloaking thing, but they'll see the blood that you're dripping everywhere. It's a good thing you're my twin, or you'd have to go to the hospital."

"If I wasn't your twin, I wouldn't have been in a position to jump through the window in the first place," I answered automatically, tracing out the shape of a small stone box. "Whatever the mage used on this is pretty powerful. I still can't see it."

"See what?" she asked, pausing to peer into my hand. "The cuts? They'll heal in a few minutes."

"I'm not worried about that—I have been stabbed, shot, and nearly disemboweled, and I know full well I'll heal up quickly enough. It's this," I said, ducking as Cyrene shoved me into the car.

"What, exactly?" she asked, gunning the engine. "Hotel?"

"Yes, please. It's a box. Look at it from the corner of your eye."

"I can't see anything when I'm driving—oh! It's a box!" she exclaimed, her gaze flickering between my hand and the street.

"I think it's crystal. I think—" My fingers, which had been stroking the invisible box, must have pressed a small, hidden switch, for suddenly my soul sang. I felt rather than saw a luminous golden glow radiating from the box, a beautiful light of such wondrous beauty, it seemed to fill me with happiness.

Cyrene swore and slammed on the brakes, jerking the car onto a thankfully empty sidewalk, her eyes huge.

I stared down in astonishment at the source of the unseen but still tangible ethereal glow.

"What the—what is that? Gracious goddess, it's . . . it's . . ."

"It's quintessence," I said, breathing heavily as I allowed the glittering brilliance to sink deep into my bones.

"The what now?"

"Quintessence. The fifth element."

Slowly, I closed the lid of the box, the light ending with an abruptness that left my soul weeping.

"Like the movie, you mean? With Bruce Willis?"

"What?" It took a moment for her words to penetrate the fog that seemed to settle over me with the loss of the light. "No, not that. That's just Hollywood. The fifth element is something alchemists strive to find. It's the essential presence."

"Essential presence of what?" she asked, carefully pulling back onto the road, but quickly pulling over again when police cars burst out of a cross street, sirens wailing and lights flashing.

"Everything. It's the above and below. The embodiment of that force we call life. It's the purest essence of . . . being."

"Is it valuable?" Cyrene asked, a calculating expression stealing across her face.

My fingers tightened around the box. "Priceless. Beyond priceless. Invaluable. Any alchemist would kill to have it."

"Hmm."

I knew what she was thinking. Cyrene had expensive tastes, and no practical ability to save money. I was sure she was going to suggest putting the quintessence up for bid, but that was something I couldn't allow. "No," I said.

Her lips, recently plumped and now shaded a delicate pink, pouted in a manner that I knew made grown men swoon. "Why not? I bet we could get a lot for it."

"For one, it's not mine." I stroked the bumpy crystal lid with worshipful fingers.

"Well, I know Magoth will want it, but that's not what he sent you there to get, right? So he doesn't need to know we have it."

I shook my head. "If Magoth thinks I was even *near* a quintessence . . . well, the phrase 'hell hath no fury like a demon lord denied' charges immediately to mind. I can't begin to describe the horrible things he'd do to me to get it. And to you, for that matter."

She shot me a quick glance as we drove through the city to the commercial center, where our hotel was located. "Me? A demon lord can't do anything to me. I'm immortal!"

"So am I, and he could snuff me out as easily as a candle flame."

"I can't believe you never learned this, but demon lords can't kill elemental beings, naiads included," she said with gentle chastisement. "Everyone knows that."

"So the lore goes, but do you seriously doubt you could escape Magoth's wrath?"

"Er . . ." She thought about it for a moment, her lips thinning. "No."

"I didn't think so. No, dear twin, this little box is not going to Magoth . . . and we're not going to sell it. There's nothing else for it—I'm just going to have to return it to the mage."

"It seems such a pity," she said, pulling into the underground parking lot that sat beneath our modest hotel. "Maybe he won't know it's gone. I think you should just hold on to it for a bit and see if he even notices that you have it."

"Did you give up morals along with your common sense?" I asked.

Cyrene parked the car, turning to me with an exaggerated roll of her eyes. "My morals are just fine, and you can stop making that face at me. I just think we should talk this over a bit. It's invisible, so maybe the mage has forgotten about it."

I leaned forward until I could peer directly into her blue eyes. "Priceless, Cyrene. Literally . . . priceless."

Avarice lit her face for a moment.

"Even if I was the sort of person to steal something for myself—and I'll reiterate the fact that I'm not, since you seem to conveniently forget that whenever temptation raises its head—there's no way I'd keep this. It's just too valuable. That mage is going to move heaven and earth to get it back, and frankly, I could do without having anyone else after my head."

She sighed and got out of the car. "You take life too seriously. We definitely need to work on getting you a sense of humor, not to mention a sense of fun!"

"There is little time for fun when you have my job. And speaking of that, I wonder what the mage will do since his people heard my name," I said, slowly getting out of the car. My skin was hot and tight at spots where dried blood pulled at it. The cuts I'd received going through the glass were mostly healed, but I still looked like hell.

She spun around, her hand at her mouth. "Oh, May! I'm sorry! I didn't think of that—do you think they'll connect Mei Ling with you?"

I let the corner of one side of my mouth curl into a rueful smile. "I don't see how they can. They didn't get a good look at me, and they think it was Mei Ling, infamous international cat burglar, and not a simple doppelganger from California."

She grimaced. "Me and my big mouth."

"Oh, it's not that bad—it means less attention on me if everyone is looking for an Asian woman. Ugh. I can't go into the hotel like this. I'll shadow walk to my room. Will you be OK?"

She'd had a century to practice the long-suffering look she bestowed upon me, but my lips twitched at it nonetheless. "I'm not inept, May! I am perfectly capable of entering a hotel and making my way to my room without encountering any assassins, thugs, anarchists, or muggers, thank you."

"Sorry," I said, contritely.

"Honestly! You treat me like I'm the child and you're the parent, when it's the other way round. I'm almost twelve hundred years old, you know! Just because I need a little help now and again doesn't mean I can't do *anything* without you. . . ."

She marched off to the elevator with an indignant twitch of her shoulders. I followed more slowly, avoiding the overhead lights and taking the less-used stairs as a question danced elusively in my mind.

How on earth was I going to get the quintessence back to the mage without being caught?

Chapter Two

"Good morning. Is Magoth in?"

"Yes." The female demon looked up from its laptop, using a wicked-looking stiletto to poke a strand of errant blond hair back into an otherwise tidy French twist, all the while eyeing me with obvious disdain. "You're not a demon."

"Er . . . no, I'm not. I'm a doppelganger. I don't believe we've met—I'm May Northcott."

"Sobe," the demon answered, its mouth set in a prim line. "I've never seen a doppelganger. You are a dark being?"

"Not really, no. I'm a twin, the shadow image of a normal person. Well, not a mortal—she's a naiad."

"A twin?" Sobe's expression turned even more sour. "How does this happen?"

"Oh, you know, the usual way," I said, trying to be bright and perky. It never worked—I just wasn't a bright and perky sort of person. "Someone decides they want an exact copy of themselves, they invoke a demon lord, sacrifice one of their character traits, and poof! A doppelganger appears, after which there is usually much merrymaking and quite possibly an orgy."

Sobe just looked at me, its lips pursed now. I made a mental note that attempts at humor were wasted on demons.

"I see. What are you doing here if you're a naiad's twin?"

"It's a long story, and one that would probably bore you to tears," I said, not wanting to get into my history with a strange demon. "Let's just leave it at the fact that I do some work for Magoth now and again. How is he today?"

"The master? He laughed. Twice."

I flinched.

Sobe nodded, tapping a couple of keys on the computer with long, rose-tipped fingers. "You don't have an appointment, doppelganger. If you work for him, you must know how he gets when his servants approach him without an appointment."

"I'm expected," I answered airily, trying to quell the bile that inevitably rose within my gut whenever I was summoned before Magoth. He might be the lowest of all the demon lords, but my meetings with him were fraught with . . . well, dread.

"It's your life," Sobe answered with a shrug, returning its attention to the laptop. "What's left of it."

I squared my shoulders, gathering up my strength before I knocked gently on the door that led into a large office. Magoth on the best of days wasn't easy to deal with. . . . A happy Magoth boded ill for everyone.

"Entrez!"

A little shiver ran down my spine as I opened the door. Low, smoky music drifted out of invisible speakers as I negotiated the candlelit narrow hallway that opened into Magoth's living quarters, which he used as his office.

"Ah, May, what a delight to see you again. You look as delicious as ever." Magoth shimmered into view, dressed in a dark blue shirt open three-quarters of the way down his chest, tight black leather pants, and a bullwhip wrapped around his waist.

I cocked an eyebrow at the sight of the whip. "Been watching Indiana Jones movies again?"

His smile was blatantly sexual, right down to the devilish twinkle in his black eyes. "Just indulging myself in a few fantasies. Speaking of which . . ." He threw himself down onto a white leather couch, patting the seat. "Come sit with Papa."

"Are we ever going to be able to do this without sexual harassment?" I asked, primly seating myself on a chair as far away from him as I could get.

"Sweetness," he cooed, rolling over onto his back and giving me a playful look. "Come. And I do mean that literally."

I thinned my lips and stayed put.

"Hey, little girl." He unbuttoned the last few buttons on his shirt and waggled his eyebrows suggestively. "Can I interest you in a piece of candy?"

I lifted my chin.

His fingers drifted down to his waistband as he pouted slightly. "I'm going to think my little loveykins is mad unless she gives her daddy some sugar."

"Oh, for mercy's sake . . . Magoth!" I said, exasperated.

He sighed and propped himself up, his shirt gaping open in a way that allowed me to see his entire masculine chest. As a demon lord, Magoth had the ability to don whatever form he chose, but oddly enough, the one he had used ever since I had been bound to him was his true form—that of a black-haired, black-eyed, incredibly handsome man who unabashedly oozed sexuality. "If I didn't know better, my dear, I'd swear you had no soul. What can a little wicked indulgence hurt?"

" 'Hurt' being the key word," I said, crossing my arms over my stomach and reminding myself that no matter how human he looked, he was still a demon lord.

Magoth propped himself up on one arm, his tight leather pants emphasizing every line of his well-muscled thighs. He smiled. "You don't know you won't like it unless you try it."

I kept my mouth shut, having learned the hard way that Magoth was more than happy to spend hours attempting to seduce me into his arms. The sooner I could get his mind to business, the better.

Magoth's eyes sparkled, a fact I had only a moment to notice before he was suddenly standing before me, having pulled me into his arms. "Why don't you let me show you just how fine the line is between pain and pleasure?" he murmured, his breath cold against my skin as his mouth nibbled a line along my jaw.

One hand slid along my back, his fingers leaving an icy trail that sent shivers up and down my flesh. His eyes promised much, and for a moment, I sagged into him, pulled into an erotic vision of tangled limbs, heated flesh, and pleasure so exquisite it hurt.

"You have so much promise, sweet May, so much to learn, and there is so much I wish to teach you. Let me show you the truth behind that which you can only imagine. Let me bring you to the heights of ecstasy," he murmured against my neck, his fingers dancing lower, following the line of my behind, and nudging my legs apart with his thigh.

His words spun a spell around me, my mind filling with images that simultaneously aroused and repulsed me. "That's it," he urged, supporting me as he backed up to the couch. "Give yourself over to the pleasure. I am a very good lover, my sweet May. You will have no regrets."

The erotic images danced in my brain, seducing me even as his words and caresses did. I fell backwards, sinking into nothingness as his icy fingers skimmed down the buttons of my shirt, parting the material, his head bending over my chest. The cold of his body as he slid himself across me caused my skin to prickle painfully, my nipples hard and sensitive as his bare chest rubbed against them.

"That's it, my darling. Let me have you," he purred against my neck, one hand slipping up between my thighs to part them.

It was his cold touch on the heated center of me that broke the spell he'd so carefully woven. My eyes snapped open as I realized I was a few seconds away from an irreversible step.

"No!" I shouted, shoving him off me as I scrambled to my feet, snatching up my shirt and backing away.

He looked up from where he had fallen on the floor, his face hard for a moment before it softened into a rueful grin. "I almost had you this time."

I said nothing, just buttoned my shirt with hands that shook.

"I get closer and closer each time," he added as he hoisted himself back onto the couch, grimacing slightly as he rearranged the obvious bulge in his pants. "Why don't you make it easier on both of us and give in to the inevitable?"

"I told you the first time you tried to seduce me that I wasn't interested in that sort of a relationship with you," I said after I'd pulled myself together. I picked up my bag and sat down again, more shaken than I wanted to admit. I had a horrible feeling he was right, and sooner or later, he'd complete his conquest of me.

"Would that be so very bad?" he asked, leaning back.

"Stop reading my mind," I said, ignoring the question.

"I can't read minds, my sweet one. But I am very, very good at reading expressions, and yours displays so much delicious righteousness, I cannot wait for the moment when you realize your fall is inevitable," he said with another smile.

I couldn't help myself—I knew that what I was about to do was tantamount to baiting a bull, but I couldn't stop myself from asking. "Why me?" I made a vague gesture. "Why do you want me so badly when there are so many others whom you could have?"

To my surprise, he didn't brush the question off with a slick answer and a leer. He looked thoughtful for a moment, snapping his fingers. A demon appeared, bowing low to him, its gaze lowered as it offered a silver box. Magoth selected a slim brown Russian cigarette from the box, allowed the demon to light it, and then dismissed it with a wave of his hand. "I asked myself the very same question after your twin first brought you to me. As you know, I've sampled her particular wares."

My gaze slid off of him. He knew the rules as well as I did—I didn't discuss Cyrene.

"Thus it would be perfectly reasonable to assume that as I'd had her, I had no reason to taste the pleasures you have to offer . . . and yet, there is something about you, something . . . *unique* . . . that calls to me. It is as if you alone can quench a particular thirst. I find myself intrigued by you."

Uncomfortable, I shifted in my seat, looking just beyond his ear in an attempt to not be caught and held by that knowing gaze. "I'm Cyrene's twin. You know as well as I do that doppelgangers are identical copies of their twins. There is no difference between Cyrene and me—with the exception of the fact that she's a naiad and I'm not, we're absolutely identical."

"No," he said slowly, taking a long drag on the cigarette as his eyes caressed me. "That you are not. And that fascinates me even more. . . ."

I cleared my throat, wishing I'd kept my mouth

shut. A distraction was called for. I sorted through my head for anything to take his mind off a seduction, but came up empty-handed. With nothing to lose, I fell back upon the obvious. "I assume you had a reason for summoning me?"

He was silent for a moment, letting me know that he was allowing the change of subject only because it suited him. "I heard an interesting piece of news this morning."

"I assume it must have been something important for you to have summoned me back to Paris. What is the news?" I asked cautiously, surreptitiously rubbing my arms against the chill in the room. Despite the Parisian spring sun seeping into the room, the air was cold enough for me to see little puffs when I spoke.

His lips twitched. "It seems that a certain individual has put a price on your head."

"Another one? Lovely." I closed my eyes for a moment, my frequent companions of regret, despair, and hopelessness leaving a bitter taste in my mouth.

"Dr. Kostich appears to be very upset at the loss of a precious item, stolen from his home in Greece late last night."

"Dr. Kostich?" The name rang a faint warning bell in my head.

"He is an archimage, one of the most powerful men alive," Magoth said, his voice fat with pleasure as he crossed one leather-clad leg over the other.

"*Agathos daimon,*" I groaned, slumping in the chair when I realized why that name sounded so familiar. I wanted to ask him why he would send me to steal something from an archimage, leader of the committee that ruled the L'au-delà (Otherworld), when he knew the repercussions would be heavy, but the answer was all too clear—Magoth considered the end result worth the risk.

"Yes. It would seem that you have made a very dangerous enemy." His gaze turned calculating. "The price he put on your head was a high one."

I swallowed down a lump in my throat. "Money?"

"Some. A few million dollars," he answered, waving a dismissive hand at the thought of something so mundane. "Along with a benefaction."

My heart sank, my tongue turning to lead as I stammered, "A . . . a benefaction?"

"Yes. Evidently Dr. Kostich doesn't take kindly to people stealing his valuables. He's called out the thief takers, in addition to which he has promised not only a monetary reward, but his services, as well."

Oh, dear goddess. A benefaction—people have died for mages' benefactions. Wars have been fought, lives have been forfeited, countries have changed hands, all at the intercession of a benefaction. And here was this mage—no, *archimage*, the highest of the high— offering not only a couple of million dollars for my capture, but also what amounted to a magic genie willing to grant any wish. "I am so dead," I murmured, my forehead in my hands.

"Fortunately, that is not the case. It does make one wonder, however. . . ." Magoth's eyes narrowed on me as he flicked cigarette ash onto the top part of a skull that had been inverted and turned into an ashtray. "Why would Kostich be quite so upset at the loss of Liquor Hepatis?"

I tried very hard not to fidget, and met his piercing gaze with one I prayed showed nothing but serenity. "I thought Liquor Hepatis was valuable."

He took another deep drag on his cigarette. "It is, my darling, it is. Especially that which Kostich possessed—it was the purest form, the arcanum of the soul. Only a master alchemist can make it, and it takes many years to cure it to the clarity of the liquid I assume you now possess."

There was both a question and a demand in his lightly spoken comment. Silently, I removed the bottle from my inner pocket and rose to give it to him. He took the bottle but, before I could withdraw, grabbed my hand, pulling me onto his lap.

"Stop struggling; your virtue is safe from me. For the moment," he added with a leer before turning over my hand so he could examine my palm.

I shivered at the chill that seemed to seep from his flesh to mine.

"You are hiding something from me," he said in a low, soft voice that would have been beautiful but for the very real undertone of threat.

"I couldn't do that," I answered, trying not to squirm nervously on him. "I'm bound to you. I must follow your orders."

His forefinger traced a curlicue over my left breast. "I can hear your heart racing, sweet May. What is it you fear I will learn?"

"I don't like being held by you," I said, praying the truth of that statement would satisfy him.

"Hmm." His finger brushed along my lips. I turned my head away and tried to escape his hold. To my surprise, he didn't fight to hold me.

"This deception I sense in you is new and fascinating, but I'm afraid I cannot allow it to continue," he said calmly as I shakily gathered up my purse.

"If I had the power to disobey you, do you think I'd be here now?"

A slight smile played about his lips, his eyes half-closed. "You *are* hiding something from me, May Northcott."

I backed up a step at the use of my full name, the

hairs on my arms rising as my brain screamed a warning. Unable to speak another denial, I simply shook my head.

He got to his feet with languid grace, strolling toward me with an expression that might seem pleasant, but which scared the crap out of me. He stroked the curve of my cheek with one finger. "Such a lovely face. You offer such temptation, and yet I believe you truly do not understand what you possess. Ah well, that time will come, and I look forward to introducing you to pleasures you can't even begin to imagine."

"If that's all, I'd better be going," I stammered, backing up toward the door.

"Do you know what I will do if you attempt to keep something from me?" he asked just as I got my hand on the doorknob and was turning it.

I paused, my stomach tightening. "Kill me?"

"Tsk. The image you have of me," he said, pretending disappointment even as his eyes danced with amusement. "Sweet May, I am a lover, not a fighter, as the mortals so quaintly put it. I would not kill you, although I admit that the thought of lessoning you brings me"—he closed his eyes for a moment, breathing deeply—"much pleasure."

I had a momentary image of what his idea of lessoning was. It shook me to my core. No doubt my horror manifested itself in my expression.

Magoth laughed. "Alas, that enjoyment must await another time. But do, I beg of you, keep it in mind as I ask you this question—have you seen something at Dr. Kostich's that I will want?"

I almost sagged with relief at his question. I had been on the verge of admitting everything, figuring I might avoid the heinous fate he had planned if I could bring him the quintessence, but his own choice of words saved me. I lifted my chin, looked him dead in the eye, and said with absolute honesty, "No, I have not seen something that you would want."

He ground out his cigarette on the carpet. "I will rephrase my question—what did you find out about the archimage Kostich?"

"Not much," I answered, my fingers tightening around the doorknob as I sorted through my memories of the previous night for anything of interest. "He seems to favor Greek and Roman antiquities, has two original Renoirs and one fake hanging in a reception room, and possesses a mistaken belief that arcane magic will protect his most valuable objects."

Magoth lit another cigarette, watching the flame on the lighter for a moment before snapping it closed. "Where was the vial?"

"In a case in his study."

"What else was in the case?"

"The only things I saw were a couple of old vases, some gold jewelry that looked to be Etruscan in origin, and a fertility figure."

He was silent for a moment, his eyes hooded, but I knew he was examining me for signs I was lying. My stomach revolted for a moment at the thought of what he'd do if he found out I was picking my words carefully to avoid lying.

"Very well," he said at last. "If you are sure I cannot tempt you to stay and enjoy the gratification that only I can bring you, you may leave."

I stifled the urge to whoop and dance for joy, bowing my head in a show of submission.

"I will have need of you again in a few days, once I transmute this Liquor Hepatis to Balsam of the Soul. Come naked next time, hmm?"

I shot him a startled look.

He grinned. "It was worth a try. Until we meet again, my delectable one."

I inclined my head again, and left the room, collapsing against the door as it closed behind me.

"Still in one piece?" Sobe asked, glancing up from the laptop. The demon looked vaguely surprised, its perfectly shaped eyebrows rising a little. I felt a familiar twinge of irritation that something that wasn't human could look so much better than myself. From all appearances, Sobe was a gorgeous blonde, perfect in every way. "That didn't take long."

I curled my lips in a faint smile and told the demon that I would be back in a few days.

"You'll need to come to Madrid, then. We're leaving for Spain tomorrow," it answered, flipping through an appointment book. "We'll be there for two weeks. After that it's a week in America, and a month in Brazil."

"I'll find you," I said, gathering up the things I'd left in the outer office.

Sobe considered my well-worn duffel bag that I used when traveling, a slightly wistful look in its eyes. "I almost envy you. You get to go places and see things. We travel, but . . ." It shrugged. "We're always limited to the Abaddon side of things, and I never seem to have time to go out and see the mortal world for myself. Where are you going now?"

"Back to Greece."

"Really?" It eyed me with enough interested speculation that I assumed it had somehow listened in to the conversation Magoth and I had.

"My twin is there," I explained, forcing myself to smile. "She wants to have a little vacation, and since Magoth won't need me for a few days, I figure I'm due for some time in the sun."

"I wouldn't have thought that was quite your forte," it said slowly, eyes still speculative. "I didn't think your kind liked the sun."

"Anything is bearable with proper precautions," I said lightly, waggling a bottle of sun block at the demon. I hurried out before it could ask me any more penetrating questions, muttering under my breath as I left the house. Unless a demon lord was very power-ful, he or she could not step foot in the mortal world, although most of them maintained domiciles that had an intrusion into our world, serving as more or less a conduit for their minions. As I skipped down the steps of Magoth's Parisian house, I breathed another sigh of relief, and hunted down a taxi.

Magoth didn't mind his servants going to the trou-ble to summon me via a portal or rip in the fabric of being, but he frowned on them expending any such energy when I wanted to leave. It was up to me to make my own way out of Paris, and although there was a sticky moment when the passport official balked at my lack of proper entrance documentation, eventu-ally I was on a plane headed back to Greece.

". . . so I'm back, still alive, and haven't had any-thing stripped from me, like my soul or brain or any of the other things Magoth will remove if I cross him," I told Cyrene a couple of hours later.

She turned from where she had been looking out the window of my hotel room while I told her of my trip, her face twisted with anguish. "Oh, May, I'm so sorry you had to go through that! I'm just sick to death that I ever agreed to bind you to him! It's just that he was so incredibly handsome, so overwhelm-ingly sexy, and I had no idea—"

I pulled myself up from where I had collapsed ex-haustedly on the bed and held up a hand to interrupt the apology. "I didn't tell you that to make you feel bad. Your sexual thrills aside, I know full well you had no real grasp of what you were agreeing to when Magoth seduced you into creating me, so stop beating yourself up for it. I'm coping well enough, and managing to stay a step ahead of him, so there's no need for you to continue on this martyr kick."

That was true so far, but as my near seduction earlier had proven, the future didn't hold much hope for me. That thought nibbled away at me as Cyrene paced past.

"I will never forget the look on your face when you were created, and Magoth told you that I'd given you to him. I thought my heart would break."

Her distress was very real, as real as the tears rolling down her face.

"Oh, Cy," I said, stopping her to give her the hug she so obviously needed. "I know you weren't to blame for what happened with Magoth. I have never thought you would willingly bind me to him, so you can let go of that guilt."

"But he makes you do things you hate! You have to steal for him, and I know how much that distresses you!"

It took another ten minutes of Cyrene alternately begging my forgiveness (which had been granted many decades ago) and sobbing over what had been done before she managed to dry her eyes and pull herself together enough to hold a conversation.

"May . . ." She fussed with the telephone cord, twirling it around and around as I unpacked my bag.

"Hmm?"

"You remember when I called you last week?"

"Yes. You got terribly excited when I said I was going to Greece. Hold this, would you? I can't find my hand lotion, and the air here is so dry I feel like my skin is going to flake away."

She took the cosmetic bag I held out, biting her lip as I sorted through the mishmash of belongings I'd tossed into my duffel bag. "Do you remember me saying there was something I needed a little help with?"

"Yes," I said again, this time much more cautiously. I plucked a tube of ginger-and-orange hand lotion from the bottom of the bag, applying it while I watched her closely. Her eyes, which offered the only means to tell us apart (hers being a clear blue while mine were blue with a black ring around the edge of the iris), were clearly unhappy . . . and quite obviously avoiding meeting mine. "Oh, Cy," I sighed, sitting down on the edge of the bed. "What sort of trouble are you in now?"

"It's not my fault this time!" she exclaimed, tossing the cosmetic bag down to sit next to me. "I swear to you it isn't! And . . . and I tried, I really *tried* to take care of it myself, because I know how much you dislike having to fix things for me."

I patted the hand that was clutching at mine, a small pit of worry forming in my gut. Cyrene seemed to attract trouble the way dung attracted flies. "I don't mind helping you out when you need it, you know that."

"I know, and I'm so grateful for that. It's why I was excited when you said you were going to Greece on a job—I thought that, at last, here was a chance for me to help you."

"That's very generous of you," I said, giving her another pat before picking up all the clothing I'd tossed out in the hunt for the hand cream. "What exactly is troubling you now?"

She was silent. I glanced over my shoulder to see her face set in stony unhappiness. "I . . . I . . . I need to take a bath!"

I grabbed her arm as she dashed past me toward the bathroom. "Oh, no, you don't. I know all about you and your three-hour-long baths. You're not going to escape something unpleasant by hiding in the tub again."

"I'm a naiad! I can't help it if water makes me feel better."

"You're only going to make things worse if you don't tell me everything," I pointed out, releasing her arm to lean one hip against the low chest of drawers. "Go on, get it over with."

She sighed, her head lowered as she peeked up at me. "I'm . . . I'm being blackmailed."

"Oh, Cy, not again!" I said. "I thought that after the last time—"

"This has nothing to do with that!" she said quickly. "Well . . . not so much. Really, it's barely connected with the unfortunate incident."

"You're the only woman I know who could refer to the act of taking an aquarium hostage as an 'unfortunate incident.' How many fish did you kidnap this time?"

"I didn't!" she protested, a righteous look on her face. "I promised you faithfully after that incident I wouldn't try to free any more ocean mammals, and I haven't, I swear I haven't. It's just that . . . I . . . we might have blown up a couple of helicopters and maybe two or three ships."

My jaw dropped a few inches as I stared at her. "You *what*?"

"They were baby-seal hunters!" she said, crossing her arms over her chest. "Horrible, evil, cruel people who wanted to go out and kill innocent, sweet, furry little baby seals."

"Oh, my god," I said, sliding down the chest of drawers to the floor. "How many people did you kill?"

"May!" she gasped, her face horrified. "No one! What sort of a person do you take me for? We bombed the helicopters and ships when they were empty."

"Well, thank the twelve gods and all their little minions for small miracles," I said, relaxing slightly. "I take it the 'we' you mentioned were your usual cohorts in crime?"

She lifted her chin. "My fellow naiads and I only have the best interests of the planet at our hearts."

"Uh-huh. So who's blackmailing you?" I asked, willing to forgo a lecture on the impropriety of bombing things in order to get to the bottom of the situation.

"I think it was one of the people at the fur processor. Last weekend when I was in London, I received a note saying that there was a film of myself and the other naiads at the airport in Nova Scotia, bombing the helicopters."

I groaned and rubbed my forehead.

"The blackmailer said that unless I give him something, he'll turn the tape and other evidence over to the mundane police."

"Oh, gods." I closed my eyes, imagining the horrible hue and cry that would follow if Cyrene and her fellow naiads were brought to trial in a mortal police court. "What is it exactly the blackmailer wants you to give him?"

She was silent for so long, I opened my eyes again to see what she was doing.

"He wants you," she said, watching me closely.

"Me?" I asked, confused.

"Yes, you. He said he knew you were my doppelganger, and—"

"What?" I interrupted, my mind reeling with shock. "No one knows I'm your doppelganger. No one but Magoth and a few of his demons. How could he have found out?"

"Oh, May . . ." Her lower lip quivered as her eyes filled with tears again.

I sighed and put my arm around her, sitting her down on the bed. "Let's have it from the beginning. What exactly did this blackmailer say?"

"He said he'd been doing a job in Chicago, and he saw you."

"Chicago?" I thought furiously. Four weeks ago Magoth had sent me to Chicago to steal an arcanum— an ancient book detailing some ritual or other used by mages centuries ago. "Magoth sent me there to get an arcanum. I didn't get it, though—it was gone when I got to the oracle's library where it was housed. Did he say who he was working for?"

Cyrene shook her head, sniffing and wiping at her eyes with the back of her hand until I got up and got her a box of tissues. "He just said he was working for a dreadlord."

"Dreadlord?" I frowned in thought. "That's another name for a demon lord, isn't it?"

"I don't know. I think so."

"It's got to be Asmodeus," I said, sliding that piece of the puzzle into place. "Magoth is always going on about how Asmodeus tries to beat him to all the good things. I bet you this blackmailer of yours works for Asmodeus, and he was sent to take the arcanum just like I was. Only he beat me to it. That doesn't explain how he knew I was a doppelganger, though."

"He said he saw you shadow walk."

"Oh, great," I said, my shoulders slumping. Only doppelgangers could shadow walk, and if this demon or whoever it was Asmodeus had hired to steal the arcanum saw me slipping out of the shadows, it wouldn't be impossible for him to put two and two together. "I suppose he followed me back to the hotel?"

"Yes. That was the weekend I was in Chicago for the Wiccan festival. Evidently he saw us when we got together for dinner, and . . . well, you can guess the rest."

"All too easily, yes." My stomach was tight with anger.

Cyrene continued with obvious hesitation. "He said that he could use your services, and that if I didn't get you to agree to do what he asked, he'd see to it that I went to mortal prison. Mayling, I don't want to go to any prison, let alone a horrid mortal one!"

I bit back the urge to tell her she should have thought of that before bombing the helicopters and ships, but I knew it wouldn't do much good. Oh, it was true that Cyrene had stepped over the line—even naiads had to have limits—but it was *my* carelessness in being seen that escalated the situation from an annoyance to something potentially deadly.

"Are you angry with me?" Cyrene asked a few minutes later in a soft little voice.

I clasped my arms around my knees, resting my chin on them. "No, I'm not angry. In a way, it's kind of funny that I'm in so much demand. I wonder if the other doppelgangers get so many requests for their talents."

"I don't know. Could you ask them?" she said, seriously considering my question.

"I haven't ever talked to them, and I doubt if that's a suitable reason to contact any of them," I pointed out gently.

"You don't talk to them?"

I shook my head.

"I can't believe you don't ever talk to them. I'm always in contact with the other naiads."

I was well aware of the fact that the naiads, all forty-eight of them, had banded together in a sisterhood that resembled a sorority more than a collection of elemental spirits, but that was neither here nor there. "There are six doppelgangers in the world, Cy, and we're spread out all over the place, so I'm afraid getting us together isn't very likely. Back to the problem at hand—or one of them—what sort of a deadline did this blackmailer give you?"

"A week. That was three days ago."

"Which gives us four days . . . hmm. I wonder if he knows about the connection to Mei Ling?"

"I don't think so. He'd mention that if he did, wouldn't he?" Her expression held a faint flush of hope.

I sighed again. "I suppose that's one small blessing to be thankful for."

"What are you going to do?" Cyrene asked, watching as I took out a small notebook and made a few notes about the blackmailer.

"Nothing right now. I have to take care of this situation first, then we can decide what to do with your blackmailer. We have a little bit of time to figure out what we'll do."

"All right. I feel much better knowing you're going to take care of things for me," she said with a sincere smile.

"Do you have the original letter he sent you?"

She nodded. "It's in my room."

"If he doesn't have any idea of who I really am, then I don't think we have much to worry about. I'll probably be able to fob him off one way or another. Bring me the letter, and I'll take a look at it a little later. Right now we have to focus on the immediate task at hand. Did you call that holiday rental place for me?" I asked.

She perked up at the change of subject. Cyrene might be a trouble magnet, but she really did have a pure heart, and was quite happy at the thought of being of use to me. "Yes. They said the house is empty now, but people are expected in late tonight or tomorrow."

"Hmm. We'll have to go scout it out and see if the renters have arrived. Let's hope not, because it'll make life so much easier if we can use their gardens to get into Dr. Kostich's." I hoisted myself to my feet and rustled through my bag, pulling out what Cyrene called my cat burglar outfit—black pants, shoes, and shirt, topped with a leather bodice containing several inner pockets, and a small dagger that I wore at my ankle.

"I still don't see why you're going to all this trouble when you could simply pop the quintessence thingie in the mail to Dr. Kostich," Cyrene said as she plopped down on the bed.

I disappeared into the bathroom, one eye on the clock as I quickly changed clothes. "For one thing, I'd never mail something so valuable. You don't seem to understand just how important quintessence is to alchemists—it's the above and below."

"Huh?"

"Everything. It's everything to them, everything they strive for, everything they want to achieve, everything they want to know. It is the living thing that breathes life into all their processes. I didn't actually think it existed until I saw it. Its importance demands that I replace it where I found it."

"Pooh. I say let the mage go without it."

"Cy, you don't seem to understand—this isn't just an ordinary mage. This is Dr. Kostich, the man who runs the entire L'au-delà. And let me tell you, there are a lot of other things I'd rather do than mess with the guy who leads the Otherworld."

"He doesn't rule naiads," she said indignantly. "We're elemental spirits!"

"And naiads are a part of the L'au-delà. Since Kostich heads up the committee that rules it, that means he has the power to affect even you."

"Oh, how bad can he be? He's a mage," she said dismissively. "They're all about arcane magic, and that doesn't affect you or me."

I emerged from the bathroom, tucking my knife into its sheath before donning the leather bodice. "No, it doesn't, but there's something he can do that is very much a problem."

"Oh? What?"

"He has thief takers after me now, Cy."

Her eyes opened wide.

I nodded at her look of horror. "Do you think the mysterious Mei Ling is going to remain so very mysterious with a couple of thief takers on her butt? They'll track me down in less time than it takes you to get dressed unless I get Kostich to call them off."

"I don't quite see how you're going to arrange that," she said, frowning as I lay prone on the floor, reaching under the heavy oak dresser to find the small box I'd taped to its underside.

"That's the easy part. He'll do anything to get the quintessence back, even calling off the thief takers. The hard part . . ." I got to my feet and tucked the precious invisible box away in my bodice. "The hard part is going to be getting to him. He's sure to have tons of security after last night, and I can't trust the quintessence to anyone but him. You know what you have to do?"

"I'm the distraction. I show up at the front door and attract everyone's attention while you slip in the back via the garden connecting to the rental house next door. Then you find Dr. Kostich, give him back the thingie, and assumably have him call off the thief takers." Her face was unhappy for a moment before a sunny smile broke through. "You need me, May. You *really* need my help."

I smiled back. "Kind of mind-boggling, isn't it?"

"Unprecedented, but it won't be the last time, you'll see," she promised, gathering up her things as I headed toward the door. "I'm taking a vow. This blackmail is the last time I will cause you any trouble. From here on out, things are going to change. I'll be the best twin you ever had, see if I'm not!"

It's kind of scary how declarations of that sort come back to haunt you.

Chapter Three

"This is ridiculous. I can't . . . oooph . . . urgh . . . can't get in . . . ow! Stop pulling my hair; that's not going to do any good!"

"Sorry. I was just trying to help." Cyrene stood in the open doorway and frowned at me as I struggled to enter. "I didn't have any problem walking through it. What do you think the matter is?"

"It's . . . warded . . . gah." I gave up trying to shove myself through the ward, panting with exertion.

"Warded? Oh, one of those drawn spells that Summoners and Guardians use? The sisterhood doesn't hold with those."

"There are a lot of other beings in the L'au-delà, Cy. Even if the naiads don't see the use in warding places, most of the rest of the Otherworld does. Diviners, oracles, Guardians—they all use wards. Ow." I stopped and rubbed my head where it had hit the wood of the door. "Why couldn't a mage have taken the house? Arcane magic has no effect on me, but this . . . Someone who really knows wards drew this one. I can't get through it."

"Why can I get through it?" Cyrene asked, puzzled.

"You're not bound to a demon lord," I said succinctly, and backed up a few steps to survey the front of the house. "Why would a rental agency ward a house?"

"To keep dark beings out? Not that you're a dark being, but you work for one . . . which I'm really, really sorry about . . ."

I made an impatient gesture to cut off yet another apology, and examined the windows. "I just don't understand why a rental agency would take that sort of precaution. I wonder if it has something to do with Dr. Kostich living next door? Perhaps he arranged for the wards?"

"That could be," Cyrene said thoughtfully. "Although why would he care about this house?"

I shrugged and continued my examination. The property consisted of a two-story stone house, covered in pink and red flowering bougainvilleas and climbing ivy, flanked on either side by a tall white fence. I eyed a fig tree branch that hung over the fence. "I don't suppose it really matters. I need to check out Dr. Kostich's garden. You stay put while I go take a quick look."

"I'm not going to stay here while you have all the covert fun! I'll go, too."

I gave her a little push back into the house. "Fine, but you don't have to climb the fence with me. Go out to the back garden. Use your flashlight, and don't turn on any lights in case a security guard is doing a drive-by. I'll meet you out back."

Her brow wrinkled. "May . . . what if the people who rented the house show up?"

"It's after midnight, and it's a good hour's drive from the airport, so I think it's safe to say that no one will be arriving here tonight." I grabbed the keys from the front door and tossed them to her. "I guess it's good we borrowed these, given the trouble the wards are posing me. I'll have to return the keys to the rental agency in the morning before they notice they're gone."

It took me a couple of tries to get over the tall fence, but I managed it without damaging much more than my ego. I limped through the back garden, a wonderland of citrus, olive, and fig trees that bordered immaculately groomed lawns, a small swimming pool, and long terraced stretches that led down to the shore. The night air was heavy with the scent of lemon and orange blossoms mingling with the tangy breeze that lifted from the sea a few hundred yards away. It was a tiny bit of paradise, and I paused for a moment, breathing deeply and wishing to the depths of my soul that I could turn my back on everything and live quietly in this beautiful garden.

"Fish pond!" Cyrene squealed, disturbing my thoughts as she hurried off to commune in the ways of the naiads, something that overtook her whenever she was near bodies of freshwater. I sighed for a moment at the fact that I'd never be able to live in such a beautiful spot as this, but cut short the pity party when my watch made an almost imperceptible peep.

"No time for dallying, May," I told myself as I flicked on a penlight and examined the brick fence that divided the property from that of Dr. Kostich. Midway down the fence, a small wooden gate was set into an archway, clearly put there so the neighbors could visit with ease.

"No wards. Hmm. Interesting." Dr. Kostich may have been concerned enough about his neighbors to see to the warding of the house, but he obviously didn't fear intrusion via the gate. There was a small padlock on this side, but it didn't require much finessing at all to open it. I let the padlock drop to the ground as I shook my head at the door. "Just a few arcane protection spells . . . ineffectual at best."

"Totally lame," a male voice agreed behind me.

I shadowed immediately, spinning around to see who had managed to creep up on me unawares.

A large furry black dog gazed at me with its mouth slightly opened, its tail wagging gently in the balmy evening breeze.

I looked around quickly for the dog's owner, but my eyes slowly returned to it as I realized the truth.

"Yup, that's right, you're not seeing things. I'm a demon. Sixth class, if that helps. Whatcha doing?" The demon dog took a step closer to me, snuffled my legs, then tipped its head to the side. "Wow. Doppelganger. I've only seen one other of you guys. I didn't realize there were two of you in Europe."

"There are three of us, actually. One is in France, and one is in Rome," I answered, my gaze trying to pierce the shadows cast by the trees. I didn't see anyone else out there, but if there was a demon here . . . "Who are you, demon?"

"Now, you know, I could refuse to answer that, since you didn't summon me and all, but Ash gets annoyed when I display what she calls bad manners, so I'm going to play nice. Name's Jim. Effrijim, really, but no one calls me that except Aisling when she's really pissy. What's your name?"

"That's not pertinent," I said firmly, thinking as fast as I could. If there was a demon here, someone must have sent it . . . but for what purpose? And who had set the demon to watch the gate? Dr. Kostich? That didn't make any sense—mages could technically summon demons, but I'd never heard of one doing so, not while they had arcane abilities at their fingertips to achieve whatever they wanted. "Who sent you, Effrijim?"

"No one sent me. I'm just doing my walkies," the demon answered, sniffing my legs again. I stepped back, pulling the shadows tighter around me. I knew it would do little good—experienced demons could sometimes sense even those who shadow walked—but it made me feel less open to prying eyes.

"Your . . . walkies?"

"Yeah, you know, walkies. Constitutional. Pinchin' a loaf," it said with a particularly annoying chuckle.

I opened my mouth to point out . . . well, I didn't know what to point out, so many thoughts were tumbling through my mind. Instead I shook my head at my own folly, and with a firm look, asked the demon who its master was.

"Aisling. She's inside, if you want to have a chat with her, although she's a bit cranky because Drake made her come home early from the theater," the demon answered, nodding toward the house. I spun around, alarm skittering down my back at the sight of the house Cyrene had crept through—now aglow with lights.

"*Agathos daimon,*" I swore under my breath, reaching for the switch on the radio pack strapped to my belt. "Psst! Stop swooning over the fish pond and get over here. Carefully! The people who rented the house are here, and . . . and . . . oh, just get over here."

"What? Goddess! I'll be right there," her breathy voice whispered in my ear.

"I didn't realize your master had taken over the house yet," I told the demon named Jim. "I mean her no harm, and I'll leave in a minute, I swear."

"I'm here, I'm here," Cyrene said as she hurried out of the shadowed edge of the lawn. "What happened? I thought you said the people wouldn't come this late at night. Oh! A doggy!"

Jim turned its head and winked at her. "Hiya, babycakes."

Cyrene clapped her hands in delight. "A demon! May, where did you find a demon? Can we keep it? I've always wanted a demon of my own."

"No, you haven't," I told her, pulling her away from where she was patting the demon on its head. "And thank you so much for using my name in front of it. Come on, I have to get you out of here without anyone else seeing you."

"But—" she started to say as I grabbed her wrist and pulled her after me, sticking close to the fence in an attempt to avoid being seen from the house. "But, May—"

"Shh!"

"I wouldn't go that way, if I were you," Jim called out after us.

I gritted my teeth and turned back toward it. It ambled over to us with a raised eyebrow.

"Why not?" I asked.

"Drake takes his protection very seriously," it answered, pausing to scratch at its shoulder. "Pál and István always go over the perimeter before they set the alarms."

I swore under my breath again, spinning around to eye the garden. The opposite side was no use—the house was butted up against a cliff. If we couldn't go out the way I came, there were only two choices—Dr. Kostich's garden, or the beach.

"Beach," I said quickly, doing an about-face as I hauled Cyrene toward the water.

"They set up motion sensors out there this morning," Jim said, following. "In case, ya know, someone tries to get in from the water."

"Who is Drake?" Cyrene asked the demon. "Who are Pál and István?"

"Drake's bodyguards," it answered, laughter visible in its eyes as I did a circle trying to find another way out of the garden. "Drake is a wyvern. Green dragons."

"Dragons!" Cyrene gasped, her eyes widening in delight. "May, did you hear that? Dragons! He must be that dragon who married the Guardian we read about! You know, the one who's a demon lord. Can we—"

"No! OK, new plan. We're both going into Kostich's garden. He only seems to use arcane magic, none of this high-tech stuff the dragons favor," I said with a frown at the demon. It smiled at me. "I'll get you out, and we can resume the plan. OK?"

"Well, all right, but you know, I'm willing to bet that the dragons and this Guardian can help us—" She started to walk toward the house.

"Cy, no!" I said, stopping her. "We don't need help! We'll be OK so long as we stick to the plan."

"Cy, huh?" Jim asked, making me swear at myself for the slip of my tongue.

"It's Cyrene, really. Only May calls me by the abbreviation," she told it.

"Oh, great. Now it knows both our names," I groaned, wanting to bang my head on the brick wall until this farce of an evening ended.

"So?" she asked, rubbing its ears as it leaned into her, groaning with pleasure.

"So now it's going to go back to its master and tell her everything."

"Would I do that?" Jim asked, its eyes closed in bliss.

I frowned at it as it peeked at me.

"Yeah, OK, I would," it said with a laugh. "Guess the only thing you can do to keep me quiet is take me with you."

"For the love of . . . no!"

"Oh, but May!" Cyrene said, patting it on its furry head.

"Absolutely not. We've got enough trouble without having a demon tagging along."

"It could help us!" she protested as I moved over to the door, feeling it again for signs of any magic I might have missed earlier. There was nothing but the arcane spells the mage had bound into the door.

"How can a demon help us?" I asked, hoping to point out the irrationality of her statement.

"Distraction," the demon answered quickly. "You want to get your twin out, right? What could cause more attention than a demon? I drag everyone over to one side of the yard, and bingo! You take the lovely Cyrene out the other side."

"Yes! What a good plan!" she said, nodding vigorously.

"Uh-huh. And who's to say that Jim isn't going to sound an alarm when I'm getting you out of the garden?"

Cyrene's face, filled with hope, fell. Before she could answer, the demon snorted. "Are you kidding? Kostich almost killed Ash last year. There's no way I'm going to do him a favor."

"Then why did your master take a house next to him?" I couldn't help but ask.

"She didn't know until we got here who lived next door." Jim smiled again. "She went all potty mouth when she found out, too, but Drake pointed out she wouldn't have to see Kostich unless she wanted to. You don't have to worry that there's any love lost between Aisling and Kostich."

"There, you see?"

The triumph in Cyrene's voice was an indication that I wasn't going to rid her of this idea without a whole lot more trouble than I was prepared to go through. Rather than argue the situation for the next fifteen minutes—increasing the chances that the dragons would come out to see what was keeping their demon—I gave in to the inevitable, and opened the door to Dr. Kostich's garden.

"Stay back and out of sight until I tell you to cause a distraction," I told the demon, grabbing it by its collar as it nodded. "And so help me, demon, if you betray us, I will hunt you down and—"

"Yeah, yeah, do horrible things to me with a small fruit knife and a couple of nipple clamps. Heard it before, sister," it said, brushing past me to enter the garden.

I was about to order it behind me when a blast of blue-white light exploded in front of me, knocking me backwards against Cyrene. There was little noise, but an intense heat and light that blinded me for a few minutes.

"Agamemnon's balls!" I heard Cyrene exclaim from beneath me. I rolled off her and scrambled to my feet as my vision slowly returned.

"Are you all right?" I asked.

"Yes. Except I'm seeing stars."

"It's from the explosion. It'll pass."

"I think it's more from your head hitting my chin," she said, rubbing her jaw as she got to her knees. She looked up, gasping. "May! The demon!"

I turned to look. I don't know what sort of magic was in the trap that the mage had evidently laid just beyond the gate, but it left the demon's form in flames.

"Help it! It'll die!"

"Demons can't die, you know that," I answered, snatching Cyrene's lightweight jacket to smother the still-burning blue flames. Although there hadn't been much noise, evidently the blast of light was enough to alert members of Kostich's household to a possible intruder, as lights started appearing at the back of the house.

"Help me move it back to the other side before they see us," I hissed, hoisting the demon dog's heavy front end in my arms. Cyrene stumbled over to us, half lifting, half dragging its back end.

I released the dog as soon as it cleared the doorway, quickly closing the gate and using Cy's jacket to tie it shut. "It's not much, but it might fool them into thinking the gate wasn't used. Or at least stall them until we can get out of here. Come on, we'll just have to chance the front fence."

"Mayling!" Cyrene jerked me back to where the inert form of the demon lay. "We can't just leave . . . what did you say its name was?"

"Jim, and yes, we can. It's not going to die, Cyrene. It's a demon."

"But look at it!" she protested, pointing. "It's hurt! Because of us! We can't just abandon it when it's unconscious!"

Smoke curled up from various spots on the demon's body. Blood was smeared across its face, its coat partially singed, the scent of burning hair hanging heavy in the air.

"What if we destroyed its form?" Cyrene asked, kneeling beside it.

"We can't . . . ," I started to say, but stopped. She was right. It was harmed doing something for us, and I couldn't just walk away. "I don't know what we can do, Cy. We can't take it up to the house. The dragons—"

"Are no friends of Dr. Kostich," she interrupted. "Come on. And stop making that face—you may work for a demon lord, but I know you. I created you!

You're not a heartless person, so let's just get this poor demon to its people and then we can leave. All right?"

"Why do I have a feeling you're enjoying this?" I grumbled as I picked up the front half of the dog.

She giggled as she lifted its rear legs. "I have to admit I'm looking forward to seeing real dragons. And famous ones! This Aisling Grey person was the subject of conversation at the Elemental Beings conference last month. It was a very romantic story. She met this wyvern and became a demon lord and then she had something happen to make her a prince of Abaddon . . ."

We were puffing heavily by the time we got the heavy demon to the flagstones marking the edge of the patio area. Cyrene continued to tell me some convoluted story about the demon's master—to be honest, it sounded far too bizarre to be real—but most of my attention was focused on how I was going to explain the situation to strangers, and more important, keep the existence of the quintessence secret. I might have never met any dragons, but their love of treasure was legendary; the quintessence would surely present a temptation they couldn't ignore . . . and one I couldn't let them have.

Chapter Four

"Remember your promise," I reminded Cyrene in a low voice as we set the demon on a chaise longue.

"Which one? Oh! That one." She nodded and made a gesture over her lips. "Locked tight, Mayling."

"Good. I think we're about to have company." I straightened up and tried to adopt an innocent expression as two red-haired men burst out of the house, their body language (not to mention expressions) intimidating. I lifted my hands to show I was unarmed. "Good evening. I assume you are Pál and István?"

"I am Pál," the taller of the two men said, stopping in front of me. He nodded to the stockier man, the one who watched us with hard, suspicious eyes. "He is István. What are you doing here?"

I moved aside so the men could see the body of the demon lying on the chaise. The one named István started and gave a little cry, immediately kneeling down next to the demon. Before I could tell him the demon's form wasn't destroyed, it was just unconscious, the other man jerked me forward, twisting me around so his beefy forearm crushed my windpipe.

"What did you do to Jim?" he growled in my ear.

"Nothing. It was the mage next door—"

"Stop it! Stop hurting her!" Cyrene cried, leaping onto Pál's back in an attempt to pull him off me.

He snarled something in another language, tightening his arm around my neck until large, wavering black spots began to eat at my vision. I struggled desperately for air, both hands clawing at his arm, but it was like he was made of steel.

Cyrene screamed as István pulled her off Pál, flinging her halfway across the patio. She slammed into a glass and metal table, cracking her head on the edge with a horrible gut-wrenching sound, her body falling limp to the ground.

Adrenaline spiked my blood at the sight of my twin lying in a growing pool of her own blood. I twisted away from Pál, but István caught me before I could reach Cyrene. Angling my head, I clamped my teeth over István's arm, biting down and throwing myself backward at the same time. István yelled, slamming his free hand down on my head as I slid out of his grip.

"What's going on out here?" a woman's voice asked. "Who's . . . good god! Is that Jim?"

I swung a metal chair at Pál as he leaped for me, István lunging at the same time. There was a flash of black, and I was slammed up against the stone side of the house, the furious green eyes of a dragon burning straight through to my soul.

"What do you think you are doing?" the dragon asked in a more menacing tone than I'd ever heard from anyone who wasn't a demon lord. Over his shoulder I could see István advancing toward Cyrene's inert form. I didn't have time to explain what had happened to the demon—I knew that bastard would do something more to harm her. Without thinking, I wrapped my hands around the dragon's arms and swung both my legs up to kick him in the chest. He was knocked backward into a couple of chairs, falling with a crash of metal and glass. I raced toward Cyrene, screaming, "If you touch her again, I'll kill you!"

The woman spoke a couple of words, and I stopped, rooted to the ground by a binding ward just a few feet away from Cyrene. István had reached her and was hauling her upward, her head lolling at an unnatural angle. I screamed again and shadowed, slipping out of the ward to leap onto István.

I heard the woman gasp. "Good lord! Did she just disappear—"

Before I could reach István, I was knocked off my feet onto the grass a good ten feet away. I shadowed again, trying to roll out from under my assailant, but the man pinned me down with a knee on my back, his grip on my shoulders pressing me into the grass.

"Stop fighting," he said in my ear. "You will only harm yourself and your friend if you continue this."

"If you hurt her again, I'll—"

"We will not hurt you or her unless you continue to fight. Drake! I have this one. I have promised her no injury will come to the other."

I snarled into the ground as the man named Drake spoke to his men, trying once again to slip out of the grip holding me.

"I will turn you over, but you must not attempt to escape. Drake is overly protective and will not hesitate in destroying you if you make a move toward his mate."

"I don't give a damn about anyone's mate," I said, spitting out blades of grass and a bit of dirt. "Just let me go to my twin. That gorilla broke her neck."

"I am a healer," the man said, removing his knee from my back. "I will see to any ills she has suffered."

I rolled away from him, but he was on me again before I could get up, lying across my chest in a manner that would have been intimate in any other situation.

Eyes of liquid silver bore down into mine, a look so intense it momentarily stripped all thoughts from my mind but one. "Quicksilver," I said without thinking, reaching to touch the glittering mercury eyes that glowed with some inner light.

A foot descended on my hand before I could touch him, painfully grinding it into the ground.

"Release her," the man on top of me growled, glaring at the person who had suddenly appeared next to me.

Reluctantly, the man standing on my arm stepped off. I made a fist and tried to punch his leg, but he stepped out of my way.

Oddly, that seemed to amuse my captor. He smiled, dimples marking his cheeks, mobile, sensitive lips revealing teeth that for some reason reminded me of a wolf.

"We will get up now," he said, his gaze never leaving mine. He had a faint accent I couldn't quite place—it was vaguely singsong, with occasional hints of an Australian twang. Wherever he came from, it left him with a beautifully lyrical voice, the sort of voice that could mesmerize. . . . "You will not try to attack Drake's men or Aisling. Your twin will not be harmed. Do you understand?"

"Perfectly, although I would like to point out that we did not attack them—they attacked us."

He said nothing, but moved off me, being careful to keep hold of my arms. Two other people stood around us, the man who had stomped on my arm, and a woman, both dark haired and gray eyed, and dressed identically in black. The woman held a wicked-looking knife, her eyes glittering angrily at me. I allowed the man to pull me to my feet, but wouldn't let him brush me off. "I must see my twin. She's injured. Badly."

He nodded, and with one hand holding tight to my arm, gestured toward the patio. The two others followed us. I tried to shrug him off and run to Cyrene, but he held firm.

"I will tend to her, do not fear," he said in that beautiful voice as I sank down next to the chaise where she'd been laid. The dragon with green eyes stood at her feet, his face hard and watchful, his arm around an obviously pregnant woman. His two goons stood on the other side, István bleeding profusely from the arm. I smiled at that, but the smile withered away as my gaze dropped to my poor twin.

"Agathos daimon," I gasped, my hands shaking as I reached for her. Her face was deathly white, blood matting the thick, glossy black hair that she wore an inch or so longer than mine.

"Will you allow me?" the silver-eyed man asked.

I didn't want him to touch her, didn't want any of them to have anything more to do with her, but I didn't even know where to begin fixing whatever damage István had done when he'd knocked her into the table.

"I am a healer," he said again, his voice caressing me.

I hesitated a moment, wanting nothing so much as to hide Cyrene from their prying eyes.

"You don't have to worry about Gabriel—he's very good," the pregnant woman said. She must be Aisling Grey, the demon lord who had wed a wyvern. I glanced at her, unsure of what I should do. I couldn't get Cyrene out of there without doing more damage to her, but to trust her to strangers . . .

"He did wonders for me when I was gutted with a sword," Aisling added.

I eyed the man kneeling next to me for a moment. Those beautiful mercurial eyes considered me with calm assurance.

"All right," I said slowly, scooting back a hair to let him have access to Cyrene. "But I'll be watching you."

A slight smile caused his cheek to indent in the beginnings of a dimple. "I would expect nothing else."

"What's going on?" A furry black head was inserted between the man and me. Jim the demon was back on its feet, a shocked look on its face as it peered down at the inert form before us. "What happened to Cyrene?"

"Jim! You're OK?" Aisling asked, hurrying over to it.

"Yeah. Uck, what happened to my coat? Oh, man! That's gonna take forever to grow out!"

"I'm so glad you're not hurt," Aisling said, hugging it. "I thought they'd destroyed your form."

"They?" Jim asked, looking from me to Cyrene before turning back to the woman still hugging him. "You don't think Cyrene and May did this to me, do you?"

"They didn't?" she asked, giving me an odd look.

I didn't pay her too much attention—that was taken up with watching the velvet-tongued healer as he worked over Cyrene.

"Nope."

"We saw them attacking István and Pál," Drake said, nodding toward us. "The one kneeling bit István."

"Hard," István muttered, having taken off his shirt to wrap around the arm in question.

"Really?" Jim's eyebrows rose as it looked back at me. "Nice job, May! I couldn't have done better myself."

"Nice—Jim, are you insane?" Aisling asked, ruffling the fur on the top of its head.

"Naw. But you guys are confused. May and Cyrene weren't attacking anyone. May just wanted to get Cy out of the garden, but I told them about Drake being a gadget freak, so they decided to go out through Kostich's yard. That's where we were nailed . . . or rather, I was. Fires of Abaddon, his arcane traps are downright nasty! He owes me a whole bunch of fur."

"Will she be all right?" I asked the man who was evidently named Gabriel.

He nodded without looking at me, his eyes on Cyrene's face as his fingers manipulated her neck. "She has a superficial cut to the scalp, but you were correct that her neck was broken."

My stomach lurched at his words. Cyrene might be immortal, but there was still such a thing as brain damage. If she didn't get sufficient oxygen and blood to her brain, she would be left in a coma . . . a permanent coma.

"It is a good thing she is a . . ." He glanced at me, his eyes questioning.

"Naiad," I answered.

"Ah. That would explain much. Elemental beings do not cope well with injuries to the head. Their center is in their heart, is it not?"

Cy certainly thought with her heart more than her head, but I wasn't about to admit that to the stranger . . . A thought struck me. I looked more closely at him. Like the other men present, he was dressed in evening clothes of a black jacket and pants, but unlike the others he had a gorgeous silvery vest heavily embroidered with fantastical creatures. His skin was a warm brown, like a very dark tan, but his high cheekbones and narrowed nose pointed to mixed ancestry. The shoulder-length dark brown dreadlocks hinted at some African blood, while the narrow mustache and goatee simply drew the eye to his mouth, which seemed to hold an unholy fascination for me. But there was something else, something exotic about him that I found it hard to pinpoint. . . . "You're a dragon," I said suddenly, the pieces of the puzzle sliding together.

"I am," he said, nodding acknowledgment.

"Gabriel is not just a dragon," the nasty man who stepped on my arm said in a deep voice heavy with an Australian accent. "He is *the* dragon. The silver wyvern."

Wyverns, I knew, were leaders of dragon septs. Great. Now we had gotten ourselves tangled up with not one wyvern, but two. And a demon lord, a demon, and a couple of homicidal bodyguards.

My expression must have shown my feelings, for Gabriel shot me a little smile, saying, "You needn't look quite so wary. I won't bite. Unless you ask me to, of course."

I blinked at him in surprise.

"Did you just flirt with her?" Aisling asked, an interested light in her eyes as her gaze rested on me. "Would you mind . . . I hate to be rude . . . er . . . May, is it?"

I nodded.

"This is always so awkward, but there's really no way around it. What exactly are you? I've never seen anyone who can get out of my binding wards, but you just—*poof!* Disappeared. Then suddenly you were a few feet away."

"Oh, geez, Ash," Jim said, covering its eyes with one paw. "I just can't take you anywhere, can I?"

"What?" she asked, turning to her wyvern. "Stop looking like you all know what May is! You do, don't you? Admit it—you all know, except me! I *hate* that!"

"You've seen her type before, Ash," Jim said, pushing itself forward to look at Cyrene. I shoved it back, not wanting anything else to disturb Gabriel.

"I have? Where? No, wait, let me think. . . ." She sat when Drake gently moved her toward a chair, her face scrunched up as she thought. "Immortal, definitely. But not a naiad, like the woman on the chaise—she's got a definite glimmer to her that May doesn't have. Hmm. She's not bound by wards, and can do that disappearing thing . . ."

"It's called shadow walking," I said, unable to stand any more of her scrutiny. "It is a trait common to doppelgangers."

"Doppelganger!" Aisling said, her eyes wide in surprise. "Wow. I thought you guys were really rare."

"We are," I said, turning back to Cyrene.

"But . . . shadow walking? I've never heard of that. What exactly . . . er . . ."

I stifled a sigh, not really irritated with the woman so much as I was with the whole situation. I hated having to explain my origins. "Doppelgangers are created from their twin. We are identical in every way, but individual beings, and wholly separate from our twins. Because we are literally created from the twin's shadow, we can slip into that form and move amongst people without being seen—except in brightly lit places. We cast no shadow ourselves, and have no reflection. Here endeth the lesson. Is my twin going to live or will she be in a coma?" I asked the question of Gabriel as he sat back on his heels, his eyes intent on Cyrene's face.

Cyrene's chest rose in a deep breath as her eyelids fluttered, a long exhalation of her breath bringing joy to my heart. Her eyes opened, puzzlement evident as she looked first at Gabriel, then at me. "Mayling?" she asked, her voice reedy.

I grasped her hands and squeezed her fingers, relief swamping me as I smiled down at her. "I'm here."

"Mei Ling?" Drake asked, and I froze, my fingers

tightening around Cyrene's until she made a noise of protest. "Mei Ling the cat burglar?"

"Mei Ling?" Gabriel said as well, his warm voice filled with speculation as he considered me with those lovely quicksilver eyes. A smile spread slowly, his dimples becoming evident as amusement filled his eyes. "How propitious."

I released Cyrene's hands, edging away from him. I wanted to bolt, to get us out of there, but Cyrene wasn't in any condition to move yet. "How so?"

His dimples deepened. "You're just the woman I've been looking for."

Chapter Five

" . . . think you'll be just fine here. Jim, get off the bed and let Cyrene have some rest."

"Hey! Belly scratches happenin' here!" the demon protested, its back legs kicking as Cyrene obediently scratched at the hairy stomach.

"Off!" Aisling ordered, pointing to the door. She gave me an apologetic smile as the demon left, muttering under its breath. "You'll have to forgive Jim. I think its nose is a bit out of joint because of all the attention focused on the baby. Is there anything else you need?"

Cyrene, reclining against a mountain of pillows, waved a wan, pale hand. "No, thank you. I'm comfortable, but tired, very, very tired." She punctuated her sentence with a gigantic yawn.

"All right, then. Shout out if you need anything," Aisling said, glancing across the room to where her wyvern stood leaning against the wall, silently watching us. "Drake?"

"We would like to see you downstairs when your twin can spare you," he said to me before walking over to his wife, holding the door open for her.

I didn't bother replying since he clearly was issuing an order, not a request. I simply waited for the door to close behind them before hurrying over to the two windows in the room.

"*Agathos daimon,*" I swore as I tried to open them. They were both warded against dark beings, which meant I wouldn't be able to get out of them.

"What's wrong? Mayling! You're not thinking of leaving?" Cyrene asked.

"Well, I'm not thinking about staying, if that's what's on your mind. We have to get out of here, Cy." I spun around, eyeing the room to consider possible avenues of escape. There wasn't much in the room but a bed, two chairs, a couple of dressers, and two doors—one that led to the hallway, the other to a shared bathroom.

The bathroom!

"Why?" Cyrene asked as I hurried toward it. The window inside it was too small to climb through, but there was another room on the other side of it. Obviously Aisling had warded the windows to this room with the intention of keeping me prisoner, but hope rose within me that she might have forgotten the connecting room's windows.

"Mayling?" Cy's voice followed me as I persuaded the lock on the door to the other room to release, swinging open the door to find myself face-to-face with the healer named Gabriel, who was tending to a shirtless Istvàn.

"Oh! I'm . . . sorry. Just . . . uh . . . carry on," I said lamely, quickly retreating through the bathroom to Cyrene's room before either man could say anything.

I was extremely aware of an amused silver-eyed gaze on me as I backed out.

"May?" Cyrene's brow furrowed. "Whatever is the matter with you? You're beet red!"

"Nothing," I said, locking her door to the bathroom. "Er . . . what was it you asked me a minute ago?"

"Why?" she repeated.

"Why what?"

"Why do we have to get out of here so quickly? That Aisling seems very nice, not like a demon lord at all. I can't wait to tell the sisters that I met her—they'll be thrilled. Do you think she'd give me her autograph?"

"I have no idea, but as nice as she is, those dragons are nothing but trouble. I'll feel much better when we're out of here."

"Oh, I don't know," she said with a dreamy note to her voice, a little smile on her lips as she smoothed out the blanket covering her. "That silver dragon Gabriel is absolutely stunning, don't you think? He has such a nice voice, and those dimples just make me want to pounce on him."

I stared at her for a moment, a strange unhappiness twanging my consciousness at her words. Why shouldn't she find him attractive? I certainly did. But down that path I could not go, so I pushed down the unhappiness, focusing on what was important. "He's also a wyvern, and you and I both know that means trouble. Wyverns are all-powerful, and frankly, they make me nervous."

"I think he liked me, too," she continued, her eyes shining as she gazed at the ceiling. "His hands were so gentle on me, Mayling; you have no idea how wonderful it felt to have him stroking my neck."

Something awfully close to a spike of jealousy stabbed through me. I squashed it mercilessly. I'd never been jealous of Cyrene's romantic interests in the past, and I certainly wasn't about to start.

"How do you feel?" I asked, sitting on the edge of the bed to scrutinize her face. "How do you really feel? Do you think you can walk if I help you?"

The dreamy look left her face, replaced with a frail-looking expression. "Oh, Mayling, you're going to think I'm the most horrid creature ever, but I truly do feel tired. Gabriel said that my body went through so much energy to start the healing process, it might take me a little bit before I'd be back to normal."

I'd been standing right next to her when he said that, but I didn't point that out. I frowned down at my hands, wondering what the best plan would be. Should I trust the dragons and leave Cyrene in their care while I managed the situation with Kostich? My instincts said that she was all right, but she was still very pale, and apparently quite weak. What if she had been permanently damaged by the attack? Would even a healer as competent as the silver wyvern be able to help her?

Those questions and a thousand others chased around in my head as I watched Cyrene drift toward sleep.

"You go see what they want," she murmured, her eyes drooping shut. "More specifically, see what Gabriel wants from you."

My lips tightened at the reminder of his comment earlier. Oh, I knew what he wanted: the same thing every other unconscionable being in the Otherworld wanted from me. I waited until I was sure she was asleep, then squared my shoulders and mentally girded my loins to face the dragons in their den.

"—had no idea that doppelgangers could become invisible like that. That's an incredibly powerful ability. It's no wonder she abuses it, although—oh, May. I'm . . . er . . . this is embarrassing," Aisling said as I entered the room that opened onto the patio, a faint flush pinkening her cheeks. "It seems I'm doomed to put my foot in my mouth around you."

I gave her a little smile. She seemed nice enough, quite pleasant for a demon lord, displaying none of the traits common to Magoth. "Don't let it bother you," I said politely, hesitating at the entrance of the room. Aisling and Drake were sitting together on a sofa, Pál standing in the background, talking quietly with a now-bandaged István.

Gabriel stood leaning against the wall, a glass of red wine in his hand. His dimples deepened slightly as he spotted me, gesturing with the glass to the bar beside me. "May I offer you a beverage, May?"

"Whatever you're having is fine," I said, obediently taking the seat that Aisling waved me to. Behind me, the man and woman who seemed to be accompanying Gabriel took seats. I had a feeling they had chosen their spots with care.

"I don't think that would be wise at all," Gabriel answered with an enigmatic smile, pouring out a glass of a local red wine.

I accepted it, my gaze flickering from him, to Aisling, to the silent but watchful Drake, and back again. Aisling chatted for a few minutes about the pleasant evening and the area we were in. I took a couple of sips of my wine, making noncommittal replies whenever it seemed called for.

"Have we met before?" Aisling suddenly asked, a smile on her lips as she added, "I'm sorry, that came out terribly rude, didn't it? It's just that you look so familiar . . ."

"Louise Brooks," I said, with a half smile of my own.

"I beg your pardon?"

"I look like Louise Brooks. It's the hair, mostly, I think," I said, smoothing my hand over my short bob.

"I like it," Gabriel said to my astonishment. "Your hair is glossy and black, like the wing of a blackbird. You are small like a bird, too."

Momentarily dumbfounded by both the comments

and the warm undertone almost imperceptible in his voice, I was silent for a few seconds before continuing. "Louise was a silent movie star. Cyrene fell in love with the flapper styles of the early 1920s and was a dead ringer for Louise. Thus, when Cyrene created me, I looked like Louise as well. Cy usually wears her hair differently than me, but a couple of months ago she went to a costume party and decided to re-create her flapper look."

"She . . . *created* you?" Aisling asked, looking astounded.

"Yes. Doppelgangers are created when their twin gives up a part of themselves. In Cyrene's case, she sacrificed her common sense in order to create me." My lips tightened. I didn't mind talking about doppelgangers in general, but I was not going to go into any more details about my creation, or subsequent bondage to Magoth.

"That's very interesting," she said. Jim the demon wandered in from the yard, taking up a spot at her feet.

"Are you finished?" Drake asked her.

My stomach tightened uncomfortably at the hard look he turned on me.

"Yes, but you could have made more of an effort to participate in a little polite conversation," she told him, pinching his thigh. "Please forgive him, May. Dragons normally have the most exquisite manners, but for some reason, tonight Drake seems to have misplaced his."

I avoided looking at István. I wasn't feeling guilty about biting him—he had done far, far worse to Cyrene—but that was clearly not going to be a welcome subject of discussion.

"I'm sure you're all tired, so why don't I save everyone from dancing around the issue," I said, wincing at the abruptness of my tone. My eyes went over to where Gabriel had resumed his position. He seemed relaxed enough, but there was a sense of tension surrounding him that seemed oddly out of place, despite the events of the evening. "You want me to do something for you. Why don't you just tell me what it is?"

The humor that seemed so comfortable in Gabriel's eyes faded, the gray in them dulling. He glanced toward Drake. "There is a . . . situation."

Drake's eyes narrowed on me.

Jim pursed its lips.

"What sort of a situation?" I asked, not really wanting to know.

Cicadas chirped in the silence that followed.

Aisling looked from one dragon to the other, sighing and heaving herself over a bit on the couch so she could lean toward me. "Honestly, dragons! Here's the deal, May—Drake is the wyvern of the green dragons."

I nodded.

"His brother was the wyvern-in-training of the black dragons."

"His brother? I didn't think families could be split like that," I said slowly.

"It's a long story, but basically, Drake was claimed by his grandmother's green dragon family, while Kostya, his brother, was in line to take over as wyvern of the black dragons. Only there was a problem with Baltic, the wyvern at the time. You see, the silver dragons were once part of the black dragon family, but they left to form their own sept."

"After several hundred years of abuse by Baltic," Gabriel said, his eyes still dull.

"Baltic didn't want them to be off on their own, and he basically destroyed his own sept trying to get the silver dragons back."

Katie MacAlister

"I see." I wondered what all this had to do with me.

"The few existing black dragons who survived—how many, sweetie?" she interrupted herself to ask Drake.

"Less than ten," he answered, his hand stroking gently on her back.

"The few existing black dragons who survived went into hiding, Drake's brother Kostya included. Because he'd sworn to uphold Baltic's plan to bring the silver dragons back into the fold, you see."

I didn't see, but I wasn't about to slow down the information dump.

"So, long story short—"

"There isn't anything short about your stories," Jim muttered.

"Long story short," Aisling repeated in a louder voice, "Baltic was killed by Kostya, but it was too late—the damage had been done and the sept was destroyed. Kostya went to ground. Later he was kidnapped and held prisoner, although no one seems to know by whom. Drake found him and we rescued him a couple of months ago."

Unbidden, my gaze went to Gabriel. He took a long pull on his drink, then strolled across the room, setting his glass down on the table next to me. His face was shuttered and absolutely expressionless as he looked down on me.

"I take it that this Kostya is making your life hell?" I asked him, dread building within me. I began to see what it was he wanted me for.

"That would be an understatement," he said, turning to look out into the darkness.

I set down my own glass carefully lest I end up snapping the thin stem. "I think I should tell you all that I am not a hit man. I will not kill anyone, let alone a dragon."

"Oh, we don't want you to kill Kostya! He's

Drake's brother, no matter how annoying he may be," Aisling said quickly. "It's the phylactery. We want you to steal it back from him."

"What phylactery?" I asked, my heart sinking. Why was it that people saw me only for my talent, and never for who I truly was?

"Kostya took a phylactery from me. He intends on using it against the silver dragons in an attempt to annex them," Drake said.

"I see," I said again.

"You're Mei Ling, the cat burglar everyone is talking about," Aisling said, her face worried. "You can get the phylactery back for us, can't you?"

I lifted my hand in a vague gesture, unsure of what I wanted to say. With the intention of stalling for a few seconds, I snatched up my glass instead, but the moment the wine hit my tongue, I realized I'd taken Gabriel's glass instead. It was as if I was drinking liquid hellfire.

"*Agathos daimon*!" I yelped, dropping the glass and jumping to my feet as flames burst out around my feet.

"Not me," Aisling said when Drake looked at her. "That fire isn't mine."

Gabriel spun around, his eyes glowing with a sudden light as he watched me stamp out the flames that licked my toes.

"Holy cow," Aisling said, watching me with openmouthed amazement. "Did she just drink what I think she did?"

Gabriel picked the glass up off the floor, running his finger around the now-empty glass, tasting the remnants with an indescribable look as I put out the last of the flames. "Yes."

"Oh, man, two in one year?" Jim asked, an odd expression on its face. "What're the odds?"

"I'm sorry about the rug," I told Aisling, grabbing

a couple of napkins to try to soak up the spilled wine. "I must have grabbed the wrong glass. That's a heck of a drink. What is it?"

I could still taste the heady beverage on my lips, a spicy mix that had a hint of cloves and cinnamon, and a heavy red wine that was blended with something indefinable.

"It's called dragon's blood," Gabriel answered, his eyes glittering brightly as he took a step nearer to me. "Would you like more?"

The man in black who was sitting behind me jumped up and said something in a language I didn't recognize.

Gabriel ignored him, watching me with close attention that left me feeling somewhat flustered. "Um . . . sure. That would be nice."

No one spoke a word as Gabriel took a dusty bottle out from behind the bar, pouring out a glass of wine.

"Thank you," I said, accepting it, uncomfortable with the way everyone was watching me so closely. With nothing else to do, I took a sip of the drink. I was ready for it this time, but even so, the drink roared through me, setting my blood afire with its heat.

"Would you mind if I tried a quick experiment?" Gabriel asked, breaking the silence.

"I suppose not," I said, looking around nervously. Everyone in the room, everyone from the demon dog on down to the two people who sat behind me, watched me with an intensity that made my palms sweat. What on earth was wrong with them all?

"Good." Gabriel held out his hand for me. I accepted it, but rather than releasing me as I expected, he pulled me into an embrace, his body hard against mine as he suddenly kissed me.

I stiffened for a moment, unsure of what I should do. My first instinct was to shadow and break his grip on me, but the feeling of his mouth on mine had a curiously numbing effect on my brain. I couldn't seem to think as his tongue licked the corner of my mouth, urging my lips to part. Without conscious thought, they did so, allowing him entrance. He tasted like the drink, spicy, but with a faint woodsy note that I found very pleasing. His tongue twined around mine for a moment, then suddenly, I was filled with fire—*his* fire! Instinctively, I shadowed, but the fire still filled me, overspilling to spiral around me, its intensity building and building until finally, it burst out of me and spun back around him. It was an exhilarating feeling, one that left me both stunned and incredibly aroused.

"Holy cow!" I heard Aisling exclaim. "She's OK! She's . . . she's . . ."

"A wyvern's mate," Drake said, a note of wonder in his voice.

Their words sank into my head as I put both hands on Gabriel's chest, shoving back hard enough to separate us. I stared up at him, my brain still lost between confusion and a rising passion.

His eyes positively glowed, like lightning trapped in a crystal sphere. "No mate shall be born to any members until a black dragon is accepted as wyvern," he said.

"Pardon?" I asked, trying to pull my wits together.

His arms tightened as I tried to move out of his embrace. "It's a curse. Our sept was cursed by Baltic. Until the day when a black dragon is accepted as a wyvern, no mate will be born to any of its members." His lips curved into a smile, and I found myself watching his mouth, remembering just how delicious he tasted.

Suddenly Gabriel whooped, and scooped me up in his arms, spinning us around in a circle. "But you're a doppelganger, May! You weren't born!"

"I'm not quite . . . I don't understand—" I stammered, confused as to what on earth he was so excited about.

"Good lord," Aisling said, getting to her feet, a huge smile on her face as she hurried over to hug me despite the fact that I was still being held by Gabriel. "You're a wyvern's mate! *Gabriel's* mate! I never thought I'd see the day!"

"Gabriel's . . ." The sentence dribbled off as I looked with astonishment at the man who was beaming at me.

His dimples deepened, his eyes alight with a wicked glint that made me feel like I was drinking dragon's blood again. "A mate at long last. *My* mate."

Oh, gods! *Now* what was I going to do?

Chapter Six

"Mate—"

"Will you please not call me that?" I interrupted, backing away from the silver-eyed dragon who could kiss all semblance of wits right out of my head.

"You are the wyvern's mate," the woman in black said suddenly from behind me, causing me to spin around. I felt trapped, surrounded by all number of threats, and I wanted nothing more than to slip out into the night and find a dark corner to sit and think about what had happened.

Everyone knew that it was impossible to take a dragon's fire and live . . . unless you were a dragon's mate. Wyvern's fire was supposedly more potent than a regular dragon's, and the fact that I'd kissed Gabriel without being burned to a crisp seemed to indicate that there was, in fact, something going on between us. But I was a doppelganger! I'd never heard of one being a wyvern's mate. . . . I shook my head at my foolish thoughts. The question of whether or not a doppelganger could be a mate diminished in importance when there were so many other things claiming my attention.

I took a step toward the woman. "Look . . . er . . . I'm sorry, I don't know your name."

"This is Maata," Gabriel said smoothly, coming forward to do the introductions. "And that is Tipene. They are members of my guard."

"You're obviously an intelligent woman," I told Maata, hoping to make her see reason. "I know this situation appears to indicate one thing, but I assure you that I'm no one's mate. I'm a doppelganger, not human, not an elemental being like Cyrene, not even a spirit. Strictly speaking, I'm made up of shadows."

"You felt like flesh and blood to me." Gabriel was right behind me, the warmth of his body reaching me even though the night air was balmy. A little shiver went up my back as his breath caressed the nape of my neck. For a moment I was reminded of Magoth's repeated seductions, but where he was icy cold, Gabriel radiated heat. "There is no other who could withstand my fire, May. It is a shock to me, too—a joyous one, I assure you, since I never expected to have a mate—but we will explore this new phenomenon together."

I turned slowly and looked at him, really looked at him. His eyes were still bright with an emotion I realized was part sexual interest and part jubilation. But there was something else in his expression, something unyielding that hinted of trouble to come. He was a dragon, a wyvern, a healer, yes, but also a man who was a leader, someone who would quite likely fight to the death to protect his sept. He would be focused, relentless in his pursuit of whatever stirred his interest, and also possessive, since that was reported to be a trait common to all dragons.

An oddly deflated feeling possessed me, a sadness that I couldn't risk experiencing what it would be like to be cherished by such a man. Sooner or later, however, reality would catch up to me, and that would be the end of everything. As much of a temptation as

Gabriel represented, it would be better for us all if I didn't give in and see what a dragon had to offer.

"No," I said simply, with as much kindness as I could. "There is no phenomenon. There is nothing to explore, at least not between us. I will arrange to have Cyrene moved. We will not impose upon your kindness any longer."

I made it across the room, my foot on the stairs before the two bodyguards caught me, one on either arm.

"You are the wyvern's mate," Maata said, her face set. "You cannot reject him."

"Excuse me?" I asked, unable to believe what she said.

"You are his mate. You can't leave."

I looked at the other guard, Tipene, the one who had stepped on my arm. His face was just as impassive as Maata's. "You are the mate," was all he said, just as if that was the end of the discussion.

"Even if a doppelganger could be a mate, and even if I was that doppelganger, it doesn't matter. I can't stay."

"Let her go," Gabriel ordered. As soon as they released my arms, I twisted around to face him. He stood a few feet beyond me, incredibly handsome in his evening clothes, his eyes drawing me in and making me want to lose myself in them. He was still, but a coiled sense of power seemed to surround him, as if he was a panther about to pounce.

"I'm sorry," I told him. "This is no reflection on you. You seem to be a very nice man . . . dragon . . . but unfortunately, even if I agreed that somehow, I was meant to be your mate, there are circumstances that prohibit me from taking that role. I hope you understand."

"I understand," he said after a few moment's silence, his voice rubbing along my skin like velvet.

Before I could stop myself, I took a step forward toward him. "Thank you."

The rest of the world seemed to recede until only a small stretch of wool carpet bearing Gabriel and myself existed. His eyes searched mine, searing a silver path straight down to my soul. It was as if our souls touched for one blinding moment of glory.

Drake's voice lashed across me with the violence of a whip crack, dragging me back into reality with a painful jerk. "There is still the matter of Mei Ling."

I backed away from Gabriel, not trusting myself to be near him. For a moment I wished . . . but that was folly. I needed to stop moping over wishes that would never be realized, and instead work on getting us out of the situation. The doorway loomed behind me. Oh, how I wanted to race through it, grab Cyrene, and escape this house. But I couldn't, not yet. Slowly, I examined everyone in the room, silent and still as if they'd been frozen into place. I avoided looking at Gabriel's bright eyes, looking instead at the man who'd spoken. "What about it?"

"You are the thief Mei Ling." Drake frowned for a moment. "You don't look Asian."

"I'm not. Or rather, Cyrene isn't, hence I am not."

"Then why are you called Mei Ling?" he asked.

"Mayling," Aisling said suddenly, smiling. "It's a nickname."

I nodded, and decided to brazen it out rather than offer up a denial none of them would believe. "And if I said I was the thief Mei Ling? What would you do? Hand me over to the watch? Burn me at the stake? Wrap me in chains and toss me into the nearest dungeon?"

"There is a price on her head," István said. "A *large* price."

"That's right," Aisling said thoughtfully. "I heard about that earlier. You stole something from Dr. Kostich, and he put a whopper of a bounty on your head."

"Is this the point where you blackmail me into doing your bidding?" I asked, shifting my attention to Gabriel. "Are you going to threaten to turn me in if I don't steal for you, too?"

"*Too?*" he asked, jumping on the word, his eyes curious. "You do not steal for yourself?"

I paused for a moment, damning my verbal slip before tightening my lips. Why did I care what he thought of me, what any of them thought of me? Why did I want to explain to them how I had been bound to Magoth even before I'd been created, how I had no freedom in my life, no ability to make my own decisions. Why did it matter that Gabriel's words stung me until I wanted to scream my innocence? I owed them nothing. They were no different from anyone else who tried to use me. "I am a doppelganger, a shadow walker. There is no end of people who have offered to hire me for one illegal purpose or another."

"Then you will have no difficulty undertaking this task for Gabriel," Drake said.

To my surprise, Gabriel turned to the other wyvern with a frown. "Drake, you are interfering with my mate."

"I'm not your mate! And you needn't couch your demand in such polite terms, dragon. There are those in the world who don't bother with the niceties. They are the ones who use force to make me do their bidding."

"I am not interfering," Drake told Gabriel, totally missing my sarcasm.

"You are, and I don't appreciate it. May is mine,

not yours. I won't have you giving her orders or threatening her."

"Oh, for mercy's . . . I am not *anyone's* mate!"

Everyone ignored me. The green wyvern looked surprised at Gabriel for a moment. Aisling covered up a little chirp of laughter by suddenly taking a sip from her glass.

"Might I point out that you have interfered with *my* mate on numerous occasions?" Drake said. "You even planned to challenge me for her."

A little spike of pain stabbed inside me. Gabriel flashed a glance toward me that I had no trouble deciphering as embarrassed. "That was before I knew . . . That doesn't matter. The fact remains that you are interfering, and although I know you mean well, I would appreciate it if you would allow me to handle my mate in my own fashion."

"The situation concerns us, as well. I believe that we have a right to ensure that matters are concluded satisfactorily."

"You know, I think I'm with Gabriel on this," Aisling said, putting her hand on her wyvern's arm. "Maybe we should just butt out—"

"Kostya is not Gabriel's problem alone," Drake told her.

"We are the only ones who are threatened by him," Gabriel argued, taking a step toward the other dragon. "You are not fighting for your survival as we are ours. We are the ones who must deal with Kostya."

"That doesn't mean—"

"Yes, it does!" Gabriel interrupted, the two men now toe to toe.

Their respective bodyguards lined up behind them as the wyverns slipped into a language I didn't understand.

"What are they speaking?" I asked Aisling, as she hoisted herself to her feet.

"Bah. Baby's sitting right on my bladder. Hmm? Oh, that's Zilant." She smiled at my look of confusion. "I only just found out about it myself. It's a language that all dragons were taught centuries ago, so that members of different septs could understand one another. It's pretty much unused now that most of them speak English. Zilant had something to do with the origins of the black dragons—it's a region in Russia, evidently, and took the name from there."

The two wyverns were still going at it, arguing with occasional intercessions from their bodyguards.

"Are they always like that?" I couldn't help but ask.

Aisling smiled at me. "Pretty much so. They're arrogant to a man, and bossy, and they always think their way is the only way. . . ." She tossed a fond look toward the dark-haired green wyvern. "But they're also absolutely unswerving in their devotion. I know this whole thing with Gabriel has probably made you feel like the rug has been pulled out from under you, but he really is a sweetie, and I doubt if you'll have the trouble with him that I had with Drake. He was absolutely impossible when I first met him."

"I heard that!" the man in question said, interrupting his argument long enough to shoot a potent glare at Aisling.

She blew him a kiss, then excused herself and went off to the bathroom.

I started to edge my way out of the room. I made it to the stairs before Gabriel turned his head to notice I was nearly out of the room.

"Mate!" he said, frowning.

"Mate?" A voice came from behind me on the stairs. Cyrene stood there, her face puzzled as she glanced around the room. "You can't mean . . . May? A mate? A dragon's mate?"

"I thought you were tired and taking a nap," I said, hurrying up to her.

"I had a quick bath instead. I feel much better, although I'm confused about what's going on here. Did that delicious Gabriel call you 'mate'?"

I opened my mouth to explain, but found it hard to put things in a manner that sounded like anything but mindless babble. "Er . . ."

"That is correct," Gabriel said, moving over to stand next to me. He didn't touch me, but he didn't need to—to my embarrassment, I found myself leaning toward him, as if he was a lodestone and I was a magnet. "May is my mate."

"But she can't be!" Cyrene said, shaking her head as she marched over to us.

"She can't?" Gabriel asked, looking from her to me. "Why can't she?"

Gods, he was handsome. That warm brown skin, those liquid silver eyes, along with a strong jaw and gently squared chin that for some reason made me feel suspiciously weak in the knees. But he was a dragon, a wyvern, and I was Cyrene's shadow. I moved a step away and tried to ignore the sorrow that filled me.

"Why can't she?" Cyrene looked at him as if he was insane. "Because she doesn't like men, that's why. She's never had sex."

My face burned as I closed my eyes for a minute, fighting with the desire to shadow. "Cyrene, no one is interested in this."

"Well, I certainly think Gabriel is going to be interested if he's under the delusion that you are his mate! I know it's hard for you to be open about this, but evidently there is a major misunderstanding about you. We owe it to them to be truthful; these people are our friends, after all."

"István broke your neck," I pointed out, momentarily sidetracked from the hell my life had suddenly become.

"Ycs, but I'm sure he didn't mean it," she said, turning to him. "You didn't, did you?"

István nodded, frowned, then shook his head. "I thought you were attacking Jim."

"There, you see? You know I would never want to put you on the spot, dear Mayling, but now is not the time for shyness. Do not be afraid to admit the truth."

"Oh, gods," I swore to myself, sinking into the nearest chair. *Why me?* my mind shrieked. Why did Cyrene pick now to bring up this issue?

"I . . ." Gabriel looked as stupefied as just about everyone else. "Are you sure?" he finally asked Cyrene, his confused gaze on me.

"Oh, yes," Cyrene answered, taking up a position next to me in order, undoubtedly, to show support. "I'm quite sure. May's never been with a man physically, even though more than a few have wanted her."

"The things I miss while I'm in the bathroom," Aisling murmured as she took her seat again.

I hunched over, dropping my head to my hands in mortification, regretting to the very depths of my being the day I had the bright idea of telling Cyrene that I had never had, and never would have, a sexual relationship with a man. "Please, Cyrene! No more!"

"So wait, she's a virgin?" Jim asked in an awestruck voice, coming over to snuffle my hands. "Wow. I haven't seen a professional virgin since we were in Hungary."

"Well, not strictly speaking, because when she was created, I wasn't . . . er . . ." Cyrene had a rare and lamentably late moment of circumspection, and thankfully stopped that line of thought before I died of embarrassment right there before her.

I could feel Gabriel's speculative gaze on me. I

peered at him through my fingers. He examined me for a moment, then winked.

I wanted to die all over again.

"Well, that's really . . . um . . . I'm not quite sure what to say to that," Aisling said.

"You said she hasn't been with men, but you guys aren't . . . you know, *girlfriends*, are you?" Jim asked, continuing to sniff me.

I smacked at its nose, glaring at it before I turned the look on my twin as she said in an indignant tone, "Of course we're not lovers! I *created* her! Making love to her would be like . . . like . . . like having sex with my own clone!"

"Well, you know, some people might find that kind of kinky and yet oddly attractive. I, myself—ow!"

"Silence!" Aisling said, shaking a rolled-up magazine at the demon.

"Cy, please!" I begged. "Now that you've shredded what remains of my dignity, can we move on?"

She patted my hand. "I'm just trying to help clear things up. It's not fair to Gabriel that he not know the truth if he believes you are his mate."

My lips twitched as I tried to decide if I wanted to burst into laughter or tears.

"That's OK," Jim said, leaning against me, leaving a little puddle of drool on the top of my shoe. "We won't think bad of you just because no one's ever parked the pink Plymouth in your garage of love."

"Jim!" Aisling said, whapping it on the butt with the magazine.

"What? I said it politely! Would you have preferred 'ride the skin bus to Tuna Town'?"

"No!"

I wondered if it would be possible to strangle a demon to death.

"Windsurfing on Mount Baldy?"

"That's it!" Aisling bellowed, pointing a finger at the demon. "One more euphemism, and you're spending a week in the Akasha."

"I think it's time we leave," I said at the same time, standing up to grab Cyrene's arm.

"I'm so sorry for Jim's rudeness," Aisling apologized.

"Her twin started it," the dog said, although it shut up quickly enough when Aisling shot it a look that promised retribution.

"I don't see what you're so upset about," Cyrene told me, frowning slightly. "It's nothing to be ashamed of—"

"Cy!" I yelled, praying the ground would open up before me and swallow me whole.

"May's sexual experience, or lack of it, doesn't matter at all," Gabriel pronounced, his voice wrapping itself around me as he moved closer, not quite touching me, but close enough that I could feel his body heat again. "She is my mate regardless."

"No, you don't understand," Cyrene interrupted, tugging his sleeve. "The problem isn't that she hasn't been with any men before . . . the problem is that she doesn't *like* men."

You could have heard a feather drop in the silence that followed. Every single pair of eyes but Cyrene's turned to me.

I groaned to myself and thought seriously of murdering my twin.

"She . . . doesn't?" Gabriel asked, disbelief rife in his voice.

"No, she doesn't. She told me so herself. But you know that she's my twin, yes? My identical twin? An exact copy of me? So perhaps I'm the real mate, and you just got confused because May is so much like me."

Chapter Seven

"So let me get this straight—May's a virgin lesbian doppelganger wyvern's mate?" Jim pursed its lips as it looked me over before turning to its demon lord. "I think she's got even you beat, Ash."

I had finally had enough. I stood up and looked sternly at everyone present, but mostly at the man standing next to me. "I am *not* a virgin, nor a lesbian! I *am* a doppelganger, but the wyvern's mate question is not proven."

"You drank the dragon's blood without any ill effect," Drake mused, his arm around his wife.

"I'm immortal. It can't kill me like it could a mortal," I pointed out.

"Yes, but you kissed Gabriel without any problem," Aisling said. "Even an immortal would have been affected if she wasn't a mate. I'm afraid that's a pretty good indicator."

Hrmph. "Do you mean to say that no other woman has ever survived a kiss from you?" I asked Gabriel, disbelief dripping from my voice.

"On the contrary, I've never killed a woman I've kissed." He leaned closer to me, his eyes blazing like sunlight off a polished mirror. "But there have been a few close calls."

Gods, but he smelled good. My body went into a

full-fledged battle with my mind, the former wanting to grab his head and kiss that knowing half smile right off his face, the latter pointing out that one kiss could hardly be decisive.

"You're right," he said, almost against my lips. "More is definitely better in this case."

"Stop reading my mind," I whispered, groaning to myself when his lips curved into a smile.

"No woman has ever taken my fire," he murmured as I stared into those glorious eyes. I teetered on the brink of indecision, wanting more than anything else at that moment to taste him again, to feel his body pressed against mine, to revel in his closeness, but the sane corner of my mind worried that if I gave in, I'd have to face facts that I'd be much better off avoiding. "Tell me you want it."

I tilted my head just a smidgen, just enough to allow my lips to caress his. That's all it took. With a low-pitched primal noise that seemed to emanate deep from within his chest, his mouth claimed mine, the fire pouring out of him and into me. His lips were hotter than I remembered, hotter than I thought possible, moving over mine in a fashion that left me both satisfied and craving more.

"More," I murmured, my hands in his hair, tugging on the dreadlocks. I was dimly aware that I was behaving in a manner wholly at odds with my normally unemotional self, but there was something about him that seemed to release all the inhibitions I usually held.

That thought scared me to my toenails.

Dragon fire whipped around me, spiraling up from my toes to my waist as Gabriel kissed me with a thoroughness that left no secrets undiscovered. I was shocked at the depths of my desire for him, a man I'd just met. I couldn't hide from the fact that I wanted him, all of him, with a hunger that left me weak with sudden need. I moaned into his mouth as his fingers dug into my hips, pulling me tighter against the hard lines of his body. He tasted like fire, hot and exciting and dangerous, and I wanted more. The fire grew around me, twisting my desire higher, building my need until I thought it was going to burst from me in a primitive cry. The fire roared from me back to him, leaving me a blazing brand that threatened to burst into a million incandescent sparks.

"Sweet May," he groaned into my mouth as he rubbed my hips against his. "Sweet, sweet mate."

The words pierced my being like little bullets of ice, slicing through my almost out-of-control desire and returning me to reality with a shock that left me reeling.

With a cry, I pushed back, pulling my mouth away from his. "Don't call me that," I said, my voice hoarse and shaky.

Confusion filled his eyes.

I shadowed and twisted out of his arms, backing away a few steps. I touched my lips with a trembling hand, feeling empty inside, as if I'd lost something integral to myself.

"May?" he asked, taking a step toward me, evidently seeing me despite the darkness of the evening. "What's wrong?"

"Nothing. I just . . . I just don't like that word," I answered, clearing my throat and glancing around.

Everyone was standing where they had been before Gabriel sucked all my attention from the room, their faces displaying varying emotions.

Cyrene turned shocked eyes to me, but I sensed an underlying emotion that didn't make any sense to me: pain.

"I'm sorry," I said, feeling the need to apologize. "I didn't mean to turn the evening into a peep show."

"You—" Cyrene started to say, then stopped, biting her lip as she looked away.

"I liked it," Jim said, plopping its big butt down next to a chair. "You don't often get to see a wyvern claiming a mate. It's better than Skinemax. Is there going to be an encore? If there is, can you hold off until I make some popcorn?"

Aisling spoke a few hurried words and, before the demon could do more than open its mouth in protest, banished it to the Akasha. "I'm sorry about Jim. I think a little time-out is in order. I'm afraid, though, that it might be right about one thing."

I slid a glance toward Gabriel. He was watching me with an intensity that both flattered me and made me uncomfortable. "Yes, I'm afraid that it is. . . . It would seem that despite the fact that I'm a doppelganger, I appear to be your mate."

"I don't understand how . . ." Cyrene's voice trailed away to nothing as she sank rather less gracefully than normal into a nearby chair.

"The how is not important," Gabriel answered, his dimples slowly emerging. "What matters is that the impossible has happened. I'm delighted that you understand the significance of being able to share my fire, May. I never expected to have a mate, but now that I've found you, I am very pleased."

I wanted to shadow, to go find a quiet spot where I could think over recent events by myself, without any other distractions. I was a thief, dammit, a shadow walker, servant of a demon lord, keeper of Cyrene's common sense, and responsible only for myself and her well-being. And now I found myself bound to a stranger? I shook my head. I just didn't have experience with men, let alone dragons. The situation seemed untenable at best.

"I don't understand any of this," Cyrene said, giving me a hurt look. "You *do* like men?"

"I'm sorry," I said, dropping to my knees next to her. I took her hand and gave it a squeeze. No matter how scatterbrained she was, no matter how many times she got herself into scrapes and expected me to pull her out, she was still my twin. I owed my very existence to her. "I didn't like deceiving you, but it seemed like less stress for everyone if you thought I wasn't interested in men at all."

"You're a dragon's mate," she said slowly, as if she was absorbing this new image of me. "I still don't . . . Are you sure we're not both your mate?"

Gabriel considered her for a moment.

"We are identical," she told him, her expression earnest. "May is an exact copy of me. Well, she's not a naiad, but other than that, she's my duplicate."

I have never minded being called her twin, but for some reason, her insistence on referring to me in de-humanizing terms rankled a bit. I stifled that as best I could; with the exception of her common sense—a trait that had been given over to me at my creation—she wasn't saying anything that wasn't absolutely true.

"You were born," Gabriel said gently, taking her hand from me. "The black dragons are cursed to never have a mate born to them."

"But if May—" she started to argue.

"This is a question easily settled," he interrupted. His fingertips suddenly burst into flame, causing Cyrene to squawk and leap backward, yanking her hand out of his when he touched a spot on her wrist.

"My apologies if I hurt you," he said, bending his head over her arm. Cyrene watched with open-mouthed amazement as he first breathed on the small burn mark, then lowered his mouth to it, his tongue lathing the spot.

Rage burst into being within me, startling me with both its presence and its intensity. Gabriel was *licking* Cyrene.

"Er . . . ," I said, taking a step closer.

"It's all right, don't be alarmed," Aisling said, watching them with interest. "Gabriel has the most amazing saliva. All the silver dragons do. They make a wonderful healing ointment out of it, but it's not quite as potent as when it comes from the source."

"Um . . ." I tapped Gabriel on the shoulder. He looked up with a distinct twinkle in his eyes. "That doesn't look very hygienic."

"I assure you, it will do her only good, and no harm," he said, smiling as he returned Cyrene's hand to her with a little bow.

We both looked. The small red burn mark had disappeared.

"That was amazing," Cyrene breathed, gazing at him with wonder.

I stifled the last little bubble of irritation, reminding myself that he was just doing his job.

He didn't have to enjoy it quite so much, though, did he?

"And now May," Gabriel said. I looked at him a moment, wondering what sort of a man it was that fate had bound me to. I held out my hand, watching with dispassionate interest as he traced a symbol in flames on my wrist. It burned merrily on my skin, although I felt nothing more than a mild heat.

"Dragon mates have the ability to share dragon fire. They can use it, mold it to their own desire, drawing power from it when needed," he said, watching me as I coaxed the little flame to my fingertips. It shimmered there, as if it was about to go out. I held my other hand out over it, willing it into a small ball, smiling to myself when it obediently formed a sphere. I held it in the palm of my hand for a moment, admiring the beauty and power held within it, before throwing it directly at Gabriel.

A slow smile spread across his face as the flame ball exploded against his chest, bathing his upper body in fire for a few seconds before it evaporated into nothing. "I believe that answers your question, Cyrene."

"It doesn't even begin to cover the questions I have," she said softly. I took a few steps away from Gabriel, startled by the undertone I had heard in Cyrene's voice.

"Well, as you said, what does it matter how it happened—it did, and it's a miracle. I hope you both will be very happy," Aisling said as she gave Gabriel a hug before turning to me to do the same.

I frowned. "I'm not sure I follow you. Happy doing what?"

Her smile slipped slightly as she glanced quickly at Gabriel. "Er . . . happy being together."

It took me a few seconds to understand what it was she was talking about. "Oh, we're not together. At least, not in the sense you mean."

"You're not?" she asked, looking downright confused.

"No. I can't. It's just not possible," I answered, turning to Gabriel. "I'm sorry if you assumed there would be some sort of a . . . for lack of a better word, romantic relationship between us."

His eyes turned to molten silver. "You have just accepted that you are my mate."

"Yes, it seems foolish to deny it when all the evidence points to that conclusion. But that doesn't mean we are . . . you know, a couple."

Drake looked at his wife. "You've infected her."

Aisling's mouth dropped open a smidgen. "I have not!"

His green eyes narrowed upon me. "You have an American accent."

"Yes," I answered, wondering what that had to do with anything. "Cyrene was living in Louisiana when I was created. I moved to the West Coast shortly thereafter." I didn't mention the reason for my sudden move away from my twin—Magoth, fascinated with the early movie industry, had based himself in Hollywood, and bound to him as I was, I had little choice but to follow.

"I miss New Orleans," Cyrene said wistfully. "I'm living in London now, and of course, it's very cultural, but there's none of the je ne sais quoi of the U.S."

"I knew it," Drake said, nodding at Aisling. "It's something in the water that makes American women the most stubborn beings on the planet. Try to deny it."

She smiled at me. "We're not stubborn, sweetie— we're smart. We simply want to know what we're getting into before we agree to anything."

"Well . . . there is that, yes," I said slowly, unwilling to say too much. "But there are certain obligations I've got to consider, and I'm afraid that right now, I'm just not in a position to maintain anything but a distant relationship."

"You are my mate," Gabriel said with an obstinate glint to his eye.

"Yes, I believe we've established that fact," I said, glancing at my watch. "It's very late. Since Cyrene appears to have recovered from the injury, we'd better be on our way."

"You can't leave!" Maata burst out, her disbelief evident.

"I'm afraid I have some prior commitments that I must attend to." I turned my attention to Gabriel.

"We should probably stay in touch. Do you live here in Greece?"

"No, we are here simply to make plans with Drake and Aisling while they are on holiday. My home is in Manukau."

I frowned in question.

"New Zealand," he answered. "I have taken a home in London since that is where Kostya is believed to be basing himself. I cannot address the obligations you mention until I have more information, but I assure you that the job of wyvern's mate will require much more time and attention than can be conducted by a *distant relationship*."

The emphasis he put on the last couple of words was unmistakable. So was the light in his eyes.

"The sheer hell she's going to put you through," Drake muttered, shaking his head.

Aisling whomped him on the chest. "For what it's worth, May, I think you have the right idea. Take your time to get to know Gabriel. Don't let anyone rush you into anything. Being a wyvern's mate is time-consuming, yes, but there's no reason you can't do your own job as well as take care of Gabriel and the silver dragons."

"She is a thief," Drake pointed out.

"Well, so are you," she countered, leveling a look at him that I'd have been afraid to even think of. "And I'm sure she has a very good reason for being a thief, too. Cyrene and May probably have an ailing mother, or there's someone else May has to take care of, and doing a Robin Hood act is the only way she can get by."

All eyes turned to me. I lifted my chin and smiled at no one in particular. "It's something like that. Now, if you'll excuse us, Cyrene and I should be on our way. Do you have a phone number where I can reach you in London, Gabriel?"

Silently, he pulled out a card and handed it to me. I tucked it away in an inner pocket of my leather bodice. "Thank you. I'm sorry about disturbing your evening. It's been . . . a pleasure. Good night."

I grabbed Cyrene's arm and started to hustle her through the door, but I had a feeling we weren't going to be able to make an escape without hearing from the quicksilver-eyed dragon.

"We will accompany you to your hotel," Gabriel said, suddenly standing in front of us, holding the door open.

Aisling murmured something about erasing the ward on the front door, scooting past us to do so. I looked behind me. Maata and Tipene wore matching expressions . . . neither gave me much hope they'd listen to reason. "Weren't you . . . weren't you just back there?" I asked Gabriel.

"Dragons can move quickly when they so desire. Drake, Aisling, my thanks for a very enjoyable evening. I will be in contact with you regarding the phylactery. And now, my dear . . . ," Gabriel said, gesturing toward the open door.

I tried to exchange a glance with Cyrene, but she was looking at the floor, apparently avoiding my eye. "You don't know where we're staying," I said. "We could be greatly out of your way."

"You are my mate," Gabriel said, a sudden flare of emotion in his eyes making a hot flush start at my belly and move upward. "Nothing you can demand of me will be too great."

"Excellent. I demand you leave us alone. I'll call you in a few days, when we're back in London," I said, pushing Cyrene out the door as I slipped past him.

"Alas, I wish it was that easy, but I am bound by sept tradition to see to your welfare," he said, following us out to the driveway. Tipene went off to where a black BMW sat. I eyed Cyrene for a moment, unsure if I should trust Gabriel with her. I hadn't seen anything in him that led me to believe he would harm her, but dragons were strange beings—they looked human, but clearly didn't operate in the same manner. Still, he didn't strike me as the type of man who'd take out his wrath on an innocent person.

I tried to catch Cyrene's eye, but she continued to avoid looking at me. That hurt, but now was not the time to smooth her obviously ruffled feathers. I allowed Gabriel and Maata to escort us toward the car, but the second we were far enough away from the lights of the house, I shadowed, spinning around in the opposite direction, merging myself with the blissfully dark shadows.

Gabriel shouted my name, but I paid him no heed as I dashed alongside a high hedge, keeping myself immersed in the densest parts of the shadows. He might be able to see me at a close distance, but I was willing to bet he couldn't when more than a few yards separated us.

I ran down the street, through yards, around gardens, moving in a direction opposite the mage's house until I could no longer hear signs of pursuit. I doubled back, slowly picking my way, cautious of every looming shape, but no one leaped out to grab me.

Gabriel, it seemed, didn't bother to try to find me. I was oddly disgruntled by that fact, but decided it was foolish and immature, and there were much more important matters to concern myself with than the puzzle my heart wanted to solve.

Steeling myself, my chin high, my shoulders set, I made my way back around to the mage's house.

Chapter Eight

The voices drifted out on the night air, just loud enough to be audible as I crouched on the window ledge outside of the archimage Kostich's living room.

". . . could guarantee that you were compensated for the loss, would that make a difference?"

It was a man's voice . . . a familiar man's voice, one that slid along my body like satin. I froze, frowning at the beige stone wall to which I clung. What on earth was Gabriel doing talking to Dr. Kostich? Why wasn't he seeing Cyrene home, as I had expected?

"The item that was stolen from me is irreplaceable," the mage answered. "No amount of money could compensate me for it."

"Is it safe to assume that you know the whereabouts of the thief Mei Ling?" a third voice asked, one that was unknown to me.

I risked peeking around the edge of the window. Gabriel sat with his back to me, calmly watching as Dr. Kostich paced back and forth across the room. I didn't see a third person at first, but suddenly, a silhouette moved in front of the window. I ducked to the side, flattening myself against the stone of the building. Although technically no one should be able to see me when I shadow walked at night, some beings were more perceptive than others, and until I knew whom I was dealing with, I felt it wiser not to take chances.

"No, I don't know where she is," Gabriel answered. "I know how to contact her, however. And I believe I can convince her to see the error of her ways."

I snorted to myself at that. Gabriel had a sad comeuppance due if he truly believed that he could control me simply because it turned out I was his mate.

"I find it rather peculiar that a dragon of your stature, a wyvern, should interest himself in the doings of a common thief," the nameless man said slowly. He had an English accent, but I was at a loss as to who he was, or how he was involved with Dr. Kostich.

"I interest myself in a great many things, thief taker," Gabriel said with calm assurance.

I froze at the words. Kostich had made good his threat and called in a thief taker, the Otherworld's version of bounty hunters. Thief takers were notorious for ignoring or disregarding laws in order to achieve their end goal. They were reputed to be intelligent, persistent, and very, very dangerous.

"Do you have some connection with Mei Ling?" the thief taker asked.

I wanted badly to lean forward so I could peer into the window and see who this man was—in order to stay far, far away from him—but every time I thought it was safe to do so, movement next to the window warned me off.

Gabriel's voice was smoothly noncommittal. "What connection could I possibly have?"

"That is the question, isn't it?"

"A question that has no pertinence, hence I do not feel obliged to answer it," Gabriel said.

"Methinks the dragon protests too much," the thief taker answered quickly.

Gabriel rose slowly from the chair. "If you are insinuating—"

"Enough!" Kostich interrupted, marching over to stand in front of Gabriel. He said, slowly, "I am torn with the need to have returned that which was stolen from me, and a hesitancy to involve someone else with an individual who clearly poses a danger. Although your kind are not under the umbrella of the L'au-delà, dragonkin have long been considered our friends. It is for this reason that I will refuse the temptation you offer, and instead warn you not to have anything further to do with Mei Ling."

"You do not need to fear for my safety," Gabriel replied with no attempt to hide the amusement in his voice. "Dragons are notoriously difficult to destroy, and I have no qualms acting as a go-between for you and Mei Ling."

The thief taker snorted.

"I must admit that I, too, am curious about why you are willing to do such a thing," Kostich said smoothly.

Gabriel turned his head just enough so I could see the dimple in one of his cheeks. "You have offered a generous reward. I'm sure your thief takers are"—his pause emphasized the stress he laid on the next word—"*adequate*, but you should not underestimate the interests dragons have in rewards of the nature you are offering."

My fingers tightened around the smooth stone of the casement as anger flared at the thought of him turning me over to Kostich in order to receive the benefaction. Was this, then, how he chose to achieve his goal of acquiring the dragon phylactery? Was he willing to betray me in order to gain it? I felt sick to my stomach at the thought, enough so that even my brain, when it pointed out that it wasn't terribly likely a wyvern would so endanger his mate, had a hard time discounting the idea.

"Adequate?" Amusement was rife in the thief taker's voice. The shadow that had blocked light from the window shifted, and I risked a quick peek to see that the man had moved off to the side, away from me.

Sickened by what I was overhearing, I slipped past the two windows, moving beyond the room. Everyone had settled down to sleep; even the night birds were muted as I crept down the ledge to a darkened window. Wards had been etched into the glass, but they were the wrong type of ward to keep me out. That gave my spirits a short-lived boost—evidently no one had seen me long enough to guess my origins, which made it all that much easier for me to simply ignore the arcane magical traps Dr. Kostich had laid around the window.

The study was dark except for a dim light set high in the case I'd broken into earlier. I kept myself shadowed as I moved carefully around the furniture, which I could dimly make out, heading for the corner where I remembered seeing the surveillance camera. I stopped underneath it, listening intently.

From the room next to me, I could hear the low rumble of masculine voices. Damn that Gabriel, he was probably telling Dr. Kostich just what he wanted for his benefaction. I thinned my lips and thought of what I'd like to say to him at that moment, reluctantly setting that aside to deal with the problem before me. From the inner pocket of the bodice, I pulled out a small, flattened disk of silver-backed utility tape, using it to cover the camera's lens before heading for the case. I also withdrew the quintessence, my fingers caressing the invisible edges of its case, a strange yearning suddenly possessing me. I wanted to feel its glory again, to revel in its beauty, to absorb all that it had to give me. Why should I give it back to Dr. Kostich when the man clearly didn't know its true value?

I'm ashamed to say that for five seconds, I considered the possibility of keeping the quintessence for myself. It was tempting . . . but I sighed as I carefully opened the case, placing the unseen box onto the shelf where I had originally found it.

"I may be a thief," I said softly as I closed the case, watching with mild amusement as the arcane symbols of protection drawn across the front resealed themselves as if they'd never been disturbed. "But I don't have to be a dishonest thief."

Righteousness filling my heart, I turned to leave, but was unable to move.

"What the . . ." My feet appeared to be rooted to the ground, stuck to the rug as if by some industrial-strength glue. I peered down at my feet, horror crawling up my arms as I realized there was a pattern woven into the rug upon which I stood . . . a pattern that was not arcana based, as was all the other magic the mage had used. This was something older than that, something with an elemental basis that held me in place just as firmly as if I'd been bolted to the ground.

Panic filled me as I shadowed, hoping against hope it would break the bond of the spell that held me to the ground. I struggled, squirming against it, twisting one of my feet in an attempt to break free. The spell wasn't meant to hold someone who could shadow walk, allowing my foot to slowly gain freedom. I had just wrestled one foot out of the binding when the door suddenly opened, the figure of a man looming up in its place.

"Perhaps you wouldn't mind showing me where it was taken from? I have a curiosity about these sorts

of things," Gabriel said, flipping a switch near the
door that turned on a standing lamp. I froze, my heart
racing as I realized the direness of my situation: I was
directly next to the case, one foot stuck to the floor,
unable to free myself. The light was near the door,
but it illuminated the room enough to allow someone
to see me even if I could move. I was trapped good
and proper.

"That's an odd sort of thing to be curious about,"
the thief taker said in an aside to no one.

Gabriel ignored him, as did Kostich.

"I don't see what good that will do," the latter said
as he entered the room behind Gabriel.

"I've found that there are some things that you least
expect which can provide the most enlightenment."
Gabriel strolled toward me, his silver eyes flickering
over me impersonally before sliding away, leaving me
wondering for a moment if the room was dark enough
that he couldn't see me. If he hadn't, he surely would
as soon as he was closer. But if he had . . . My poor,
confused brain had no time to work on the puzzle that
Gabriel presented. Before I could move so much as a
finger, he was directly in front of me, so close his arm
brushed me as he turned to face Dr. Kostich and the
thief taker.

"You have some lovely things here. That fertility
statue is Irish, is it not?" Gabriel asked, gesturing
toward the case, his body blocking my sight of the
two men.

Which meant that Dr. Kostich and the thief taker
couldn't see me, either.

"Welsh, I believe." Kostich's voice held an edge of
irritation that Gabriel seemed to ignore.

"Indeed. And this is the case? I see there is one
shelf empty. Would that be where the item was stolen from?"

"Yes. Now that your curiosity is satisfied, perhaps you wouldn't mind leaving? It is late," Dr. Kostich said abruptly.

"I see you have used arcane runes for protection," Gabriel said, ignoring his comment. "Very wise. Few beings would not be affected by them."

For some reason I had yet to fathom, Gabriel was providing me with cover. I didn't stop to wonder at that, just struggled to free my bound foot.

"Is there a point to this catechism?" Kostich asked, all signs of politeness thrown by the wayside.

Gabriel's cheek curved as he smiled. "I am a dragon. We are all very interested in security methods when it comes to treasure. I have not had the opportunity to try arcane magic to guard my own lair, but I can see from your spells and runes that it is something I should consider. Although I must admit I dislike relying upon one type of magic only, preferring the security that multiple types offer."

"Nor would I be so foolish. If you were to take a step five inches to the right, you would find yourself held tight in a binding earth element."

"Clever," the thief taker murmured. "Very clever."

"Earth element? You are an alchemist, then?" Gabriel asked, shifting his weight slightly, I assumed to block me a little better.

"I am interested in it, yes."

"Ah. And can I assume that the item which was taken from you was of an alchemical nature?"

Kostich's voice left no doubt that he was irritated. "A Liquor of Hepatis was stolen from me, as well as another element."

My foot was almost free. I twisted it with a strength that made my muscles cry out, dropping to my knees as Gabriel suddenly leaned toward the case to peer into it.

"I could have sworn I'd seen something . . . but now it's gone. Must have been a trick of the light."

I peered around Gabriel's hip. All I could see was Dr. Kostich frowning at him for a moment before the latter ran over to the case, his hands gesturing quickly as he undid the binding element. I almost fell over at the sudden release of my foot.

"What . . . it's here! The quintessence is here!"

Dr. Kostich's hands came into view from where I crouched. He cradled an object invisible to all sight but that of the most peripheral nature. He flipped open the lid for a moment, filling the room with that brilliant warm glow. "But how . . . I was sure it was gone. No, it was gone, stolen. I *know* it was."

"What is it?" Gabriel asked as Kostich closed the lid again.

"Quintessence," Dr. Kostich answered in a distracted way as he frowned at the case. "It is that which is invaluable. I don't see how I could have overlooked it . . ."

"Very confusing, indeed," the thief taker said.

I ground my teeth at the smugness in the man's voice. I still hadn't gotten a look at him, but I didn't dare try to get an unobstructed view of him lest he see me, as well.

"Perhaps in the confusion over the theft of the other object, it escaped notice," Gabriel said.

"No. I would not have done that. It was not on the shelf."

"But it is now," Gabriel pointed out in his smooth, silky voice. "And since you now possess it, perhaps you would reconsider your actions with regard to Mei Ling?"

"I know I searched the case . . . hmm? Oh. No," Dr. Kostich said slowly as he replaced the quintessence, redrawing the binding element on the ground. I had moved a couple of steps away, keeping Gabriel between me and the two men, praying that the former and the dim light would continue to keep me hidden. "She must be caught. She has robbed too many people in the L'au-delà."

Gabriel clearly wasn't happy with that, but I realized there was little he could say without attracting too much attention from both men.

"And now I must insist that you be on your way," the mage said just as I was trying to get a peek at the two men. I ducked down behind Gabriel's broad shoulders, holding my breath. "I have a great many things to do before the sun rises."

Gabriel smiled and gestured toward the door. "After you."

Dr. Kostich hesitated, but moved toward the door.

The thief taker evidently still stood in front of the cabinet, but he, too, left after a moment's pregnant silence. Gabriel followed. As they went through the door, he paused long enough to turn off the light, shooting me an unreadable look as he did so. "I am sure you will be able to rest knowing that your precious things are safe from any further theft."

I made a face at such an obvious warning, waiting until he turned off the light and closed the door before hurrying toward the window.

There was no denying that Gabriel had saved my butt from a very unpleasant situation. But everyone knew that dragons never did anything without expecting to be compensated. Just what was Gabriel going to demand as payment?

That thought worried me all the way back to my hotel.

Cyrene was nearly asleep when I tapped on her door.

"You all right?" I asked when she opened it.

"Yes." Her shoulders slumped as she crawled back into bed, leaving me standing awkwardly.

Everything about her twanged at my conscience, from her dejected, downturned mouth to the way she wouldn't meet my eye.

"How does your neck feel?" I asked.

She gave a little twitch of her shoulder as she pulled the blankets up. "Fine. It doesn't hurt."

"You don't look happy," I said, miserable.

"I'm not." Her eyes lifted to meet mine for a moment, hurt mingling with accusation in them. "You lied to me."

"Yes, I did. And I'm sorry, but . . ." I let my hands fall and walked over to the window, twitching the curtains aside to look out on the sleepy town. The sun would be up in a few hours, heralding the dawn of yet another day. "It just seemed so much easier that way. Do you remember in the 1960s, when you kept bringing men to my house and urging me to jump into bed with them?"

"Everyone was doing it then," she said, her mouth tight. "I just wanted you to be happy. You seemed so lonely then. You still do."

"I appreciate the thought now as I did then, but rampant sex with anything bearing the appropriate equipment and a libido to match has never been—and alas, never will be—my idea of a path to happiness."

"But why didn't you just tell me that?" she implored, slapping her hand down on the bed. "You should have just told me that you didn't want me to try to set you up with someone. When I think of all the trouble I went to finding men for you . . . and later women . . . I could just cry, Mayling, I really could."

"Cy!" I said, spinning around. "I did tell you. Repeatedly. But every time I brought up the subject, you started screaming and ran away."

She blinked at me in stupefied disbelief. "I did? Mayling, I've never once screamed and ran away when you talked to me about men, or the lack of them, in your life."

"No, not men, *man.* As in one man. The one man who is the reason why I can't have casual relationships with anyone, man or woman, not that my tastes are anything but traditional in that line."

I knew the moment she understood what I was talking about. Her face turned cold and hard, her eyelids drooped down, shadowing her eyes as she turned her head from me. "I don't want to talk about it."

I was silent for a few moments, sharing in her pain. "It doesn't matter," I said finally, moving toward the door.

"Mayling, wait . . ."

I turned. Her eyes were bright with tears now, her face flushed.

"It *does* matter. And you're right, I have avoided . . . that subject . . . but what happened to me has nothing to do with you."

I raised an eyebrow. "I'm here. I think it has something to do with me."

"No," she said sharply, her color deepening as she bit her lower lip. "You're right, you always are, and I see now that I'm partially responsible for you feeling you couldn't be open with me. But that's all over. We can talk about it."

I raised my hand and let it fall with a sense of futility. "I don't see that any good will come of talking about what's past. What's done is done, and there's nothing we can do to change it."

"But, Mayling, you don't see," she said, scooting out of the bed, taking my hand and giving it a little squeeze. "Just because I was . . . I had . . . because Magoth . . ."

"You were enthralled, about to be made consort," I said, finishing the sentence she was so clearly unable to say for herself.

"Yes. And because of that, you were created, not that I've regretted that at all. You're like the sister I never had."

I couldn't help but smile. Sometimes I wondered what she would have been like if she hadn't given up her common sense.

Her expression turned dark, her gaze dropping as she added in a lower tone, "And . . . people died."

"It's over, Cy."

"No," she said stubbornly, shaking her head. "I have to say it. Because Magoth enthralled me . . . because I had given in to him, he made me kill my lover."

I watched as she wrapped her arms around herself, sinking onto the edge of the bed. I hated for her to indulge in emotional flagellation, but she needed to understand once and for all just what sort of situation I was in.

"But that doesn't have anything to do with you," she said after a few moments of silent weeping.

I handed her a box of tissues from the nightstand.

"My downfall, my sins, are not reflected on you, you know that. And just because you work for Magoth doesn't mean he'll try—"

"He already has," I interrupted.

Her eyes grew large as she looked up to me in horror.

"No, he hasn't succeeded yet; I've managed to keep my wits about me despite his seductions. But it's been a very close thing the last couple of times, Cy, and to be perfectly frank, I don't know that I'll be able to withstand the next one."

Her mouth formed a perfect O.

I nodded. "So you see why it is that I can't get involved with any man. The minute Magoth pulls me into his thrall, he'll use me to destroy a challenger to his domination . . . and that means any lover, any boyfriend, any husband, would be doomed."

"Oh, my poor Mayling, my poor, innocent Mayling." Huge tears rolled down her cheeks. "But . . . this evening . . . the wyvern . . ."

"Picked the wrong woman to have a future with," I said, my face placid despite the fact that my soul was weeping tears of the purest sorrow.

Chapter Nine

"It's not fair," I said, closing the door to my room, intent on venting my spleen the only way I could—to an empty room.

"Life, you mean? No, it isn't, although we do the best we can to compensate for that fact," a male voice answered, causing me to utter a little shriek, shadow, and spin around to face the bathroom from which the voice emerged.

I had a horrible feeling my mouth dropped open a little bit at the sight of the man who stood there. The room was lit by candles on every available surface, casting a lovely warm glow that seemed to caress his body as he leaned against the door frame. He wore a calf-length black silk robe, matching sleeping pants . . . and nothing else but a smile. My eyes flitted from his beautiful eyes to his delectable lips, now curved in a sensual smile, to a bared chest that so fit my idea of male beauty, it left my mouth dry. "What are you doing here?" I finally managed to ask, my voice a hoarse croak.

Gabriel's dimples deepened as he held up a familiar dusty bottle. "I brought a little libation."

I managed by an intense output of will to drag my eyes off him, adopting what I hoped was a sophisticated expression of nonchalance. "How is it you can see me when I'm shadowed? The room is dark enough that you shouldn't be able to see me unless I'm right next to you."

"You are my mate," he said, strolling across the room to where a couple of wineglasses sat on a tiny table. "You cannot remain hidden from my eyes." He lifted his head for a moment as if he was scenting the air. "Nor from my nose."

I let the shadow drop, frowning. "I apologize if I offend your delicate senses."

"On the contrary," he said in that deep, velvet voice that made me shiver, "your scent is quite intoxicating."

Intrigued despite myself, I took a couple of steps into the room. "Intoxicating how?"

He poured the dragon's blood wine into two glasses, offering me one. I shook my head.

"You smell of . . ." He paused for a moment, closing his eyes as he breathed deeply. "You smell of the woodlands, but not of the bubbling golden stream as your twin does. You smell as if you were born in the dark, hidden glens, cool and mysterious, but infinitely deep. You smell of smoke and shadows, just like a little glossy-headed bird who flits between the darkness and light. Your essence is an intricate tapestry woven from the scents of the earth itself."

He moved toward me slowly as he spoke, his words wrapping themselves around me in a silken cord of sudden need and desire, forbidden to me, but no longer denied.

"You smell like a woman, *my* woman, and I will be grateful to the end of my time that you have chosen me to be your mate."

Who could resist such alluring words? I swayed against him, my body coming to life in a way that I never knew it could. Deep, hidden parts of me that had only been utilized in a most mundane fashion suddenly began to tingle at his nearness. When his breath brushed against me, I didn't back away, as I knew I should. I lifted my chin to meet his mouth, allowing my lips to caress his, the skin of my arms burning where they touched the bare flesh of his chest.

The sane part of me, the part that knew who I was and what would happen should I forget it, screamed dire warnings, but I seemed to be unable to do anything but focus on the sensations Gabriel brought to life deep within me. "This isn't right," I murmured against his mouth.

"It was meant to be," he answered, his hands at his sides as I let more of my body lean against him. I had a feeling he was deliberately holding himself back, allowing me time to get comfortable with him. How he knew I was nervous about my lack of experience with sexual intimacy escaped me, since I had tried to present a mien that, while not worldly, was not one of utter stupefaction where things sexual were concerned.

Nerves be damned, I thought to myself as I let my lips wander along his jawline. Although he had a mustache and goatee, both trimmed short, the rest of his face was clean shaven, leaving a long jawline to nibble along. And nibble I did, enjoying both his scent (deliciously woodsy) and taste (hot and fiery, leaving me wanting more). But headiest still were the soft little groans of pleasure he made, and the way his breath hitched as I bit gently down on his earlobe.

"Mayling, I don't think I will be able to keep from possessing you if you do that again," he murmured, his chest and arms twitching beneath my questing hands.

My stomach tightened at his use of "Mayling." Cyrene had called me by the nickname ever since I'd been created, but never had the word stirred such a warm glow of happiness as when Gabriel said it. Perhaps it was as he said—we were meant to be. Who was I to turn my back on fate? Would it be so wrong to give in to temptation just once . . . ?

"Mayling, my sweet one. I have prayed to the gods that one day I would find you. . . ."

A little chill touched my spine as the air-conditioning found my suddenly bared skin, but it wasn't that which froze me. Magoth's image rose in my mind, impossibly handsome, coolly calculating.

"No," I said, almost sobbing as I pushed back from where Gabriel was peeling my clothing off. He'd gotten both the leather bodice and my shirt off without me being aware of it. I snatched up the shirt and hurriedly buttoned it, backing away from him as I did so.

"What is it, sweet May—" he started to say.

"Stop," I interrupted. "Don't call me that. Don't ever call me that. He uses that word. It makes me feel . . . sick."

Gabriel watched me for a moment with eyes that seemed to see too much. I turned away, feeling soiled by the association with Magoth. What was I doing giving in to my base urges when I knew the outcome could only end in tragedy?

"Which word is it that upsets you? Sweet?"

I nodded, telling myself to stop being such a coward and face him. Slowly I turned back around, dreading the expression I knew would greet me.

To my surprise, he wasn't even looking at me. Instead he frowned at the bottle of wine, wiping off dust with a hand towel from the bathroom. "Do you object to me calling you by your pet name?" he finally asked, glancing up at me with nothing in his face or eyes but interest in the question.

"No, I don't mind. Cyrene has called me Mayling for as long as I can remember."

He nodded. "Then I will do so as well. Will you sit

and have some wine? I will move to the balcony if you do not wish for me to be near you."

Oh, gods, how had things come to this? I sagged down onto the edge of the bed and let myself slump into a ball of unhappiness. "I think we both know that I have no aversion to being near you. I nibbled all over you, if nothing else."

"No," he said, sitting beside me, close, but not so close that he touched me. I straightened up and looked at him. He was smiling a bit ruefully. "You did not nibble all over me, only my face. Which I enjoyed greatly, you understand. But as for all over?"

He glanced downward. I followed the movement, swallowing hard at the sight of his delicious chest so close to me. He didn't have a lot of chest hair, whether due to his mixed heritage or just by chance, but what there was looked as soft as silk. An intriguing little trail started below his belly button, leading down into the waistband of the pants, leaving me wanting to follow the trail with both my hands and mouth.

"I have scared you. I apologize for that. I know that this must all seem overwhelming to you, and I will endeavor to move at a pace which will ensure your happiness."

My cheeks burned as I realized he had seen me ogling his belly and below. "Do you mean sex?" I asked with bluntness. "If so, you're wrong. Oh, it's true what Cyrene said, not that I am in any way pleased that she felt it necessary to share that fact with everyone. I haven't had sex with a man before. But I'm not a shy, innocent virgin, either. I've seen movies. I've read books. I even attended a series of Our Bodies, Ourselves seminars during the 1970s. I'm not a prude or a stranger to sex; I've just never engaged in it with another person."

"I see." His eyes twinkled at me in a way that made

me want to melt into a puddle of goo. He leaned over slightly and nudged me with his shoulder. "Do you like flavored massage oils? There is a passion fruit oil that I would very much like to try on you."

A vision rose in my head of Gabriel doing just that, which made it difficult to swallow. "The issue I have is not one of sex," I repeated. "It's sex with men."

"You are not going to try to convince me that you prefer women, are you? Perhaps you enjoy both sexes? I do not share that ability, myself, but I will not condemn you for it. However, I will not share my mate with any other, woman or man . . ."

"No," I interrupted, inadvertently putting my hand out. It touched his chest. Little flames broke out at the ends of my fingertips where they rested against his flesh.

He looked down. "You have already gained a control of my fire. That is very good. Aisling could not control Drake's fire for months. It still gets away from her every now and again. It pleases me greatly that already you are so in tune to me that you can master my fire."

I jerked my hand back, jumping up from the bed, pacing to the door and back again before stopping in front of him. "Please just let me talk. I have something important to explain, and it's not in any sense of the word going to be easy."

"Very well," he said, nodding. He leaned back on the bed, propping himself up on his arms. "Proceed."

I wanted to fling myself on him, rip that robe right off his body and lick every inch of him. I spun around, marching over to the window in order to get a grip on my libido.

"I would be more than happy to acquiesce, not to mention reciprocate, but I doubt if you'd get much explaining done," he said.

"Will you stop reading my mind?" I asked, exasperated. "I didn't know dragons could do that."

"My sept can't, not normally, but my mother was from Australia."

I blinked at him a couple of times, as if that would help me understand.

"She was an Aborigine, her roots firmly in the Dreaming."

"I don't know what . . ." I frowned.

"The indigenous peoples of the Australian region believe there are two realities . . . this one, and the Dreaming. Those people who can inhabit both equally often exhibit abilities that mortals consider supernatural."

"The ability to read minds is one of them? That must be handy in a wyvern."

His lips quirked. "Thus far, you are the only person other than my parents whose mind I can read."

I wasn't sure I bought that, but it wasn't something pertinent. "I don't want you to use the word 'sweet' because the demon lord who is bent on seducing me uses that," I said in a rush, the words tumbling over themselves in my haste to get it all out.

That had him sitting upright. "A demon lord wishes to seduce you?"

I nodded.

His eyes narrowed, the silver in them turning glacial. "Which one?"

"Magoth. I am bound to him, Gabriel." My stomach balled itself up at the startled look that flitted across his face. "I am a servant of Magoth. Do you understand now why I can't be anything to you but a mate in name only?"

He stood up slowly. "Why did you bind yourself to him?"

"I didn't." I hesitated a moment, not wanting to

bare my dirty laundry, but knowing he wouldn't accept anything but the complete truth. "Last century Cyrene ran into Magoth. I don't know where, she never told me, but it really doesn't matter. He is a very handsome man, and she is prone to falling in love, and . . . well, despite the fact that she was quite happy with a troll from Austria named Hugo, he seduced her."

"That is regrettable, but not unknown," he said.

"It wouldn't be anything but a sign of Cyrene's weakness for handsome men if Magoth hadn't decided that she was worth keeping for a bit. He enthralled her. Do you know what that is?"

He pursed his lips slightly. "Is it a spell of some sort?"

"More or less, yes. He placed his thrall on her, and used his will to get her to kill off his competition, her lover, Hugo." I looked down at my hands for a moment. They were balled into fists. I forced myself to relax my fingers. "Cyrene, in a drunken orgy that I really don't want to know about, decided that it would be a good idea to have a doppelganger, and since you need to have a demon lord to create one, and she was considering becoming Magoth's consort, she went ahead and started the ceremony."

"It did not go as planned?" he asked.

I shook my head. "Magoth was growing tired of Cyrene. He lifted the thrall and agreed to the creation, on the condition that she bind her doppelganger to him. Since she'd sacrificed her common sense to my creation—why she couldn't have picked a trait like ticklishness or even irritability is beyond my understanding—but since she sacrificed that, she said yes. Thus I was created, an instant servant of Magoth."

"Who uses your ability to shadow walk to his own benefit?" Gabriel asked.

I nodded again. "He seeks to gain a hold on the mortal world, and sends me out to acquire for him those things which might give him power here."

"And you thought I wished to use you the same way he does," he said, then checked himself. "I suppose in your eyes there is little difference. I understand now why you refused to help me."

"I never refused to help you," I said wearily, slumping into a chair. "I just can't have sex with you. I can't . . . love you."

"Love is not an emotion that is so easily commanded," he said, his fingers wisping across my cheek.

I looked up. His expression was unreadable.

"I would not demand declarations of love from you. I would hope that the emotion would follow, as it does for most mated pairs, but I believe you already feel for me an attraction that would be enough. To start," he added with another brush of his fingers across my cheek.

I resisted the urge to lean into the gesture. "That point aside, the fact remains that I can't be the mate that you want. Or deserve. Magoth is bent on seducing me as he did Cyrene, and has even offered me the position of his consort. It is becoming increasingly . . . *difficult* . . . to resist him," I said carefully, wanting him to know the whole ugly truth. "He is not someone I would choose to have that sort of a relationship with, but he is very powerful, and I know the day will come when despite my best efforts, he will succeed. And once that happens, it will be child's play to cast a thrall upon me, and then . . ."

He looked thoughtful as my words trailed off. "Then he would order you to kill me."

"Yes." I rubbed my fingers. "I like you, Gabriel. I think you're probably a very good wyvern, and a good man. I believe that if my situation was other than it is, I would be happy to be your mate—in all meanings of the word. But I will not risk your life for just a few fleeting moments of sexual gratification."

His dimples suddenly appeared. "I assure you, there will be more than just a few fleeting moments."

"You know what I mean."

"Yes, I do." He suddenly dropped to his knees before me, pulling me from the bed into his arms, my legs straddling one of his silk-clad thighs. "Mayling, my little bird, so used to carrying the burdens of the world upon your delicate shoulders. Do not speak that reproach I see your lips ready to form." His head dipped and he kissed me quickly, his fire roaring through me for a moment before it withdrew. "I am wyvern of the silver dragons. I am not so easy to kill."

"But—"

"Do not worry about it, Mayling. You are my mate. I will not give you up to anyone, not even a demon lord."

"I'm *bound* to him," I said, wishing I could just give in to what he offered me. "It's not so simple as me having a choice, don't you understand? He is repugnant, evil personified, the being I most dread on the planet, and yet more than once I have found myself slipping under his seductive spell. To say you won't give me up is neither here nor there. . . . I'll give myself up in the end."

"You have resisted his attempts upon you for a hundred years," he said, his eyes bright with emotion. "I will teach you ways to continue to do so."

A faint surge of hope blossomed within me. "You know a way to avoid his spells?"

"Well . . . not as such. But there are others who do, and we will find them. Do not worry about this, little bird. You are mine, and I do not give up what I hold."

I looked deep into his eyes, and for a moment, I believed him. His belief in himself was unshakable, as was his interest in me. But there was something else, something that was even more intriguing, a brief glimpse of a gentler emotion that found an answering chord within me. "Even if we do find someone who can teach me, we've only known each other . . . well, for a few hours. And much as I enjoy kissing you, and touching you—"

"And wishing to feel me slide into your body, possessing you as only I can—" he said, echoing my thoughts.

I clapped a hand over his mouth, glaring as his dimples emerged.

"Even if all that were true, and I'll thank you very kindly to stop reading my smutty thoughts about you, even so, I am not the sort of a person who is comfortable with the idea of physical intimacy the very day we met. Just because I haven't slept with a man before doesn't mean I'm the sort of girl who jumps into bed at the first seductive and incredibly arousing smile a man gives her."

To my surprise, the aforementioned smile faded. "You are a wyvern's mate."

"Yes, I know—" I started to say, but he stopped me.

"More to the point, you are my mate, but to ensure that you are not, for lack of a better word, poached by another, I must claim you. Physically. After which, you will accept me and the sept, and only then will you be safe from everything but *lusus naturae*."

"What do you mean, poached?" I asked. "*Lusus* what?"

He took a deep breath. I was momentarily distracted by the feeling of his leg pressed so intimately between mine, but managed to wrestle my mind away from that to what he was saying.

"Wyvern's mates are rare. They are born—or in your case, created—to be the mate of a wyvern."

"And?" I asked, waiting for the penny to drop.

"*Any* wyvern," he said.

The penny hit the floor with the impact of an atomic bomb. "You mean I'm not *your* mate . . . I'm any wyvern's mate?"

"Any wyvern who does not yet possess a mate, yes. There are four wyverns in the weyr . . . two of them are mated, two are not, although we're not quite certain about whether or not one of the wyverns is still alive."

"So there's another wyvern out there who could zoom along and . . . what? Grab me for his own mate?"

Gabriel looked vaguely uncomfortable.

"What? The other wyvern isn't a man?"

"No, he is, it's just . . . it's a long story, one which I really don't wish to go into right now, but the blue wyvern was challenged and overthrown by another wyvern, the true wyvern, so now you could say there are two blue wyverns."

"You dragons are very strange," I said, apropos of nothing.

"And then there's Kostya," he said, his gaze a thousand miles away.

"That's the guy you want me to rob?"

"Yes. He claims to be the wyvern of the black dragons, but as such, they do not exist."

"Great. So there are now three other possible guys on the snatch-and-grab list?" I asked.

He hesitated. "Possibly four, if Chuan Ren is not confined to Abaddon after Aisling threw her there."

"Pregnant Aisling tossed a wyvern into Hell?" I asked, astounded.

"She is a Guardian," he said with a slight smile, his gaze returning to the here and now. "A very powerful one."

"I guess so. But none of that explains why any of those possibly four other wyverns would want to pick me to be their mate. I mean, you and I . . . well, we kind of hit it off."

His arms tightened around me, pulling me flush against his upper body. "You are mine, Mayling. No other wyvern will have you. But until you are properly claimed and accept me as your mate, you are vulnerable. We must mate tonight. You must accept me as your wyvern, and the silver dragons as your sept, or I will be forced to spend all my time keeping you from other wyverns rather than helping you escape your bondage to Magoth."

Tears pricked at the back of my eyes. I seldom cried, unlike Cyrene, who wept at the drop of a hat, but the thought that Gabriel would go to the immense trouble of trying to free me from Magoth touched my heart in a way I did not know was possible. "You'd do that for me?" I asked in a breathy voice.

His eyes promised so much. "I will move the heavens and earth if you so desire."

The romantic moment was almost too much to bear, but I would not be Cyrene's twin if I did not bring forth all the common-sense arguments against an instant relationship. "Can't I accept you and your sept without us having sex?"

A slow smile pulled up the corners of his mouth. "Yes. But it wouldn't be nearly as much fun."

Chapter Ten

"I owe you much this first time, but unfortunately, I may not be able to show you the tenderness and gentleness you deserve," Gabriel murmured into my collarbone as his fingers deftly stripped my upper body of shirt and bra.

I shivered as the chilled air hit my fevered skin, then gasped as my breasts, heavy and sensitive with wanting, brushed against his chest when his hands slipped lower, tugging off my pants. I rose to my feet, kicking off the pants, watching with increasing concern as he shucked his own sleeping pants.

"I'm short," I said, looking up as he stood naked in front of me.

His lips twitched. "I wouldn't say short. 'Petite' was the word that first came to mind."

"Yes, but . . ." I stared in dismay at his penis. It was slightly darker than the rest of him, possessing all of the usual attributes, but also startlingly . . . well, large. "You're much taller than me. At least a foot."

A lovely soft chuckle twined itself around me. He took my hand and wrapped it around himself. "We will fit, do not fret, little bird."

"I'm not fretting. I'm just concerned."

"I assure you that in this regard, I am no different from any other man."

I narrowed my eyes at his penis. "You don't have to patronize me. I've seen naked men before. I'm no stranger to sex, either, just not with a man."

"I would not dream of patronizing you. Would you like me to lie down so that you may explore my body?"

"I have toys," I told his penis, rather enjoying the heat of it in my hands. Since he invited me to do so, I allowed my fingers to explore the scenery. The results confirmed my suspicions. "I can say in all confidence that none of them even approach this level of . . . er . . . girth. I know women are built to accommodate all sorts of sizes and shapes, but there has to be a limit, Gabriel. And with the difference in our body sizes . . . well . . ."

"May."

I dragged my gaze off his nether regions up to his face. "What?"

"Are you stalling?" he asked, his eyes alight with amusement.

"Is it that obvious?"

"Yes. But I understand. You are nervous. You are not sure you are ready to commit to this. And I wish I could give you the time to become comfortable with the idea of being my mate, but this is a time of war. I must claim you tonight."

"You're aroused," I blurted.

"Yes, I am."

"But we just met. I'm not aroused."

His arms slid around me, his head lowering to the breast nearest him, his mouth hot on a suddenly aching nipple as he took it into his mouth, lashing it mercilessly with long, soft swipes of his tongue. The sensation lit fires all over my body, causing my back to arch. A low moan of sheer pleasure ripped from my throat as I clutched his shoulders. "Oh, dear god. All right, I take it back, I'm aroused! Do the other one!"

I moaned when his mouth descended on my waiting breast, my hips moving urgently against him as I squirmed with the odd mixture of pleasure and pain when he sucked the nipple. His fingers left trails of fire along my skin as he slid my underwear off, opening me up to his burning touch.

Overcome by the sensation, I bit his shoulder, moaning my ecstasy as he probed and teased, building the fire inside until it roared in my ears. I'd never felt anything like this, amazed and dazzled by the strength of my emotions as his mouth burned a trail along my jaw. His whole body was hot as if he was fevered, his skin a silky brand as I moved restlessly against him. "I want . . ." I stopped, unable to put into words the sensations that held me in a vortex of desire.

"What do you want?" he asked, his voice sliding along my flesh like water. "Tell me what you want."

"I want . . . more," I said, acknowledging the deep need that dwelled within me. I didn't just need his body in mine; I needed him, all of him, merged with me in a way that went beyond sexual.

He tipped my head back, burning my lips, the pupils in his eyes mere slivers of black set in the purest molten silver. I knew then that what he said was true: we were meant to be mated; I was meant to be there at that moment, accepting him into my life and body, binding myself to him for all time.

"Little bird, I must . . . we must do this in the manner of dragons," he murmured, his normally beautiful voice hoarse with passion. "I must claim you this way."

We sank to the floor, Gabriel's mouth and hands building the inferno that raged within me even higher as he turned me over, his body covering mine. One arm was braced next to me as I clutched the carpet, arching my back against his chest, his free hand spreading my legs.

I reached behind me to find him, guide him to where the fire burned the hottest, and he growled low and deep in his chest as he thrust into my body, a hard, burning invader that I welcomed with a cry of joy. The stretching sensation as he pushed his way in turned to one of pure pleasure as he moved. He claimed me with hard thrusts, his breath ragged as he wrapped an arm around me, pulling my hips back against him. I closed my eyes for a moment, so over-come with feelings I wanted to weep with joy, but a sudden burst of searing heat on my shoulder blade had me jerking backwards with a cry.

"It is my brand, the mark of the silver dragons," he said, as he licked away the sting, his hips pistoning against me. "Now you are mine."

An orgasm was building within me, deeper than I'd ever experienced, a tension that was familiar and yet different, seeming to draw energy from everywhere at once, focused at one brilliant point.

Gabriel thrust harder into me, reaching a depth I didn't imagine possible, pushing me past the point of cognizance into a realm of blazing rapture.

He bit my neck, roaring wordless pleasure as he approached his own climax, the arms that were braced beside me suddenly shimmering for a moment as my eyes filled with tears of rapture.

He thrust into my body again, his back arching as he yelled out my name. I welcomed the fire that licked my flesh, reveling in it for a moment before reluctantly returning it to him. Beneath me, the carpet rubbed roughly against my sensitized breasts as Gabriel col-lapsed onto me, his weight a welcome feeling. I lay for a moment, stunned by the power and depth of the experience, protesting weakly when he pulled himself off me, rolling me over into his arms.

"Mayling, did I frighten you? Are you hurt?"

His voice was back to being velvet and satin. I opened my eyes, looking down from where I rested against his chest, a thousand little muscles inside me still quivering with exultation. "I'm not hurt. You were right about that, although I still don't know how we fit together."

He laughed and shifted me up higher, so my head rested on his collarbone, his hands splayed wide across my back. "You have the most delightful mind. I have never met a woman like you."

"Nor are you likely to, unless someone you know is sleeping with a demon lord," I said dryly.

"I'm sorry if the mating frightened you," he said, his voice a lovely rumble in his chest.

I hesitated a moment, picking my words carefully. "It startled me. I wasn't expecting such intensity. You seemed so powerful, so . . . forceful."

"Like an animal?" His voice was light, but there was an undertone that had me pushing back off his chest so I could peer at his face.

"You're not an animal, Gabriel." One corner of his mouth went up. "Well, not in the traditional sense of the word. You're a very enthusiastic lover, but you seem so human, it's just hard to remember that this isn't your real form."

"I am still the same being no matter what form I wear," he said slowly, his eyes filled with warmth. "And you are my mate, the woman who has completed my life. Dragons frequently shift in the throes of sexual ecstasy, but if my dragon form makes you uncomfortable, then I will endeavor to control it."

I bit my lip, hating to make such a big deal about

it, but at the same time, pathetically grateful that he would stay in human form. "I'm sure it makes me the worst sort of bigot to say that I'm uncomfortable around something that doesn't look human."

His dimples popped into life. "Do you know that you shadowed at your moment of climax?"

I gazed at him in surprise. "No! I did? I didn't feel it. Are you sure?"

"Sure that the woman I held in my arms suddenly became almost entirely transparent? Yes."

"I'm sorry," I said, feeling the need to apologize. "Did it unnerve you?"

"No. There is nothing about you that I could ever find disagreeable."

I held my tongue, not wanting to ruin the moment of intimacy, allowing him to pull me back down against his body, still hot, but now dampened by our experience.

Lazy fingers drew patterns along my back, slowly moving up to my shoulder. A sensitive spot of skin reminded me of the burning sensation. "What was that brand you burned into me?

He traced out a pattern on my shoulder blade. "It is the mark of the silver dragon. It signifies you are my mate."

I frowned. "I'm not sure I like being treated like a piece of cattle. Couldn't you have asked me first if I wanted it?"

"All members of the sept wear the symbol, here, in the small of their back." He touched a spot on my lower back. "Only wyverns and their mates wear them higher, on the shoulder."

"Let me see yours."

He obliged by sitting up, turning to the side so I could see the emblem that had been burned into his skin. I touched it, following the pattern. It was in the shape of a hand bearing a crescent moon. "That's actually quite beautiful. What does it symbolize?"

"Our relationship with the sept, and nature," he said enigmatically, pulling me up as he got to his feet. "It is morning. I wish I could let you have the rest you deserve, but you must first accept me as your mate so that I can make the preparations to present you to the sept."

I glanced down to the floor, where a few minutes before I had been writhing in ecstasy. "Didn't . . . er . . . our lovemaking qualify as me accepting you?"

He shook his head, his eyes still almost glowing. "You must formally take me as your mate."

"All right," I said, extremely aware that I was standing naked next to a beautiful—also naked—man who could shift into dragon form at the merest whim. My mouth went a bit dry. "What words do I need to repeat?"

"Whatever is in your heart."

"Are you sure?" I asked him after a few seconds of silence. "There is Magoth to consider—"

"He will be taken care of, I promise you that, Mayling."

My better judgment warned me against accepting what he offered, but my heart leaped at the thought of having my cake and eating it, too.

I would trust him, trust that he was the one person who could survive being in a relationship with me. "I am May Northcott, doppelganger, and your mate. Your life is bound to mine, and mine to yours. I accept you into my life, and will do my best to make you and the silver dragons happy."

He pulled me into an embrace, my breasts immediately turning into strumpets as they pressed themselves against the flesh of his lower chest. "I, Gabriel Tauhou, wyvern of the silver dragons, take you as my mate, to guard and protect, to care for and cherish, to the end of my days."

The kiss he shared with me burned with dragon fire. I welcomed it, rubbing myself against him as it blazed through me, igniting fires I'd assumed were slumbering. With a growl, he tossed me onto the bed, following to kiss a blazing path from my neck to my breasts.

"We're going to do it again?" I asked, amazed but pleased to see his penis beginning to swell.

"Now we will mate like humans," he said, lifting his head from the valley between my breasts. His gaze scorched along my flesh, leaving me trembling with need. "But this time, we will take it slowly. I will pleasure you at length, giving you the time you need to—"

I grabbed his head, wrapping my fingers in the thin, soft dreadlocks, pulling his mouth down to mine at the same time I wrapped my legs around his hips. "Now," I yelled into his mouth, biting his lower lip.

He laughed even as he shifted his hips, thrusting into my waiting flesh. "My demanding little bird."

"You have *no* idea," I groaned, thrusting my hips up to meet him, my tongue twining around his in an erotic dance that begged for more. "Give me your fire. *Please.*"

He didn't say anything more, just released his dragon fire until it consumed us, sending me soaring once again into a world that consisted only of Gabriel and me, and the blaze that we built between us.

Chapter Eleven

"Let me see if I have this straight."

I rubbed my forehead and wished for the fiftieth time in the last ten minutes that a portal would suddenly open up next to me to take me a thousand miles from this spot.

"Despite the fact that you had just finished explaining to me why you could not get involved with any man—"

Cyrene's voice was drowned out for a moment by the arrival of another fire engine.

"—to the wind and slept with Gabriel? Oh, Mayling, *really!*"

In the blissful silence that followed the siren being silenced, Cyrene's voice was clearly audible.

I closed my eyes and wondered what would be the worst thing that would happen if I was to suddenly shadow in front of the twenty or so people who now turned interested faces upon us. Luckily, the crowd gathered had other things to capture their attention, and turned away from us almost immediately. All but one person, a tall, wiry man who examined Cyrene and me with speculation I found almost offensive.

"I don't think *everyone* in the entire country heard you," I said in a low, dangerous voice, giving the man a thin-lipped look. He blinked a couple of times, then moved off.

Cyrene rolled her eyes. "The point is that despite everything you had just told me, you slept with Gabriel, and had such incredibly wild sex that the bed was set on fire. Am I correct in that summation of the evening's events?"

I grabbed her arm and pulled her as far away from our audience as was possible, my cheeks hot with embarrassment. We were standing a block away from the hotel, huddled with other guests in various states of undress as the fire department put out the blaze that had damaged part of the floor my room was on. "It wasn't like that!"

"And unless that very handsome fireman who brought out my things was mistaken, your little love-fest with Gabriel not only caused the furnishings in your room to burn—a fact that evidently went unnoticed by either of you—but the fire spread to adjoining rooms?"

I ground my teeth.

"Do I have all that correct?"

I lifted my chin and gave her a look of my own. "There were extenuating circumstances. Not to mention the fact that the hotel's fire prevention practices are clearly out of date. The sprinklers didn't go on until the curtains were almost gone."

She eyed me with a curiously flat look. "Gabriel must be one hell of a lover."

"That is neither here nor there," I said with as much dignity as I could muster, which admittedly wasn't much.

Cyrene was silent for a few minutes before turning back to me, her voice much lower. "You slept with him. You really slept with him?"

"I didn't intend to. I meant everything I said to you. I still do—but somehow . . . somehow Gabriel made me believe that there may be a way around the situation with Magoth."

"So"—her hands made a vague gesture—"does this mean you're a dragon?"

"I accepted him as my mate," I answered warily. "I don't believe that changes me in any way other than my life is now bound to his."

Another fire truck arrived. We scooted back as more refugees from the hotel were released by the medical folk. "What do you think Magoth will do?"

"Probably try to seduce me yet again, but I think . . ." I remembered the feeling of Gabriel's body with a warm flush that started at my belly and rippled upward. "I think it will be easier to refuse him. Rather than being a weakness Magoth could exploit, I think that this relationship with Gabriel may end up giving me strength."

"I'm still trying to get over the idea of you having sex. After all those years when I tried to find a man for you . . ."

"I haven't exactly been chaste," I said with a little smile. "As you should know, since you were the one to give me the Pink Bunny Tinglator."

She smiled fondly. "That was one of my better finds, wasn't it? But not as good as a man."

"No, definitely not."

She digested that for a moment. "Was he in man form, or dragon form?"

"Really, Cy, does it matter?" I draped the blanket I'd been holding tight around me onto a nearby shrub, pulling on the leather bodice that I'd grabbed, along with my pants and shirt, before Gabriel had rushed me out of the blazing room.

"No, of course not, although I can't help but be curious. I've never had sex with a shape-shifter before, so I wasn't sure how they . . . er . . . did it."

"They do it like any other *human*," I answered, emphasizing the important point.

"Yes, but dragons aren't human, are they? They're . . . well, I suppose they're animals."

"Gabriel is not an animal!" I said in a furious whisper. "He's a dragon, yes, but they aren't animals. They're just . . . dragons. Usually human in form, sometimes appearing in another form."

"So . . . did he do it in dragon form?"

I scanned the crowd of people for the tall, gorgeous man who'd gone off to explain to the fire department why my room was ablaze. "This really isn't anything I'm comfortable talking about."

"No, I can't imagine that admitting to engaging in bestiality is something that you want bandied about, but it's fascinating nonetheless."

I spun around to glare at my twin, keeping my voice low. "It was *not* bestiality!"

"You had sex with him in dragon form—that's certainly not plain old missionary-position sex," she pointed out with cheerful disregard of anything I said.

"He was *not* in dragon form. He said he could, but he didn't, and frankly, I'm glad. . . . Oh, this is silly. I'm not going to discuss this any further with you."

Cyrene patted me on the arm. "Don't get me wrong—I admire you, I really do. I remember in the old days, when Zeus was always flitting around in swan form, trying to seduce the sisterhood. Have you ever had a swan hump your leg? It's not the least bit alluring, let me tell you!"

I gaped openmouthed at her. "You . . . *Zeus*?"

"Oh, yes, he was always after us naiads. Had some sort of a fetish about doing it in the water, so the rumor went. We won't go into what he did with his beak."

There just wasn't much I could say to that, so I closed my mouth and made a mental note to read up on Greek mythology.

"There he is," Cyrene said, looking intently as Gabriel emerged from the crowd. Her voice held a note I couldn't pin down, but that made me uncomfortable.

"Cy, you're not angry that I turned out to be his mate rather than you?" I asked slowly.

She thought for a moment, then shook her head, her eyes unusually sober. "I was at first, but then I thought of what it would mean to you if I snatched him away, and I decided I couldn't do that to you. You deserve a man of your own."

I bit my lip against replying that she wouldn't have been able to take him from me, feeling she deserved a little face saving.

Gabriel stopped in front of me, his expression grim.

"What's wrong?" I asked immediately.

"Have you seen Maata or Tipene?"

I looked around, trying to find the two rather large bodyguards in the mass of people still milling around outside the hotel, but it was difficult to see over everyone. "No. Didn't they go back to wherever you are staying?"

He shook his head, frowning. "They took rooms here, in order to keep a watch on you."

"*Me?*" Anger rose quick and hot, aided by a deep feeling of pain that he didn't trust me. "You thought I was going to steal something of yours and run off?"

"You've already stolen something of mine, but that's not the point."

He scanned the crowd, his eyes worried. I grabbed his arm, glaring up at him. "How dare you. I have not stolen anything from you. I'm not a real thief, which

I thought you would have understood after I explained about my relationship to Magoth."

"Mayling—"

"How could you possibly do the things we just did and then tell me you think I'm a low-life, common, ordinary thief—"

He stopped my tirade by the effective method of yanking me up to his chest and kissing me with a passion that stripped the breath from my lungs.

"My heart, little bird—you stole my heart."

I closed my mouth on the protest I was about to make, a lovely warm feeling glowing in my belly.

"I would be offended that you could imagine I'd have such a low estimation of my mate," he continued, "but I do not have time for that now. If Maata and Tipene are not here, they must have perceived a threat to you and followed it up. Which can only mean one thing."

"What?" I asked, startled by the strength of a sudden need to fling myself upon him and kiss away his worried frown.

He said the name as if it was an oath. "Kostya."

"Who's Kostya?" Cyrene asked, yawning as she wandered over to us. "When can we go back into our rooms? I must have my morning bath, or I'm just not fit for the day."

"He's a black dragon who doesn't want Gabriel to be wyvern of his sept," I said absently. Something didn't make sense. "Why Kostya?" I asked Gabriel. "Or rather, how Kostya?"

"How?" He shot me a confused look.

"Yes, how. You said that your bodyguards were protecting me, but why would they need to when no one knows about me? I mean, we just met each other"—I glanced at my watch—"less than twelve hours ago. How would Kostya know who I am, let alone the fact that I am now your mate?"

"She has a point," Cyrene said.

"He is Drake's brother," Gabriel reminded me.

I raised an eyebrow. "I thought Drake and Aisling were your friends. They certainly seemed friendly enough. Would he rat you out to his brother like that?"

He looked uncomfortable for a few moments. "Our relationship has been a bit . . . strained . . . of late. There were recent regrettable incidents for which, unfortunately, my part was seen only in a suspicious light."

"Regrettable incidents?" I asked, watching him closely. "What sort of regrettable incidents?"

He took my hand and started down the sidewalk. I grabbed Cyrene's arm and pulled her after us.

Gabriel's gaze darted here and there as he searched for his two missing bodyguards. "It is an involved story."

"Uh-huh. Why do I have the feeling that it involves Aisling more than Drake?"

He flashed me a quick grin. "Are you jealous?"

"Oh, yes."

He stopped for a moment, surprise chasing delight on his face. "You are?"

"She's pretty, powerful, and a wyvern's mate. Plus Drake said something about you interfering with her, which makes me think that she made a play for you."

He laughed, giving my hand a squeeze. "I am flattered that you think so, but the truth is much less prone to inflaming your jealousy. Aisling has always been in love with Drake."

"Then what was the regrettable incident?"

"Will you be all right if I leave you here for a few minutes?" he asked, parking us next to a small clutch of policemen.

I made a little face. "I've managed to exist for more

than eighty years on my own, and Cy is over twelve hundred years old, so yes, I think we'll just be able to manage standing here without attracting catastrophe."

Cyrene whapped me with the end of her blanket. "Don't tell him how old I am! You know how sensitive I am about that."

"What was the regrettable incident?" I asked again, my curiosity getting the better of me.

"I betrayed Aisling and Drake. Stay here while I go talk to that taxi driver."

He dashed off into the crowd before I could do anything but gawk.

"Did he say he betrayed them?" Cyrene asked me.

I nodded. "Yes. What a very interesting man he is."

"Dragon."

"He has such layers. Just when you think you have him pegged, you discover another layer."

"Goodness," Cyrene said with a thoughtful look. "He sounds so very exotic. And then there's the shape-shifting. I imagine that would be incredibly erotic. Hmm. I wonder who I know who can do that . . ."

Gabriel returned looking more worried, and swearing under his breath. Before I could ask what was going on, he escorted us to a taxi.

"No luck?" I asked once we got in.

"No. I'm going to have to ask Drake for help."

"Is that wise if he's working with his brother?"

"I never said he was working with Kostya—but it is entirely likely that he told his brother about you. He might have thought it would encourage Kostya to give up his attempt on us." He shook his head. "Damnation. I didn't want to involve Drake in this any more than I have, but I don't see an alternative."

"I'll be more than happy to help," I said, touching his hand.

The smile he turned on me could have melted steel. "I count upon your support, Mayling."

I couldn't resist his dimples . . . or anything else for that matter. I leaned to the side, brushing my mouth against his. "Have I told you how beautiful your eyes are?"

"I'm going to look out the window now," Cyrene announced, "because voyeurism is never a pretty thing, although it can be oddly exciting if you are in Rome with a dashing Italian, and he flings you into a fountain on New Year's Eve, and subsequently licks the water off you."

"No," Gabriel answered, nibbling my bottom lip. "But they can't be anywhere near as fascinating as the lovely pools of mystery that you bear, little bird."

"They're plain old blue eyes," I said with a little laugh, doing a little nibbling of my own.

"Hello! Those are *my* eyes you're denigrating, and I've had odes written to them! Well, one ode, and a sonnet, and a couple of limericks, although now I think on it, those weren't really about my eyes so much as other parts."

A half hour later we stood in front of the lovely rental villa, which was even lovelier by daylight.

"It's still pretty early," I told Gabriel as he paid off the taxi and marched up to the double doors. "Do you think they're up yet? We had kind of a late night."

"They're up," he answered in a voice that was rough with grit.

"How do you know?" I asked.

He pointed toward the garage, off to the side of the house. The nose of a sleek black car was just barely visible. "That isn't the car Drake is using."

Cyrene and I stood a few feet back as Gabriel pounded on the door.

"These dragons are awfully intense, don't you think?" Cyrene said, watching him with a concerned eye.

"I think there's a lot going on that we're not aware of," I answered, wondering if that car belonged to Drake's brother. "But on the whole, yes, they are intense. Which isn't necessarily—"

The doors were opened by István, who didn't look the least bit surprised to see us on the doorstep. He didn't look happy, either, although he said nothing, just bowed and stepped back to allow us to enter.

Cyrene touched her neck as she sent him a little frown, but managed on the whole to sail through the doorway with her usual grace and elegance.

I slammed up against a ward and felt my body distort in what I was sure was a gruesome manner as I attempted to force my way through it.

"I'm sorry," I said finally, backing away. "I can't get through it."

"It is for dark beings," István said, giving me a suspicious look.

"Aisling will simply have to remove it again," Gabriel said, going in ahead of me. "Is she here?"

"On the patio."

"Aisling? Could you unbind the ward so May can enter?" Gabriel called out in a loud voice.

The person who appeared from the patio wasn't Aisling. It was a man, dark haired and dark eyed, slightly taller than Gabriel, but leaner, with much less body mass. That fact didn't seem to matter, though—he took a flying leap at Gabriel, slamming them both against the nearest wall.

Chapter Twelve

"What—" Cyrene started to ask, looking confused as the two men hit the floor, fighting for all they were worth.

I didn't wait around to see what happened—I shadowed, raced around the side of the house, and leaped over the fence, running around to the patio with a burst of speed I doubt I'll ever be able to match.

Drake was assisting Aisling to her feet, Jim in front of them heading for the house. I ran past the two of them, hurdling the third as I headed for the hallway where I could hear Gabriel yelling.

"What on earth—what was that? Drake, did you just see someone—" Aisling was saying as my feet hit the slick stone tile of the entryway. I threw myself onto the back of the man who was trying to strangle Gabriel. István had him by one arm, Pál by the other, but they weren't having much luck in stopping him.

I grabbed his hair with both hands, and using my knees as leverage on his back, flung myself backward, dragging him with me.

The man screamed as I rolled out of the way, throwing myself across him and slamming his head down onto the stone floor.

"What is going on—good lord! Is that May on

Kostya? It's so hard to see her, she's almost translucent. Gabriel, are you all right?" Aisling's voice asked.

"Stop!" Drake bellowed, but I ignored him, continuing to slam Kostya's head onto the tiles. "Gabriel! Control your mate!"

"Mayling, you must stop. Kostya's head is too thick to harm; you'll only break the stone floor."

I glared down at the man, noting with satisfaction that one of his eyes was swelling shut. Gabriel must have connected with his fist before I'd made it around the back of the house. "All right, but only because if he got seriously hurt, you'd have to heal him."

"Your consideration boggles the mind," Drake said dryly as Gabriel, weaving slightly, took my hand and pulled me up next to him.

I looked him over carefully. There was a faint trickle of blood from his upper lip, and some nasty bruising on his throat, but the latter were fading before my eyes. "Are you OK?"

"Yes," he said, clearing his throat at the roughness that resulted from the throttling. "I'm fine, although I would appreciate it if Kostya would tell me in advance when he declares a kill-on-sight status upon me."

The man I'd correctly surmised was Kostya got to his feet, assisted, I was secretly pleased to note, by no one. He listed a bit to one side, and his face had a battered appearance, but already his black eye was beginning to recede. He spat something out in a language that sounded Slavic.

Drake sighed and took Aisling's arm. "Your assault on him *was* unwarranted, Kostya. We've already told you that Gabriel does not have the phylactery."

"The phylactery?" Gabriel looked startled for a moment, then frowned. "What game is this, Kostya?"

"Come out onto the patio and we'll explain it," Aisling said, sounding and looking a bit weary. I thought Drake was going to carry her out there, but she gave him a warning look and made her own way out to the comfortable rattan couch that overlooked the garden and beach.

I wondered what it would be like to be so cherished. Despite my relationship to Cyrene, I'd always been alone most of my life—she had her sisterhood of naiads, and I had Magoth.

"What's wrong?" Gabriel asked, his voice warm against my ear as I took a seat. He stood behind me, one hand on my shoulder in a little display of possession that I found oddly appealing. "You look as if you'd just bitten a dung beetle."

"I was thinking about Magoth," I answered quietly.

"Do not worry about him, little bird. All will be well there, you'll see."

I didn't correct his mistaken impression that I was worried about the likelihood of Magoth convincing me to destroy Gabriel—now that I'd felt the strength of the bond that connected me to Gabriel, I had little fear that Magoth's seductions would fall upon anything but fallow ground. But I did wonder what it would be like to live with Gabriel, to bear his child, to have him treat me as if I was the most precious thing on the planet. And there was something else about Drake and Aisling, an awareness that I found both curious and intriguing. They didn't touch each other often, didn't even appear to be looking at each other much, but if Aisling shifted slightly to get more comfortable, Drake was instantly there, adjusting a pillow or sliding a glass a little closer to her.

I wondered if the obvious sympathetic bond they shared was something unique to them, or whether a version of it would come as I spent time with Gabriel.

His fingers brushed the back of my neck lightly as if in unspoken answer.

"Kostya insists that you have the phylactery," Drake said without preamble.

His brother, who was pacing along the far edge of the patio, whirled around and glared at Gabriel. "There is no one else who would steal it! He must have it. I demand it be returned to me."

Gabriel's fingers tightened on my shoulder. "Disregarding the fact that I do not, in fact, have the phylactery, your claim to it is asinine. Drake found it in Fiat's lair—if anyone has a claim on it, it would seem Drake does . . . or at worst, Fiat. But not you, Konstantin Nikolai Fekete."

The black dragon did not like hearing Gabriel use his full name, and I didn't blame him. Everyone knew that names have power, and I certainly wouldn't want a wyvern I was more or less warring against invoking mine.

Kostya snarled and would have lunged toward Gabriel, but István and Pál had taken up positions on either side of him, grabbing him when he started toward us.

I leaped to my feet, ready to shadow and go after him if Drake's men couldn't control him.

"I begin to think you are more like a falcon than like a blackbird, Mayling," Gabriel murmured gently, pushing me back into the chair. "Do not trouble yourself over Kostya."

"Mei Ling?" Kostya asked, the anger in his face giving way to surprise. "Mei Ling the thief?"

"She is not a thief, not a real one," Gabriel said with a flash of his silver eyes. "She simply acquires objects for her employer, nothing more."

"And yet you claim you did not steal my phylactery?" Kostya turned to his brother with an angry gesture. "What more proof do you need? She is a thief, and his mate. Obviously, she stole it to please him!"

"She couldn't have," Aisling said, shaking her head.

"Gabriel and May met last night for the first time," Drake explained.

"Bah! That was what they wanted you to think, in order to excite sympathy for their cause. But I am not so easily fooled as you are, brother. They are working together, and I will not allow them to succeed with their infamous plans."

The sudden calculating look he shot me sent cold chills down my spine. "Gabriel," I whispered, leaning toward him, "I think we may have a problem."

"I will not allow him to harm you," he answered in a louder tone of voice than was strictly necessary. "Do not fear for your safety, mate. He will not touch you."

"That's not quite what I meant," I said, intending on pointing out that as Dr. Kostich hadn't lifted the price on my head, it was entirely possible Kostya might turn in information about me in order to gain the benefaction. I hated to think what he could do with a powerful archimage on his side.

Before I could mention all that, Kostya started ranting about the injustices done to him. "I swear to you that the black dragon sept will regain what we once held but was taken from us!"

"Oh, not that again," Aisling said, whispering to her husband, "Can we hit a fast-forward button, do you think?"

"We will face death to restore to the sept the pride, the glory, the true essence, of what it once was," Kostya declared with a dramatic sweep of his hand.

"Enough!" Gabriel suddenly roared, taking everyone aback. "I have had enough of your games, Kostya! I can only assume you are trying to turn Drake against me with these outrageous claims, but I will not waste my time any longer defending myself. There is a more important matter at hand that must be attended to."

"Drake—as a neutral party—got Kostya and Gabriel to agree to come here and talk about things," Jim said softly as it ambled over and sat next to me, leaning its bulk against my leg. "That was before you tried to bash Kostya's brains out all over the entryway, naturally. Things are probably a bit dicier now."

I shot the demon a look. It grinned back at me, pink tongue lolling.

"I suppose now is as good a time as any to begin the talks between you two," Aisling said, looking dubious.

"I will not talk peace with Kostya until he returns Maata and Tipene," Gabriel said, his fingers tightening again on my shoulder.

I could swear there was a momentary flash of surprise in Kostya's eyes before they returned to their familiar belligerent cast. "I do not know what you're talking about."

"Maata and Tipene are gone?" Aisling asked. "I wondered where they were. Kostya—"

"I do not know what he's talking about!" Kostya repeated, louder. "I have had nothing to do with any of his sept, as per our agreement prior to meeting here."

"An agreement you saw no problem in ignoring when you saw the chance to take my guards," Gabriel snapped. I leaned slightly toward him, nudging his leg with my shoulder.

"If I wanted to take out a silver dragon," Kostya said in a low, threatening voice, "he would not be missing—he'd be dead."

Gabriel's body twitched as he restrained himself. "I don't believe you," he said after he got himself under control.

Kostya shrugged. "It matters little to me what you believe. Perhaps you are simply claiming they are missing in order to garner Drake's sympathy."

Gabriel flinched as his own accusation was flung back at him. "I see that we are at an impasse again." "And it will stay so until you return my phylactery to me," Kostya almost yelled.

"You will return Maata and Tipene unharmed, or I will finish what was started centuries ago!" Gabriel returned, his eyes positively glowing with anger.

I stood up and took his arm as Pál and István closed in on Kostya again. The two wyverns glared at each other. I could feel the dragon fire within him, raging to be freed, but he had immense control, and kept it back when I probably would have burned down the entire block.

"Then there is nothing more to be said. This meeting has been a waste of time." Kostya stiffly jerked his arms from the two green dragons, bowing to Aisling. "I bid you good day, Aisling, brother."

He took a step toward Gabriel, but his ebony gaze was narrowed on me, sending a little skitter of fear down my back. "As for you, thief . . ."

Gabriel stepped in front of me, a ring of fire bursting to life around the two of us. "Do you threaten my mate?"

I stared at Gabriel's back in astonishment. I'd never heard such raw fury in a man's voice before, and that it came from velvet-tongued Gabriel . . .

"You should not *have* a mate," Kostya snarled, spitting little balls of fire at our feet. "No silver dragon deserves a mate since they are responsible for stealing that of the black wyvern."

"We did not steal her! We took back that which was stolen from us! Ysolde de Bouchier was a silver dragon!"

"That history does not have importance at this time," Drake said, stepping between the two furious dragons. Gabriel immediately backed down, wrapping an arm around me and pulling me tight against his side. Drake sent his brother a warning look, which, after a moment or two of antagonistic posturing, Kostya acknowledged.

"Discussing the issue of a future agreement between Kostya and the silver dragons is useless until Maata and Tipene are returned," Gabriel said.

"I have nothing to do with them!" Kostya yelled, slamming his hands down on a metal table.

"If you have not, then who has?" Gabriel argued. "Who would wish to do harm to the silver dragons? Fiat? His battle has nothing to do with us. Bastian and his blues are on friendly terms with the silver dragons. Neither do we have a grievance against the red dragons, no matter if their wyvern is Chuan Ren or another. The green and silver septs have long had a history of mutual friendship and trust."

"Which is why you sided with Fiat to destroy Drake and claim Aisling as your mate?" Kostya asked in a sneering voice.

My gaze went to the man at my side. He flickered a brief look at me, his jaw tightening as he said slowly, "My intention was never to destroy Drake or the green dragons. Fiat was intent on doing both, and I simply did what was necessary in order to lessen the massive destruction that was sure to follow if he proceeded unchecked."

I looked thoughtfully at the very pregnant Aisling. A faint smile twitched her lips. "He never really wanted *me,* you know. He just wanted a mate."

A painful knot gripped my stomach as I wondered if it was merely for a mate that he had so enthusiastically embraced me.

"No," he said, watching Kostya.

It didn't matter . . . or rather it did, but now was not the moment to examine the basis of the man I'd bound myself to. As Gabriel said, there were more important things at hand, such as the whereabouts of Maata and Tipene.

All the same, the words echoed in my head: *He just wanted a mate.*

Chapter Thirteen

"Well. I'll say this for Gabriel—he has good taste in houses." Cyrene dropped the handle of her suitcase with an audible thump on the rich carpet of the entrance hall. "I hope the rest of the house is as nice as the entrance. It's much nicer than my flat, and certainly better than that dark little hole you inhabit. How many rooms did he say it has?"

"Seven bedrooms." I closed the front door, consulting a small card to punch in the code needed to pacify the security system.

"I shall graciously accept Gabriel's invitation to stay with you until he gets here, then," she said, opening up the door nearest us. "Sitting room. Kitchen back here, do you think?"

"I guess." I stood for a moment in the hallway, noting absently that Cyrene's assessment of quality was, as ever, dead on. The house mightn't be a huge mansion, but it was located in Marylebone, right in the center of London, and it appeared to be furnished simply but elegantly. I touched a finger to the half-paneled wall before slowly following Cyrene. She explored the house, scattering excited little oohs and ahs of pleasure behind her as she ran from room to room. I paused to look in the sitting room, decorated with antiques of cream, rose, and gold, admired the kitchen with its huge marble-topped center block, and finally stopped at the back of the house, in a parquet-floored conservatory sporting tall palms and a beautiful blue-gray granite fireplace that had to be at least three hundred years old.

It was all lovely, perfectly charming . . . and utterly lifeless. It was as if Gabriel had never even been there at all, as if his presence hadn't touched the house in any way.

"The master bathtub is divine!" Cyrene announced, coming down from the second floor. "Would you mind . . . ?"

"Go ahead," I said, sitting gingerly on the edge of a spindly legged chair.

"You know how a bath always makes me feel better." She started to go, but paused, looking back at where I sat. "Is something wrong, Mayling? You have the oddest look on your face. Don't you like the house?"

"The house is beautiful. It's just . . ." I hesitated, finding it difficult to put my strange mood into words. "It just seems so bare, as if it was just here for show and no one has ever really lived in it."

"Well, Gabriel did say he wasn't in London much. Maybe he hasn't had time to make it feel like a home yet. Besides, that's what you're for, isn't it?"

Her words brought to the surface all the feelings of doubt that I'd successfully pinned down during the last twelve hours.

"Mayling?" Cyrene took a couple of steps into the room, her brow furrowed. "You are going to be happy with Gabriel, aren't you?"

Her concern touched me, making me forget my earlier annoyance with her. That had always been the pattern of our relationship . . . she got into trouble, and, exasperated, I ran to her aid, forgiving her when faced with her genuine affection and gratitude. "Of course I'll be happy. How could I be otherwise? I have a man so sexy he literally burns down a hotel room, a gorgeous house in a prime spot in London, and carte blanche to do with it what I want. I'd have to be insane not to be happy."

"Yes," she said, touching my cheek lightly. "You would. Those dragons are incredibly sexy, don't you think?"

I glanced up quickly, but she had a dreamy look in her eyes, not one that hinted of jealousy. "That's one way of putting it."

"I think it's because they're so . . . oh, I don't know . . . exotic. You know what I mean? There's a sense of danger about them, as if they are barely just holding back the beast that dwells within them."

I couldn't deny her assessment, although I was more than a little reluctant to have this discussion. "I suppose so, although Gabriel seems much more even tempered than Drake or his obnoxious brother."

"Obnoxious!" Cyrene gaped at me. "How can you possibly say that about Kostya? He's not obnoxious! He's just . . . intense. Very, very intense. And so handsome, don't you think?"

Relief mingled with disbelief as she continued to sing Kostya's praises. I recognized the signs all too well, having lived through a good hundred or so of Cyrene's relationships. "He doesn't seem terribly stable, emotionally speaking," I said slowly.

"Who doesn't? Kostya?" She wandered over to a palm, absently stroking its leaves in a manner I knew would have the plant sprouting new branches (plants love naiads). "There's a reason for that, you know. I had a long talk with Aisling earlier, and she told me all about how Kostya had to go into hiding after he killed his wyvern, and then how he was kidnapped by someone unknown, and left to starve in a horrible prison until Drake and Aisling rescued him. So you see, he's been through a lot in the last couple of hundred years. Allowances should be made for his rather brusque manner."

I stifled a little smile at the word "brusque" being applied to Kostya, but kept silent, feeling it was better for her blossoming infatuation to burn itself out without help from me.

"I wonder if he's going to be wyvern of his sept," she said, looking out of the floor-to-ceiling window to a darkened garden.

"I was under the impression there was no sept to be wyvern of."

"Aisling said she thought there were a few black dragons still left, but they are in hiding." Cyrene turned back toward me, making a contrite face. "I'm sorry, here I am chatting on and you're obviously tired and should get some rest. Bath for me, and then the master room is all yours."

She hurried off to take her restorative bath, leaving me to my murky thoughts.

My emotions were too raw to dwell much on the last few hours I'd spent before Cyrene and I had left Greece. Most of the day had been spent kicking my heels at Aisling's house, waiting to hear what Gabriel and Drake had found out about the disappearance of Maata and Tipene. I had been frustrated being kept out of the way, but knew too little about the ways of dragons to know if it was a case of being kept from underfoot, or if Gabriel and Drake were putting themselves in a situation that would have been dangerous to me.

"Anything?" I had asked when Gabriel returned after four hours.

"No." He took my arm and edged me away from

where Aisling was grilling Drake. "No one has seen them. Their things weren't touched, and they didn't leave any message for me. I'm afraid the worst has happened."

I put my hand on his chest, wanting to comfort him. "You think they're . . . dead?"

He was silent for a moment before shaking his head. "No. I'd feel it if they were dead. But someone has taken them against their will, and that someone is Kostya."

"He says he didn't."

Gabriel's eyes were as bright as mercury, his face suddenly frightening in its austerity. "He lies. He's tried to sway Drake over to helping him against us before. This is just another attempt to put me in a bad light, and himself in the role of a victim."

"I have to say," I said slowly, unsure how he'd take my comment in his present unyielding mood, "that he looked to me to be surprised when you accused him of harming your guards."

"He is a very good actor. He's had time to perfect that skill . . . but it doesn't fool me. The silver dragons are at war with no one. There is no reason anyone would want to take my guard. It has to be Kostya."

"So what do we do now?" I asked.

His eyes warmed several degrees as he looked down at me. "You, little bird, are going to London with your twin as you originally planned."

I was both surprised and hurt at his dismissal.

"Do not think I don't want you near me," he said with a flash of his dimples, his fingers soft as he brushed back a strand of my hair. "There are some green dragons who live in the north of Greece—Drake has called on them to help us search."

"Aren't there any silver dragons around here?"

He shook his head. "They populate mostly Africa,

and the South Pacific, although recently more have moved into the Caribbean, and the West Coast of America. Very few silver dragons live in Europe."

"Why? Is there something here that keeps the silver dragons away?" I asked.

"Not at all. I myself prefer the southern climes, but business concerns frequently keep me in the Northern Hemisphere. I do not wish to part with you, Mayling, but it will relieve my mind to know you are safe at home. There is enough room for your twin to stay as well—I'd be easier in my mind if you had company with you there. I expect to follow you tomorrow, at the latest. Until then"—his head dipped down as he bit my lower lip—"I will miss you greatly."

The scene played in my mind as I sat alone in the empty, echoing conservatory. Rain pattered down lightly on the windows as indigo claimed the sky. I touched my lips, shivering, but whether it was from the relative cold of an early spring London night, or from a suspicion that what Gabriel would miss was his mate rather than me specifically, I couldn't say.

"This isn't doing you any good," I said aloud, my voice eerily thin. I cleared my throat and tried again. "What you need is a plan of action. Let's put that mind to work and come up with something useful."

Cyrene's faint voice, chirping happily away in the bathroom upstairs, drifted down as I pulled out the blackmail letter she had given me earlier. It was brief and to the point, demanding that I render a service or else the blackmailer would hand over the videotape to the appropriate authorities.

With reluctance, I punched in the phone number the blackmailer had given.

"What?" a gruff male voice answered.

"This is Cyrene Northcott's twin. I understand you wished to speak with me."

"Oh, the doppelganger." The man's voice had a harsh midwestern U.S. twang to it. "About time you called. There's a job I want you to do for me. Something I want you to steal."

I was no stranger to bluntness, so I ignored everything but what was important—I needed to make sure that he didn't know I was also Mei Ling. "What makes you think I'm going to condone an illegal act?"

The man grunted. "Saw you at that oracle's with your hand up his ass, didn't I? You were there for the same thing I was—the arcanum."

"I would hardly refer to being in the oracle's book room as having my hand up his ass, but we'll let that go."

"You're a doppelganger. I looked that up—you can go invisible and get into places normal people can't. So don't come over all high and mighty on me."

I bit back any number of responses, relieved that he hadn't mentioned anything about Mei Ling. The arcanum I was sent to get wasn't particularly valuable—Magoth simply had a desire to see it—and it certainly wasn't of the same quality of items that the infamous Mei Ling had previously stolen, so it was entirely within reason that this person didn't connect a shadow-walking doppelganger named May with a Chinese cat burglar. "What is it you want acquired?"

"Not going to deny it, eh?" The man chuckled, his laugh just as unpleasant as his voice. "Smart girl. There's a piece here in London, a small golden amulet. It's well protected, so you'll need to use your wits to get it. You got a pencil? Here's the address."

I took down the information, wondering what the amulet was, and how I was going to get out of stealing it. For now, I'd let the blackmailer think he had me by the short and curlies, but I would not commit myself to stealing something about which I knew nothing. Perhaps if I knew a little more about who he was working for, I'd be able to assess what it was he wanted stolen. "All right, I have that. My twin said you were working for a dreadlord. Which one?"

"Who I work for is none of your business," he said sharply, on a quick intake of breath.

"Well then, who owns this amulet you want stolen?"

The silence that followed was rife with suspicion.

"Look, I don't know what you think doppelgangers can do, but we can't turn invisible, and we can't walk through walls. We're flesh and blood just like anyone else . . . more or less . . . and we can trigger alarms and set off security systems. The more I know about the person who has this amulet, the better I can protect myself and ensure success."

"Just steal the damned thing. You don't need to shove your nose into anything else. Get in, get it, and get out. Call me when you've got it."

"I'm not a miracle worker—" I started to protest.

"If you're caught, he'll kill you," the man interrupted. "So don't get caught."

"But who—"

He hung up before I could finish asking him who it was he intended for me to rob. I sighed and slumped back into the chair, staring blindly at the piece of paper I held. I had a bad feeling about this whole thing, but I wasn't in much of a position to do anything. I'd just have to go to the target's house and assess the situation there.

It wasn't until I was in my room, donning my working outfit, that I realized something odd about the address he'd given me.

"I'll be damned," I said a few minutes later as I

looked at the card Aisling had given me. One side of
it had her address in London, and on the back, she'd
written the location of Kostya's lair.

It was the same address the blackmailer had given
me.

An hour and a half later I slipped out of the back
door of Gabriel's house, casting an eye upward to the
window of the room Cyrene had claimed. A faint light
flickered through a gap in the curtains, indicating Cyrene was happily tucked into bed, yakking on the
phone to one or another local naiad while she watched
late-night TV. I hadn't told her my plans lest she wish
to accompany me . . . and where I was going, she
definitely couldn't follow.

Why was the blackmailer trying to steal something
from a dragon? No wonder he didn't want to tell me
whom I was supposed to steal from—no one in their
right mind would ever try to get something out of a
dragon's lair.

"More intriguingly, who is he working for?" I murmured aloud to myself. "And does this have anything
to do with that phylactery Gabriel wants?"

"What's that?"

I came to myself with a start as the taxi driver
pulled up outside a dark and rather grimy warehouse.
"Sorry, just talking to myself. Is this it?"

"It is. That'll be five pounds."

I paid the man, hesitating for a moment as I glanced
at the warehouse. I wasn't normally a fearful person,
but I had to admit there was something about the
hulking black building that left me feeling a bit
twitchy. "I don't suppose you'd like to wait for me?"

"Here?" He shoved my change in my hands. "Not
for five times that. Good luck."

He sped off into the darkness without even a backward glance. "Talk about your foreshadowing," I muttered as I slipped into the shadows.

The lock on the door to the warehouse posed no problem to me. I smiled as I laid my fingers across the front, gently urging the tumblers within it to turn until the lock obligingly clicked open. I've never been sure why, exactly, doppelgangers had the inherent ability to open locks, but it was such a useful talent, I figured it was best not to question it. As the door opened, I shadowed and made my way cautiously into the lower level of the empty warehouse. A small amount of dim light from the buildings on either side filtered through the high, grimy windows, giving me enough light to make out a couple of large boxes in an otherwise empty room.

"Kostya lives in an abandoned building near Greenwich," Aisling had told me earlier in the day, when Gabriel and Drake were off looking for the two missing bodyguards.

"Does he?" I'd asked, a little bit surprised by the sudden change in what had been up to that point innocuous conversation.

"Yes. I'm telling you now because if Gabriel is anything like Drake, he's not going to want you to do anything on your own. Dragons are like that: very protective, and the wyverns especially so—it's sweet, really, but they just don't realize that we are professionals, and sometimes, we need to be given some space to do our own thing."

I nodded. I had a suspicion I was being kept out of the way, which was already rankling.

"You have quite a reputation as being able to take . . . well, just about anything, I guess. I mean, anyone who can break into Dr. Kostich's house and take something valuable has got to be pretty good at what she does."

I squirmed a little in the chair, my eyes on the figure of Cyrene and the demon dog Jim as they wandered around the garden. "Er . . . thank you. I think."

"Oh, that was a compliment," Aisling said, laughing. "I have nothing but respect for strong women who go after what they want. But that's neither here nor there—I'll write down Kostya's address for you. If you're going back to London tonight, you'll want to have a look around his place to see just what's what."

I slid her a curious glance. "Do you think Kostya is lying about the phylactery, and Maata and Tipene?"

"I don't know," she said after a moment of thought. "It's hard for me to read Kostya. In some ways, he's very much like Drake, but in others, he's a complete stranger. His emotions are so volatile. My uncle believes that stems from a prisoner-of-war mentality, but I am starting to believe that it's just his personality. Either way, I know you'll want to look around at his place, and figured I'd give you what information we have."

I made a mental note to thank Aisling again for her help. I hated to think what I might have done if I'd been forced to rely on just the blackmailer's information.

The amulet was bound to be with the rest of Kostya's valuables, which meant I needed to go to a small room on the second floor that Drake—the only one besides Kostya who had actually seen it—had told Aisling was protected pretty heavily by a variety of electronic alarms and locks.

"Nothing like killing two birds with one stone, I guess," I said to myself.

There was a sort of mezzanine in the warehouse, a flight of rickety stairs leading upward to what probably had been administrative offices. I walked carefully down the narrow hallway, avoiding both the rats, which

couldn't see me when I shadow walked, and the broken
office furniture, which had been piled along the inner
wall. A faint red blinking light high up near the ceiling
warned of a security camera. I paused in front of the
door to the last office, eyeing it carefully. I knew that
to normal eyes it would look like a perfectly normal
wooden door, equipped with an electronic lock linked
to a retina-scan unit attached to the wall next to it.
But the door bore things that the casual observer
might have missed, such as the illegible words that
were apparently etched into the door's surface.

"Dragon's bane," I said softly, looking at it carefully
from different angles. I'd never seen one before,
Magoth (wisely) never having demanded I burgle a
dragon, but Aisling had warned me that any treasure
Kostya held might be guarded by a bane.

This one looked powerful, glowing gold against the
dark wooden door. I sighed, trying to remember what
else Aisling had said about it.

"They're really tricky, and can be deadly if you
don't know what you're doing," I recalled her saying,
leaning close and speaking quickly as Cyrene and Jim
approached. "I went through four demons breaking
Fiat's bane, but honestly, I wouldn't advise you to
mess with anything Kostya has protected with a bane.
It's just bound to be too dangerous."

Those words came back to me now as I examined
the door for signs of any weakness. There were none.
A quick look at the other rooms, locked by conven-
tional means, yielded nothing as well. I climbed out
of the window of the room next to the sealed one,
moving carefully along the narrow six-inch stone
ledge. I had serious doubts that Kostya would be stupid enough to ignore any entrance into his lair, but
figured it couldn't hurt to check.

The window was guarded by not one, but three dif-

ferent security systems, brands I recognized as being
nearly impossible to overcome. As I stood plastered
against the side of the building, I thought furiously of
any means to get into the room. Via the ceiling? From
the floor below? Perhaps through the wall of the office
next to it? Those and other hopeless ideas were squir-
reling through my brain when I noticed something odd
about the window. . . . One of the panes of glass
shimmered slightly in the stiff breeze that was coming
off the river.

I laid a hand on it, prepared to make a fast getaway
if the alarm gave any sign of a blip. But it didn't. The
glass gave way under my hand, swinging open silently,
the little electronic box attached to it not giving the
slightest indication that the alarm had been triggered.

I opened it a bit more and poked my head into the
room to get a good close look at the electronic
box. . . . It had been disabled.

"Well, now. How about that?" I murmured, taking
a fast look around the room with a penlight. The room
itself was small and musty, with a curious airless feeling as if it had been sealed for a thousand years. It
was empty of furniture, but one side of the wall was
lined with three wooden chests, each bound with iron.
Cautiously, I let myself down out of the window, bracing myself for sirens as I landed on the floor.

The room was as silent as the tomb of which it
reminded me, every noise magnified. Even the breath
I drew sounded oddly amplified. I checked all available surfaces for any other electronics, breathing a
sigh of relief when I found none. Either Kostya had
been imprisoned so long he'd forgotten how to guard
the treasures in his lair, or . . . well, perhaps this wasn't
his lair after all.

I frowned at the door. "Then why bind a bane into
the entrance?" I turned to look back at the window,

trying to piece together the contradictions. I had taken
a step toward the window when a very slight vibration
shook the floor of the mezzanine.

Someone had closed the large metal door directly
below where I stood. I had to get out of there . . .
but could I count on such easy access to the lair any
other time?

I didn't debate the issue. I figured I had about thirty
seconds to find both the phylactery and the amulet
before Kostya—or whoever it was who had just come
into the warehouse—made it upstairs. I flicked the
penlight over the first of the three wooden chests. It
was locked with a bright, shiny new lock, but nothing
else. The second bore several powerful wards, and a
couple of arcane spells keeping it shut. The latter
wouldn't stop me, but the former would slow me down
considerably. The third chest was oddly unprotected.

The faintest of vibrations warned of someone coming up the metal staircase. Even a standard lock would
take me too long to open—I crouched down before
the third chest, my heart sinking as I realized that no
one in their right mind would leave something so valuable as an amulet or the dragon phylactery sitting
around unprotected. There were various antique art
objects in the chest, mostly gold, but a few bejeweled
pieces that looked valuable. Tucked down beneath
them all was a small box, which, when opened, re-
vealed an ugly gold lump wrapped in a piece of blue
silk. I almost sighed in relief. The gold was shaped
roughly in the form of a dragon, although it had a
very primitive feel to it.

"One down, one to go . . . but no time left," I
murmured almost silently.

A sound at the door had me stuffing the gold lump
into my bodice before hurriedly replacing everything
in the chest.

I shadowed and was almost to the window when all hell broke out. Brilliant blue-white fluorescent lights— bane of doppelgangers since they eliminate all shadows— lit up the room like spotlights. I reached the window just as the window alarm suddenly came to life, a grid of lasers glowing red as they made a crisscross pattern across the glass. I had a horrible feeling they were there for more than just sensing movement.

"You!" a man's voice bellowed behind me. I didn't need to look to tell it was Kostya. I just leaped for the window, slamming open the glass and ignoring the horrible searing sensation as the lasers burned through my clothing to my flesh. Kostya yelled something, but I wasn't about to stay to find out how he dealt with intruders to his lair—I threw myself out the window, my arms and legs cartwheeling as I plummeted to the pavement below.

The shock of hitting the ground stunned me for a few seconds, but luckily, self-preservation had caused me to shadow as I fell, aiding the darkness to keep me hidden from Kostya as he leaped out after me. I managed to roll a few feet away until I was wrapped around a cement post that supported a heavy chain fence to keep pedestrians from tumbling the few feet into the river.

Dimly, I was aware of the fact that Kostya passed within a foot of me, where he was joined by another person. My brain was still muzzy from the fall, but it had enough sense to know I couldn't lie there and wait for them to step on me. I half slid, half rolled down a shallow slope into the river. The cold water hit me with the force of a semi-truck, but it served the purpose of yanking me into full consciousness.

The Thames River isn't my idea of an ideal swim- ming location, and especially not when it's the part of the river that runs past industrial areas. I kept my face out of the water, oil, muck, and gods only knew what else had been pumped, dropped, or otherwise deposited into the river, swimming silently away from the warehouse. The laser burns on my chest and arms screamed in agony as the water hit them, but the sound of Kostya and his companion as they called to each other behind me kept me moving despite the almost overwhelming need to curl up into a ball and pass out.

Time passed. How much time I don't really know; it all tended to blur into one long moment of pain and discomfort that stretched into an eon. At some point, however, I found myself clawing at a set of slimy stone steps that led out of the river to a small area that overlooked the river.

"Need some help?" a man's voice asked from the darkness.

I froze for a second when I realized I wasn't shadowed any longer, eyeing the man who stood in the pool of light cast from a streetlamp.

He looked vaguely familiar, but I couldn't quite place his face. I took a step closer, and I relaxed a smidgen as I saw he wasn't a dragon.

"Um . . . yeah. Thanks." I took the hand he offered, grateful for his strength when he helped me up the narrow, slippery steps.

"Take a tumble into the river?" he asked when I stood at the top, shivering with shock, cold, and pain, my hair dripping horrible slimy blobs onto the pavement, my clothes reeking of waste of so many forms, I couldn't begin to separate them into individual elements. I was filthy, stinking to the skies, with bloodstains clearly visible on my clothing despite the swim.

"Something like that, yes," I muttered, uselessly trying to brush off the worst of the mucky residue left by the water. "Thank you for your help. I'll be all right now."

"My pleasure." The man had a pleasant face with dark blond hair, blue-gray eyes, and one of those little clefts in his chin that seemed to drive women wild. "You are a mess, though, aren't you? Here, let me help you. My car is right over here."

I shook my head as the man carefully took my arm, escorting me toward a small parking area next to a restaurant that sat on the river. "Thank you, but there's nothing wrong with me that a gallon of disinfectant and a long shower won't cure. Er . . . by any chance, have we met? I normally have a good memory for people, and something about you is very familiar, but I can't seem to recall just where it is we've met."

"We haven't met. I'd have remembered if we had," the man said with absolute conviction, but despite that, there was an oddly unplaceable note in his voice that had a little warning bell going off in my head. "Here; wrap yourself in this. I don't mind being a Good Samaritan, but this is my employer's car, and I don't think he'd appreciate waterlogged leather seats."

Numbly, I accepted the blanket he took out of the trunk of a car and thrust into my arms. I knew I should just walk away, but the events of the evening had left me feeling more than a little bit out of it. I touched my head, wincing when I found a huge lump on the side. I must have hit my head on the ground when I'd gone out the window, knocking myself out for a few seconds. "Well . . . if you're sure. I don't want to be any trouble."

"No trouble at all; it's what I'm here for!" He held open the passenger-side door, carefully tucking the blanket around me (no doubt more to protect the up-holstery of the car than to warm me), snapping me in with the seat belt before going around to the driv-er's side.

"I'm May," I said as he started up the car.

"Savian." He shot me a quick look, which changed into a smile. "You look like hell, May. You need something hot to drink."

"I'll be fine, thanks. I'm staying in Marylebone, on Wimpole Street. It shouldn't be too long a drive from here."

"That's a nice area," he said agreeably.

I tried to think again why he seemed so familiar, but gave it up as being a lost cause with my wits so apparently scrambled from the fall. I closed my eyes for a moment, reliving the last hour of the evening, and wondering what it was I'd found in Kostya's lair. I didn't feel the least pang of guilt at stealing from him, not when he so basely attacked Gabriel. I had no doubt the phylactery was locked in the chest with the wards, which made Kostya's attempt to shift blame to Gabriel all the more reprehensible.

A police siren passing by us jerked me out of the doze I'd fallen into. I sat up, looking around confus-edly at the bright lights of the area in which we were driving. "Savian? This . . . er . . . this appears to be the airport."

"That's right," he said, flashing a smile as he whipped us into an airport parking lot.

Suspicion took its own sweet time dawning, but at last the warning bells went off in my head.

"You led me on quite a chase, let me tell you, Mei Ling. I can't name the number of times you slipped away just as I was about to nab you, and I have to admit, you'd probably have gotten away from me

again this time except you seemed to knock yourself
silly jumping out of that window. Still, all's well that
ends well. If you would come this way, please?"

"What . . . ? Who . . . ?" My brain was still slug-
gishly processing his words when he unbuckled my
seat belt and pulled me out of the car, his hands hard
around my wrists.

"Sorry, didn't I introduce myself properly earlier?"
he asked with a little chuckle. He kept ahold of my
wrists with one hand, the other going to his chest as
he bowed in the elegant manner that only the people
of the Otherworld seemed to be able to master. "Savian Bartholomew, L'au-delà thief taker, at your service. And you, fair thief, are my prisoner."

Chapter Fourteen

The members of the Otherworld, in general, get along well with the mortal world. We all have to live in it, after all, so it makes sense we've learned to adapt to mortal foibles and whims, but the people of the Otherworld who bear an official capacity tend to take the time and effort to make sure that the mortal world sees them in an appropriate light.

"I don't suppose it would do me the least bit of good to yell?" I asked as Savian the thief taker flashed an official-looking card at an airport official.

"None whatsoever. I have the diplomatic authority to take prisoners in and out of this and seventeen other countries, so I'm afraid that any protests you make would fall upon deaf ears. Ah. I see we are to have the first three rows to ourselves. Excellent. Do you need to use the loo?" he asked politely, stopping before a bank of tiny airplane bathrooms.

I shook my head, clutching my now-sodden blanket around myself, my spirits as damp as the rest of me.

"All right, then. If you'd sit there, please."

I glanced around the section of the plane that he'd evidently managed to keep clear, but there was no hope for it. The lights were too bright—I'd never be able to get away by shadow walking. I plopped down in the seat he indicated, furiously trying to think of a way out of this horrible dilemma. "No handcuffs?" I asked acidly as he reached for my seat belt. I slapped his hands and buckled it together myself, glaring at him as he chuckled again.

He took his seat, drawing a binding ward on me. "I don't need them, Mei Ling. It took me some time to come up with a ward that would hold a doppelganger, but as you can see, it's quite effective."

Horror crept up my spine as I realized he was right—I couldn't move from the seat. I slumped back defeated, wondering what the L'au-delà committee was going to do when Savian the sexy thief taker handed me over.

"At least I know now why you are so familiar," I grumbled to myself as the plane took off.

He looked curious. "Did you catch me tailing you this evening?"

"No, I'm ashamed to say I didn't know there was anyone watching me," I said with much regret. "I heard you at Dr. Kostich's house last night."

"Ahh," he said, enlightenment dawning in his eyes. "You were there? I wondered at the time what the dragon was doing there, and why he was so interested in you. I thought perhaps he was trying to smuggle the quintessence back into the case. But obviously you did that."

"Yes." My poor abused head throbbed, but I sternly ordered it to sort through the facts and come up with a plan of action. "What I'd really like to know is how you found me to begin with. If you didn't see me at Dr. Kostich's, how did you know where to find me?"

"Well, you see, it's like this," he said, getting comfortable after signaling the flight attendant. He waited until she served him a glass of wine before continuing. "Kostich hired me to find you and his quintessence. I thought it was a bit odd that the silver wyvern should be interested in apparently the same thing, so I followed him. He went to earth in a hotel, and didn't appear until this morning."

A sudden flash of memory had me sitting up straight. "You were the man outside the hotel. The one who stared so rudely at Cyrene and me."

"If I was staring, it was in astonishment, and meant no offense," he said with a warm smile. "Picture the scene: a dashing, roguish hero—that's yours truly—has been hunkered down all night, waiting for his prey to emerge from what was evidently quite the love nest."

I refused to blush. I kept my face unmoving, my expression placid.

He just grinned. "And then all of a sudden, whoosh! The hotel starts to burn, people pour out, including a dragon and his luscious bit o' fun."

"If you think that's going to get a rise out of me, you're going to be very disappointed," I said tonelessly.

His grin deepened. "I had a feeling you'd be good at this."

"That explains how you found me, but not how you know about my connection with the thefts," I said, lowering my voice.

"That's where the story gets good," he assured me. "There I was, faced with not only the man I've been following, but also a lovely woman. Imagine my surprise when the lovely woman is joined by an identical twin. Imagine that surprise turning to complete and utter astonishment when, as I was strolling past in an attempt to identify the ladies, I heard the name of one of the most sought-after criminals in the history of the Otherworld."

I cast my mind back to the morning, groaning to myself. "Cyrene called me Mayling."

"Right out in the open, where anyone could hear," he said with cheerful agreement. "Once I got over the shock of hearing her say the name of Mei Ling, I did a little bit of investigating, and found out that the woman with the loose lips was twin to one May Northcott. Two and two and two . . . well, they make six, May."

I shook my head, disgusted with myself for being so distracted by Gabriel that I hadn't been aware of Savian. "And you simply followed us to London, and then later on, tracked me down at the warehouse. I can't believe I didn't see you."

"I'm very good at following people," he said with no pretense of modesty. "It's my specialty, if the truth be known."

I digested all of that on the flight to Paris, ignoring his further attempts at conversation, preferring to dwell in the horrible inky pit of despair that wrapped me firmly in its embrace.

"Don't think that there's any chance you're going to get away from me," Savian said as we deplaned at Orly Airport.

He waited until everyone else had left the plane but the flight attendants, all of whom watched me with interested eyes. I had no idea what story he'd concocted to tell them; to be honest, I didn't care. I just wanted to get away to somewhere dark, somewhere I could make my escape.

"Do you know, I'm almost sorry I caught you," he continued in a conversational voice as we walked up the long ramp to the concourse. "It's been rather exciting trying to keep up with you. Are you really mated to the silver wyvern?"

I stopped to give him an astonished look.

"Word gets around fast," he explained, giving me a little push to get me going again.

"You are a very strange man," I told him, thrown off guard by his entire demeanor. I expected the thief takers to be harsh, ugly little men with no souls and less humanity. But Savian was . . . well, charming. And handsome. And judging by the glint in his eye, probably also quite the ladies' man.

"I've been told that. I consider it a compliment, actually. Wouldn't want life to become boring and staid, now, would we?" he asked, gesturing me toward a room marked with a private notice. I entered the small room, most likely used for interviews of suspicious people by customs officials, and tipped my head as I watched Savian gesture to someone at a desk. He came into the room, closing the door behind him. "Won't be but a minute, and we'll be through customs. I expect you're anxious to be through all this, hmm?"

"I don't suppose you're open to bribes?" I asked, ignoring the charm he was so clearly trying to wield upon me.

That took him by surprise for a few seconds. "What did you have in mind?"

I ran a mental accounting of my checkbook, disregarding both it and my credit cards—Magoth didn't mind paying my travel expenses when necessary, but he certainly didn't pay well for the rest of my services—then musing for a few moments on the amulet, which was tucked away under my left breast in the inner pocket of my leather bodice, but I dismissed the thought almost immediately. I hadn't been strafed by lasers and given myself a concussion just to hand over the amulet to the first thief taker who managed to grab me.

Which left only one thing I had with which to barter my freedom. I toyed with the leather laces of my bodice. "What about me?"

His eyes opened wide at that, his gaze turning calculating as he examined me thoroughly from my toes to my crown. "What would your wyvern say to that offer?"

I swallowed back the bile that rose in my throat at the thought of having sex with Savian. "This has nothing to do with him. It's between you and me."

"Indeed it is," he said, taking a couple of steps closer to me. I forced myself to stand where I was, lifting my chin to meet his gaze.

"You're positively rank, woman. You reek of things I don't really want to name."

"Thank you. There's just nothing like being told you smell like a sewer to make a woman feel wanted."

He laughed. "Hmm. Despite your current state, I have to admit I'm very tempted. Beneath all that muck you're really quite lovely, in a silent movie sort of way." He reached out to touch my hair. I had to steel my arms to stay at my side, not flinching when he trailed a finger down my jawline. "*Very* tempted. Oh, what the hell, you only live once."

He turned back to the door, opening it to call something out to the official who was approaching with a clipboard.

I tried to calm the gorge rising within me, but my repulsion must have been evident, for when Savian turned back around he burst into laughter. "Good lord, woman, you look like you've been asked to do the most heinous things imaginable to babies. I take it you've had a change of heart about your offer?"

I slumped into one of the three wooden chairs, which, along with a small table, were the room's only furnishings. "I'm sorry. I thought I could do it, but I just can't."

Savian looked thoughtful for a moment. "Is it me? Or are you in love with the wyvern?"

"I'm not in love with anyone," I muttered, my forehead resting on my hands as I hunched over the table, unsure of whether I should cry or laugh at the ludicrous situation I found myself in.

"Then it's me? You don't find me . . . dashing? Attractive, in a roguish sort of way? Kind of a cross between Han Solo and MacGyver?" Savian asked, a note of worry in his voice.

I looked up, a smile twitching my lips. He looked almost devastated. "No, you're very Han Solo. It's just . . . well, I did promise to be Gabriel's mate, and I know it's silly to take fidelity seriously these days, but I guess I'm just one of those people who is faithful whether they want to be or not."

He was silent for a moment, then nodded. "He's a lucky dragon. Was there anything else you wanted to try to bribe me with? Or was that it?"

"That's it," I said, wiping back a few tears of hilarity that had squeezed out of my eyes.

"Ah, well. Perhaps another time you might have a priceless gold treasure hidden upon your lovely person."

My gaze shot to his, but he was already back at the door, calling for the official.

"This won't take—"

Suddenly he was jerked out of the door. I leaped up, racing for freedom, but shrieked when the doorway was suddenly filled with a large, hulking man with dirty dark hair, shrewd eyes, and a wicked-looking scar that started beneath his eye and curved down to his earlobe. "—long," the man said, his lips curling up in a smile as he clamped one hand around my wrist, my bones protesting as he yanked me out the door after him.

"Who the hell are you?" I asked, trying desperately to free myself. To the right I saw a small group of people bent over a prone form, one person on a radio obviously calling for medical aid. "And what did you do to Savian?"

The surly man tightened his hold on my wrist until I howled my protest, beating on his arm to let go of me. "Stop your bitching or I'll stop it for you! Here." He thrust an identification card at a customs official who hurriedly backed out of the way.

"Help!" I yelled, trying to simultaneously claw the man's grip off my wrist and twist myself free. "I'm being kidnapped! Someone help me! He—"

The last thing I remember before a white pain exploded in my head was the man turning toward me, his fist raised. After that, blissful darkness claimed me, welcoming me with a familiar comfort. I wandered the pathways of the shadow world for a bit, that place between realities that few can reach, and fewer can leave once they get there. It was a dreamworld, a place of sanctuary for those for whom reality had become too much, and I was tempted for a few moments to just remain there, safe from the pain and strife that made up my world. But the image of Gabriel's bright eyes rose in my mind, the memory of his burning kisses stirring the slumbering embers of my desire.

A cold shock of water dragged me out of the shadow world and back into my body. I sputtered and choked, rolling off my back and into a sitting position as I wiped water from my face. *"Agathos daimon!"*

"You will please to come to the chamber," a voice said with a complete lack of emotion. I shook the water from my eyes well enough to see the slight young man speaking.

"Who are you? And where am I?"

"I am Tej, apprentice to Monish Lakshmanan. This is Paris."

"Paris," I groaned, getting painfully to my feet. The

laser burns had long since healed, but my wrist was still sore and discolored. The scene with the thief taker and the dark-haired brutish man rushed back. "What happened to the thief taker?"

"Porter? He's claiming his reward. You must please to come this way."

I staggered out of the small room, taking quick glances around me to look for an escape. Our footsteps echoed down a long hallway dotted with occasional chairs and small tables. "Where exactly in Paris?" I asked my escort.

"Suffrage House," he answered.

My spirits dropped. Suffrage House was the mansion of a long-dead suffragette, bought by the L'audelà, and now used as their headquarters. Although I'd been locked in a small, dark room that was clearly used as a holding cell since it contained no furniture whatsoever, I had to admit that I'd been in much worse places.

"Who's Monish Lakshmanan?" I asked, sliding an appraising glance at Tej. He appeared to be Indian, his soft brown eyes watching me warily as we walked down a long gold and white hallway.

"Monish is an oracle, and a member of the watch."

Oh, wonderful. The watch was the police force of the L'au-delà, and their members were not people with whom I ever desired to cross paths. "I hate to do nothing but ask questions, but where are we going?"

"The almoner's chamber. You must make a phone call, yes?"

He threw open a door to what appeared to be an office containing four desks, three of which were occupied by women who bore all the appearances of secretaries.

In front of the nearest one, a familiar man stood arguing. "—after which he stole her from me. Porter has no right to claim the reward when I did all the hard work and caught her to begin with."

"Stop your bellyachin'," the nasty dark-haired man snarled from where he stood to the side. I followed Tej into the room and took the chair at the empty desk that he indicated. "You know the rules as well as I do—he who brings in the suspect gets the reward. I'll take that voucher for the benefaction now."

"That only applies if the suspect escapes one thief taker, a fact you know very well," Savian said, slamming down his hand on the table. "The fact is that you stole her from me. You didn't pick her up after I left her; you *stole* her from me. As if that wasn't enough to disqualify your claim on her, there's the little fact that you were about to conduct an illegal search upon her person when I found you."

"An illegal search?" The woman at the desk frowned.

"What sort of illegal search?" I asked, sick to my stomach at the thought of the man named Porter touching me while I was unconscious.

"You keep your nose out of what doesn't concern you," the nasty man (evidently named Porter) snarled.

The words echoed horribly in my head. I took a step back, surprise overwhelming the repugnance he had generated. I'd heard something very like those words before, only a few hours ago. Cyrene's blackmailer was a thief taker? What on earth was all that about? And why had he all but kidnapped me from his colleague?

"He was about to strip-search you, my dear. You may thank me later for saving you from that particular indignity," Savian told me with a little wiggle of his eyebrows.

"Strip-search me? Why?" I asked, my mind reeling as I tried to sort out the confusion.

Porter's expression turned sly as he picked his ear. "Your word against mine that I did any such thing."

I gave a mental shake of my head. Why would he want to search me? The only thing of value I held was the amulet he sent me to get. It didn't make sense for him to kidnap me in order to get what he'd sent me to retrieve. Not unless he knew that I wasn't about to hand it over without knowing exactly what it was.

"This is a problem." The secretary frowned again, shuffling some paperwork on her desk. "I'm afraid I can't disburse the reward if it is being contested. Both your claims will have to go before the committee for settling."

Porter swore loudly and extremely profanely, sending me a look that, by rights, should have struck me dead.

"There's nothing to be settled," Savian started to say, but the secretary cut him off by a lengthy recitation of the rules regarding claims.

Porter swore again and started stomping his way from the room. I moved quickly to intercept him, speaking in a tone low enough that it couldn't be overheard by the others. "Just exactly what game are you playing at?"

His eyes were hooded and wary. "What're you talking about?"

"Let's try the fact that you blackmailed me into taking a dragon's amulet, and yet you're supposed to be upholding the laws of the L'au-delà. You're a thief taker, but at the same time you're working for a demon lord stealing who knows what."

For a moment, his eyes held a startled look. "You're crazy."

I leaned closer, tamping down the sick feeling in my gut that being so near him generated. "It wouldn't be that hard, you know, to ask around and find out which

demon lord you work for. I can't imagine whoever it
is would be happy to know you hold a position in the
L'au-delà. Nor would the committee be happy to find
out one of their own works for a prince of Abaddon."

To my surprise, a slow, ugly smile split his face. He
grabbed my arm in a grip that made me yelp, pulling
me up against his body until his breath stung my face.
"You think you're so smart, but you're not even close.
You breathe one word about that amulet to anyone,
and you're dead. You got that? If I don't kill you
myself, the dreadlord will."

"If you kill me, you won't get the amulet," I pointed
out, keeping mum about the fact that I already had
the item in question.

He snarled something anatomically impossible.
"You'll get it."

"And if I don't?" I asked. "You can hardly expect
me to steal something for someone who treats me this
way. Frankly, at this point, I'd almost rather deal with
the repercussions if you exposed Cyrene's actions in
Nova Scotia."

His breath was foul. "Get the amulet back, or you
won't have a twin to protect."

I stared at him in openmouthed horror, but before
I could rally a response to his threat, he pushed me
away, storming out of the room. Savian reached my
side, frowning after Porter. "Are you all right? I saw
him grab you. Are you hurt?"

"I'm fine," I said, rubbing my arm. "Just a little
confused."

He gave me a long, considering look. "I suspect
you're not the only one in that state. I don't suppose
you'd like to tell me what all that was about?"

I shook my head and returned to the desk where
Tej stood watching with bright, interested eyes. "Exactly who am I supposed to be calling?"

The young man looked vaguely surprised. "You are to make a call. It is the rules."

"The rules? What rules?"

The woman at the desk behind me dropped a couple of sheets of paper on the desk before me. "Would you mind signing this receipt for your personal effects, Miss Ling? You were unconscious during the sentencing, or I would have had you sign it then."

I stared down at a piece of paper listing the items I'd had on my person: wallet, three passports, cell phone, assorted money, cinnamon gum, two keys, and a small golden figurine.

The last object leaped to mind as I hurriedly checked the inner pocket of my bodice. The lumpy gold dragon amulet was gone. I thought it was odd they got that and not the small knife I wore strapped to my ankle, but I wasn't about to point out their omission.

"Where are my things being kept?" I asked the secretary, worried that Porter might have figured out I was bluffing and was even now on the way to get the amulet.

"All effects of prisoners are kept in the vault, naturally," she answered, twitching the paper at me.

"And is the vault secure? I mean, really secure?"

"It is the L'au-delà vault!" she answered indignantly. "It has not been violated in at least a century."

Somewhat relieved, I signed my name where she indicated.

"Convicted persons may petition for the return of those items not deemed to be dangerous," she added.

"Convicted?" A headache suddenly blossomed to life. I rubbed my forehead, trying to figure out just what was going on. "I was convicted?"

"Oh, yes," the secretary said. "Earlier, when you were brought before the committee. You were charged, tried, and sentenced, and now if you would just sign these forms as well, I can initiate your transfer to the Akasha."

"The Akasha?" I felt like some sort of deranged parrot repeating things the woman was saying, but I was beyond confused. My blood turned to ice at the thought of the Akasha—it was what mortals sometimes thought of as limbo, a place where demons and others who had been banished were sent. It meant an eternity of nonexistence, a perpetual torment, a punishment so heinous, it was reserved for only the most serious of crimes . . . or people who sufficiently pissed off the heads of the committee.

And this woman wanted me to sign papers that would send me there? "I don't think so," I said aloud, snatching up the phone. I didn't have to think about who to call; I pulled out the small card with Gabriel's cell phone number, and punched in the appropriate country code and number.

"It would be my utmost delight to speak with you," Gabriel's smooth voice assured me. "But unfortunately, I am unable to take your call at this time. Please leave a message."

I wanted to cry right there in front of everyone, but as I've mentioned, I'm not a weepy sort of person. "It's me. Er . . . May. I'm in Paris, and apparently was unconscious when I was charged by the L'au-delà committee to be banished to the Akasha. I'd really appreciate it if you could do something about it before they send me there." I gave the phone number that was printed on the phone and hung up, despair welling up inside me.

"Do I take it you refuse to sign the forms?" the secretary asked, her mouth thin with irritation.

"That is absolutely correct. I won't sign anything until my . . . er . . . wyvern checks it out."

She snatched the papers back and marched to her desk, muttering about unreasonable people who had no concept of the amount of work she had to do.

Tej watched me for a moment with sad eyes before escorting me back to my cell, allowing me to make a bathroom stop on the way.

"The windows have been barred," he pointed out as I was about to enter the bathroom, and sure enough, they had been. The air duct was too small to climb through, the ceiling was made of solid plaster, not tiles with access to a ventilation shaft, and there was no exit other than the door that led straight to Tej.

I sighed, made use of the facilities, and prayed to as many gods as I could name that Gabriel checked his voice mail in time to keep me from being sent to the Akasha.

Chapter Fifteen

I have no idea how much time had gone by since Tej had deposited me back in my airless, barren cell of a room. For that matter, I had no concept of how much time had passed while I was in the shadow world—evidently enough to conduct a trial, although why no one bothered to bring me around during that was a question I very much wanted to ask. I suspected the answer would not be complimentary.

Time did pass, enough that Tej brought me a plate of food for which I had no appetite. Since my room had no windows, I couldn't even tell if it was day or night. I considered slipping back into the shadow world, but I knew that was no solution to my problem.

By my best guess, about four hours later, the door to my room was suddenly opened. I'd curled up on my side, figuring I might as well rest in case the opportunity to escape presented itself, and I looked up with surprise at the person who was shoved into the room.

"—know who I am? I'm a naiad, you idiot! A member of the Sisterhood of Hydriades! You can't arrest me!"

The door slammed shut behind Cyrene.

"What on earth did you do?" I asked, getting to my feet as she pounded on the door.

"Shhh," she said over her shoulder, before turning

back to the door and yelling, "I demand to speak to the committee! You can't treat me this way! I'm a water elemental! I have rights!"

"Cy?"

She gave the door .one last slam of her fist before turning a delighted face upon me. "This is fabulous! I'm sorry, Mayling, you know I love you dearly, but this is ever so much more fun than hiding in a tree watching in case of intruders. I sounded very convincing, didn't I? I knew I should have stayed in Hollywood after you were created, but Magoth was being so unpleasant, and . . . well, you know. But this! I'm a natural at this, don't you think?"

I leaned back against the wall, my arms crossed over my chest. "I take it you have some sort of plan going? Something that calls for you to be arrested?"

"There, now, you see? I told Drake you'd grasp the gist of things right away, but he had his doubts."

"Drake?" I straightened up. "Is Gabriel with him? Did he get my message?"

"Of course he got your message. That's why I'm here. Is there no chair?" she asked, frowning around the empty room.

"No. I hate to let down the team and all, but what exactly are you doing here? Is Gabriel going to be able to get me out of being sent to the Akasha? Is he going to appeal the conviction?"

"Better than that," she said with smile, glancing around quickly before leaning in closely, her voice dropped to almost a whisper. "We're going to bust you out of here."

"Bust me . . ." I closed my eyes for a moment. "You've been watching too many old westerns. No one conducts jailbreaks these days. Especially not when the jailers are the L'au-delà committee."

"That's why this plan is so incredibly cunning," she

said, giving my arm a little squeeze. "They're all expecting you to try to escape—they'll never expect us to break you out of here."

"Oy," I said, sliding down the wall to the floor. "This has 'doomed from the start' written all over it. You didn't think up this plan yourself, did you?" I asked suspiciously.

She looked offended. "No, I didn't, and you can stop being such a negative Nelly. Gabriel thought up the plan, and Drake and I are helping. I'm the decoy, you see."

"Of course you are. What, exactly, is this grandiose escape plan?"

Her mouth set in a prim manner. "I can't tell you."

"Why not?"

"There could be bugs. We don't want them to know our plans."

"If they were listening in, you just told them there's a plan, so they'll be expecting something to happen," I pointed out.

"Yes, but they won't know what," she said, pulling off her jacket. Her shirt followed almost immediately, as did her jeans, shoes, and the sparkly pink socks that she was so prone to wearing despite the fact they would look more at home on a twelve-year-old.

I watched her striptease with confusion for a moment before a thought struck me.

"You don't mean—"

"Shhh," she said, waving a vague hand around as she pulled off the scarf she wore to confine her bangs. "Bugs, remember?"

I bit back an obvious reply, thought for a moment, then decided that although the plan Gabriel had come up with was too *I Love Lucy* for words, I didn't have any alternative. I stripped.

A half hour later the door opened to Tej. "Cyrene Northcott? You may see the committee now."

I turned from where I was pacing back and forth across the small room, ignoring Cyrene dressed in my clothing as she sat in a corner hunched over her knees.

I wasn't sure that our trick would fool anyone, especially since Cyrene's hair was a bit longer than mine, but Tej didn't give me a second glance as I marched out the door. "It's about time," I said, adopting Cyrene's light, fluty voice. "I've been in there forever! You don't have any right to hold me! I haven't done anything wrong!"

Tej said nothing, just opened a door and gestured for me to go in.

My stomach quailed for a moment as I saw that one of the three men who sat at a long table was Dr. Kostich, but I remembered that Cyrene, as a naiad, had no special fear of him. Chin high, I stormed forward in my best impression of her at her most outraged. "This is an obscene injustice! I demand to be released immediately. If you do not, I will alert the sisterhood to this travesty, and then you'll all be sorry!"

The man at the end of the table, a dark-skinned man with lovely brown eyes, grimaced as he glanced at the papers before him. "I am Monish Lakshmanan, currently acting head of the watch. You are Cyrene Northcott?"

"I certainly am!"

"I am pleased to inform you that the charge against you of assault has been dropped due to lack of evidence."

"And rightly so, since I never did assault . . . er . . . that person." I backed out of the corner from which I found myself with as much aplomb as was possible, which admittedly wasn't a whole lot.

"The *dragon* in question," Monish said with a slight emphasis, his eyes watchful, "refused to make a statement, and in fact, left the building rather hurriedly."

"He was a liar," I said, tossing my head in a trademark Cyrene gesture.

"*She* did not say much to allow us to make an assessment either way," he said.

I forced a light, lilting laugh. "You fell for that cross-dressing act? I would have thought someone in the watch had more sense. You can take it from me, Mr. Lakshmanan—that dragon was no lady."

The moment of silence that followed was pregnant with unspoken words.

Monish cleared his throat and slid a glance toward the mage next to him. "Indeed. We cannot help but find your presence here somewhat of a coincidence, Miss Northcott. Your sister is arrested and tried for crimes against a number of individuals, and that very same day you are brought in on an assault charge that is mysteriously dropped."

I tried to school the surprise I felt at his words from showing on my face, arranging my features to display vague indifference, instead. *Sister?* Monish had said *sister*, not twin. The word "sister" was never used to indicate a doppelganger, except occasionally by the originating twin as a form of affection. But everyone else always referred to the two people as twins, not sisters—which could only mean that Monish and the others did not realize the truth of our relationship. Savian knew I was a doppelganger, as did Porter. Why did neither of them tell the committee? I gave a mental head shake—the whys weren't really important now. What did matter was that the two thief takers and Cyrene had managed to keep my origins quiet, and *that*, I saw, was the key to Gabriel's plan for my escape.

"Well, of course it's not a coincidence," I said, thinking as quickly as I could. I allowed outrage to fill my voice. "She's my sister! Do you think I'm going to stand around and let you guys do who knows what with her? This whole thing about poor May being a thief is ridiculous. Ridiculous! She's as innocent as I am!"

The second the words left my lips, hindsight pointed out that that claim wasn't, perhaps, the most judicious to make at the moment.

"Indeed," Dr. Kostich said, speaking up for the first time since I'd marched into the room. He gave me an appraising glance that I had a horrible feeling saw much more than I would have liked. "I find that statement difficult to believe."

I lifted my chin in haughty scorn, allowing a slight sneer to enter my voice. Mages and elemental beings had a long history of disagreement, and I knew that Cyrene was no fonder of him than I was. "Do you question my word, mage?"

"It is not your word I question, naiad," he answered smoothly. "It is, perhaps, your identity that I wonder at."

"My *identity*?" I scoffed, throwing as much disbelief as I could into the word. "You don't believe that I am a naiad?"

"You are very much like your sister," Monish said slowly as both men eyed me. "Are you twins?"

I couldn't lie. Both men looked too savvy to not sense an outright untruth when spoken. Subterfuge was one thing—that was natural to a doppelganger. But I seldom spoke lies simply because I didn't do it well. "Yes, we're twins. But there are obvious differences between us!" Such as the fact that I was a doppelganger, while Cyrene was an elemental being.

"In that case, I'm sure you wouldn't mind proving

you are who you say you are?" Dr. Kostich said with a slight smile.

"Oh, for the love of the twelve gods . . . you question me? Me, the ninth sister of the house of Hydriades? I am a naiad, a daughter of Tethys, and you have the audacity to question me? I have never been so insulted!"

"It is not meant as an insult," Kostich said, the belligerent look easing as I slammed my hands down on the table in front of him. "More as a way to verify—"

"Fine!" I bellowed, my voice echoing off the walls. "You want to verify I am a naiad? You wish for me to summon water to prove to you, a mage, one who knows nothing of the ways of the elements, my worth? You want me to prove it?" I pushed up my sleeves and spread my hands out, palms down. "Fine! I'll summon water. I'll summon enough water to flood this ridiculous room, and you with it! And when your head is pressed up against the ceiling with two inches of air left, then perhaps you'll believe me!"

"Wait!" Monish interrupted, looking nervously from me to Kostich. "Er . . . with all due respect, sir, I believe such an extreme act might have repercussions. This room has not been warded to contain the contents."

Kostich's eyes narrowed, but before he could reply, the doors behind me slammed open. My stomach did an odd little flip-flop at the sight of Gabriel storming into the room, accompanied by Drake and his two bodyguards.

"I demand the release of my mate," Gabriel snarled, his gaze impassive as it passed over me. For a moment, I thought he didn't recognize me, but I shook that thought away.

"It's about time you got here," I told him, tossing my head again.

"Be quiet, woman," he snapped at me, not moving his gaze from where it bore into Dr. Kostich.

I was shocked for a moment by the anger in his voice, trying to keep a step ahead of him. What role was I supposed to take as Cyrene? Submissive? Should I leave all the talking to him? No, that wasn't Cyrene. When she was outraged about something, she let the world know about it.

I snatched up the stack of papers on the table in front of me and threw them at Gabriel. "Be quiet? *Be quiet?* I'm the only one here who cares enough about May to get her released, you big . . . big . . . dragon! Don't you 'be quiet' me! I demand that you listen to me and not him," I said, turning to Monish.

He made a tching sound, gesturing to a clerk, who scurried over to pick up the papers that had fluttered all over the floor.

"You will not speak to me that way!" Gabriel roared, grabbing my arm and jerking me back, his eyes blazing.

I grabbed another handful of papers and threw them at his head. "I'll speak to you any way I want to! You're not *my* mate, thank the gods! You're nothing but trouble! I blame you for letting poor May be arrested in the first place!"

"And you're a danger to yourself and others! You are hereby banned from seeing May unless in my company!"

"Oh!" I screamed, and grabbed for the pitcher of water in front of Dr. Kostich.

"Cease!" Kostich yelled, his face red with anger as I stood with the pitcher over my head, poised to throw it at Gabriel. "This behavior is unacceptable. Bailiff, remove that woman from our presence."

"I will not be treated in this manner!" I yelled, tossing the water onto the small man who had been picking up papers. "And you have not heard the last of me, mage. The sisterhood will hear of this treatment, as will the Council of Elementalists! I will have justice!"

I turned on my heel as the now-sopping clerk headed for me, marching out of the room with my head held high. Drake, a silent figure with his two men, raised an eyebrow as I passed them. I gave him a head toss and strode angrily from the room.

"As for your demands, Tauhou—" Kostich said, but I didn't hear any more. The clerk didn't touch me, but herded me unceremoniously downstairs and out of the building with a murmured request to not return unless summoned.

"Hrmph," I snorted at him as he went back into the building, heaving a sigh of relief at my freedom.

I wasn't quite sure what I was supposed to do once freed, but I didn't have long to wait. Before I'd taken a couple of steps, the dragons burst from the building, Gabriel yelling curses at Monish as he stood with the little clerk barring the door.

Gabriel stormed by me, Drake and the two others hot on his heels. None of them looked at me as they passed. "Hey!" I yelled, running after them. "I'm not finished with you, either!"

The men stopped at a sleek black 1930s limo. I didn't wait for an invitation; I pushed Gabriel aside to get into the backseat, praying someone wasn't going to run out of the building calling for my immediate arrest.

It wasn't until the car turned the corner and headed down a busy Paris street that I slumped back in the seat, but my slumpage was short-lived. Gabriel wrapped one arm around me and pulled me onto his lap, his lips finding mine in a way I could only applaud.

"You make a hell of an actress," he murmured against my mouth.

I smiled and bit his lower lip, my heart beating wildly. Part of it was from the adrenaline generated by the scene with Kostich, but most of it was due to the man from whose lap I was gently pushed.

I made a little noise of unhappiness as Gabriel's mouth parted from mine.

"I appreciate your enthusiasm, little bird, but now is not the time," he said, nodding toward where Drake sat opposite us.

I pinched his hand. "You can't kiss your own mate in front of another wyvern?"

"It is not fitting," Drake answered, his face passive, although I could have sworn he was fighting a smile.

"Fitting?"

"Dragon etiquette demands that mates be treated with the utmost respect in public," Gabriel said solemnly. "Excessive shows of affection are frowned on when in the company of other dragons."

Gabriel's words might have been staid, but his eyes were downright molten with desire.

"Screw etiquette," I said, grabbing his head and pulling him over to me. I groaned into his mouth as his tongue immediately twined itself around mine, sliding with sinuous, teasing movements that made me want to crawl on top of Gabriel.

"Fire," I whispered, tugging on his hair, and I felt his lips curve as I was bathed in dragon fire, filled with it, consumed by it. I reveled in its heat, in *his* heat, returning it to him with a joy that threatened to set my very soul on fire.

"I hesitate to point out that the upholstery, while fireproofed, does have its limits, but this car is a favorite of Aisling's, and I would hate for it to be out of commission."

Drake's voice acted as water on the flames of our desire.

"I should chastise you for such a breach of etiquette," Gabriel said, his lovely voice husky with all sorts of sensual promises.

"It won't do any good," Drake said, sighing. "I have tried many times to school Aisling, but she refuses to listen. It's a very annoying trait in American women, I've found. Perhaps you will have better luck with May."

I snorted, giving Gabriel a gimlet eye. "Don't even *think* about going there."

He grinned. I melted.

"American women," Drake said, shaking his head.

"What's going to happen to Cy?" I asked Gabriel as the gravity of the moment returned. "Does this plan of yours that she couldn't tell me about include her rescue, as well?"

"She will rescue herself in about"—he consulted his watch—"two hours. Enough time for us to get you safely to England. Then she will reveal herself as the true naiad, claiming you drugged her in order to escape."

"Won't they notice that she hasn't, in fact, been drugged."

"She will be," he answered cheerfully, his fingers stroking my leg. "She has a small vial containing a sleeping draught, which she most likely took as soon as you left the cell. Once she wakes up, she will no doubt make a demonstration of her naiad abilities, and since the committee has nothing with which they can charge her, she will be released."

"That is pretty smart," I said, giving him an admiring glance before doubt returned to worry the edges of my mind.

"We thought so. And now that you are free, perhaps you would tell us how it is you came to be there in the first place?" Drake asked.

I hesitated a moment, unwilling to tell them about the blackmailer and amulet, but knowing the connection to Kostya might have some importance. As succinctly as possible, I told them about Cyrene's blackmailer, and how he'd sent me to retrieve an amulet.

"From Kostya?" Drake's expression was thoughtful.

"What amulet was it, did the blackmailer say?" Gabriel asked.

"No. He didn't tell me anything at all about it, not what it was, why he wanted it, or even how Kostya came to have it." At the thought of the amulet, a question arose. "What will happen to my things the committee took when I was arrested?"

He considered the question. "They'll remain locked up with them, I suppose. It would be rather awkward to request them to be returned now."

"Yes, but . . ." I bit my lip.

"Did you have something of value?" Drake asked, his eyes glittering as he sniffed the air a couple of times.

"Not really, although I will be in a world of hurt if I don't get my passports back," I said slowly. "I use them when I don't wish to be recognized."

"We will have another made for you," Gabriel said.

Drake sniffed the air again, then suddenly lunged forward, his face pressed into my breasts. I squawked and threw myself backward at the same time Gabriel snarled something.

"I meant no disrespect," Drake said as Gabriel shoved him back into his seat. "Your mate has been wearing gold. Recently."

Both dragons turned thoughtful gazes upon me. "Gold?" Gabriel asked, the pupils of his eyes narrowing. "You have gold?"

"No, I don't have gold," I said, amused at both of their reactions. "I touched a few of Kostya's things when I was going through his chest—he has gold."

"What sort of gold?" Drake asked, an avid light in his eyes.

"Was the amulet made of gold?" Gabriel asked at the same time.

"I think so. I don't know anything about the quality of gold, so I'm afraid I can't give you an estimate of its purity. It looked like Kostya had a lot of things, and almost certainly the phylactery was in one of the locked chests. There were three chests in all, two bound and locked. I didn't have time to look at them. I found the amulet at the bottom of the unlocked chest."

"Unlocked," Drake said, sitting back with a dismissive gesture. "He wouldn't keep anything valuable in an unlocked chest. This amulet must not be worth much."

"But it was gold," Gabriel said. "What else did you find in the lair?"

I couldn't help but smile at him. "I knew dragons liked gold—I didn't know it was a borderline obsession with you."

"It's not an obsession . . . well, a little one . . . but we do find gold incredibly . . ." He lifted my hand to his lips, his tongue painting my fingertips with fire.

"Expensive?" I asked, wondering that men who obviously had so much wealth could pant after a few bits of gold. "Precious?"

"Desirable," Drake said, his face aglow with avidity.

"Arousing," Gabriel corrected him, the sensual velvet tones of his voice affected not in the least by the fact that he was nibbling on my fingertips. I shivered as his tongue made little circles at the tip of one of my fingers.

"Yes, arousing. Very, very arousing." Drake frowned for a moment and whipped out his cell phone. "I must call Aisling."

I turned to Gabriel to give Drake a little privacy during his phone call.

"And what about you?" I asked, another shiver sweeping over me as Gabriel bit the pad of my thumb. "Does gold have an erotic effect on you, too?"

His quicksilver eyes scorched me. "Most definitely. I look forward to seeing you wear some of my gold pieces . . . and nothing else."

I was perilously close to flinging myself on him, so it was a feat of strength to drag my mind from the promise he so temptingly offered back to the present. "Um . . . what was it you asked me?"

It took him a moment to gather his thoughts, as well, a fact that pleased me to no end. "Er . . . what you found in Kostya's lair?"

"Oh, yes, that." I thought for a few moments. "There wasn't much else in the unlocked chest. Some necklaces, the amulet, a couple of old-looking pieces of tapestry, and that's about it."

"You had no difficulty getting into his lair, then?" Drake asked, putting away his phone. "Did the black-mailer let you in?"

"On the contrary, he said it was going to be difficult to get in. But . . . well, there's a bit of a story about that. Someone was there ahead of me." I explained about the dragon's bane on the door, and how I'd gone around to the window to find it open.

"Kostya came in as I was going through one of the chests, the unbound one. Judging by his surprise, he wasn't expecting anyone there, which means someone else must have opened that window and disarmed the security system."

Drake glanced at Gabriel.

"I was with you all day trying to find out what happened to Maata and Tipene," the latter pointed out.

Guilt prodded me painfully. "I'm sorry, I've been so caught up in my own troubles, I didn't ask you about them. Did you find out anything?"

Gabriel shook his head. "No. They have just disappeared."

"And someone has broken into Kostya's lair," Drake said thoughtfully.

Gabriel's handsome face grew cold at the mention of the black dragon. "Fiat?"

"Possibly. Or one of the red dragons," Drake answered. "It could be that Chuan Ren has been released from Abaddon. Although I believe she'd first come after Aisling and me."

"It must be Fiat. He would stop at nothing to regain control of the blue dragons." Gabriel's hand was warm as it took mine. "Just as Kostya has nothing to lose but everything to gain by keeping Maata and Tipene from me."

"You don't think he'll hurt them?" I asked, a sick feeling making my gorge rise.

He didn't dismiss that idea nearly as quickly as I would have liked. "To do so would bring an all-out war against him, not only by the silver dragons, but by others as well." He sent an inquisitive glance to Drake.

The latter nodded. "Killing your guards would constitute an act of war against a sept of the weyr. The members would be obligated to uphold the terms of the treaty and destroy him in return."

"You know, Porter looked surprised when I asked him what demon lord he worked for," I said slowly as I mused over the facts. "I wonder if Cyrene heard correctly when he said he was working for a dreadlord."

"Dreadlord?" Drake asked, pouncing on the word. "He said that specifically?"

I nodded. "What's the significance of that? It's just another word for demon lord, isn't it?"

Drake and Gabriel exchanged glances. "In modern usage, yes, but in centuries past, it meant many things . . . including a wyvern," the latter said.

"Oh. You think Porter was working for a dragon? One of the ones you mentioned?"

"I don't know," he said, his eyes dulling slightly. "It is an interesting thought nonetheless."

"So what are we going to do?" I asked, suddenly swamped with exhaustion. I tried to remember the last time I'd slept, and couldn't.

Gabriel pulled me up against his side. I leaned into him, feeling warm, safe, and cherished. "First we get you out of the country."

"You are welcome to stay with Aisling and me," Drake offered. "The thief takers evidently have found your house, Gabriel."

The latter nodded. "Then I think we will need to have a look into Kostya's locked chests. The phylactery must be contained in one of them."

"And the amulet?" I asked.

"It poses many questions, but I do not see that it is of much importance," Gabriel said after a few moments' thought. "It was kept in an unlocked chest, and Kostya would never put it there if it held value. It is possible that the thief taker was deliberately trying to mislead you into believing he was not in the employ of a demon lord."

"Or he could be operating for purposes of his own," Drake said.

Gabriel nodded.

"What if it turns out that he's working for a dragon after all?" I had to ask.

Gabriel pulled me tighter against him. "Then we will deal with that situation, too. But of first importance is the phylactery. It is the only thing I can use to barter for the release of my guards. I *must* have it."

"Agreed," Drake said, hesitating a moment. "He will in all likelihood be expecting such a move, you know."

Gabriel didn't answer, but the smile that curled his lips left me shivering again . . . this time with cold.

Chapter Sixteen

"Alone at last," Gabriel said in his best dramatic voice, his dimples at odds with the lascivious grin he was giving me as he closed the door and leaned against it.

I stopped admiring the room and eyed him slowly. Although Drake seemed to wear the color of his sept frequently—mostly in his shirts—Gabriel wasn't clad in silver. Instead he wore a pair of faded jeans and a scarlet shirt, opened just enough to show a beaded necklace from which hung a silver version of his sept emblem. He was the sexiest man I'd ever seen, and I was just a fraction of a second from leaping upon him when there was a knock at the door. It opened, bumping against him.

"I'm so sorry, I didn't know you were there," Aisling said when Gabriel moved away enough for the door to open completely. She smiled happily at us both. "I just wanted to check that everything was all right. There's a bathroom attached, in case you didn't know, just through the door opposite."

"Thank you. I'm sure we'll have no problem finding it," I said, trying not to drool on Gabriel.

She bustled into the room, tweaking the cover on the bed before going over to a large antique wardrobe. "There should be some extra blankets in here, if you get chilly. Oh, and everything's been fireproofed, so you guys can . . . well . . . I'm sure I don't need to explain it."

"Everything is lovely," I said, feeling awkward. Gabriel ignored Aisling to watch me with the intensity of a panther about to pounce. It just about blared his intention to indulge in wild, unbridled lovemaking, and although I had every intention of fulfilling that thought, it was a bit embarrassing to have everyone know it.

Drake suddenly appeared, herding his wife out of the room and down the hall with an apologetic glance at Gabriel. "*Kincsem*, you should have been in bed an hour ago. You will tire yourself."

"I'm pregnant, not an imbecile, Drake! It's quite obvious they want to be alone, but I just wanted to make sure they had everything first. There's nothing more annoying than being caught short during the middle, if you know what I mean . . ." Aisling's voice drifted down the hall after her.

Gabriel sighed, closed the door, and leaned against it in a repeat of his earlier action. His eyes blazed with blatant promise as he examined me thoroughly. "Alone at—"

The door thumped open again, hitting him hard enough that it sent him staggering forward a few steps. He whirled and glared at the black dog that stood in the doorway.

"Heya. Cy just showed up, May. Thought you'd want to know since you were worried and all. I think Aisling's putting her in the room down the hall. You want to see her before you and Gabe go off to Boinksville?"

I hesitated, feeling that I should make sure Cyrene was all right.

"Is she harmed in any way?" Gabriel asked before I could answer.

Jim pursed its lips and shook its head. "Nope. Said she came close to flooding the place before they let her go, but she's fine. István told her there was a pool in the basement, and she was headed that way when I left her."

"Then we will see her in the morning," Gabriel said firmly, pushing the demon none too gently out the door.

"Suit yourselves, although she said she had something to tell May. If you need help shifting the furniture so you can do it in dragon form, just give me a yell—"

The door slammed shut in its face.

"Just tryin' to be helpful!" it yelled.

Gabriel growled at the door for a moment before turning back to face me.

I decided such a show of restraint deserved a reward. I pulled off my shirt and pants, allowing my hands to run sensually down my ribs and hips.

Gabriel's eyes widened, the pupils almost nonexistent as he gazed upon my exposed flesh. He swallowed a couple of times, his voice thick when he spoke. "Alone—"

"We bring your luggage," someone said behind him. Gabriel leaped out of the way to avoid being whacked on the back yet again as István kicked open the door, depositing my bags from Gabriel's house. I didn't have time to snatch up a shirt before Gabriel was in front of me, blocking István's view.

István's eyebrows rose at the sight of my clothing on the chair. "Oh. Sorry. The door locks, you know."

"I will be sure to see that it's used," Gabriel answered.

István surprised me with a grin, and then he was gone. Gabriel locked the door, counted to ten, then sighed when no one knocked on it. "Shall we try this again?"

"I don't know—it's taking on the feel of a scene from a Marx Brothers' movie, don't you think?"

His smile warmed me to the tips of my naked toes, but it was his gaze that left me feeling as if I was burning. "You are so delicious, I don't know where to begin." His gaze moved along my exposed skin.

I laughed, propping my foot up on the chair and nodding toward the knife I wore at my ankle. "Why don't you start by helping me out of this?"

He looked at my leg. He looked at my breasts, straining to get out of my bra in a manner hitherto unbeknownst to me. He went back to my bare leg, with a brief stop at my hips and belly.

"No?" I asked, amused, aroused, and slightly confused by his hesitation.

He swallowed, his Adam's apple bobbing as he shook his head. "I want you," he finally said, his voice sounding somewhat strangled.

"I can see you do," I said, glancing toward the bulgy front of his pants.

"I mean I really want you. I need you. Right now."

"Well, I don't see a problem with that, unless Cyrene has suddenly developed a skill for lock picking," I said, unbuckling the knife sheath.

I stood up, wondering what on earth was keeping him from all the pouncing I could have sworn he was going to do the second we were alone, and decided to give him a little encouragement. I unhooked the front of my bra and let it fall to the floor.

Gabriel swore in what I assumed was his native language, his eyes huge.

I watched him closely for a moment. He was as stiff

as a board, only the liquid silver of his gaze as it leaped from my breasts to my legs and back again offering a sign he was still actually alive. He'd even stopped breathing.

I shucked my underwear and stood in what I hoped was an attractive pose that wouldn't let him see quite how large my backside was.

A strange gurgling noise emerged from him, but nothing else.

"Am I doing something wrong here?" I finally asked, raising my hands and letting them fall in frustration. "You don't want me naked?"

A little whimper escaped his lips. He swallowed again, his hands tightening to fists at his side. "I can't think of anything I want more at this moment, including the phylactery, Kostya's head on a platter, and peace in the weyr."

"Then why are you standing over there, making odd little noises of unhappiness, while I'm standing here feeling extremely insecure, exposed, and like I need to go on an immediate diet to lose at least ten pounds?"

He closed his eyes for a moment, his face twisted in pain. "I may be a dragon, but I am not an animal, Mayling. You clearly wish to arouse me by performing this . . . incredible . . . striptease, and I will stand here and allow you to proceed if it kills me. Which it very likely may do."

"Gabriel," I said, smiling at the fact that he thought I was performing for him.

"Don't," he said, his eyes still closed. His body trembled.

"Don't what?"

"Don't say my name. I don't think I can bear it."

I shook my head, laughed a little, then walked over and unbuttoned his shirt so I could put my hand on his bare chest. "I don't understand you at all. You're acting like you want to make love to me, but I can't say your name?"

"No," he answered, piercing me with a look so hot it made my toenails steam. He swallowed again, his voice rough around the edges. "When you say my name, all I can think about is joining with you. You are my mate, Mayling. I don't just wish to make love to you; I need to join with you. I hunger for you the way a mortal hungers for food."

"Then why . . . ?" I asked, sliding my hand down his chest to his belly. He gasped, his muscles contracting underneath my fingers. "Why are we standing here talking when we could be on the bed indulging in wild, steamy dragon lovin'?"

"I am not an animal," he repeated. "But I *am* a dragon, and our matings tend to be intense. You are a woman, and thus you need time to become aroused to the point where our mating will not hurt you."

"Are you talking about foreplay?" I asked, finally seeing the light.

"Yes. You deserve foreplay, but if I touch one tiny centimeter of that deliciously satin skin of yours, I will lose the little control I have. I cannot give you foreplay at this time, Mayling. I'm sorry, but I just can't."

"But you can stand here and discuss the issue," I pointed out.

"Only because I am determined to prove to you that I value you more than anything else in my life. I would greatly appreciate it if you didn't explore any more of my stomach, because that too will send me over the edge. In fact, I'd be eternally grateful if you would arouse yourself, and tell me when you are ready."

His eyes were closed again, as if looking at me hurt too much.

"You want *me* to arouse myself," I said, trying hard not to laugh.

"Yes. Normally I would enjoy performing that function, or at worst, watching you do it, but I cannot at this time."

I smiled, amused and touched at the same time. He was trying so hard to reassure me that he was more a man than a beast, but I had needs as well, and they weren't being met with us standing there talking. I grabbed his shirt with both hands and literally ripped the rest of it open, yanking it off him. "Take me!" I demanded as his eyes popped open in surprise. *"Now!"*

I didn't have to ask twice. Before I could so much as blink, I was on the bed, splayed out on my side, a suddenly naked Gabriel half covering me.

"I will give you foreplay when this is over," he said, his breath hot on the back of my neck as he slid one arm underneath my waist, pulling my upper leg back over his thigh. "I will arouse you then, but first, I must join with you."

I wanted to point out that any such activity would technically be afterplay, not foreplay, but my brain was too overloaded with the sensations he was generating to form words. The position was a little awkward, leaving me to clutch the sheets as he searched for entrance, and then found it, his body hard behind and in me, muscle and tissue parting to allow him access to areas that went beyond a mere physical body. Gabriel had used the word "joining," and as his hips flexed, making long, slow strokes into me, his mouth hot on my neck while his hands found my breasts, I understood just what he meant by it. I arched backward, tilting my hips back to take in more of him in a wordless demand. He growled against my neck, the long, tanned fingers tightening on my breasts.

I sucked in my breath not only at the sensation of his hands, but at the feeling of fullness deep within me. Gone were the long, slow movements meant to arouse—his body pistoned into me in an act of possession, my body welcoming each blow with a thousand little jolts of pleasure. I gasped again, a tight ball forming that seemed to draw in every nerve in my body.

Gabriel's breath was harsh, coming in primitive little groans as he sucked the skin of my neck, his tongue leaving long, wet streaks.

One hand slid off my breast, down to my belly, probing and parting delicate flesh to find the center of my pleasure.

"Mayling, I cannot wait," he moaned.

I tightened every muscle I had around him, arching my back, my hands clawing at the sheets as the ball of passion deep inside me threatened to explode. "Fire," I gasped, barely able to form a coherent sentence. "I want your fire. I *need* your fire."

He gave it to me then, fed me his dragon fire until it washed over us in a blaze of ecstasy. He was the dragon fire, surrounding me, on me, inside me, every inch of my being bound so tightly with his, we were the flames, dancing higher and higher until we burst into a million little sparks, separate, but whole.

Pain, sharp and hot, lit the back of my shoulder, but it faded almost instantly as I let myself go, drifting slowly back down into my body as an ember from a bonfire lazily wafts it way back to earth.

The bed was not on fire, I was pleased to note. Neither were the curtains, chair, or wardrobe.

Flames licked down the length of Gabriel's body as he collapsed onto his back, the fine sheen of sweat that covered him instantly vaporizing.

My body felt heavy and dull as compared to the bright phoenix we had been together, even as little tremors of pleasure, orgasmic aftershocks, made me cognizant of the truth of Gabriel's warnings of rough lovemaking.

"You're on fire," I said, rolling onto my other side in order to face him.

His eyes were closed, his chest heaving as he sucked in huge quantities of air. He cracked one eye open to look at me, his dimples popping into life as he closed it again. "Thank you. I endeavor to please you, little bird, although you are a demanding woman. It takes my full energy to sate your many desires."

I rolled my eyes at that gross exaggeration, stroking my hand down his still-burning chest. "I meant literally."

He opened an eye again, this time to glance down at himself. "Am I? How very curious. It must have something to do with you."

I patted out the flames on his chest and belly, the rest of the fire dying out. "Me? I don't see how. You're the dragon—you're the one who has dragon fire."

He wrapped an arm around me and pulled me up close to his body, arranging me so that I lay draped over him before closing his eyes again, sighing in happiness. "This has never happened to me with another woman. It must be because you are my mate. When you give the fire back to me, it's more than what it started out as."

"More?" I drew a lazy circle around the pert brown nipple that lay next to my mouth, considering whether or not I had the energy to taste it.

"More." One hand lifted and made a vague gesture. "It's . . . purer. More powerful. Something more than what it starts out as. I can't really explain it. It's just . . . more."

"Ah." I smiled at his nipple, oddly proud.

"What are you doing?" he asked suspiciously, lifting his head to peer down at me.

"Smiling at your nipple. I was wondering what you taste like."

His eyes, a sleepy, slumbering silver, sparked with interest. "Foreplay?"

"This, my dragon, is afterplay," I said, moving so that I straddled his thighs. I leaned down to lick his nipple, but before I could capture it, a familiar tingling started up my back. Dread swept over me as I swore, threw myself over the edge of the bed, blindly grabbing for the blankets we'd pushed off the bed during our lovemaking.

"May? What's the—"

The tingling increased to a painful pitch as the world seemed to give a shudder, then twisted into a gut-wrenching parody of reality. I was jerked out of the room at Drake's house, and deposited naked, clutching a blanket, onto a cool tile floor.

"I see you've changed your mind about me. I'm delighted, although I would have preferred a little warning of your intentions," a smooth, suave voice spoke.

The chill from it caused my skin to prickle as I twisted the blanket around me toga-style. My dignity was shredded, but I managed to get off the floor with the blanket intact. I glared at the man who stood in front of me, his hair slicked back from his forehead, his dark, deep-lidded eyes promising all sorts of carnal pleasures.

I said the first thing that came to mind. "I never liked you in that movie about the Arab chieftain, you know. You were bearable in the sequel, but the first one? The word 'ham' comes to mind."

Magoth bristled, the air cooling at least ten degrees.

"That was my greatest picture!" he said in a near hiss. "It *made* my career!"

"I thought your depiction was clumsy, brutal, and extremely heavy-handed."

He did hiss this time, his face hard. "Women the world over swooned whenever I was on the screen. *Swooned!* Several committed suicide because of me!"

"That was just the Hollywood hype," I said nonchalantly, aware that I was playing with fire (so to speak), but unable to express my fury in any other way at the untimely summons. "You had a very good manager, as I recall. I always did think he was smart to have you pretend to die just when you did. I doubt if you'd have kept your precious mystique if you'd been around much longer."

Magoth's face worked for a moment before he regained control. I knew I was perilously close to being punished for my flip comments, but they served their purposes: they distracted him from thoughts of seduction of my nearly naked self, and they gave vent to my much-aggrieved spleen.

He strolled over to a bar, pouring himself a glass of sangria. I took the wicker seat across from him, ignoring the fact that two demons were also present in the pretty courtyard of what I assumed was his villa in Spain. "I find myself wondering if there is a purpose in your slanderous comments about my brief movie career," he said with perfect suavity.

"Just an idle thought. You haven't worn your hair slicked back like that for a number of decades—it reminded me of when I first saw you."

He smiled. It wasn't a pleasant thing to behold. "I have toyed with the thought of returning to the screen, but alas, my schedule allows me little free time. Which brings me to an interesting bit of gossip I have heard."

His gaze dropped to the top of the blanket, the edge
of which was tucked securely under my arm. "The
word on the street is that you have mated with a
dragon. A wyvern, to be exact."

"Yes," I said, fighting to control the fear that rose
inside me. I knew this moment would come, and
counted on Gabriel's strength to see me through it.

One sleek black eyebrow rose. He sat, crossing one
leg over the other, the glass of sangria dangling from
his fingers. "That is all I am to expect from you on
the subject?"

"There's nothing to say. I met a wyvern, agreed that
I was his mate, end of story."

"Oh, I think not," he said with amusement. My
stomach contracted. Gabriel would probably be furious and worried about my sudden disappearance from
his bed. What if he came after me? What would
Magoth do to Gabriel if he managed to track me down
in order to rescue me? "There is another rumor that
I have heard, one that I find even more intriguing."

I frowned, running my mind back over the last couple
of days. With the quintessence returned to Kostich, there
was nothing I'd done in the last few days that would be
of any interest to Magoth. "What rumor?"

"It is said that a thief taker finally caught you." He
leaned back along the rattan chaise, patting the cush-
ion next to him. "Let us not be so formal. Come sit
with me."

"I'm fine where I am," I said, oddly relieved that
he didn't seem to be trying to enthrall me.

"This is not an invitation," he answered, the force
in his voice compelling me to move from the sanctuary
of my chair. Reluctantly, I clutched the blanket tight
around myself and perched on the edge of the chaise,
as far away from him as I could manage.

"There, now, isn't that more comfortable?" He

dropped a hand on my blanket-covered knee, lolling back. In an instant, the demons moving silently around in the background were gone . . . as were Magoth's clothes.

"I believe I will start a clothing-optional hotel on the southern coast," he said with studied nonchalance. "I find the human form so much more pleasing when it is not hidden away behind garments."

I slapped his hand away from where it had crept toward the knot of the blanket. "That depends on the body in question. I prefer to remain clothed, thank you."

"Sweet May. Sweet, adorable May. Does my form please you? I have thought of changing it, but there is no other which can match the original, don't you think?" He waved a languid hand to indicate his body.

He clearly hoped to shock or frighten me. In an effort to deny him any satisfaction on either account, I forced myself to glance over him with what I prayed indicated indifference. "It's very nice, as you well know, given the number of women you've seduced, enthralled, and damned to eternal torment."

" 'Torment' is such a harsh word for it. I prefer 'enlightenment.' "

My curiosity, always bothersome, got the better of me. "You said this was your original form . . . did you have to beat the women off you with a stick when you were mortal?"

His lips quirked. "From the time I first grew hair between my legs, women have chased me. Few have resisted me when I have set about to charm them. You are one of my failures, but even you are not, I think, immune to me?" He gestured toward his bare chest with a wicked glint to his eyes. "Perhaps you find my body not to your taste? My chest is too broad for you?"

"It's fine, although a little hirsute for my tastes," I answered, clearing my throat. He wasn't turning the full power of his charm on me, but just being this close to him—naked—was reminding me that even a mate to a dragon could be susceptible to his power. The key was to keep him from feeling he had to prove a point. "I know other women like a furry chest, though."

"And my belly. No—abs. That is the current trend, is it not? My abs are rock hard, are they not?"

"Six-pack," I agreed, nodding at the body part in question.

"I can do things with my cock that would make you faint with pleasure," he said with half-closed eyelids. "What do you think of it?"

I bit my lip and gazed upon his privates. His penis was enlarged, bobbing gently in the breeze. "It looks pretty much like any other male genitalia, although I doubt if many men would tolerate having their penises tattooed."

"That was not my choice," he said with a shrug. "It was the first curse bound to me by a very jealous diviner years before I rose to power. If you trace out the words of the curse, they will glow," he added with a leer.

"I think I'll pass on the opportunity to see a glowing penis curse. Is that it, or would you like me to admire your legs, as well?"

He sighed in a highly dramatic fashion. "I do my best to please you, and still you spurn me. Tell me, did you enjoy the bestial act with your dragon?"

"Very much so," I said, refusing to rise to the bait. "But you didn't summon me here to discuss my love life, did you?"

He wrapped his fingers around my neck and started pulling me down to his bare chest. "You wound me with such harsh words. Let us kiss and make up, and then I will discuss just why I have summoned you before me."

"Do you really want to invoke Gabriel's displeasure over something so trivial as a kiss?" I asked slowly, hoping he would stop and think before he did something rash.

He paused, his eyes thoughtful. I used the opportunity to slip out of his grip, edging away slightly.

"This dragon of yours . . . he is jealous of you?"

"He is a dragon. They are extremely possessive."

"Interesting." He leaned back again, his thoughts masked as he watched me for a few seconds. "I wonder how far he would go to reclaim his mate?"

I shifted slightly, uncomfortable with the thought of Gabriel going up against someone as powerful as Magoth.

"Tell me of this second rumor, sweet May," he continued. "Did a thief taker finally catch up with you?"

"Yes. I was arrested, tried, and sentenced to imprisonment in the Akasha."

"And yet you are here, in the glorious flesh," he said, his gaze dropping to my breasts.

"Gabriel helped me escape."

"Again the dragon," he mused, a little smile playing around his lips. His eyes were as cold as ever, though, coolly calculating. "I did hear that the thief taker caught you robbing the lair of another dragon. Tell me, minion, what did you take from him?"

Chapter Seventeen

"I haven't taken anything from Gabriel," I said, purposely misinterpreting his statement in order to give me time to think. Why was he interested in the dragons? I ran my mind over the items I'd seen in Kostya's lair again. Could the golden dragon amulet be valuable after all? It certainly wasn't anything else in the unlocked chest, which meant it had to be the amulet or something in the locked ones that piqued Magoth's interest.

A horrible thought came to me—what if Porter was working for Magoth? Was this some sort of a test? Was I about to be replaced? I dismissed the notion almost immediately; if Porter was in Magoth's employ, he would certainly know exactly what I was. His threat of the dreadlord killing me if I mentioned the amulet just didn't fit.

None of which explained why Magoth was so interested in the contents of Kostya's lair.

"You play games with me, and yet, they are not the games we can both enjoy," he said in a light tone, but the undercurrent of menace was enough to turn my blood cold. "Answer the question, *servant.*"

The word stunned with the force of a lash. I didn't want to tell him the truth, but I could not refuse to answer a direct question. I could, however, censor out any information not specifically questioned. "I didn't have much time to spend in the dragon's lair. I took only one thing away, a gold amulet in the shape of a dragon."

"An amulet?" He frowned, sitting up. I was pleased to notice that his erection had ceased being quite so rampant. "What sort of an amulet? Describe it to me."

"It was nothing special," I said, relieved that he hadn't asked me either what I'd gone there to find, or who had sent me to take the amulet. It was far, far better that he think Gabriel had sent me to rob another dragon than to hear of the phylactery. "It was about so big, made of gold, but not made very well, as if it was a child's toy."

He froze. "Describe it."

"I just did." Why was he so interested in the amulet? I shook my head at his odd reaction. "It's just an amulet. Gold, shaped roughly like a dragon, very primitive and quite honestly, not attractive in the least sense. It was in the *unlocked* chest, so it can't be worth much to anyone."

"The Lindorm Phylactery," he murmured, his gaze filled with disbelief and confusion.

My jaw just about hit the floor at his words. "The . . . the *what*?"

"Could it be?" His eyes narrowed as he thought about it. "I had not heard of it surfacing. It was in an unlocked chest, you say? That does not seem right, not right at all."

"The phylactery? Are you saying that ugly little lump of gold was the *phylactery*?" I shook my head. "It can't be. It's not at all like the Gulden Phylactery you made me take from that oracle in South Africa.

That was a lovely crystal vial. The thing I'm talking about is an amulet, a primitive-looking amulet of a dragon."

I hurriedly scooted out of the way as Magoth rose from the chaise, mindlessly pacing back and forth as he thought out loud. "What would a dragon be doing allowing the most valuable artifact of his kind to sit in an unlocked chest? It does not make sense, and yet the description matches."

"It doesn't make any sense at all. I might not have a great knowledge of dragons and their society, but from what Gabriel told me—" I stopped in horror of what I'd said, one hand going to my mouth.

Magoth spun around, his gaze so intense it slammed me backward a good six feet to the wall. My ears rang with the blow, giving me a moment of disorientation.

"The wyvern spoke to you of it?" The temperature of the room dropped ten degrees as Magoth took a deep breath. I'm not a cowardly person in general, but at the look of unabated fury on his face, I crumpled into a ball on the floor, covering my head with my hands. And not a moment too soon.

"You were sent to take it!" Magoth roared with a fury I'd never heard, loud enough to shatter every bit of glass in the room. Glass shards from the windows, pictures that hung on the wall, light fixtures, and assorted other sources rained down to the floor, several pieces piercing my skin.

I stayed curled in a protective ball until the worst of it was over, then carefully lifted my head and eyed Magoth.

His eyes were lit with a glow that left me terrified. "Where is the Lindorm Phylactery, May?"

"I don't have it," I said quickly, my gaze darting around the room for a possible escape.

Magoth eliminated that idea by simply grabbing my

neck in one hand and lifting me a good two feet off the floor. "Where is the Lindorm Phylactery, *servant*?"

"I don't know."

He shook me as effortlessly as if I were a dish towel. I clutched at his hand, trying to ease its grip enough to allow air into my lungs. "Where?"

"The L'au-delà has it!" I cried as wavering black blotches appeared before my eyes. "They took it from me. It's in their vault."

He opened his hand, allowing me to plummet to the floor. I lay stunned for a few seconds, rubbing my neck as I dragged in huge, gasping breaths. Before I could do anything else, he jerked me onto my feet, his eyes boring twin holes into me as he spoke.

"You will find the phylactery and bring it to me."

My voice came out as a croak. "You can't possibly want it. It's a dragon artifact—"

"You will find the phylactery and bring it to me," he repeated, but this time, the power he put into the words stung my skin like a million little snakes.

"Why?" I cried, ignoring the pain.

He released me, strolling back to the chaise, where he took up a reclining position. He didn't answer for a few minutes, but finally he turned his head to me and gave me his usual sardonic smile. "I want it."

"It has no power you can use," I said, still massaging my neck. "It can have no value to you."

"It does not have power over mere mortals, true . . . but it is the basis of all power to dragonkin."

I shook my head, retucking the blanket that was wrapped around me. "If that's so, the item I saw wasn't it. I would have been able to feel something with that much power in it, and I'm telling you that this lump of vaguely dragon-shaped gold did not have any sort of emanations other than age."

"You are not a dragon." His eyelids dropped halfway, shielding his gaze. "It has no power for you to feel because it is not connected to you as it is to them."

"All right. Let's say for the sake of brevity that the gold blob was the phylactery—not that it looks anything remotely like a vessel—"

"It is a vessel," he interrupted. "It is part of the dragon heart, that which holds the essence of the first dragon. Your wyvern didn't tell you that when he ordered you to steal it for him?" He shook his head in mock sorrow. "Regardless of what you think, it is of value to me."

My head was still reeling from the last few minutes, leaving me feeling particularly stupid. Now it made sense why Porter had wanted me to steal the amulet, but it didn't explain why Kostya would keep something so precious in an unlocked chest. Nor did it explain why Magoth wanted a dragon relic when it held no power over mortals—over whom he was always trying to gain control—or over any other beings in the Otherworld. Other than the dragons, of course . . . The light dawned at last. "You're going to use it against the dragons," I said, horror mixing with bile in my gut.

The long, slow smile he gave me would have stripped a few decades off the lifetime of a mortal.

"You can't control them," I said quickly, fear bitter on my tongue. "They're dragons, Magoth. They do not bow to Abaddon. They never have."

"Never before has a demon lord held the Lindorm Phylactery," he said in a soft, sinister voice that left me sicker than ever. "With it, and with the other pieces of the dragon heart, the weyr will come to heel . . . and I will have the chance to establish a presence in the mortal world."

My legs gave out. I fell to my knees, sick to the very depths of my soul with what he was saying.

"Bring me the phylactery, sweet May."

I shook my head, knowing full well he might strike out for such insubordination.

"Bring me the phylactery, and you will be rewarded."

"There is nothing, nothing you can give me that would make me betray the dragons in that manner."

His fingers tilted my head up, forcing me to look into his obsidian eyes. What I saw there scared me to the depths of my being. "Not even your freedom?"

I looked at him, unable to speak.

His mouth curved in a wicked, knowing smile. "If you bring me the phylactery, I will grant you a temporary rescindment of your bondage for . . . shall we say a century?"

A century. A hundred years of freedom from Magoth and his demands. A hundred years of happiness with Gabriel, untainted by the stain of Abaddon that clung to me. A lifetime of servitude for the dragons.

I couldn't do it. There was nothing he could offer me that would induce me to betray Gabriel and his sept, of all the septs, in that way. "No," I said softly, bracing myself for a blow.

Pain lashed through me with sharp precision. I doubled over, clutching myself against it. "Sweet May. Lovely May. It would be such a shame to lose a servant as devoted as you."

He lifted me up, his eyes blazing as he pulled me against his body, but for once, there was no erotic intent in his expression. "Do not fail me, May, lest I be forced to recall you to Abaddon, where you will remain until the end of your days."

* * *

"—too early to do anything. I haven't had my breakfast yet!"

"You're just going to have to wait, Jim. Finding May is more important than feeding you. Gabriel, are you sure she didn't say anything before she disappeared?"

The voices reached me even before I fell through the rip in reality that Magoth's minion had created. I hit the floor, disoriented as I always was when shoved through a tear in the mortal plain.

"Speak of the devil. Ouch. Looks like you've been to Abaddon and back," Jim said close to my ear. I felt a faint moist sensation on my shoulder. "Oh, yeah—hellfire and brimstone. Well, back safe and sound, that's all that matters. Now can I have my breffy?"

I hadn't shaken the dizziness from my head before I was yanked upward and slammed against a hard surface . . . a warm hard surface, one with arms that tightened around me, which smelled like heaven, and tasted even better. Gabriel didn't wait to ask me what happened—his mouth took possession of mine with a need that demanded all. I let him plunder away, ignoring my guilt for a moment in order to give him everything I had.

His lips and tongue pulled away from me with violence, his eyes literally scorching me as he looked down, his face set in hard planes. "I need you," he said in a low, intimate growl.

I blinked for a moment in surprise, glancing to the side where Drake stood next to Aisling. It would appear the demon had dropped me off in Drake's kitchen. Behind the two of them, Drake's men, and a woman I remembered being introduced as István's girlfriend, stood watching with silent interest. Surprisingly, Cyrene wasn't present. "Er . . . right now?"

"Yes." Gabriel didn't hesitate—he simply scooped me up in his arms, blanket and all, and headed in long strides toward what looked to be the back stairs.

Aisling glanced at her wyvern. "I know it's none of our business, but does May look to you like she's up to the sort of activities Gabriel is clearly planning?"

Drake leaned down and kissed her. "She has been taken from him and returned. It is the way of dragons, *kincsem*."

The last thing I saw before Gabriel leaped up the last of the stairs was Aisling giving her husband an odd look. "Really? You never did that with me. I wonder if I could get someone to kidnap me for a bit . . ."

"Is that true?" I asked as Gabriel pounded up a second flight of stairs.

"Yes. You are not harmed in any way?"

"No, I'm fine. Just a little . . . er . . . taken aback by your sudden passion."

He slid me a look that was part desire, part amusement. "I'm sorry, little bird, but you are my mate. I must possess you. It is a primal need, not one that can be controlled. A mortal man might do so, but I cannot."

"Oh," I said, not wanting to admit that I found it immensely flattering that the second I was returned, he felt the need to join again with me.

He kicked open the door to our room, setting me down on the bed before locking the door. I was trying to get up so I could untangle myself from the blanket, but before I could, he was on me, unrolling me deftly, his hands trailing little paths of fire as he caressed my thighs, my belly, my breasts.

I don't know how he got his own clothes off so quickly, but I wasn't about to ask. His eyes were molten, brilliant with desire. "Mayling—"

218   *Katie MacAlister*

"I know," I said, pushing him onto his back. "No foreplay."

"I swear to you, we will do this slowly the next time," he answered, pulling me over him. "But I must have you now."

"It's not like I've had a lot of foreplay before," I pointed out as I leaned down to nibble the nipple I'd wanted to molest earlier. "So I'm not bound to miss— *agathos daimon*!"

He took me at my word, not waiting to even find out if I was ready for him, just lunged upward as he pulled my hips down. The sudden shock of his intrusion caused a burst of pleasure that left me bucking against him. He was right, this was a possession, pure and simple, but it was a possession that went both ways. I leaned down to nibble on his neck, savoring the feel and scent and taste of him. I didn't have to ask for his fire; he gave it to me as I rode him, our mouths finding each other despite the wild dance.

I closed my eyes as he pulled me down onto his chest, the warm, damp skin beneath me burning me outside even as the fires within flared to new heights. I tilted my head to nuzzle the sweet spot behind his ear, making him groan when I bit down gently, a groan that changed to a roar that bathed me in fire as he found his pleasure. The sensation as he slammed himself into me was enough to send me over the edge, too. I let go of my guilt, of the worry about what would become of us, let go of everything but the joy of joining myself to the man who had somehow become a part of me, giving myself up to the spiral of flame that spun up and around us.

There had to be some way to stop Magoth. There just had to be.

Chapter Eighteen

The urgency of Gabriel's needs—and my immediate and overwhelming response to them—had driven from my mind the discussion I'd had with Magoth.

"The phylactery!" I yelled suddenly, pushing myself off Gabriel's warm, limp form.

"What about it?" he asked sleepily, his face relaxed and bearing a sated expression that gave me no little amount of feminine pride.

"I know where it is."

"What?" He sat up so fast I slid off him and onto the floor. "Mayling!"

"It's all right, I'm fine," I said, laughing. "I should have known better than to startle a dragon."

He knelt beside me, his eyes grave. "Where is the phylactery?"

"Paris. In the L'au-delà vault."

His eyes widened at the same time his pupils narrowed. "The amulet you stole from Kostya?"

"Yes."

"Why did you not tell me this when we were there?"

"I didn't know that's what it was," I answered, getting to my feet. The memory of Magoth chilled my flesh, causing little goose bumps to rise along my arms. I pulled out some clothing from the bag István had brought, holding it to me as I faced Gabriel. He wouldn't harm me—I knew that. But I still dreaded telling him what had happened between the demon lord and myself. "Gabriel, I . . . Magoth knows."

"He knows what?"

"He knows about the phylactery." I lifted my chin to look him dead in the eye. "I had no idea that the amulet was the phylactery. It was in the unlocked chest, after all. What sane person would keep something so valuable in a place like that? And I swear to you that Porter never gave a hint as to what it really was. I wonder now if he knew."

Gabriel looked confused for a moment. He gently pushed me into the chair and knelt at my feet, his hands on my knees. "Explain it again. Slowly. And do not leave anything out."

I went over again my phone call with Porter, the visit to Kostya's lair, the conversation with Porter in Paris, and the pertinent parts of my conversation with Magoth. I was sick with the knowledge that my ignorance had set Magoth onto the trail of the phylactery, but Gabriel brushed aside my pathetic apology.

"The blackmailer poses no problem. We can deal with him so that he will offer no threat to Cyrene or you." He rose and began pacing the room. "As for the demon lord . . . I would have preferred to keep knowledge of the phylactery's whereabouts confined only to us, but as we cannot undo what has been done, we will simply have to make the best of the situation. Our first and foremost priority must be to get the phylactery before Magoth can order you to retrieve it for him." He paused to give me a long look. "Or has he already done that?"

Bile rose, burning the back of my throat. I wanted to admit the truth to Gabriel, to cling to him and sob out my sorrows, avoiding all the unpleasantness that was woven into my life, but I couldn't do that to him, not while there was the slightest shred of hope that I could avoid Magoth's command.

I touched my throat where Magoth had almost succeeded in throttling me. "He attacked me when he realized what the phylactery was. I was on the verge of passing out—"

Gabriel, distracted as I had hoped he would be, was instantly at my side, probing my neck with gentle fingers. "You were bruised here. Your flesh still remembers the trauma. I will ease its memory."

His lips caressed my neck, building the banked fire within me until I moaned at the sensation of his skin against mine.

I tossed aside the clothing I was still holding, falling into his arms, kissing a line along his jaw.

"I cannot seem to get enough of you, little bird," he murmured as his tongue swept broad strokes across my neck. I'd never been licked before by a man, but the sensation wasn't even remotely repugnant. Gabriel positively hummed with pleasure as I slid my hands down his silky skin, tracing out the hills and valleys that made up the planes of his back. "You are so good, Mayling. You taste so good."

I let my forehead drop to his shoulder, guilt spiking through my desire until the latter all but evaporated. "I'm not good. I'm not good at all, Gabriel. Even assuming we have nothing to worry about with Porter and whomever he's working for, Magoth will move mountains to get that phylactery."

"Then we shall simply have to get to it before he does," he answered, lifting my chin until my lips brushed his. "We must get you into the vault before Magoth can summon you and give you a direct order. We will have to share this news with Drake and Aisling—I do not wish to involve them, but without

Maata and Tipene to help us, we are in a weak position."

I said nothing, just snuggled into him, savoring the scent and feel of him pressed so closely against me, thinking with irony of the many times I'd comforted Cyrene when one of her romantic relationships had failed. I'd always been somewhat skeptical about heartache, but now I knew the full extent of how a person could feel they were dying inside. Worse, I had no one but myself to blame for my present circumstance—I knew it was folly to become involved with Gabriel so long as I was bound to Magoth. I knew it, and yet I'd ignored the reality of the situation. And now the true price was uncovered as I acknowledged that over the span of just a few days, my emotions had deepened significantly.

I was falling in love. It was an odd sensation, a sort of prickly excitement that alternated with the absolute depths of despair. I'd never felt love before—other than affection for Cyrene—but even that was tinged with a sense of duty because I owed my very existence to her. But Gabriel was different . . . which would make it all that much more agonizing if I did not find a way out of obeying Magoth's order.

"It is almost morning," Gabriel said, glancing at the clock. He scooped me up and stood, carrying me to the bed. "Magoth cannot assault the L'au-delà vaults himself, can he?"

I shook my head. "He doesn't have the means to leave Abaddon. Even if he did, the Otherworld officials sealed their offices and vaults from the demon lords long ago. Magoth can't get to them himself— he'll need an agent to do that." I almost choked on the last few words, but managed to keep my voice steady.

"As I thought. Then we shall rest. You need sleep,

and I must think. We will consult with Drake and Aisling in a few hours."

He lay on his side, pulling me up tight against him, tucking my leg between his as he rested his chin on the top of my head.

I allowed myself to relax into him, seduced by the warmth of his body and the comfort he brought me just by holding me. He was becoming infinitely dear to me, more precious even than my own life. I must find a way out of the situation I was in—Aisling was a demon lord. Rumor said she was once a prince of Abaddon, but had been removed. She would know of a way to get around Magoth's command. She would help me . . . she had to. The alternative was not to be thought of.

I awoke confused, the echoes of an alarm followed by a man's voice piercing my uneasy slumber.

The door was just closing as I sat up and shook the hair from my face. "Gabriel?"

Our room was empty, but judging by the shouts filtering up from the floor below, I gathered others were up and about.

A woman's scream drifted up. I leaped out of bed, jerked on a pair of pants and a shirt, and went racing barefoot down the hall to the stairs.

Cyrene stood midway down the stairs, holding a blanket around her much as I had a few hours before. Behind her, with his back to me, Kostya stood, clutching her tightly to him. I suspected that from the way everyone else present stood as still as statues on the floor below, he held some sort of a weapon on Cy.

"I'm in deadly earnest, Gabriel. Your mate may be immortal, but even she won't be able to long survive a neck slit from ear to ear."

I shadowed, not waiting to find out why Kostya believed Cyrene was me, creeping down the stairs until I was within a hairsbreadth of him. It was morning, but a dull, overcast morning, and the chandelier that hung from the ceiling above the stairs hadn't been turned on. No one saw me until I was just behind Kostya.

"Mayling, no!" Gabriel yelled, leaping toward me.

Kostya realized his mistake too late, half spinning around toward me as Cyrene lunged forward, tripped over her blanket, and hurtled down the stairs to the floor below.

I threw myself on Kostya, my thumbs digging into the pulse points on his neck. Cyrene screamed as Gabriel caught her. I didn't get to see more than him setting her abruptly aside before Kostya swore and swung around, slamming me into the wall and knocking the breath out of me.

Gabriel's roar of fury rattled the windows. I'm just about completely certain that if he had made it to Kostya, he would have ripped the latter's head off, but fortunately for us all, Drake's two bodyguards grabbed Gabriel before he could enact his rage.

Drake himself jerked me from Kostya's grip, pinning his brother to the wall, ably assisted by a snarling Jim.

"This will cease now!" Drake bellowed, sharing his glare between his brother and Gabriel.

"Do not interfere in matters concerning my mate," Gabriel growled, his normally lovely voice pitched low with warning as he struggled with the two green dragons.

"I would not dream of doing anything of the kind, but this attack was not prompted by May. Kostya, if you do not behave in a civilized manner, I will allow Aisling to perform as many wards upon you as she can think of, and she has become quite inventive the last few months."

Kostya spat out what I assumed were some nasty oaths, but ceased fighting his brother's hold. I shook the stars from my eyes and ran down the steps to Gabriel, wrapping my arms around him both for comfort and to keep him from attacking Kostya.

"If I said this was getting old, would anyone pay attention to me?" Aisling asked as most of the occupants in the room—the dragon occupants—stood seething and glaring at one another.

"No," Gabriel answered at the same time Drake did.

"Well," she said with an injured sniff, "it is. I'm certainly getting tired of the dragon brand of testosterone, and I imagine May and Cyrene are as well."

Gabriel's muscles relaxed slightly, enough that he slid his arms around me. "Your brother-in-law seems to make a habit of assaulting my mate, Aisling. I will not tolerate that."

"You began this when you stole my phylactery!" Kostya yelled, shoving his brother aside. "The black dragons will regain that—"

"Oh, no," Jim moaned, shaking its head. "He's gone off on his Bravehcart speech again."

"—which we once held but was taken from us."

Both green dragons instantly leaped in front of him as Gabriel tried to move me out of the way.

"Aisling's right," I said, digging in my heels to keep him standing still. "This is getting old."

"We will face death to restore to the sept the pride, the glory, the true essence, of what it once was!" Kostya yelled.

I gave him a look so sharp it should have drilled a hole in his head. "Are you through now? Good. I think we need to have a talk, Gabriel. *All* of us. Without anyone assaulting anyone."

"Amen," Aisling said. "Jim, escort Kostya to the living room. If he makes any sort of move toward Gabriel or May, take him down."

"You got that, bad boy?" Jim said, nudging the back of Kostya's leg. "I'm going straight for the noogies, too. Just so you know."

The look Kostya shot the demon was almost comical in its indignation, but I didn't feel much like laughing. It took a few minutes more of cajoling, reasoning, and outright threats from Aisling before the entire party was settled in a pleasant living room.

"May is absolutely right. We need to have a talk, but since Drake has been nagging me to learn to delegate—"

"I do not nag," Drake interrupted, a thin trickle of smoke emerging from his nostril as he shot his wife a quelling look. "I am a dragon. We do not nag. We suggest."

"As Drake has been suggesting quite heavily, in a repeated fashion that would be nagging in anyone else, that I share tasks with others, I am more than happy for May to take the lead here."

"Me?" I asked, startled into sitting up straight. I'd been snuggled up against Gabriel, the two of us and Cyrene sharing a couch across from Aisling, who was curled up next to Drake. The two bodyguards leaned against the wall behind them, their faces wary as they alternated between watching Gabriel and Kostya.

The black dragon paced back and forth in front of the windows, reminding me of a caged panther I'd seen in a tired traveling circus many decades before.

"Why me?" I asked.

"Well . . . it really is your show. Gabriel's and yours,

that is, but since Gabriel looks like he could happily murder Kostya, you're clearly the one to take the lead. Don't worry, we'll ride shotgun."

"Yeah. Shotgun," Jim said, narrowing its eyes at Kostya.

"All right," I said after a moment's thought. "I think the first question that needs to be answered is, where are Maata and Tipene?"

Kostya made a show of sighing. "I told you I do not know where they are. I have not taken them."

"We only have your word that you didn't," I pointed out.

"You have no proof otherwise," he snapped back.

I thought about that a moment, then admitted, "He has a point."

"He lies," Gabriel said.

"Unless we find some proof to the contrary, I don't see that standing here arguing about it is going to get us any closer to finding your guards," I said.

"He must have taken them. No one else would," Gabriel insisted.

"I did nothing!" Kostya bellowed.

"I think we will come back to that point," I said after the echoes died down. "The next question is whether the man named Porter is in your employ." I had a hard time figuring out why Kostya would hire me to steal something he already held, but I figured we needed to exclude as many possibilities as we could.

"Who?" Kostya asked.

I looked at Gabriel. "Truth or lie, do you think?"

Kostya made a wordless noise of displeasure that I would call his statement into question.

"Truth, I'm afraid," Gabriel said with reluctance.

"I second that," Aisling said. "I'm pretty good at

telling when people are lying, and Kostya isn't. Not that he usually does," she added quickly at a sharp look from her brother-in-law.

"I agree with the consensus," I said. "The next question concerns the phylactery."

"Why you deny taking it when I caught you in my lair, you mean?" Kostya growled.

"No, that's not the question," I answered.

"Why Kostya insists you took it when he still has it?" Aisling asked.

I shook my head. "No, although that's part of it."

Kostya snorted and continued pacing.

"Where the phylactery is right now?" Drake asked slowly.

"That's not an issue right now, either," I said, sliding a glance to Gabriel.

He watched Kostya pace with half-closed eyes, deceptive in their appearance. Beside me, his body was tight with tension, as if he was going to spring at any moment. I put my hand on his leg and squeezed it gently to remind him of his party manners.

"Is the question why Kostya couldn't tell the difference between May and me when I clearly wear my hair differently?" Cyrene asked with a righteous jerk of her blanket.

Everyone pretty much ignored that.

"No," I said. "The answer I want is why Kostya kept the phylactery in an unlocked chest."

That stopped him dead in his tracks. He spun around to look at me, surprise clearly evident in his dark eyes. "What? What unlocked chest?"

"There were three chests in your lair."

It was his turn for a little bit of smoke to escape him. I leaned into Gabriel and asked softly, "Can you do that too?"

His eyes never left Kostya, but his lips parted

slightly. A tiny curl of smoke emerged. For some reason, it delighted me, but that delight was short-lived.

"You admit you were in there!" Kostya said, storming toward me. "You admit you stole my phylactery!"

Instantly Gabriel was on his feet in front of me, István and Pál moving in. I stopped Gabriel as Kostya backed off, snarling.

"Yes, I did take it," I said with a little glance at Gabriel. "But I didn't know what it was at the time."

"I think perhaps you'd better explain again what happened while you were in the lair," Drake said slowly.

"It's nothing beyond what I told you before. But those alarms were disabled, and someone had to do it. I can't see Porter doing that without just taking the phylactery for himself."

Kostya shot me a fierce look. "That's ridiculous! That alarm is always set! You lie."

"Mayling never lies! Well, almost never," Cyrene said with a cutting look.

"Thanks for the support," I murmured, my lips twitching wryly before I continued. "I found it hard to believe that you'd leave the window unprotected that way. But when I looked at the alarm, it had been disabled."

"You disabled it!" Kostya accused.

I shook my head. "I didn't. I couldn't—it's inside the window."

That stopped him for a moment.

"But there's more than the window alarm that doesn't make sense. Why did you leave the phylactery in an unlocked chest?"

"I don't *have* an unlocked chest. You broke the wards binding it, and unlocked it three nights ago, when you stole the phylactery."

"Three nights ago I was in Greece," I said thoughtfully.

230   *Katie MacAlister*

"You stole the phylactery then!" he insisted. "Then you returned to steal more of my treasures. I found the chest you'd broken into days earlier nearly empty after you leaped out of the window," he snapped, making short, jerky little motions with his hands as he paced back and forth in front of the window. "You stole many things from me that night, but it's the phylactery that matters the most. I want it returned!"

"If May is speaking the truth—and I do not doubt for a moment she is—then I begin to see the point of her question," Drake said. "Kostya claims the phylactery was stolen three days ago. You are certain of that, brother?"

Kostya snapped a "yes" at Drake.

Aisling breathed a little "ahhh" of enlightenment. "So, if the phylactery was stolen when we were all in Greece, then someone else must have taken it."

"And if May didn't disengage the alarm and unlock the chest, and likewise Kostya didn't . . ." Cyrene said, frowning in puzzlement.

"Then who did?" I asked, looking around the room. "And is the person who burgled Kostya the night I paid his lair a visit the same one who took the phylactery? Was it Porter? If it was him, why did he blackmail me? How did the phylactery get back into an unlocked chest? Why was it returned? And most importantly, is the person who did all that also responsible for the disappearance of Gabriel's guards?"

"I don't believe these lies," Kostya said, shooting me an evil look. "She is the thief Mei Ling. She admits to taking my phylactery. She has concocted this smoke-screen to hide her actions."

"If May had given me the phylactery, do you think I'd be sitting here now tolerating your abuse of her?" Gabriel asked, his muscles tensing up again.

Kostya was about to answer, but stopped, clearly baffled.

"Despite my better judgment, I am willing to concede that I was wrong about Kostya," Gabriel continued. "At least so far as him having the phylactery was concerned, although I reserve judgment about Maata and Tipene. It would seem that there is another player to this drama, one who has not yet unveiled himself. Someone who first removed the phylactery from Kostya's lair, then returned it for some unknown reason. Someone who has employed the thief taker Porter, although whether he ordered Porter to retrieve the phylactery is not known. It could be Porter was acting on his own. Whoever is behind it, he had no difficulty in disabling either Kostya's alarms or the protections he bound into the chest containing the phylactery. In other words, someone who appears to be manipulating us all without our knowing it."

"Who?" Cyrene asked.

The dragons all exchanged glances.

"No," Drake said, shaking his head. "What you suggest is impossible."

"Who?" Aisling asked, pinching the back of Drake's hand. He covered her hand with his, still shaking his head at Gabriel.

"It is not impossible. You found signs in Fiat's house," Gabriel said.

"Signs of whom?" I asked Gabriel.

"He's dead," Drake said, still shaking his head. "We all know he's dead . . . Kostya most of all."

Kostya looked frozen, his face a mask. The two bodyguards had a similar frozen look. Who was it who could make two wyverns and a couple of dragons react in such a manner?

"Who?" Cyrene and I said at the same time.

The dragons were silent.

"I'll say it if no one else will," Jim announced, standing up and shaking itself. "The person in question is a wyvern, reportedly killed a couple hundred years ago by his right-hand man and heir to the wyvern throne, and is, in fact, the same wyvern who stole a silver dragon's mate and made her his own. He is also the one responsible for the deaths of thousands of dragons, and not incidentally the one who cursed the silver sept. Yes, it's the big kahuna, the whole enchilada, the dread wyvern himself—Baltic."

Chapter Nineteen

"Baltic is dead. Kostya cleaved him in two long ago." Drake's voice, pleasant enough although not even close to being as delicious as Gabriel's, seemed to hang in the thick silence that followed Jim's statement.

"That would seem to me to be pretty final," I agreed. "I haven't known anyone who could survive it."

"That doesn't explain the fact that someone is manipulating events to his wishes," Gabriel said.

"I don't claim it does, but it doesn't necessarily imply that the person behind the recent movements of the phylactery is Baltic," Drake answered.

"There is someone out there leading a group of dragons with no known sept or affiliation. You know that yourself, since you and Kostya were held prisoner by them," Gabriel said.

I looked with wonder at Drake and Kostya. "Someone held you both prisoner?"

Drake made an impatient gesture. "That was an isolated incident."

"They were up a mountain without a paddle," Jim said with blithe disregard. "Aisling had to save their butts."

"It's my job," Aisling said with a humble smile. "I'm a professional."

"You do it well," Cyrene said. "I wonder if I could have your autograph later?"

Aisling looked pleased.

"So who are these dragons, then?" I asked the room at large.

Silence weighed heavy before Gabriel spoke. "No one knows. I thought they were ouroboros—outcasts, septless dragons who banded together for strength—but now I am not so sure. The way they took over Kostya's aerie, the manner in which they dealt with Drake, and now this matter of the phylactery . . . it would take more than a small group of lawless dragons to coordinate those activities. There must be someone guiding the group, Drake, someone with a wyvern's experience at leadership. It has to be Baltic—it can be no one else."

"That does seem to make sense, sweetie," Aisling said, leaning into Drake.

He shook his head a third time. "Baltic is dead. Kostya killed him."

I looked at Kostya with no little amount of speculation. "You've been awfully quiet the last few minutes, which I have to say is wholly unlike the ranting and raving manner you normally seem to adopt."

"I have not said anything because there is nothing to say that Drake has not already mentioned," Kostya said dismissively.

"So . . . you don't have anything to say about killing Baltic?"

"Such as?" Kostya's face continued to remain an expressionless mask.

"Such as did you really kill him? Or are you just saying you did?" I thought for a moment. "It strikes me that perhaps there's another explanation for this. What if Kostya didn't actually kill his wyvern? What if he made it seem like he did in order to put some grand plan into effect?"

"A grand plan whereby I am first exiled, then imprisoned for a few hundred years, abused, tortured, and starved for my own amusement?" he snapped back.

"Perhaps," I said slowly, considering the matter. "If it cemented the idea that you had killed off your wyvern, it's within the realm of possibility that you would allow yourself to suffer, knowing that an end to all that would come soon enough. Fanatics have suffered much worse for their beliefs."

Kostya snorted and turned his back on me, but I noticed he didn't dispute my comment.

I turned to Gabriel, who was watching Kostya with an equally speculative look in his eyes. "I don't believe I've ever heard the story of what happened between you and Baltic firsthand," he said evenly. "Why don't you tell us about it now."

Kostya whipped around and leveled a glare at him. "I do not recognize your right to question me, Tauhou."

"Perhaps not," Aisling said with a misleading sweetness. "But I'm interested in hearing about this as well. So if you don't want to end up with several different extremely nasty wards slapped on you, you'll dish with the details."

"Mate," Drake said with a frown, pulling Aisling back as she struggled to get out of the couch. "I have told you that Baltic is dead. Threatening Kostya will do no good."

"I want to hear about it nonetheless. And what's that business Jim said about a black dragon stealing a silver's mate? No one has ever mentioned *that* before."

"It is old history and not important at this time," he said stubbornly.

"I'd like to hear it. I find all this dragon history fascinating," Cyrene chirped. "It's kind of romantic."

Aisling directed an inelegant snort to her husband. "Cyrene is right, not to mention the fact that dragons stealing each other's mates is *always* an important topic. And don't give me that 'not pertinent' crap. You said you were there when all of this was going down . . . Did you see Baltic's body?"

Drake was silent.

"I thought so." Aisling turned back to Kostya. "You know you're going to have to go over it—we outnumber you. So why don't you just tell us and save me the trouble of prying it out of you."

Kostya didn't explode as I thought he would. He looked for a moment like he wanted to, but a glance at his brother had him marching back to the window, his hands clasped behind him as he glared out at the world at large. "I will tell you not because you threaten me with your pathetic Guardian powers—"

Jim started toward the dragon until Aisling ordered it back.

"I will tell you so that you know, once and for all, the truth of the matter. You must understand that I have always upheld what Baltic stood for—" His head turned enough so that his eyes flashed ebony at Gabriel. "He wanted the sept whole, complete again."

Beside me, Gabriel tensed, although his voice was mild in the extreme. "That will never happen, Kostya. My sept is content as it is."

The muscles in Kostya's jaw worked a couple of times before he continued. "Although Baltic's motives in fighting to regain what was once ours were correct, I began to doubt his method of ensuring success.

When it became apparent that his goals had shifted to include domination over *all* the septs, I realized he was inflamed by the idea of power into conducting acts of war that were decimating the black dragon population. By the start of the eighteenth century, I knew Baltic must change his tactics or risk the total annihilation of the black dragons."

Bitterness filled his voice. I leaned against Gabriel, taking comfort from his warmth and strength.

"I gathered my guard together, and called up aid from allies. Drake came, along with a small group of green dragons who disobeyed an order from their wyvern. The blue dragons also sent members, although they were fewer. We met to reason with Baltic, but he . . ." Kostya paused, his voice suddenly hoarse. "He was mad. It was evident to all there that he would rather destroy the sept than give up his grandiose plan of domination of the weyr. I had no choice but to kill him. But it was too late—the silver dragons had chosen that same moment to strike, slaughtering all but a handful of black dragons."

"We did not attack unprovoked," Gabriel said through gritted teeth.

I put a hand on his arm, giving it a squeeze to remind him now was not the time to start another argument.

A look of sadness tinged Kostya's dark eyes for a moment before dissipating into his normally hostile, arrogant expression. "For my attempt to save my own sept, I was almost destroyed by the man for whom I was named, a traitor who set himself above the rule of the wyvern."

"Constantine Norka was a savior, not a traitor," Gabriel yelled, leaping to his feet. I leaped with him, pushing myself between him and Kostya. "He begged

Baltic to end the foolish plan of dominating the weyr, but for his trouble Baltic named him ouroboros and cast him from the sept, claiming Ysolde as his."

"Ysolde?" Aisling asked Drake in a low voice.

"Constantine Norka's mate."

I looked up at Gabriel's face, touching his cheek. His eyes, burning with fury, bore into my own. "You can *steal* another dragon's mate?" I asked.

"It's possible, although not done frequently." His gaze shifted to Aisling for a moment. "It never used to be, that is."

"Ysolde was intended to be Baltic's mate. He had chosen her and she indicated she would accept him. But before she could, Norka stole her and made her his own mate, an underhanded trick I am not surprised you wish to keep from Mei Ling," Kostya answered with a sneer as he turned away.

"Baltic abused Ysolde!" Gabriel shouted. "She hated her life with him, and begged Constantine to take her away—"

"So you say. But we all know how much truth can be found in the words of a traitor," Kostya answered, a distinct baiting note in his voice.

"Before you boys get into another fight, why doesn't everyone sit down?" Aisling suggested.

"Sound advice," I said, nudging Gabriel back toward our couch. He gave way reluctantly. I was about to retake the seat beside him but thought better of it, plopping myself down on his lap instead. "To keep you from doing anything imprudent," I said with a kiss to his chin.

"Sweetie, I'm a little confused. Did you see the whole thing with Kostya and Baltic yourself, or just hear about it?" Aisling asked Drake.

Drake shot a look toward his brother. "I didn't actually *see* Kostya kill him, no."

"But the body—there must have been a body?"

Kostya turned his back on everyone and resumed his post at the window, as if dismissing us from his thoughts.

"When Baltic realized Kostya's intent, he used the castle bolt-hole to try to escape. The silver dragons had sieged Baltic's stronghold and were about to break down the last of the keep's defenses. Kostya caught Baltic in the caverns below and slew him. But in the turmoil of the onslaught from the silver dragons, his body was not recovered immediately thereafter. Rather than risk Baltic's body and stronghold becoming a martyr's shrine, Constantine Norka had it destroyed altogether," Drake said.

"So no one but Kostya saw what happened in those final moments," I said, thoughtful as I watched Kostya.

"I returned with his sword," Kostya said roughly, his shoulders twitching with irritation. "I cleaved him in two with it. He did not survive."

I put my hand on Gabriel's chest, where his heart was. "Did you help sack Baltic's castle?"

"Me?" Gabriel looked surprised for a moment before his dimples made a brief showing. "How old do you think I am?"

"Well . . . I don't know. Five hundred years?"

His dimples deepened.

"Six?"

"I was born in 1702," he answered. "My father was with Constantine when he made the final blow against Baltic, though. It was a victory, but one which was met with saddened and grieving hearts. The dragons who died were our family once."

"Which brings us back to the point of who it is who's doing all this," Aisling said quickly, interrupting Kostya's obvious rebuttal. "If it's not Baltic, then who is it?"

"I don't see why it matters who's doing it so long as the phylactery has been returned," Cyrene interjected. We all looked at her.

"Well, honestly, does it matter if it was this Baltic person, or another dragon, or a benevolent fairy who's pulling the strings? All that matters is getting back Gabriel's guards, not who took them."

"The question of Baltic's possible survival is of the greatest importance to the silver dragons, I assure you," Gabriel told her.

"Why?" she asked, her nose scrunched in confusion.

"Why?" Gabriel asked, aghast.

"I think I know what she means," I said. "Assuming Baltic is alive, he is no longer the wyvern of the black dragons. You said the sept was destroyed, yes?" I asked Drake.

He nodded, his gaze flickering to his brother. "It was, although Kostya intends to gather what members remain and apply for recognition of the weyr."

"Even if he did get that, though, it wouldn't mean Baltic would immediately step into wyvernhood, would it?"

"Baltic will never again lead the black dragons," Kostya said, his voice pitched low with warning. "The sept will be reborn, but I will lead it."

I bit back a retort about the wisdom of that little plan. "I begin to see Cyrene's point. Assuming Baltic is alive, he's been neutered by the loss of his sept, so why does it matter if he was the one who returned the phylactery?"

"It matters because of what Baltic is," Gabriel answered.

"A lunatic, you mean?" I asked.

Kostya shot me a nasty look and would have said something, but Aisling cleared her throat in a meaningful way.

"Not just that—Baltic wielded great power," Gabriel said with hesitation. "More power than was natural even for a wyvern. It was said he had learned the arcane arts."

"Arcane? He was a mage?" Cyrene asked.

Kostya said nothing, which pretty much confirmed that guess.

"I didn't think dragons could be mages," I said.

Gabriel and Drake exchanged glances. "None have ever been able to master the arcane skills a mage must control."

"Except Baltic?" I asked.

"That is what we believe."

"Which means if he really is alive, he's going to be one badass dragon," Jim said.

"All of this is moot. I killed Baltic three hundred years ago. What matters is the phylactery—and I want it returned immediately," Kostya said.

"How do you explain the theft of the phylactery in the first place if Baltic really was dead?" I asked.

He glowered. "You stole it from me."

"How do you explain it assuming I didn't steal it?"

"I would make no such assumption. You admitted you took it the night I caught you in my lair."

"Oh, this is useless," I said, getting off of Gabriel's lap. "We're just going round and round. Whether or not Baltic is alive, the important thing is to retrieve the phylactery, and find Maata and Tipene."

"I thought you said you had the phylactery," Aisling said.

"I did have it—and then I was arrested, and my possessions taken from me, the phylactery included. So far as I know, it's with my other things in the L'audelà vault in Paris."

I was moving toward the door when Kostya shouldered me aside.

"Where are you going, brother?" Drake asked him.

"To reclaim what is mine," he said with a dark look at Gabriel.

"Like hell you are," I said, dashing after him. "That phylactery belongs to Gabriel!"

The room emptied out after us. For a moment, everyone stood looking at one another in the large entryway, then Kostya muttered something that had Gabriel lunging at him, Drake's two men grabbed Gabriel, and Aisling started ordering her demon to stop her brother-in-law. But Kostya was gone before Jim could whip into action.

"Agathos daimon," I swore under my breath.

"Should I follow him?" Pál asked Drake.

The latter hesitated for a moment before shaking his head. "No. He would just shake you."

"May can follow him," Cyrene said. "She's very good at following people. I had a boyfriend once who I thought was two-timing me—he had the tiniest eyes, which I've always felt was a sign of a shifty nature— and May followed him around for a week without him ever knowing she was there."

"Mayling will stay with me," Gabriel said, grabbing my wrist and hauling me up the stairs after him.

"Well . . . I suppose I could do it," Cyrene said with a slight frown. "It can't be that hard to follow someone. And I've been watching May do it for years."

"Don't even think about it," I called from the top of the stairs. "He's much too dangerous, Cy. We'll keep an eye out for him, never fear."

The last I saw before Gabriel pulled me to our bedroom, Cyrene was still standing in the entryway, her lips pursed as Aisling smiled at her dragon.

"To Paris?" Aisling asked.

"To Paris," Drake replied in a grim voice.

"This is just like that wacky movie with the Black-adder guy, where they were all racing to find a treasure," Jim said, its voice following us as we hurried down the hall. "Only with dragons, an ex-virgin doppelganger, and a really attractive Newfie. Bet people would pay big bucks to see this!"

Chapter Twenty

"I'm going to talk to Aisling for a few minutes," I told Gabriel as we headed to our room to pack our things for the trip to Paris. "It's just girl talk, nothing important."

He frowned as I went straight for the bag István had so recently brought me. I had taken only one or two things out of it, so it was easily repacked. "Girl talk? Are you injured in some intimate manner?" He put his hand on my belly as if to feel some sort of internal problem. "Has our mating been too rough?"

"No, it's nothing at all like that."

"May, I am a healer in addition to being your wyvern," he said with a serious expression. "You must tell me if you are having any sort of physical problem, no matter how embarrassing you find it."

"Honestly, it's nothing—"

"Take off your clothes," he said, nodding toward the bed. "I will examine you to make sure all is well."

"*Agathos daimon!* I just want to have a little girl talk with Aisling, Gabriel! I don't need a gynecological exam! Besides, if I take off my clothes and get on that bed, you'll end up with yours off, too, and we'll never get to Paris."

"When's the last time you had your period?" he

asked, a frown furrowing his brow as he ignored the playful little nibble I gave the tip of his nose.

I went to the door and cast him a look fraught with dignity. "We are not having this conversation. And if you even *think* of following me, I will . . . I will . . . well, I'm not quite sure what I will do, but you can rest assured that it will not be pleasant. My bag is packed, by the way."

He didn't say anything to that, but I felt his gaze on me as I headed down the hallway to knock on Aisling's door.

I paused for a moment before Cyrene's door, giving a quick tap before opening it. The room was empty. "Have you seen Cyrene?" I asked Pál as he hurried past me bearing two large suitcases.

"A few minutes ago, yes. She said she had something to do, and left."

"She left? What on earth . . . ?" I pulled out my cell phone and punched in her number.

Drake left his room bearing another suitcase. Through the open door I could see Aisling gathering up a few books to tuck into a book bag.

Jim wandered out. "Funny time to call someone."

"I'm trying to get hold of Cy." I waited a few seconds before hanging up, a cold, clammy hand gripping my stomach. "Voice mail. She's not answering. I have a horrible feeling I know where she is."

"Where who is?" Aisling asked as she emerged from the room.

"Cyrene. I think she went to tail Kostya. Silly, stupid . . . He won't hurt her if he sees her, will he?" I asked Drake as he came upstairs again.

He paused to consider the question. "He has no cause to. The only reason he held a knife to her before was because he thought she was you, and he will not make that mistake again."

I relaxed slightly. "I don't know why I'm worrying—she's never followed anyone before. I'm sure Kostya will realize immediately that she's shadowing him, and won't waste any time shaking her. I just hope she has enough sense to go home rather than to try to follow us to Paris."

"I have a friend in town who I'll call to check on her if it'll ease your mind," Aisling said, turning back to her room. "Thanks, sweetie, that's everything, I think. I'll be down in just a minute."

Drake nodded and went downstairs. I followed Aisling into her bedroom, standing uneasily as she called a number and left a message.

"Nora's out right now, but I'll try her again in a bit, all right?"

"Thank you. It'll make me feel better knowing someone is keeping an eye out for Cy. Er . . ." I bit my lower lip. "Do you have a minute? I wanted to talk to you really quickly, without being overheard."

She looked mildly surprised but sat down on the end of the bed and nodded toward a chair. "Of course."

Jim ambled over, plopping itself down at her feet.

I glanced at the demon. "Er . . ."

"Jim, shoo," Aisling said, correctly reading my thoughts.

"What? I'm not doing anything!"

"You're making May uncomfortable. Go see what the boys are doing."

"Whatever it is, it won't be nearly as interesting as this," it answered.

"Oh, it doesn't matter, I guess," I said with a tight smile. "Jim might have some helpful insights as well."

"I'm all over helpful insights, sister," it told me with an oddly endearing grin. "What's the problem? You can tell Dr. Jim. Is it something in the romance department? Need some advice on how to handle Gabriel?"

"No, thank you—"

"Ah. Then it's the sex, right? Fiery, animalistic, dragon sex too much for you?"

It was difficult to keep from rolling my eyes. "Thank you, my sex life is not open to—"

"What's the silver dragon element? Earth?" Jim's face screwed up as it thought. "Oh, man, that means he's gonna want to do it outdoors all the time. Buck naked in the wilderness. My advice is to take sunscreen and bug spray. And maybe a spatula or something to dig the sand out of your butt crack, in case he takes you to a beach."

"Jim!" Aisling said, wrapping her hands around the demon's muzzle. She shot me an apologetic look. "I'm so sorry. It knows better than to offer unwanted sexual advice."

"Just trying to be helpful," it said in a muffled voice.

"Well, you're not. And you can just be quiet unless you have something of importance to offer to the conversation," Aisling told it as she released its muzzle. "Go on, May. Tell me what it is you want."

"It's about demon lords," I said softly, glancing toward the open door. No one was visible, but I wanted to avoid Gabriel overhearing us.

"Oh, that's right—your twin said you were bound to one," Aisling said, nodding. "Are you having a problem with . . . er . . . which one is it?"

"Magoth."

She thought for a moment, and then shook her head. "I don't believe I've met him."

"You'd remember if you did," I said with a little laugh. "He's very attractive."

"If you like the smoldering, sensual, silent-movie-actor type," Jim said with a sniff as it licked down the fur on one paw.

"He looks like a smoldering, sensual actor?" Aisling looked somewhat startled.

"He *was* a silent movie actor, but that was only a phase he was going through."

Aisling mentioned the name of a famous actor of the 1920s.

"That was him. He was always a ham. But that's not the issue. My problem is . . ." I checked the hallway quickly. It was empty. "Is there any way for someone to disobey a direct order you give? A demon, that is."

Aisling blinked a couple of times.

Jim's mouth formed an O. "You're gonna defy an order? You're going to go dybbuk?"

"What's dybbuk?" Aisling asked.

"In terms of folklore, it's a wandering soul that enters a living body," I said slowly.

"In Abaddon terms, it means a demon who's gone rogue." Jim's eyes were grave. "Dybbuks are usually destroyed by their masters for insubordination, although I have heard of one or two who survived in order to be perpetually tormented. Fires of Abaddon, May—lots of demons talk about it, but I never heard of one who was actually thinking about *doing* it."

"I'm not a demon," I pointed out, biting my lower lip nonetheless.

"No, you're not," Aisling said in an abstracted voice. "Defying an order . . . hmm. That's tricky. Maybe it would help if you gave me the specific circumstances."

I hesitated for a moment or two, unsure whether I wanted to entrust something so potentially dangerous to her. In the end, I decided that I had little recourse, and she was my best resource of information about demon lords. "Magoth ordered me to retrieve the dragons' phylactery for himself. He plans on using it to bring the dragons to rein."

Aisling's eyes opened wide. Jim gave a low, long whistle.

"A direct order?" she asked.

I nodded, misery making my gut grumble. "I can't do it. I just can't do it. Even if I wasn't mated to Gabriel, even if I didn't give a damn about the dragons, I still wouldn't do it. It has the potential for just too much power."

"But . . . he must have had you steal powerful items before," she said. "How did you get around those? Or did you?"

I shook my head. "He's never asked me to steal anything quite so important before. Magoth is . . ." I made a vague gesture. "He's a bit of a flibbertigibbet, if you want to know the truth. He always has a hundred different projects going, and flits from one to another without following one through to the end, which, I have to say, I encourage."

"It keeps him from becoming dangerous to the mortal world?" she asked.

"Yes. All the other things that Magoth has made me steal for him over the past eighty years weren't nearly as important as this phylactery. Although I don't like being forced into the role of thief, it eased my worry somewhat to know that the things I was taking weren't really going to matter, if you know what I mean. He was just too unfocused, too easily distracted."

"Not the brightest bean in the Crock-Pot," Jim said, nodding in agreement.

"Exactly. To be honest, I think he has a form of demonic attention deficit disorder. But this . . . this is

different. He seems much more focused on the phylactery, and that worries me greatly. I can't let him have
it. But I can't see a way out of obeying a direct order."

"Sometimes when Ash gives me an order, there's
wiggle room," Jim said. "What did Magoth say exactly?"

"He told me to bring him the phylactery. There's
no wiggle room there that I can see."

Aisling looked thoughtful for a moment. "What that
means is that if you physically have the phylactery in
your possession, you must give it to him."

"Ye-es," I said slowly, not seeing where she was
going.

"So that means we simply don't let you touch it. If
you don't have it in your possession, you can't turn it
over to him, right? Easy as pie—you may be a re-
nowned thief, but the green dragons are no slouches
when it comes to stealing things. And Drake is *especially* good at it."

"I thought of that," I said, despair digging into me
with sharp little jabs. "The L'au-delà vault is sure to
be heavily protected. It will surely be beyond the
means of even the craftiest of dragons to enter it . . .
but I can get in places where no one else can. It will
be up to me to locate the phylactery. And if I'm that
close to it without anyone else around who might con-
ceivably oppose me, it would constitute a dybbuk if I
did not take it into my possession. I just don't see a
way around it—that's why I thought you might have
an idea about defying an order."

"I'm afraid I am just as helpless," she said with
genuine regret. "Jim?"

The demon shook its shaggy head. "Nada. Dybbuk
is the only thing I can think of, and I wouldn't advise
it. Magoth may be a few dinner rolls short of a smor-

gasbord, but he's no idiot. He'll be bound to make an example out of you for the rest of his minions."

I swallowed back the hard lump of fear and guilt that made my throat ache.

"I take it you haven't mentioned this to Gabriel?" Aisling asked, casting a quick glance toward the door.

"No. It's hard enough to keep him from going after Magoth directly—I really don't want to inflame his desire to free me of my bondage."

"I'll talk to Nora about that, too," she said, looking determined. "She's my mentor, and she knows all sorts of things about what Guardians can do. I know it's difficult, but stop worrying, May. Between us all, we may be able to find a way for you to end your bond to Magoth."

"Trust Ash on this—she knows Abaddon. She managed to get herself kicked out, after all," Jim said.

Aisling tried to look humble. "It's my job—"

"—she's a professional," the demon finished.

"Sorry!" I said less than an hour later, breathing hard as I raced up the narrow stairs of a small jet. "I assumed we'd be taking a portal rather than a plane."

"Drake won't let me," Aisling said with a smile at the dragon in question as she adjusted her seat belt over her expansive stomach. "He says they aren't safe for pregnant women. Of course, he says the same thing about airplanes, but I really feel there have to be some perks that go along with being immortal, and one of those is being able to fly while preggers."

"Ah. Well, I do apologize for us holding everyone up. It's my fault, not Gabriel's—I wanted to call a doppelganger who lives in Paris to see if she could help us with the L'au-delà vault, since it's bound to be extremely well protected. It took me forever to track down her number, but she doesn't seem to be at home."

"Ophelia?" Aisling asked, causing me to gawk slightly.

"Yes, that's her name. Do you know her?"

A little smile graced her lips. "Yes. Amelie, a friend of mine in Paris, said she's left the country. Her . . . er . . . twin was banished to the Akasha, you know. Ophelia suffered from depression after that, but last I heard, she was in Africa devoting herself to charitable works."

The pilot flashed on the seat-belt warning while Aisling was talking. I dug around in the comfortable leather chair for the seat belts, wondering what the doppelganger's twin had done to leave her banished to the Akasha.

My phone rang before I could ponder much. "Oh, sorry," I said as the pilot, a dragon who had been in conversation with Drake, frowned over at me. "I'll turn it off. I just . . . Oh, thank the gods." I was about to turn off my phone, but the caller ID number blinking at me was a familiar one. "Cy? Where are you?"

"Oh, Mayling, good, you haven't left yet . . ." A loud roar from what sounded like a truck drowned out the rest of her sentence. ". . . kidnapped me, which was just about the most . . . me of all people!"

"What? Cy, I can't hear you. Where are you? And what's that about a kidnapping?"

I held the phone a few inches away from my head as a loud truck horn threatened to deafen me. The pilot and Drake both glared at me.

"I'm sorry, May, but you will have to turn off your mobile phone," the latter said.

"What's wrong?" Gabriel asked at the same time, cleverly picking up on the fact that all was not well.

"I don't quite know. It's Cy, and she's evidently standing in the middle of some horrible traffic trying to tell me something . . . What's that?"

". . . the blackmailer! Can you hear me now? He's . . ." More sounds of engines cut off what she was saying. ". . . horrible man! I tried to fight him off, but . . . please, I'm begging you . . ."

"Where are you?" I yelled into the phone, hoping she could hear me.

"Is it Kostya? Has he attacked her again?" Gabriel asked, half rising out of his seat.

My hope was in vain. I could hear Cy attempting to speak over the noise, but couldn't make out the words. Suddenly, the connection went dead and all was silence.

Everyone in the plane was looking at me. I ignored them to turn to the one person to whom I knew I wouldn't have to explain. "No, it's not Kostya. Cyrene needs my help with something else, a personal matter."

His silver eyes searched mine. I was torn between the need to help Cy and the urgency presented by the situation with the phylactery, but with Cyrene's plea for help still echoing in my head, there was only one thing I could do.

"I'm very sorry, Gabriel, but I can't go to Paris." I grabbed the small backpack I used as a purse and rose.

Gabriel's face was a study in emotion as frustration, anger, and irritation all took a turn, but as he nodded and stood, concern was all that was left. "I understand. Your twin must come first."

"You go to Paris. I'll use a portaling company to get there as soon as I find Cyrene."

Regret filled his lovely eyes for a moment before it was blinked away. He turned to Drake. "We will join you as soon as possible. I assume you will do everything in your power to keep the phylactery from falling into Kostya's possession again."

Drake's lips quirked. "You would trust me with it?" he asked.

Gabriel was silent for a moment before giving him a sharp nod. The pilot had opened the door and lowered the stairs; Gabriel and I hurried down them, heading toward the nearest hangar.

"You don't have to come with me," I told him as the plane taxied off.

He said nothing until we were in the back of a cab.

"Where is she?" he asked as we got in.

"We should go to Drake's house. That's where she was last."

He gave the instructions to the driver before sitting next to me.

"Gabriel . . . you don't have to do this."

"Your twin is in danger. That must take precedence over the phylactery," he interrupted.

I looked at the strong planes of his face, the high cheekbones sculpting lines that made my stomach tighten with happiness. The brown, elegant slashes of eyebrow set off his eyes so that they just about glowed with emotion. The phylactery was everything to Gabriel— if Kostya regained it, I knew without the slightest doubt that he would use it against the silver dragons. It was of tantamount importance that we get to it before he did . . . and yet Gabriel was willing to set aside his need to protect his people in order to help me with Cyrene.

My heart heaved a little sigh of resignation and allowed itself to do what it had wanted to do from the very beginning—I fell in love with Gabriel.

"I think that is the nicest thing anyone has ever done for me," I said once I could manage to speak around the lump in my throat.

He gave another short nod, acknowledging the fact that I recognized his sacrifice.

"Would it upset all sorts of dragon etiquette if I was to kiss you silly in a taxicab?" I asked him.

One dimple started to show despite his serious expression. "Not in the least."

"Good. Because I don't think I'm going to be able to stop myself," I said, smiling into his mouth. The second my lips touched his, fire swept through me. Mindful of the surroundings—and not wanting to have to explain to a startled cab driver why the backseat of his vehicle was engulfed in flames—I controlled the dragon fire, allowing it to pass back into Gabriel.

"You taste so good," he murmured, his hands hard on my hips as he tried to pull me over his lap. "You taste of the cool water that hides deep in a stream. You taste of the night air, soft and scented and mysterious. The taste of you drives me wild. I want to be with you, be inside you, shout to the world that you are mine at the same time I want to keep you hidden where you will exist only for me. You make me feel invincible, little bird."

"You are invincible," I whispered, nibbling his delicious lower lip. "You are my dragon in shining armor who will slay that pesky Saint George for me."

His dimples deepened even though he sighed with frustration as, aware the cabby was watching us in his rearview mirror, I settled back down on the seat next to Gabriel.

"Saint George?" he asked.

"Well, his name is Porter, and he's not a saint, but I can tell you that he has stepped over the line and done something very foolish."

"You think the blackmailer kidnapped your twin?"

"Can you think of anyone else who would do something so crazy?"

Gabriel shook his head. "No. It does seem to be an attempt to manipulate you by holding Cyrene hostage."

"Exactly. I guess he figured I needed a little push into stealing the phylactery back for him."

"You should have told me about this from the first. I would have taken care of him for you," Gabriel said with smug self-assurance that grated.

The look I gave him should have, by rights, left him babbling in apology. "Certainly not! I'm insulted you think I'm so feeble I can't deal with one little blackmailer on my own. I didn't mean you should actually slay him for me, you know. I can take care of that all right."

Gabriel grinned at the annoyed expression on my face. "Such a fierce little bird."

"I may be little, but I pack a hell of a punch," I said, nodding toward my ankle where the dagger was strapped.

"I have no doubt of that, just as I have no doubt that so long as I am around, you will never have need to prove that. What do you plan to do about the thief taker Porter?"

"I hadn't thought beyond making sure Cyrene is safe. I guess we'll have to deal with him now."

"I will take care of him for you," Gabriel said calmly. "We will rescue your twin, and then see to it this thief taker does not bother you again. After that, we will be free to move on to more important matters."

"About that . . ." I took his hand in mine. "I can't begin to tell you how much it means to me that you'd be willing to forgo the phylactery in order to help my twin, but there's a little problem—"

He brushed his thumb across my lips. I bit it.

"There is no problem. I am not giving up the phylactery."

"You're letting Drake go off to Paris without you. He'll get to it first—hopefully—which means he'll probably keep it. I know he won't use it against you like his brother would, but I assumed it would rankle somewhat that Drake would get it rather than you."

"It is not yet noon," he answered with a smile.

"What does the time of day have to do with it?"

"The vault of the L'au-delà lies within Suffrage House, the same building in which you were imprisoned. It is closely guarded, as you might expect, but there is added protection during the day in the form of all the employees who conduct routine committee business."

"Ah. So you weren't going to try breaking in during the day?"

He shook his head. "It would be folly to even try. We will attempt it this evening—which means I have a few hours that can be spent taking care of the problem with Cyrene."

A smidgen of the guilt roiling around inside me eased, but what I had to say next canceled any feelings of relief. "I'm afraid that wasn't the only problem I had in mind. Gabriel, I'm—oh, here we are."

The taxi pulled up outside of Drake's house. I used the few seconds while we got out and Gabriel paid off the driver to work out what I was going to say.

"Gabriel, you know that I'm a doppelganger," I said once the taxi pulled off. He had tried to gently push me toward the front door, but I resisted.

"That point hadn't escaped me," he said with a flash of his dimples.

"I don't know how much you know about doppelgangers—not much, I suspect, since there are

only a handful of us around—but there's more to doppelgangers than shadow walking."

"Is there?"

"Yes. We can also enter the shadow world."

Gabriel's eyebrows arched. "Shadow world?"

"That's the doppelganger name for it. It's a sort of
separate plane that coexists with our reality, rather
like an overlay. It's hard to describe what it looks like,
but things in it are slightly . . . off."

"Ah, you're talking about the beyond." Gabriel
nodded. "I thought that was the realm of elves and
the fey."

"They make up the larger population of inhabitants.
As a doppelganger, I'm one of the others who can also
enter it, despite the fact that I'm bound to Magoth."

"I understand, but what does that have to do with
this situation?"

"I don't know where Cyrene is. I couldn't hear nine-
tenths of what she said, which means I'm going to
have to track her down."

Bright man that he is, Gabriel instantly guessed
where it was all going. "And you can only do so while
you are in the beyond?"

"Yes. And I can't take you with me."

His brows arched. "You just said others can enter
the beyond."

"Some people can, yes. Elves act as kind of a conduit—
they can bring people into it, but doppelgangers . . ." I
sighed. "We're just shadows ourselves, really, so we
can slip into and out of it easily, but we can't take
anyone with us. The best I can do is to track down
Cy and call you when I've found her. I don't mind
saying I'd like to have you with me to deal with the
blackmailer, but I'm afraid I don't know of any
other way."

"How will you trail her?" he asked.

"How? Oh . . . she's an elemental being. She leaves a faint trail wherevcr she goes. It's not visible in our world, but in the beyond, faint traces linger for a few hours. So I should be able to track her from here to wherever she is, so long as too much time hasn't passed."

"Interesting." He looked curious. "Do dragons leave signs, as well?"

I smiled. "Yes. Dragon scales glitter like . . . well, glitter in the beyond. And much as I hate to offend you . . ." I ran my hand down his bared neck, showing him my palm. The faintest iridescent sparkle showed on it. "You shed. Quite a lot, actually."

"I don't know whether to be offended or to make a suggestive comment about rubbing my scales all over your naked body," he said with a flash of his silver eyes. "Proceed, little bird."

I glanced around. No one was near us on the strect. "I'll call you as soon as I find her, I promise."

He said nothing, just watched as I slipped into the shadow world and set off down the road.

Chapter Twenty-one

The trail was there on the ground, faint but still visible slightly darkened footprints, as if Cyrene had been walking with wet feet across a dry floor. There were other elemental beings in the area leaving tracks as well—London was headquarters to several Otherworld groups, including a lot of elementalists—but it was easy enough to pick Cyrene's trail apart from the others.

It wasn't until I was three blocks away that an uncomfortable feeling started pricking between my shoulder blades. I spun around to see who was following me, and gawked openmouthed at the man standing immediately behind me. "How?" I asked, poking him in the chest to be sure he was real.

My hand went right through his chest as if nothing was there. "OK, change that *how* to *what?* What's going on, Gabriel? How is it you're in the beyond?"

"Beyond, shadow world, the Dreaming . . . all different names for the same thing," he answered, his dimples showing as I waved a hand through his chest. "I told you that my mother was a shaman."

"You said that's why you could occasionally read my mind. That doesn't explain why you're a . . . what, shade? Image? You're not really here, are you?"

"No. I'm in Drake's house. Or rather, my body is.

I can walk in the Dreaming, but I can't interact with anything. My mother said it was because I was part dragon." He shrugged. "I won't be able to touch things as you can, but I can accompany you."

"Do you see Cyrene's tracks?" I asked, pointing to the ground.

He squinted. "Faintly. You look different in here."

"Different? I do?" I was a bit taken aback. I knew most things looked different when viewed from the shadow world, but I was part of this world—I shouldn't look different. "How so?"

"There is a glow about you. A sort of silver glow." He smiled. "It is the sign you are part of my sept. It pleases me that you manifest that as an aura."

I looked down at my arms. "Good gods, you're right. I'm May the Amazing Glowing Woman. How very odd . . . but we don't have time to explore my glowiness, I'm afraid. Cy's trail is starting to fade."

He nodded and gestured for me to go on. I did, my heart lightened somewhat by his presence, even if it was an insubstantial presence. We couldn't take a taxi, since it would be impossible to follow Cyrene's trail, which meant we had to cover a lot of ground on foot. About an hour after we started, we finally ran the trail to earth at a grimy hotel hidden in a back street in King's Cross. We'd lost the trail a couple of times because Cyrene had evidently gotten into a car at some point, which made the little splotches of water that dropped off her scarce, but it helped having two of us to follow possible leads.

"Do not go in, little bird," Gabriel told me as I examined the outside of the hotel. It was more of a hostel than a hotel, obviously one used by people whose minds were more absorbed with where their next trick, fix, or bottle was coming from rather than where they laid their head at night. "It could be dangerous, and I cannot help you in this form. You wait outside until I can come to you in bodily form."

"One of the perks of being able to shadow walk is the ability to take a look around without anyone knowing," I told him as I finessed the lock on the door. It gave way with even less resistance than was normal, as if the lock itself had absorbed the miasma of hopelessness that hung so heavy in the air it left an oily taste upon the tongue.

Gabriel wasn't happy, but he said nothing as we slipped through the door and up a narrow flight of stairs. There was a small room off to one side that served as a lobby and reception, although the room was barren of life. The detritus of people who had lost all hope lay scattered on the floor and stairs— empty bottles, fast-food wrappers, crushed cigarette packets and butts, torn fragments of lurid magazines . . . we picked our way around all of it as we crept up the first flight of stairs. The air in the hotel was foul, stale with smoke and urine and rodent droppings, and other, less-palatable scents that I refused to identify or acknowledge. Cyrene's trail here was sporadic as well, as if she'd been dragged up the stairs. Two clear sets of her footprints stood outside one door on the second floor, however.

I glanced at Gabriel. "Can you go through walls?" I whispered.

He shook his head. "I can't interact with anything, nor can I travel through solid substances. Doors have to be open for me to go through them."

"Then I'll just have to open this one."

"May . . ." He frowned. "I do not like this. You should wait until I can come to help you. This black-mailer is clearly dangerous. You could be harmed."

His words washed over me with a warm, comforting sensation. No one had ever worried about me when I was out on a job—it never seemed to occur to Cyrene that I could be harmed, and Magoth . . . well, Magoth didn't particularly care what happened to me so long as I succeeded.

"If you were here, I'd spend all my time kissing you and we'd never get Cy rescued," I told him with a smile. "Don't worry, I'll shadow as soon as the lock is open. This hallway is dim enough to hide me if anyone is standing on the other side of the door."

He didn't react to my light flirtation, just stood watching me with worried eyes as I persuaded the lock to open.

"Well, I guess we were worried about nothing," I said a few moments later as Gabriel straightened up from where he had been kneeling next to the crumpled form on the floor. "Is he dead?"

"I believe so. I can detect no signs of life, although I would have to be able to touch him to know for certain if he could be resuscitated."

Unwilling to touch the body, I used my foot to nudge it over onto its back. "*Agathos daimon!* It's Porter."

"The thief taker?" Gabriel asked, frowning down at the twisted face of the dead man on the floor. The handle of a knife emerged from his chest.

I avoided looking at the grimacing face and examined the handle as best I could without touching it. It was silver, carved with runes I couldn't identify. Something about it tickled the back of my mind. "I think I've seen this before."

"Where?"

"I don't remember. It just looks . . . familiar." I steeled myself and laid two fingers across the man's neck. The body was cool to the touch. "No pulse."

"If he's dead, then where's your twin?" Gabriel asked.

I rose and looked around the room with him. One corner held a grimy bed, a chair, and a three-legged table. A filthy, rust-stained sink hung crookedly off the wall on the other side of the room, below a mirror that was missing most of its glass. "That is a very good question."

I had come out of the shadow world to examine the body of the thief taker but slipped into it again to look for signs of Cyrene.

"There," Gabriel said, pointing at the window.

"Why does no one ever use doors to exit rooms?" I grumbled, moving over to the window to examine it. It was pushed down, but not latched from the inside. Sure enough, there was a footprint on the windowsill. "Looks like we're going out onto the fire escape."

"I hate to contradict a lady, but alas, there are times when duty must take precedence over manners," a voice said from behind me.

I spun around to find Savian the thief taker in the doorway. His gaze swept around the room, pausing on the body of Porter for a moment before continuing its perusal. "I see you've had a bit of excitement, Mci Ling. Why don't you step out of the shadows so we can have a little chat about it."

I froze. Although it was daytime, the room was dark enough that unless I moved, Savian wouldn't see me.

Before I could think of how to respond, he leaped across the room, straight for the window . . . and me.

"What's this? Leaving? You wound me, Mei Ling, you truly do," he said, grabbing at me. This close, he could no doubt see a shadowy image of me. "I thought we had something special between us."

I deshadowed, snarling something rude under my breath as I jerked my arm away from him.

"Take your hands off my mate!" Gabriel bellowed.

He rushed at Savian, forgot he was insubstantial, and zipped right through the thief taker.

Savian looked momentarily disconcerted. "What was *that*?"

"I am not a what!" Gabriel snapped, stalking over to Savian to stand before him, glaring. "I am the silver wyvern, and you have just touched my mate."

I raised my eyebrows a smidgen at Gabriel's show of possession. For some reason, it amused rather than annoyed me. "I didn't know you were so volatile when it concerned me."

"Volatile?" Savian repeated the word, his brows scrunching up together. "Was that intended to be a compliment about my virility?"

My gaze shifted from Gabriel to his. "You can't hear him?"

"Hear who?" Savian asked.

I looked back to Gabriel. "How can I hear you if he can't?"

"You are my mate. He is not," he answered with a growl, his eyes burning as they fixed on Savian. "Who is this man?"

"Savian the thief taker, meet Gabriel Tauhou, wyvern of the silver dragon sept," I said, gesturing toward Gabriel. "Don't let the fact that you can't see or hear Gabriel confuse you—he's in the shadow world, but he's very much here. Er . . . sort of."

Savian's gaze rested on me with speculation. "A dragon in the beyond? Didn't know it could happen."

"This seems to be the day for impossible things," I said, crossing my arms tightly. "What is it you want? Other than to haul me back to the committee, that is?"

"Well . . ." He smiled. It was a particularly charming smile, one that held a good deal of humor in it, and I thought for a moment or two that if I'd never met Gabriel, I might have followed up on that smile to see what sort of a man was behind it. "There is the matter of that little offer you made me."

I froze again, this time horrified as the memory came back to me. "That has nothing to do with anything," I said, glancing at Gabriel.

"Oh, really?" His gaze flitted around the room, and I knew for certain what he was going to say before he said it. "You don't think propositioning me in order to get me to let you go has any pertinence to this situation?"

"You're a rat," I told him. "That was downright mean."

"I know," he said, his smile widening. "But you have to admit, as rats go, I'm fairly charming."

Gabriel's silver-eyed gaze shifted from Savian to me.

"I don't suppose you'd believe me if I said that I didn't actually proposition him in order to get him to let me go?" I asked him.

"I believe you," he said without hesitation. "You are my mate. You would not be so if you did not respect and honor me as I do you."

An odd sort of constriction gripped my heart. His words were so heartfelt, they touched deep, dark parts of my soul.

"I did proposition him," I said, needing to admit the truth to him. "And he took me up on it, but I couldn't go through with it."

Gabriel was silent for a moment, his eyes shadowed. Finally, he nodded. "I would expect you to try to use whatever method you had available to free yourself. That you did not betray me to do so does not, however, surprise me."

"It was a close thing," Savian said with a wicked grin.

"Oh, it was not! I never even unbuttoned so much as one button! I couldn't! Not when I thought of Gabriel."

"You're not going to start making declarations of eternal, undying love now, are you?" Savian asked, glancing at his watch. "I'm afraid I can only give you fifteen minutes, and then we'll need to be on our way to catch the plane to Paris."

"Do not leave this room," Gabriel ordered.

I turned to him, surprised.

"I will be with you in ten minutes," he said. "Do not leave the room unless the authorities come. And do not proposition that . . . that . . . *mortal* again!"

I couldn't help but smile at the indignant look on his face, which faded along with the rest of him.

"I take it that's a 'no' on the declarations of love?" Savian asked.

I took the sole chair in the room, unfolded a bit of discarded newspaper onto the stained seat, and gingerly sat down on it. "I think I'll pass, thank you."

"Ah? The dragon's gone?"

I nodded.

"Well, then." He moved across the room and closed the door, giving me a come-hither look that was almost as good as Magoth's. "Perhaps you'd like me to show you how I can make you forget your precious wyvern?"

"I'll pass on that, too. Why don't you spend the few minutes it'll take Gabriel to get here telling me how it is you were lurking around outside the room of a murdered colleague?"

He leaned against the wall next to the window. "Oddly enough, I was curious about how you ended up here as well. Shall we exchange stories? I can give you fourteen minutes."

"And I can give you . . ." I pursed my lips as I

thought. "I'd say you have about eight minutes before a very angry dragon is going to break down the door, so why don't you go first, just in case Gabriel gets here before you have a chance to talk."

I have to give Savian credit—he didn't appear to be too worried about having to face Gabriel, although a couple of faint lines appeared around his mouth.

"Although it isn't the gentlemanly thing to do, I will go first since you so obviously desire it. I am here because I was pursuing a line of investigation, and it led me to this room."

"A line of investigation concerning one of your colleagues?" I asked.

He shrugged. "Porter wasn't so much a colleague as a rival. Thief takers . . . well, we tend to be a solitary lot, minding our own business and not mingling with one another too much. And Porter was . . . different."

"I'll say he was. Do you know that he was blackmailing my twin?"

"No, but it wouldn't surprise me," Savian said. He rubbed his chin for a moment. "That might explain some things."

"What things? Were you investigating Porter himself?"

His smile was as cheeky as ever. "Let's just say that I was following up a sense of Porter being involved in something he shouldn't have been."

"Would you happen to know whom he was working for?"

"Alas, I hadn't uncovered that," he answered, his smile fading. "To be perfectly honest—something I normally try to avoid, but I'll make an exception since I like you—I hadn't found out much about what Porter was up to. He had something going on, and it was something big, but that's all I could tell. Perhaps you have more information?"

"Perhaps, but like you, I prefer to play things close to the vest."

"Now, now, I showed you my hand—the least you can do is show me yours," he said with a cock of his eyebrow.

"There's really not much to my hand—he blackmailed me into trying to get something for him, but he didn't tell me why he wanted it, or if it was for himself, or the dreadlord he said he worked for."

"Dreadlord, hmm?" Savian chewed that over for a few minutes. "Interesting. Could be a demon lord, could be someone else."

"Exactly. And now he's dead, which means there's someone else involved. But why kill him?"

Savian shrugged again. "It would be foolish to speculate until we had some answers to our questions. And now, if you would not mind, perhaps you'd care to clarify how it is I found you with the not-at-all-lamented Mr. Porter?"

"Porter kidnapped Cyrene in order to get me to do something."

"Ah." His glance slid down to the dead man.

"He was dead when we got here, and no, I don't think Cyrene killed him. She couldn't have."

"That's right, your twin is a naiad," he said, nodding. "Although it is within the realm of possibility, I agree that it would be unlikely an elemental being such as she would harm a mortal . . . even one as reprehensible as Porter. It certainly is a puzzle."

We stood in silence for a moment before I was driven to say, "Gabriel isn't going to let you take me into custody, you know."

"I'm aware of that, yes," he answered amiably.

"Then why are you just standing here chitchatting with me while he races to get here?" I asked. "Shouldn't you at least be making an attempt to try to capture me? Not that I want you to, but it's making me curious."

"Well, it's like this," he said, scratching the whiskery stubble on his chin. "When I first saw you here, I thought my luck had turned and I'd be able to bring you in myself. Although I will say I had a moment's qualm about how I was going to get you to go peacefully. You're not a pushover."

"Thank you," I said politely. "I'm also not the sort of woman who has to wait for a man to help her, although I'm not one to turn down the offer of help if it's made."

"I completely understand. Just as I understood that when you mentioned the wyvern was present in spirit form, my chances of convincing you to come along peaceably were pretty much nil. As were any ideas of forcing you."

"Smart man."

"I try," he said with a wry twist to his lips. "The answer to your question is simply that I am hoping your scaly boyfriend will make it worth my while to not make trouble."

"He's not scaly, and if I'd known you could have been bought with something other than my body," I said, musing on the sense of humor fate seemed to have when it concerned my life, "I would have bribed you in a more traditional manner."

"But your way promised so much more fun," he said with yet another of his wickedly sinful grins. "Are you sure—"

"Quite sure. Gabriel is . . ." I stopped for a moment, not sure how to put my tangled feelings into words.

"He's warm. And strong. And concerned about people. He's very grounded, if you know what I mean—very much of this earth. I'm not elemental like Cyrene, but I am created from her, and to me, Gabriel feels right. He's also very urbane and elegant, not in the least . . . oh, I don't know, primitive. There's a sort of raw, dangerous feeling about the other wyvern I've met, but Gabriel is much more sophisticated than that. I could see him on the cover of *GQ*, if they'd ever let a dragon on it."

Savian's smile got a bit broader.

"He's also arrogant about some things, is overly confident in his abilities to control the world, and has a single-mindedness that I suspect is going to cause a lot of friction between us," I added, sure that Gabriel had appeared in the doorway behind me.

"Only if you let it," the man himself answered, moving up to stand next to me. He was a little out of breath, as if he'd run the whole way. "You left out the part about my possessiveness," he added with a warning flash of his eyes at Savian.

"You're a dragon—that goes without saying," Savian said with a shrug and a quick glance at his watch. "Shall we proceed? Time is passing."

"How much?" Gabriel asked.

"Right to the point. I like that. You know what the standard payment is for a thief taker?"

We shook our heads.

He named a figure that would keep Cyrene in bath salts for an entire decade.

"I'll triple it," Gabriel said immediately, without so much as blinking an eye at the fact that he was talking about an amount in six figures.

"That's a lot of money," I said in a low voice. "More than is necessary, I think."

"On the contrary, that's exactly the sum it would take to get me to tear up the order for your arrest," Savian said.

"Done," Gabriel said, and shook the hand Savian offered. "Send your information to the Weyr Bank and I'll have the money transferred to you."

Savian inclined his head in acknowledgment. "I feel obliged to warn you that other thief takers won't be so accommodating."

"Other thief takers? There's more than just you and Porter after me?" I asked.

"Oh, yes," he said with some amusement. "You are the first person to escape Suffrage House in . . . come to think of it, I think you're the first person to escape, period. The committee is not pleased with that fact. When you add Dr. Kostich's benefaction in with the large sum of money the committee is offering for your recapture, you will no doubt understand why every thief taker available is even now descending on Europe in order to find you."

I groaned and plopped down on the edge of the windowsill. "Great. Just what I need—even more people after me."

Gabriel looked grave for a moment, but suddenly his dimples appeared. "It's somewhat ironic, then, that Mayling will be in the last place anyone expects to find her—Suffrage House itself."

"I have to get there first," I said darkly.

He paid no attention to my black mood. "Come, little bird. As the thief taker noted, time is passing, and we must find your twin soon."

"I seldom offer my help without recompense— busman's holiday and all that—but as I find myself at a bit of a short end with regards to my current case, and as I am the best tracker in all the L'au-delà, I might be willing to help you locate your twin."

Gabriel's eyes narrowed. "What would you want for helping us?"

"Oh . . ." Savian looked thoughtful for a moment before smiling at us both. "Let's just say that all I'll ask is a favor to be granted at a later time."

"What sort of favor?" I asked suspiciously.

"I have no idea until the time comes," he answered.

Gabriel and I exchanged glances. He made a little shrugging movement that I took to mean he wasn't overly concerned about the thought of owing a favor to Savian. I was less certain as to the wisdom of putting ourselves in his debt, but there didn't seem to be much I could do about the situation.

"Very well," I agreed. "We'd be happy for the help. Cy's trail is starting to get very faint."

Gabriel nodded toward the body. "I don't suppose you are responsible for that?" he asked Savian.

"No, although I would have liked to have been. He wasn't much of a credit to the watch."

"What are we going to do about him?" I asked, nodding toward Porter's body.

"He is of no matter to you now," Gabriel said, dismissing both the body and the issue it presented.

"Not directly so, but if he was asked to employ me, then we've still got to deal with whomever he was serving."

Gabriel made a face. "We will deal with that situation after we retrieve the phylactery."

"We can't just leave him here," I pointed out. "I may not have liked him, but that doesn't mean we can just stumble over his body and not say something to someone about it."

Savian sighed and pulled out a cell phone. "Can you still see your twin's trail?"

I slid into the beyond and moved over to the window. Outside it was a frail-looking fire escape. I came back to reality with a little nod. "Just barely."

"You and the wyvern start following it. I'll call the watch and let them know about Porter, and be with you as soon as I can."

"How will you know where to find us if the trail is gone by then?" I asked.

He grinned at me. "Her trail will be gone . . . but not yours. I haven't followed you around for nothing, Mei Ling."

Gabriel made a low growling noise that secretly delighted me. I didn't want him thinking I was a weakling who needed constant protection, however, so I ignored it and lifted the window sash, gingerly climbing out onto the rickety fire escape.

Gabriel was right behind me as I made my way down to the ground.

"I can't follow you now, Mayling," he said when I had tracked Cyrene's footsteps to the street and popped back into our reality to tell him what I found. "You must walk alone. But you will call me when you find her destination."

That was a command, not a question. I nodded, wanting badly to kiss the very breath out of him, but was cognizant of the fact that we were standing on the sidewalk of a busy, if rundown, street. "Do you know what I'm thinking right now?" I asked.

His silver gaze focused on me for a few seconds. "Yes. And the feeling is mutual, although I favor honey over whipped cream. It's stickier, and requires more licking to remove it."

"A dragon with a sweet tooth—I'll have to remember that," I said, glancing around before finding a suitably empty, darkened doorway in which I could slip into the shadow world.

"You are the sweetest morsel I have ever wanted," he murmured and, ignoring propriety, pulled me into a kiss, pushing me hard against the wooden door behind me, his body aggressive and unyielding. I got the feeling he was deliberately trying to overwhelm me with his presence . . . and he was doing a damned fine job of that.

"You think I am not dangerous and primitive?" he growled into my mouth, his hands sliding down my hips. I moaned into his mouth, rubbing myself against him, the want that never left me building to the point where all I could think of was joining myself with him.

He growled again, jerking me away from the door before he kicked it open. I had a glimpse of two startled faces of the employees of an adult video store before Gabriel shoved me through a side doorway, slamming the door behind us.

We were in a dark storeroom of some sort, nearly full of boxes and broken furniture, but that was all that registered in my consciousness before Gabriel had me pinned to the door, his fingers hard on my hips as he ground me against himself.

I didn't hesitate, didn't stop to point out that now was not the time and place. I did a little shimmy as I kicked off my jeans and underwear, lunging at him even as he grabbed me again, his body a burning brand against my front, the door a cold presence on my back.

"You underestimate the true nature of a dragon, little bird," Gabriel said, his lips burning a trail along my jaw. Sharp pinpricks touched my flesh as he grabbed my legs from behind, parting them wide around his hips. I moaned again, and hurriedly undid the buckle of his belt, desperate to get to his zipper. He was hot and hard and burned in my hands even as I knew he would burn within my body. "You think me so sophisticated that I am above base needs? I may look human, Mayling, but never forget I am a dragon first. And you, my delicious morsel, are my mate."

He slammed into me, making the door reverberate as I welcomed the intrusion. His mouth was everywhere, kissing, biting, and burning me. My heartbeat drowned out all but the sound of his rasping breath as his hips flexed again and again, his penis a molten brand that should have scorched parts too delicate to stand up to such abuse, but the contrary was true. I was already teetering on the brink of an orgasm, my body tightening around him as he pumped hard and fast and deep. This was a mating, pure and simple, an act of need so basic, our bodies moved in a violent rhythm that was as old as time. It was hard and fast and there was no softness, no tenderness . . . and yet it was a joining that was just as profound as any of the others. My spirit soared as Gabriel bit my shoulder, the skin of his neck as soft as silk. Gabriel roared his pleasure, his teeth as sharp on my shoulder as the burn of fire that seared my skin. That's all it took to push me over the edge as well, and as I gave in to the climax, I knew with a soul-shaking certainty that I would not be able to exist without him.

Pounding on the other side of the door slowly returned awareness to me. I pulled my face from the crook of Gabriel's neck, smugly pleased that he was breathing just as heavily as I was.

"That was . . ." Words failed me. He slowly slid me down his body until I was standing on my own again. "That was . . ."

"That was something to remember me by while you're shadow walking," he said, his eyes as molten as mercury as he bent to retrieve my clothes.

Chapter Twenty-two

By the time I finally stood in front of a small office tucked away in a dark street of used bookstores near the British Museum, two hours had passed, I'd been spotted by—and successfully escaped from—three thief takers, and nimbly avoided a demon that suddenly appeared out of nowhere and tried to grab me.

"The demon left after I slipped into the shadow world. Thank the gods demons can't go there. I'm hiding in the alley behind the portal shop right now. I think I've given everyone else the slip. How fast can you get here?" I asked Gabriel.

"With the afternoon traffic? Probably half an hour," he answered, the sourness in his voice evident even through the cell phone. "Stay in the Dreaming, Mayling. You are safest there."

"The thief takers can follow me if they know how," I reminded him.

A muted sound of conversation followed before Gabriel's voice spoke into my ear again. "Savian is with me. He does not know how to access it, so it is quite likely the others will not as well. It is an uncommon thing for a mortal to be able to enter the beyond."

"Uncommon, but not unknown. I'll go back there as soon as I hang up. What happened with Porter's body? Did Savian tell the watch about us being there?"

"Unfortunately, he had to, yes."

I made a face at the blank cement wall of the building against which I was crouched. "I suppose it couldn't be helped. Do you trust him, Gabriel? Savian, I mean?"

The silence that followed was hard to interpret. "As a matter of fact, I think I do."

"All right. We're counting a lot on him not setting us up for a big fall. I just wish I knew why Cyrene went to a portal shop. What if she wasn't taking a portal to Paris? What if someone else grabbed her and forced her to who knows where?"

"You have no reason to believe that anyone else is with her, although I agree with your assessment that she was not responsible for the death of the thief taker. Someone else must have done it, but it doesn't follow that he or she coerced your twin into leaving."

I glanced down at my hand. "Well . . . there's actually something I need to tell you about that. When I followed Cy's tracks to the portal place, I slipped inside to have a look around. Her tracks led right up to the portal room, so I know she took one. But there was something else there . . ."

Gabriel waited for me to continue.

"Her trail was dusted with dragon scales, Gabriel."

I heard a brief intake of his breath. "You are certain?"

"Yes. I thought dragons didn't like to use portals."

"We don't. We will if it is absolutely necessary, as it is now, but if at all possible, we prefer to use alternate means of travel. Go into the Dreaming, little bird. I will be there as soon as I can."

The portal shop Cyrene had visited was one of two located in England. Portals offered individuals with large amounts of money at hand the ability to travel across the fabric of reality in the blink of an eye. Portals were quirky things, however, and even the best of the portal masters had only a tenuous ability to predict exactly where the summoned portal would open.

I remained hidden in the shadow world until Gabriel arrived, Savian in tow. We wasted no time in querying the portalist, a weaver by the name of Jarilith, about Cyrene, but true to his kind, he refused to shed any light on where she'd gone.

"Can you at least tell us if she was being forced to go somewhere?" I asked Jarilith, exasperated with his refusal to answer our questions.

"It is illegal to portal anyone while they are under duress," he said with a pointed look. "I could lose my license if I were to do so."

"You're going to lose a lot more than that if you don't tell me where my twin went," I said in a low, mean voice.

"Mayling, please. I must insist that you allow me to be the bad cop," Gabriel said as I slid the dagger at my ankle out of its sheath.

"I have never subscribed to the sexist belief that women have to be good cop," I said, twirling the dagger around one finger.

Jarilith's eyes were riveted to it. He didn't look unduly worried about me being armed, but his condescending expression had slipped just a little.

"Nonetheless, you are far more suited to the good cop role," Gabriel insisted.

"I'm going to have to go against popular opinion and side with Mei Ling on this," Savian said, watching us with a delighted twinkle in his eye. "She looks like she knows how to use that blade. What is that, a stiletto?"

"Sicilian castrating knife," I said with a smile at the portal man.

"She wins," Savian told Gabriel.

"Er . . ." Jarilith said, his expression starting to slide into worry.

"I am a wyvern! I can do far more to this man than merely remove his genitalia," Gabriel answered in an outraged tone, a little tendril of smoke emerging from between his lips as he spoke.

"Eh . . ." Jarilith said, taking a step backward.

"Hmm. He's a weaver," Savian said thoughtfully as he examined the portalist. "Those are immortal, aren't they? So he could survive a castration, but the question is would a dragon barbeque be enough to finish him off?"

"Absolutely," Gabriel said. He smiled. It wasn't a nice smile.

"Threatening a weaver is strictly prohibited by law," Jarilith said indignantly, but the fight had gone out of him. His gaze was flickering back and forth from Gabriel to Savian to the dagger I held casually. "I could have the watch on you for what you're saying!"

"Oh, please," I said with a dramatic roll of my eyes. "Just about every thief taker in this hemisphere is after me. I've already been sentenced to banishment to the Akasha. You think one little murder is going to make that any worse? Not likely."

Jarilith's eyes widened.

"It's true," Savian said. "The price on her head has already gone over six figures."

The color washed out of the portalist's face. "Erm . . ."

"Mate," Gabriel said sternly. "I must insist that you refrain from slicing and dicing this man."

Jarilith nodded quickly. "Listen to the dragon."

"It is *my* place to destroy those who stand in your way," Gabriel continued, the pupils in his eyes narrowing as he turned to the now hastily backing away Jarilith.

"Let's not lose our heads, here," the latter said in a rush.

"I don't think it's your head the lady has in mind," Savian said as he looked pointedly at the portalist's crotch.

Jarilith's hands hovered protectively over his fly. "Such an atrocity would constitute torture. You wouldn't do that to an innocent man, would you?"

"What makes you think I'd stop at the castration?" I twirled the knife around my fingers again. "This little jobby fillets, as well."

"She went to Paris," Jarilith said quickly as he dashed for a door to a back room. "I don't see the harm in telling you that as you are related to the lady. Your portal is ready in room number three. Have a pleasant journey . . ."

His voice trailed off as he bolted.

I turned a frown on Gabriel. "You really wouldn't have let me be bad cop? I'm very good at it, as you can see."

"I'm sorry," he said, his dimples belying the grave look he was trying to maintain. He gave me a gentle push in the direction of the room containing our portal. "Wyverns have some standards to maintain with their mates, and one of them is always being the bad cop. Although I do admit that you have a particularly effective manner. Would you really have castrated him to get the information about your twin?"

"Would you really have burnt him to a crisp for not answering?" I countered.

Gabriel grinned. I smiled back at him.

"Such a bloodthirsty little bird," he said fondly, giving my butt a little pinch.

Savian stood still for a moment, giving us an odd, disbelieving look before shaking his head and following. "You two are the strangest couple I've ever met. And I have to tell you—I've met some real weirdos."

It was early evening by the time we made it to the house that Gabriel said was Drake's home away from home while in Paris. The portal we'd taken had ended up dumping us in a slaughterhouse, which I am horrified to admit caused me to behave in a manner that no doubt embarrassed Gabriel by the quality of dramatics I felt necessary.

"Ironic that you'd react so strongly to a little pig's blood given that you just threatened to cut off someone's balls," Savian's voice said over my head as I hunched over a railing and vomited up my last meal.

I heaved again, scrabbling at my ankle sheath, blindly waving my dagger in his direction.

"Shutting up now," he said. He laughed as he said it, though, the rat.

"There is a mortal saying about those who live by the sword," Gabriel started to say.

I wiped my mouth on a handful of tissue and straightened up enough to glare at him. "Not the time, dragon."

"So I see," he answered, his dimples trying hard to emerge.

"I wouldn't if I were you," I told them with a black look.

He laughed and rubbed the small of my back. "Are you better now?"

"Moderately." I looked down at myself. "Ugh. I'm covered in animal blood. I need a shower, a toothbrush, and a fresh change of clothes. I don't suppose you keep a house here, too?"

He shook his head as he escorted me away from

the railing, Savian trailing behind us. "No. Our clothing will be at Drake's house. We will go there and see
what he has found out."

Luckily, it didn't take long to get to Drake's house.
I eyed it as Gabriel paid off the cab that had dropped
us at its door. "Are all you wyverns loaded like this?"
I whispered as we entered the house.

Gabriel's lips curled. "Do you fear I won't have
enough resources to keep you in the style to which
you have become accustomed?"

"Hardly," I said with a snort. "My apartment con-
sists of one room, three bookcases, and a bathroom I
share with two girls next door."

"There you are. We'd almost given up on you,"
Aisling said as she caught sight of us.

"I don't suppose anyone has heard from or seen
Cyrene?" I asked once Savian was introduced and a
brief explanation had been given of our past few
hours.

"No, we haven't seen or heard from her. Do you
think something happened to her?" Aisling asked.

"All we know is that she left London for Paris in
the company of a dragon." My gaze flicked over to
where Drake stood.

"Kostya?" he asked Gabriel.

"We do not know for certain," he answered carefully. "Although it crossed my mind."

"Why would Kostya want to come to Paris with
Cyrene?" Aisling asked.

I shook my head and trudged wearily up the stairs
to the room she had given us. I puzzled over that very
question while I washed off the effects of the afternoon. It didn't seem to make sense at all—even if
Cyrene had done the impossible and caught up to
Kostya after leaving Porter . . . or rather, Porter's
remains, why would he want to accompany her?

A thought occurred to me as I was brushing my teeth. I stared in surprise at the empty mirror as my brain chewed over the possibility that Kostya killed Porter.

"It's a tenuous connection at best, but it's still a possibility," I told the mirror. "Cyrene did set off to follow Kostya, and later, they were together at the portal shop. So who's to say they weren't together the whole time?"

If I'd been able to cast a reflection, it would have been shaking its head at the last of my words. I'd forgotten that Cyrene said Porter had kidnapped her, which meant she couldn't have been with Kostya then.

I didn't have an answer by the time I trotted back downstairs, but I didn't have much chance to mull it over before Gabriel whisked me away to Suffrage House.

"You're sure they won't have some sort of spell to catch me shadow walking?" I asked Savian. He stood with Gabriel and me across the street from Suffrage House. Drake and Aisling and their two guards were already inside the building, doing their part to reconnoiter.

"I've never heard of anything. People who could do damage to anything housed there would not have access to the beyond or shadow walking." He grinned at me. "I guess they didn't think about doppelgangers."

"We're not normally at odds with the L'au-delà," I pointed out, then shadowed and made my way across the busy street without being struck.

Gabriel and Savian strolled past me into the building ahead of me. I took my time to make sure that there were no traps or wards at the doors, but evidently Savian was correct—nothing stopped me as I made my way down to the basement. Our plan was simple—Gabriel and Savian would poke around the security offices as best they could. Drake, with an acute sense of smell when it came to treasure of any sort, would conduct an unobtrusive search for any locations other than the vault where valuables might be stored. My job was to assess the vault itself, which meant I needed to get past the security present outside it.

A half hour later, we were regrouped at Drake's house.

"Shall we start with the easy stuff first?" Aisling asked. "Drake and I hunted high and low, and there's no secondary vault anywhere. Drake said the only thing he smelled was in the basement."

"Which is where the vault is," Savian affirmed. "According to my friend in the security office, the evening shift takes over at the onset of deep night. The shift change takes place then because it's when most people are at their lowest energy, so they want fresh eyes on the job."

I smiled. "How nice it is that those of us who were born of shadow find deep night our peak performance time."

"I thought you'd like that," Savian said with a cheeky grin.

Gabriel, sitting next to me on the couch in Drake's living room, narrowed his eyes at Savian in a show of jealousy that I'm ashamed to admit utterly delighted me.

"So what about the big job?" Aisling asked, looking at me. "Is it doable?"

I nodded. "Quite doable. There's the usual run of electronic equipment, and two guards, one who roams the basement corridor, the other who wanders from above stairs to below. They may add a third for nighttime, but I doubt it. Between the guards and electronics, they seem to have everything covered."

"What about the vault itself?" Gabriel asked.

"Warded, with arcane spell protections and a couple of prohibitions. The latter concern beings of the dark powers, so I couldn't get too close to eyeball the other wards, but they didn't look like anything out of the ordinary. I assume you'll be able to remove them?" I asked Aisling.

"It shouldn't be a problem at all."

"The vault itself must be huge—it appears to take up most of the basement. But once the door is open, I should be able to shadow walk inside and disable any alarm systems within so Gabriel can enter safely."

There was a moment of uncomfortable silence as Drake and Gabriel locked gazes.

"I believe the decision of who will retain control of the phylactery has yet to discussed," Drake said.

Gabriel's eyebrows rose. "Do you have reason to believe I would abuse such an honor?"

"No." Drake hesitated. "But Kostya will not be so certain, and he will not stop at anything to regain it if he knows it is in your possession."

"I'm quite able to keep my treasures safe even from your brother," Gabriel said dryly.

"That is not my point. If you were to retain the phylactery, Kostya would continue to attack you and your sept to get it."

"It seems to me he's pretty much doing that anyway," I said.

"If he knows I have the phylactery," Drake said, "Kostya won't be happy, but he won't have cause to continue to fight you. It might even do much to keep him in line."

Gabriel frowned. "You had it once, and lost it to him. I am not comfortable knowing that it could again fall so easily into his hands."

Drake's eyes glittered emerald, but they were no match for the brilliant quicksilver fire that burned in Gabriel's.

"Do you imply that *I* cannot hold my own treasure?" Drake asked with a clear warning in his voice.

"Sweetie." Aisling put her hand on Drake's arm to get his attention. "Defluff those hackles. Gabriel wasn't insulting you any more than you were insulting him. I know you want to have the phylactery to keep it safe, but I think that in this case, Gabriel should have it."

Drake glared at his mate. She kissed the tip of his nose. "It won't hurt you to let something go," she reassured him. "Gabriel will keep it safe. He won't use it to destroy Kostya, will you, Gabriel?"

Gabriel was silent for a moment.

I dug an elbow into his ribs.

"No," he said with a resigned sigh. "The phylactery was not meant to be used as a weapon of revenge. I will honor it for what it is, and simply keep it safe."

I rewarded him with a smile and a little pinch of his thigh. He covered my hand with his, stroking my fingers in a silent gesture of acknowledgment.

It took a few more minutes of persuading before Drake reluctantly agreed to put the phylactery in Gabriel's keeping. Since there were still several hours to go until deep night, Drake ordered Aisling to rest.

I followed her out of the room, leaving the dragons and Savian to talk.

The hallway held the usual furniture—a couple of chairs, some small tables, a large mirror against one wall. As I passed a small bureau, a telephone sitting on top of it rang. I glanced around for someone to answer it, but Aisling was upstairs, and the hall was empty.

"Hello? Er . . . Vireo residence."

"I wish to speak to . . . wait. Is this the doppel-ganger?"

I recognized the voice at the other end almost im-mediately. It held a slightly Slavic accent, and for some reason, made the hairs on the backs of my arms stand on end.

"Yes, this is May. What do you want, Kostya?"

He chuckled. The door to the room I had just left opened, and Gabriel came out, followed by Drake and Savian. "The question is more what I have than what I want."

My stomach turned to lead for a moment. Had he gotten the phylactery and called to gloat about it?

"I have something of yours, shadow walker. And I am willing to return it to you for a price."

Aisling appeared at the top of the stairs accompa-nied by Jim. "Was that the phone? Is it May's twin?"

"What exactly are you talking about?" My eyes went to Gabriel, who immediately took a position next to me, his arm sliding around my waist as he leaned in to listen. Drake went across to another room, pick-ing up the receiver there.

"Are you missing a twin, perhaps?"

I sucked in my breath. "If you've hurt her—"

"I do not harm women." Kostya snorted. "Not un-less they harm me first. Your twin is safe. For now."

"Who's on the phone?" Savian asked Aisling.

She raised her eyebrows as she watched her hus-band emerge with a cordless phone. "Judging by the smoke wafting out of him, I'd say it's his brother."

"Ah. They don't get along?" he asked.

"Something like that." She came downstairs, stop-ping next to Drake.

"Why did you kidnap her?" I asked Kostya. "What do you hope to gain by this?"

"I had no need to kidnap her," Kostya told me. "She came willingly. My motive should be clear. She is in my power, and if you wish her to return safely, you will bring me the phylactery which you so recently stole."

"That is not acceptable," Drake started to say, but Gabriel, with a flash of quicksilver eyes, snatched the phone from me and snarled into it.

"I knew you would show no honor in dealing with me, but to use an innocent woman as a hostage for the phylactery is an act unworthy even of an ouroboros like yourself."

Kostya spat out an invective, but Drake interrupted before either of them could get into a verbal pissing match.

"Have you so little disregard for your place in the weyr that you would even consider such a dishonorable act?" he asked. "This is nothing short of a declaration of war, brother. To continue will destroy all chances you have of gaining recognition for your sept."

"There is no honor in the black dragons," Gabriel growled, "just as there is no sept."

"We will rise again," Kostya promised. "And we will regain all that was lost to us."

"What is he saying?" Aisling asked, trying to get Drake to let her listen in. "Is he being an idiot again? What a silly question, of course he is."

"Kostya is going off on a rant about the silver dragons again," I told her. "Frankly, I'm getting a bit tired of it."

"As am I," Gabriel said, clicking off the phone before doing an about-face to march out the front door we had so recently entered.

"Where are you going?" I asked, looking between him and Drake, who was arguing with his brother,

Aisling and Savian sharing the phone Gabriel had tossed down.

"Out," he said without stopping.

I hurried after him. "Why?"

"I have had enough of this. That Kostya would attempt to harm me, I accept. That he would strike at you, I expect. But that he would take into his hands the life of someone not related to the sept in order to blackmail me—no. Tipene and Maata, I understand. They are part of the sept. But your twin is not. This must stop now."

"I'm with you so far as that goes," I said, taking his hand. His fingers tightened around mine in an almost painful grip as he strode down the street to a busy intersection. "But how exactly are we going to stop him?"

He hailed a cab and waited until it was under way before answering me. "We go back to the portal's exit, and you follow his trail. I will end it once and for all."

I didn't like the look of unadulterated rage in his eyes, but there was little I could say that would persuade him not to take the present course of action. Besides which, I was more than a little annoyed with Kostya's ridiculous persecution of Gabriel and the silver dragons. That didn't mean I had to blindly follow Gabriel, however.

"There must be a way to end things without you indulging in the sort of violence I have a feeling you're thinking of unleashing."

"I will not give him the phylactery," Gabriel swore, his fingers tightening on mine.

"Good gods, no, I didn't mean that!" I shuddered to think of what would happen if Magoth found out I used the phylactery to save Cyrene. He'd likely destroy both of us. "I just meant that there has to be a way other than the all-out war that Drake warned him about. You can't want that."

His fingers tightened even more until I made a little wordless noise of protest. Immediately he relaxed his hold, stroking my fingers and bringing the tips to his mouth to kiss. "I'm sorry, little bird. I do not mean to take out my frustrations on you."

"That's what I'm here for, isn't it?"

The look he gave me contained no smile. "You are my mate. You are part of me now, part of the sept, but that does not mean I should unduly burden you."

He looked away, his jaw still tight. My belly ached at the unspoken rejection. I considered pushing it away, deep and dark into the depths of my own psyche, but something inside me rebelled, some newfound sense of . . . oh, I don't know, togetherness, I guess. I had spent my life alone, bound to Cyrene, bound to Magoth, but never having anyone with whom I could share things. Gabriel charged into my life with a flash of his molten silver eyes, and made me a part of something bigger, something . . . us.

"Gabriel, don't push me out. I've spent my lifetime alone," I said.

He turned a surprised look on me. "I have not pushed you out, little bird."

"You want to. I can tell you want to protect me by keeping me away from this, but you said I was your mate, and I accepted the job. That means your burdens are mine to share, and by the twelve gods, I'm going to share them."

He looked taken aback for a moment before he suddenly grinned. "I begin to see more and more why Drake puts up with Aisling's ways."

"You'd better believe—wait . . . was that a compliment or an insult? If it was the latter, we're going to need to have a long talk. If it was the former, I'll kiss you until you can't think straight."

"Former. It was definitely the former," he said quickly.

"I'm never going to be a proper wyvern's mate at this rate," I said as I flung myself across the seat to kiss him.

"I'm beginning to think the rules regarding proper etiquette are vastly overrated," he murmured as I licked his bottom lip. Gabriel allowed me to take charge of the kiss, his hands warm on my ribs as I lazily explored his mouth, the embers of desire quickly igniting under the taste and feel and scent of him. An idle part of my mind wondered for a second what it was about him that had me willing to risk everything just to be with him, but that thought didn't last long. He was what he was, and that was all I wanted.

"I'm still thinking straight," he murmured a few minutes later. His fire roared through me, seemingly setting my blood on fire, but reluctantly, I kept a tight rein on it and returned it to him lest we inadvertently set the cab alight.

"Are you, now," I purred, sliding my hands down his chest. His eyes widened as I shifted so that I was sitting astride his thighs, my body blocking the cab driver's view of him. "Let's see if you're still thinking after I do this . . ."

His nostrils flared as my hands slid lower, fingers deftly undoing both his belt and his fly. I leaned in to kiss him again, my hands busily touching and stroking and teasing, even as my tongue did the same.

"I don't know about him, but *I'm* definitely losing concentration," the cab driver said.

I released Gabriel's lip and peered over my shoulder at the man. I'd deliberately arranged myself so that he couldn't see exactly what we were doing, although I suspected he had a good idea. He winked at me in the rearview mirror, and added, "That's your address ahead of us. Would you like me to go around the block a few times?"

I glanced down at Gabriel. His eyes were hot enough to leave scorch marks. "No, I think I've proven my point," I said with a little smile as I restored order to Gabriel's clothing.

"You will pay for this torment, little bird," he promised with a deliciously wicked smile.

"Deal." Reluctantly, I slid off his thighs and pulled my mind from where it was dwelling with loving detail on the image of Gabriel wearing nothing but whipped cream, and tried to focus on the matter at hand.

"You'll pay for *that*, too," he murmured a minute later as he turned back to the cab to pay off the driver.

Fortunately for us both, Cyrene's trail was still visible just outside the portal's exit point, so I didn't have to go back into the horrendous slaughterhouse. There wasn't much traffic in the area, thankfully, which allowed me to slip into the shadows immediately.

"It's here," I told Gabriel as I returned to the mundane world. "Faint, but visible—both Cyrene and a dragon."

"Check in every fifteen minutes to tell me where you are. I'll follow you that way," he said, checking his cell phone to make sure it was on.

I nodded and prepared to move into the shadow world.

"Mayling."

"Hmm?"

His eyes glittered brightly. "Remember that you are my mate. I know you wish to rescue your twin, but you are important to me. I would not like it if you were harmed in any way."

I smiled and leaned forward to give him a quick

kiss. "You would be a very easy man to love, Gabriel."

His eyes searched mine for a moment, but he said nothing. I slipped away from him into the beyond, my attention locked onto the dim trail that was growing dimmer with each passing moment, but my heart . . . my heart was busy with other matters.

Chapter Twenty-three

"Show me," Gabriel said about an hour later.

"It's two blocks away. I had to come here to hide because I think someone from the committee saw me when I was checking out a dead end in Montmarte. At least I assume it's someone from the committee— few mortals unconnected with the Otherworld would be able to follow me when I'm in the shadow world, and I've seen the same woman three times in the last twenty minutes."

"I am with you now," he said matter-of-factly, as if that made everything right, and damned if it didn't.

"I'm not sure why, but Cyrene's trail has gone, yet the signs of the dragon remain," I said as we moved cautiously down a relatively quiet street in Ménilmontant, a working-class area in the Parisian suburb of Belleville. "I guess it just has something to do with dragon scales lasting longer because they're tangible, as opposed to signs that an elemental being passed by."

"Just so you're sure it's Kostya you were following."

"Well, it's the dragon who was with Cyrene at the portal shop. Unless he had someone else meeting them there, it's got to be him."

We stopped in front of a small bakery. Above it, curtained windows bedecked with tiny window boxes indicated modest apartments for the residents of the area.

"That's it. I didn't go in, but I did search for signs at the exits. I didn't see anything that said the dragon who went in has left."

"Good work, little bird. You will please remember that Kostya is mine to deal with," he said as he angled his body to block the view of any passersby. I persuaded the lock to open, allowing us both to slip into a narrow, dim hallway that ended in a flight of stairs leading upward.

"*Agathos daimon,*" I muttered to myself as I shadowed.

"What is it?"

"It's what's *not*—the trail. It's gone cold."

"It does not matter. If Kostya is here, I will find him," Gabriel said grimly.

I climbed the stairs slowly, examining them carefully for signs of dragon scales. Here and there I found a faint glimmer of a scale, but for the most part, the trail was gone. "Before you go bursting into all the apartments, let me look at their doors."

He didn't want to wait; I could see that. His muscles were tense and tight, the pupils in his eyes narrowed until they were thin little ebony strips. I hurried to the nearest door before he decided he would risk disturbing innocent people in his quest to get ahold of Kostya.

We hit pay dirt at the fourth and last apartment, at the far end of the building.

"Here," I whispered to Gabriel as I came out of the shadow world. The door handle had a couple of spots on it that glittered even in the dim light of the naked bulb overhead. "This has to be it."

"Get behind me and stay shadowed," he said, pulling a gun out of his jacket pocket.

I blinked in surprise at the weapon. Most people in

the Otherworld scorned the use of modern weaponry as too crass for a society that valued personal abilities over brute strength. But such things weren't unknown, although I had no idea that dragons subscribed to the use of firearms.

"I don't under normal conditions. I prefer a sword for close contact, but I do not trust Kostya to hold to such things as honor."

I didn't have time to answer that before Gabriel screwed a silencer on the gun and shot the lock three times, kicking the door open immediately thereafter.

Dagger in hand, I remained shadowed as I followed him into the apartment. It was small but neat, a tiny kitchen immediately off the entrance. That opened into a main living area, which held the usual couch, TV, and a couple of bookcases. It was empty of dragons, however . . . and anyone else.

"There?" I asked, nodding toward a closed door. Gabriel moved so fast I couldn't keep up with him, although the sound of the door being slammed back made me jump. I hurried after him, stopping in surprise at the doorway.

Gabriel knelt on the bed between two people.

"Are they all right?" I asked, coming out of the shadows to offer him my dagger. He cut the bonds holding Maata and Tipene, both of whom had been securely bound and gagged.

Maata started talking the second Gabriel had her gag off. I didn't understand what she was saying, it being in some language that had an oddly beautiful cadence. As soon as he got her arms free, she sat up and saw me, switching immediately to English.

"I knew it was only a matter of time before you found us, although it took a little *more* time than I'd hoped. Excuse me." She bolted to a room leading off the bedroom.

Gabriel cut the bonds holding his other bodyguard. Tipene looked furious as he leaped off the bed.

"We have failed you, Gabriel. I will resign my post immediately."

Gabriel looked at him with somber appraisal for a moment before grinning and enveloping the larger man in a bear hug. "Now is not the time for foolish talk. We have much work to do in finding Kostya."

"Kostya? Is he here?" Tipene asked with a puzzled frown.

"It wasn't Kostya who kidnapped you?" I asked.

Tipene shook his head. "No. It was two others, the two ouroboros who took us in Greece. They used drugs on us!"

The outrage in his voice was clearly evident.

"Several times," Maata said as she emerged from the bathroom. Tipene shot Gabriel a glance.

He nodded, and the bodyguard hurried off to the bathroom.

"How long have we been gone?" Maata asked Gabriel.

"Four days."

She swore. "We were drugged the entire time."

"You have no idea how long you've been here, in Paris?" I asked Maata.

"I had no idea we were even in Paris until I could hear the radio from the street. We woke up about six hours ago. I was getting worried that no one would come to give us water and let us relieve ourselves, at least."

I exchanged a look with Gabriel. "Kostya said he didn't kidnap them," I reminded him.

His face worked for a moment. "It fit, though."

"Possibly, but I think more and more that Porter's boss, whoever that might be, is involved in all this. Ouroboros dragons indicate it might be a dragon, but we can't know that for sure. It could be anyone, really—a demon lord, a dragon, one of the wyverns you mentioned, or even Baltic come back from the dead. Not to mention someone unknown to us."

Gabriel shook his head and questioned his bodyguards for a few minutes, but they had nothing to explain what happened other than that the original people who snatched them off the street in Greece were dragons, but dragons not known to them, and not members of any sept. We conducted a brief examination of the apartment, but there was nothing to identify the occupant.

"Did you recognize the dragon who was here in the last couple of hours?" I asked when we gave up searching for information.

Maata blinked at me for a moment. "What dragon?"

"Whoever came here a little bit ago. Possibly with my twin, Cyrene."

"I didn't see anyone, although I dozed for a little bit. Tipene?"

He shook his head. "I was awake since noon, and no one entered the apartment."

A strange chill ran down my back as I thought about the trail clearly leading to the apartment. A memory tickled my brain and sent me back to the tiny kitchenette off the entrance. A window overlooked an unkempt minute garden at the back of the building. The window was unlocked, and when I half crawled through it, I saw one little glimmer of dragon scale on the stone ledge outside.

"He left through the window," I said, climbing back into the apartment. "Probably came into the apartment and didn't bother going into the bedroom—just left via the window without being seen. *Agathos daimon*. We're being led, Gabriel."

"So it would seem," he said, looking thoughtful. "Do you think you'll be able to pick up the trail outside?"

"No. Too much time has passed. But what happened to Cyrene? If that was Kostya I was following, Cyrene must have left him at some point. Probably that spot in Montmarte where I lost the trail for a bit. I'm sorry, Gabriel."

He nodded in acknowledgment of my regret. "It cannot be helped, little bird. We will return to Drake's house and regroup. I'm sure Maata and Tipene are hungry."

Maata made a face. "You have no idea."

Our trip back to Drake's elegant house was made in silence broken only by the rumbling of Maata and Tipene's empty stomachs.

I left Gabriel, Drake, the bodyguards of both, Aisling, and Savian closeted together to discuss the assault on the committee's vault. I had no stomach for planning—I positively itched with the need to be doing something, preferably finding Kostya and Cyrene. I wandered around a small garden at the side of the house, following the line of a tall hedge to a secluded little area containing a tiny fountain and two curved stone benches. The sun had set a short while ago, the night air close and heavy, as if it was about to rain.

"Whatcha doing?" a voice asked from the other side of the fountain.

I jumped at the unexpected intrusion. "Jim! Oh, you scared me."

"Sorry. Was taking a pee. What are you doing in Aisling's outdoors sex spot?" Jim emerged from a shrubbery.

"Outdoors sex spot?" I repeated in confusion.

"Yeah. If you go over to that corner, the hedges block the view from all the houses around us. Aisling keeps a blanket out here in summer just so she and Drake can get naked. You and Gabriel going to get it on? Should I bring you a blanket?"

"I'm fine, thank you."

"Your loss. What are you doing if you're not scouting for an illicit love nest?"

"Wishing that it was a few hours from now," I answered, rubbing my arms against a little prickle of goose bumps. "All this waiting around with nothing to do leaves me feeling itchy."

"You sure it's not fleas? I had a little bout with that myself last month, and Aisling just about had a fit."

"I doubt it's fleas," I said with a little laugh. "It's just a bit . . . irritating, if you know what I mean. Everyone is so concerned about plotting and planning when the matter is really very simple: I shadow walk in, report back as to which guards are posted where, and what sort of security is in place, and the dragons eliminate them."

The demon tipped its head on the side. "You really think it's going to be that simple? The committee has had almost a thousand years to keep people out of their vaults, and I've never heard of anyone breaking in, let alone breaking in and getting away with anything."

"They've never faced a force like ours, though."

"True that," it agreed. "So what are you going to do about Magoth? You still thinking of going dybbuk? 'Cause if you are, I want to watch when Magoth gets wind of it."

"You're an evil little beastie," I said, tightening my lips.

"Hello! Demon!"

"Sixth class, which means you weren't born that way." I inspected it carefully. "What were you originally? Elemental being? Demigod?"

Jim snorted. "Ha. Like I look like I have that sort of power? I was a sprite in the Court of Divine Blood."

"Fallen angel, I should have known."

"Oh, puh-leeze," it said, rolling its eyes. "Don't even go there. It's bad enough Aisling found out. I don't need anyone else going on about it."

I laughed again and patted the top of its head. "Fair enough. To answer your question, no, I don't intend to go dybbuk. I won't have to. The situation will work itself out."

"What situation?" a silky smooth voice asked behind me. Gabriel strolled toward me, his movements controlled and graceful, like a lithe tiger. He had changed clothes and was now dressed completely in black, the darkness of the clothing and the enveloping night making his eyes glow like moonlight on mercury.

"The one concerning the phylactery. I was telling Jim that I think everything is under control, and don't anticipate any problems."

Gabriel ran his thumb along my jawline, tipping my head back so he could peer into my face. "You are keeping something from me."

It was a statement, not a question.

"Yes," I said, unwilling to lie to him.

"Tell me."

I glanced at the demon, who watched us with avidity.

"Jim," Gabriel said, and jerked his head toward the house.

"Yo. Right here. You going to suck faces? Can I get my iPhone to film it?"

"Scram," Gabriel told it.

"You're not my master. I don't have to take orders from— Scramming."

Jim hurried off to the house muttering about people not having a sense of humor. I tucked my knife back into its sheath.

"What are you concerned about, little bird?" Gabriel asked, his thumb brushing my lips.

I flicked my tongue against the pad of this thumb and gently bit it. I didn't want to tell him about the phylactery, not when we were so close to getting it. If Gabriel knew the position I was in, he would insist on challenging Magoth himself, and not even a wyvern of his power could stand against a demon lord. Much as I hated to keep things from him, it was better for all concerned if he was unaware of the true source of my worry. I answered truthfully, but with less explanation than perhaps was needed. "It's Magoth. I'm worried about him. I don't want him to hurt you."

He replaced his thumb with his lips, pulling me into an embrace that made me sigh with happiness. "Do not fret about that, Mayling. I am not so careless that I would allow a demon lord to gain an upper hand with me. And do not despair that we will fail to find a way to free you from this bondage. I've been concerned with getting the phylactery and finding Maata and Tipene, but once the phylactery is in my possession, I will put the full powers of the sept at your disposal. We will free you from Magoth."

I leaned into him, kissing his neck as guilt pricked at me for deliberately misleading him. "I just want tonight to be over."

"It shall be soon enough." He glanced at his watch. "Savian recommended we not begin until deep night starts, when the powers of any beings guarding the vaults will be at their lowest. That gives us three hours."

The last sentence was spoken with his hands squeezing my behind as he rubbed suggestively against me. My body responded immediately, my breasts becoming brazen little hussies who wanted immediate access to his hands and mouth. I tugged his shirt out of his black jeans, sliding my hands up his ribs. His skin was warm, like satin over steel. "Are you suggesting what I think you're suggesting?"

His smile was pure sin. "Three hours should be sufficient time to give you pleasure several times over."

I glanced at the house. "What about Maata and Tipene?"

"They are eating and preparing themselves for the event to come. You will have all of my attention, Mayling." His smile got a whole lot more wicked. "And this time, I intend things to go differently. I will give you much pleasure before I even think of taking my own."

"Oooh, that sounds promising," I murmured, unbuttoning his shirt. "Foreplay at long last."

He allowed me to remove his shirt before pulling off my leather bodice, his hands immediately cupping my camisole-clad breasts. I leaned into him, breathing deeply of the delicious scent that seemed to cling to his skin. "Shall I tell you what I will do to you?" he murmured, his lips busily nibbling on my ear as he peeled my shirt off.

"Oh, please, yes," I said breathlessly as his fingers slipped the front hook of my bra open, revealing my eager breasts.

"First I shall torment these lovely, plump morsels of delight. I shall taste their silky smoothness, suckling the delectable rosy tips until you scream with pleasure." He traced lazy patterns on the underside, making me shiver as he circled my breasts, avoiding my sensitive nipples until I couldn't stand it any longer, and bit his shoulder.

He laughed into my neck and gently pinched the aching tips of my breasts. "Then I shall taste the rest of you, all of you, taking my time to explore your sublime belly, your perfect hips, and the sensitive flesh of your inner thighs."

I quivered against him, positively quivered at the combination of his words, his touch, and the feel of him as I stroked the hard muscles of his back.

"I look forward to licking every inch of your legs, little bird. I want to find every little spot on you that makes you tremble with passion. I will lick my way up until I can savor your true essence upon my tongue."

I just about saw stars, and dipped my head to take one of his pert little nipples into my mouth.

Gabriel gasped, froze for a moment, and then the next thing I knew I was on my back, the cold grass pricking uncomfortably into my bare flesh. My pants, shoes, and underwear had gone flying, whipped off me at such a speed that it took me several seconds to realize Gabriel had removed them. I lay stunned for a moment, and then sat up.

Gabriel knelt next to me, his face twisted in agony. He was aroused—very aroused—but didn't seem to be able to move.

"Are you all right?" I asked, reaching out toward him.

He trembled as I placed my hand on his thigh. "Don't touch me. Please, Mayling, if you have any mercy in you, do not touch me."

"Gabriel, what on earth is the matter?" I got to my knees next to him, wrapping my arms around his shoulders. "Are you hurt?"

"I'm trying to control this overpowering, insane, undeniable . . . *need* I have for you," he said, his eyes opening to pierce me with molten light.

"I thought that need was part of you being a wyvern, and me being your mate."

"In certain circumstances, yes. But you have not been taken from me recently. I should be able to control this overwhelming drive to possess you."

"I think we'd better just give up on the idea of foreplay," I said, laughing at his tortured expression.

Irritation filled his eyes. "We will not! Dammit, May, I want to do this! I owe it to you—not just because you are my mate, but because you would like it. And I would like to see you liking it. The thought of doing it is in the top five of my sexual wish list. It's just that when you're not around, I can think about all of the many and varied ways I would like to love you, but then I see you and smell you and taste you, and it's so hard . . ."

I wrapped my hand around his penis. "Possibly hard enough to break a concrete block."

His eyes widened for a moment, and then he tipped me over backward, hoisting my legs around his hips as he thrust into me.

"Gabriel," I moaned, both at the sudden act of penetration and the unusual position. "This isn't particularly comfor—oh, dear gods, yes! Do that again!"

He repeated a delicious little hip swivel, and it was all over for me. I clutched handfuls of grass as he sent me flying, dragon fire washing over my body as I gave in to the glory of our joining. My legs, clutched around his hips, spread wider as his body thickened, the slick, satiny skin becoming rougher and harder until silver scales rippled upward to cover the flesh. Scarlet claws pricked the skin on my hips as he lifted me to meet him, the sensitive skin of my inner thighs rubbing with delightful friction against his scales. Gabriel's roar of completion startled birds sleeping in the scattered trees of the garden.

I opened my eyes when he collapsed down upon me for a moment before rolling onto his back, taking me with him. He was Gabriel once more, a man, and yet not a man. But whatever he was, I could no longer deny that I was falling in love with him.

"You shifted," I said, amazed at the experience.

"I'm sorry," he said, his eyes closed, his chest heaving beneath me. "I know I said I wouldn't, but I couldn't control myself. You are so much a part of me now, I've lost the ability to maintain a facade for you."

His words touched my heart. I savored the sweetness of them for a moment, reveling in the warmth he brought to my life. For the first time, I felt utterly cherished.

"Now," he said, interrupting my thoughts.

"Now what?" I asked, draped across him like a limp noodle. His heart beat wildly beneath my ear. I spread my fingers across his chest, marveling that such a man was mine.

"Now we will have foreplay. I believe I'm suitably sated that I can last longer than five seconds before attacking you."

"I rather like your method of attack, although I do admit I'd like to be able to indulge in a few fantasies of my own before you unleash your inner dragon on me."

He opened one eye. "What sort of fantasies?"

"I've heard so much about oral sex, and I've never had the opportunity to try it out before. So I'd really like to . . . well, I'm sure I don't have to put it into so many words. Since you're much more relaxed, why don't I just indulge myself?"

"You want to . . . ?" His other eye popped open as I started to slide down his body, intent on exploring that part of him which had given me so much pleasure.

He grabbed me before I was able to move four inches. I looked up, worried that I had done something wrong. A familiar strained, tense look was on his face, his eyes screwed up tight. I looked down at his penis. It was no longer in a resting state. "I thought you were sated?"

"I was. Until you went and mentioned doing that to me. No! Don't touch me there, woman! For the love of—grk!"

A half hour later, Gabriel, his arm wrapped around me because my legs were unusually weak, hustled me toward the house with a grim look on his face.

"I will beat this," he muttered. "I am a wyvern. I am strong. I will control my needs long enough to give you pleasure, and you will enjoy it, dammit!"

I said nothing, but I smiled. *A lot.*

Chapter Twenty-four

Deep night—the hours between midnight and four a.m.—is when the shadows are darkest, and beings of such origins strongest. As I walked in the shadow world, carefully avoiding any electronic device that might register my passing, I sought and received strength from the shadows.

On the floor above me, I could feel Gabriel's presence, a warm, comforting sort of glow that wrapped me in a cocoon of burgeoning love. I smiled to myself as I watched the basement patrol stroll down the hallway, alert for signs she might become aware of what was going on upstairs. The dragons and Aisling had little trouble dealing with the guards, for a few minutes later Jim appeared at the far end of the corridor.

"Yo! Miss Guard! I don't suppose you brought your lunch with you? You're not going to need it, and my fabulous form is being positively starved to death."

The guard, who had her back turned to Jim, whipped around to stare in momentary surprise. I zipped around behind her, deshadowing the second she reached for her radio. She hit the floor without having time to speak a word.

"Nicely done," Gabriel said as he and the others stepped over her body. "Why does it not surprise me that you have martial arts training?"

"I'm mad, bad, and *very* dangerous to know," I told him with a little smile.

"We will have to compare badness at another time," he answered with a flash of his dimples. "Is that the vault?"

"Yes." I stood back as Drake and Aisling approached the heavy steel door. "It's just the wards and prohibitions you'll need to take care of—the arcane magic won't affect me."

Aisling peered closely at the wards. "I can't unmake them, but I don't think it will be any problem to break them. Jim, get to work on the prohibitions."

"You and Tipene patrol the perimeter," Gabriel told his two bodyguards. "Drake and I will shut down any alarm systems wired to the vault."

They nodded and hurried off toward the stairs. Drake ordered his men to shut off power to all parts of the building but the basement, and to secure the entrances.

"Stay with Aisling," Drake ordered Jim as he and Gabriel were about to leave.

"Ten four, dragon buddy."

Drake turned to his wife. "Do not do anything foolish, *kincsem*."

She gave him a fond but exasperated look. "Honest to Pete, dragons! Bossiest beings in the world."

Gabriel smiled at me but said nothing until he and Drake started to leave. "You'll notice I don't have to warn *my* mate to be careful. I have full confidence in May's abilities," he told Drake.

"She's a female American. No doubt you will soon understand the true depth of hell she can put you through."

Aisling laughed as she turned back to the door. I watched with interest as Jim broke down the prohibitions (a weak version of a curse, easily unmade by beings of a dark origin). Aisling muttered under her breath as she struggled with the wards, her face turning red as they fought her attempts to break them.

"There," she said after five minutes of intense work. She stepped back, rubbing her hands. "Got the little bastards. Jim?"

"I was done before you had the first ward down. You're losing your touch, Ash."

She shot it a look. "Caribbean Battiste probably warded the vault doors. I'd like to see you take on the wards drawn by the head of the Guardians' Guild himself."

"Excuses, excuses." It smiled at her.

"The lock and arcane spells are all yours," Aisling said to me.

"Perfect, thanks." I ignored the spells as I put both hands on the lock, closing my eyes as I mentally traveled the intricacies of its mechanisms. "It's a time lock."

"Is that going to be a problem?" Aisling asked.

"No. I can persuade the inner clock to move forward. I've never seen a lock quite like this, though. There are locks within the locks, but I think I can convince them to open for us. Ah, yes. That's it. Just one more tumbler . . . lovely."

The lock didn't give me any trouble. I waited until Jim, sent to stand on the staircase, reported that the power had been cut to the upper floors before carefully opening the heavy vault door. There were no sirens or flashing lights warning that the door was being opened, but I didn't expect them—any notice that the vault was being breeched would go out silently. I just hoped Drake and Gabriel had been successful in quelling any other alarm systems.

A light clicked on inside the vault as the door opened wide enough for me to slip in.

"Here we go," I told Aisling as I shadowed.

"Good luck!" she whispered.

I entered the vault, pausing to listen for any sounds indicating security systems. There was a hum from fluorescent lights overhead, and the soft whoosh of an air system pumping air into the large vault. Ahead of me were long rows of metal cases. I touched the nearest one, but there was no lock on it. I slid the door out and rolled it back along a track. Boxes labeled "Grimoires, 1450 to 1800" filled the cabinet. The next one housed a collection of spell books. I closed both and moved down the line of cabinets. The vault was evidently created from the original storerooms of the cellar, separated by modern metal doors. Careful to avoid making any sound, I gently persuaded the door's lock to bend to my will, slipping silently through the doorway and closing it with only the barest whisper of noise.

The spotlight hit me almost at the same time as the sound.

"Aaaaaand . . . two, three, four!"

A chorus of reedy voices began to sing to an accompaniment of tinny music. Startled by the lights and noise, I shadowed immediately, although I was sure I was visible under the bright light that filled the room. Momentarily blinded, I strained my eyes to see even as I sidled out of the way of the spotlight.

"No, no, no!" The words were punctuated with a slapping noise. I blinked a couple of times, my vision slowly adapting to the light. What I saw left me speechless with amazement. The room held the same gray metal cabinets as the previous room, but these ones lined the walls rather than filled the floor space. That was taken up by a large wooden desk—or I assumed it normally would have been the case, the desk currently having been shoved to a far corner. Also dotted around the perimeter of the room were a couple of tall standing lights, the kind used by smaller theater companies. But it wasn't any of that which made me gawk.

"You have to listen to the beat! Move to the tempo! For the sovereign's sake, you're Munchkins, not lumbering baboons! It's not . . . that . . . hard!" The last three words were punctuated with the slam of a ruler against the wooden desk. A man yielded the ruler—at least I thought at first it was a man, but as I watched in openmouthed amazement, I realized he was slightly translucent. A spirit, then, not a man. Which meant . . . I turned my gaze to the center of the room.

Six imps stood in a row, clad in sequin-bedecked costumes that had only a passing resemblance to those worn by the Munchkins in *The Wizard of Oz*.

"Now we will try this again, and this time, listen to the blasted music! Everyone lift your right foot. That's your left hand. Lift your right . . . oh, let me show you. *Again*."

The spirit jumped off the desk and started for the six imps, pausing when he almost bumped into me.

"Who are you? What do you want? Can't you see I'm busy now?"

He brushed past me and took a spot next to the closest imp. "Right foot, do you see? This one is the right foot. Now you all lift yours. Well, that's two of you. On the count of four you start forward on this foot. Honestly, it's like trying to discuss brain surgery with tapioca."

This last bit was directed toward me. I figured since the spirit had already seen me, I might as well de-shadow. "This may sound a little odd, but what exactly are you doing?" I asked.

"Two by two! What did I just get done telling you? You march two by two toward Dorothy."

One imp—I was relieved to note they were the benign Australian house imps rather than the rowdier (and potentially dangerous) European variety—eeked in distress a couple of times.

"Well, I'm going to sound angry when I've told you and told you how to do this scene! This is the pivotal moment when Dorothy meets you. She's your savior, the one who has come to free you from the bondage that has held you in its steely grip for centuries. You march toward her two by two, bow, and go into the jazz number. Do you all have that?"

The unhappy imp he was addressing suddenly burst into tears, the other five huddling around it in poses of abject misery.

"Oh, for the sake of the sovereign's ten blessed toes . . . take five! Go back to your dressing room and collect yourselves!"

The imps bolted for a large cardboard box that sat next to the wooden desk. I looked from the box to the spirit. "Do I want to know why you're evidently drilling imps to play parts from *The Wizard of Oz*?" I asked him.

He crossed his arms and adopted an extremely put-upon expression. "It's not *The Wizard of Oz*. You've heard of that musical about the Wicked Witch? Well, this is my version of the Oz story, told from the perspective of the Munchkins, a much-persecuted and maligned people."

"With imps."

"Well . . . they are all I have. It's not easy being a vault attendant, you know," he said with a sniff, returning to his desk. "Not allowed to bring in guests, not allowed out for more than one day a week, hardly anyone ever comes here, and there's not even any Internet access. I would have gone insane long, long ago if it wasn't for my musical comedy troupe. We bring life to old classics—that's our motto. Snappy, don't you think?"

"Er . . . very."

He held up a colorful flyer that proclaimed "MUNCH! You've heard the witches' sides, now hear ours!" "I had hoped to open next month, but I lost most of my company when they started their own group and decided to tour America. These new imps seem to be all left feet. And so emotional! You've never seen such drama queens in your life." His eyes narrowed on me suddenly. "Who did you say you were?"

"I don't think I did. My name is May. And you are?"

"Misha," he said, nodding dismissively.

"Pleasure to meet you. I'm sorry to appear at a loss, but I wasn't expecting to find anyone in here."

"No one ever thinks of the vault attendants," he said with another sniff. "Speaking of which, the vault hours are clearly posted in the lobby. I am not obligated to serve customers after hours unless a member of the committee requests it, and I"—he made a show of shuffling through some paperwork—"do not have any such order."

"You're a spirit," I pointed out, albeit apropos of nothing.

"I'm a *domovoi*," he snapped back.

That was interesting. What was a Russian house spirit doing acting as an attendant in the committee's vault? "I'm sorry, but I'm in a bit of a hurry, and can't wait until the proper vault hours. I'll be happy to let you get back to your imp musical if you could just point me to the area where the Lindorm Phylactery is being held."

"Room C, row seven, shelf two, box K," Misha said, sitting back down at the desk. "But you can't have it."

"Why not?" I asked, wondering if he was going to make trouble.

"No one is allowed into the back storerooms. Not even Dr. Kostich himself. Besides, it doesn't belong to you," he answered without looking up.

"Actually, it was taken from me when I was arrested, and I neglected to regain my things when I left. So you see, I do have every right to it."

He pursed his lips as he considered me. "You're a dragon's mate, but you're not a dragon. That phylactery belongs to dragons."

"More specifically, it belongs to my dragon," I agreed. "That is, the wyvern to whom I'm mated. He'll be along any second to collect it, so if you wouldn't mind getting the phylactery, I'll send Gabriel in for it, and you can get on with your . . . er . . . directing."

"What was your name again?" he said with a much-put-upon sigh.

I told him.

He sorted through some of the papers, extracting one, which he read with an increasingly sour look. "It would seem your story is true. So far," he allowed. "But it is well after hours, and if I make an exception to the rules for you, I'll have to make one for everyone."

"Says who?"

He thought about that for a moment, then gave a little shrug. "You're right. I'll get the phylactery for you, but only because I really have to nail down this scene before morning if we hope to have any chance of being ready by the end of the month. Stay here and don't touch anything."

I thanked him as he toddled off, muttering under his breath about people interrupting important dramatic work. The second the door closed behind him I was out the way I came, running back to the entrance, sure that Gabriel would be ready and waiting for my report back on the vault.

I opened the door to find utter pandemonium.

Gabriel and Kostya were yelling at each other, Drake and his men trying to pull the two wyverns apart. Maata and Tipene jumped at Kostya, and everyone went down in a big mass of snarling dragons.

"What the . . . what's going on?"

"Mayling! There you are. Will you tell Gabriel to stop being so mean?" Cyrene stepped over one of the dragons and gave me a very irritated look.

"Cy? You're all right?"

She squawked a little when I hugged her.

"Of course I'm all right, silly. I was with Kostya."

I shook my head. She couldn't be saying what I thought she was saying. "You're not going to tell me that he didn't kidnap you?"

Kostya lunged free of Maata and Tipene and tried to grab Gabriel by the throat. Gabriel rolled away and lashed out with his leg, connecting with Kostya's gut.

"Kidnap me? Why would he kidnap me when he saved me?"

Kostya screamed and tried to bite Gabriel's leg, but due to the struggle, ended up clunking heads with Drake instead.

"Hey!" Aisling yelled. "Jim, stop them!"

"Saved you from what? Cyrene . . ." I pulled her out of the way as the dragons attempted to rise to their feet. I kept one eye on Gabriel in case he should need me, but judging by the blows he was getting in to Kostya—hampered though he was by Drake and his men trying to keep him from doing so—he didn't need my assistance. "Didn't Kostya have Porter kidnap you?"

"Stop them how? You want I should pee on them or something?" Jim asked Aisling.

The threat of urination had more effect than all the pleading in the world. En masse the dragons hastily got to their feet, dirty, bleeding, and furious, to a man.

"Kostya?" Cyrene all but goggled at me. "No, of course not! That man Porter, the one who blackmailed us, kidnapped me. He said he was going to give you a little motivation to get that amulet back, but he wasn't acting on Kostya's behalf. In fact, it was just the opposite. Kostya saved me from him and brought me to Paris, where I knew we'd find you. And here we all are!"

"Well, I'm glad to know that, but I don't understand why you would go willingly with Kostya after he killed Porter. I realize he saved you, but he's a murderer—"

"*What* are you talking about?" Cyrene interrupted. "The blackmailer is dead?"

"Thought that would get your attention," Jim said with a satisfied smile at the dragons.

"Yes. We found him. And since you and Kostya had evidently been there, I assumed he had killed him."

She shrugged. "You assumed wrong. Kostya followed us when the blackmailer grabbed me, and bashed him on the head, but he wasn't dead. Then we left by the window. I thought it was very gallant of Kostya."

I shook my head, more confused than ever. "Great. We're back to the question of who killed Porter. I don't suppose you have any idea?"

"I didn't even know he was dead," Cyrene protested.

"It's got to be the person who is manipulating us. And if it's not Kostya . . . ugh. I just don't know how much more of this mysterious business I can cope with."

Cyrene patted me on the arm. "Does it really matter who killed him? He was a bad man."

I shot her a look of disbelief.

"Well, don't think too hard about it, then," she amended. "It'll give you wrinkles."

"If Kostya is so gallant, why is he holding you ransom for the phylactery?" I asked, pouncing on something she'd said.

"Is he?" She looked over at where Drake and his men were (this time successfully) keeping Kostya back. Gabriel and his guards stood opposite. I frowned when I noticed that Gabriel's lip was cut, and his nose bleeding. "Well, I'm sure he has a very good reason for it. You're all wrong in thinking he's a villain, May. He's actually very sweet, and very, very misunderstood."

"I bet he is," I said, moving around her to Gabriel's side. His eyes glittered with an intensity that did not bode well for Kostya.

"We don't have time for this," I told him in a low voice.

His gaze flickered to me. "You found it?"

"Yes. But you'll need to take it. The vault attendant will only give it over to a dragon."

"The phylactery!" Kostya said loudly, wrenching himself away from Drake's bodyguards. He was at Cyrene's side before I could even think to warn her, a knife held to her throat.

"You've already done that," I told him, my fingers itching for my own knife. "You're not going to be so predictable, are you?"

"If you do not bring the phylactery to me, I will kill your twin," he said coolly.

Cyrene gasped and tried to look at him, but he held tight to her neck.

"You will not harm anyone," Drake said in a tired voice. "You may be many things, but you are not a murderer. Let go of the naiad, brother."

Kostya looked like he wanted to argue that point, but to my great surprise, he dropped the hand holding the knife, his shoulders slumping in defeat. "There is much to be said for dealing with strangers who do not know one well. No, I am not a murderer. But I will do whatever it takes to get back what belongs to me."

Cyrene turned around and stomped on his foot, then slammed a knee into his groin. Kostya yelped and doubled over, clutching himself.

"Oooh, right in the happy sacks," Jim said, wincing. "That's gonna sting."

"That's for using me! And that is for making me think you were nice when all along you're a selfish, egotistical beast!" Cyrene stormed, shoving him into the wall.

"Dragon, not beast," Kostya said with painful little gasps of air.

"Same difference." Cyrene marched over to where I stood, telling Gabriel, "I take back everything I said about Kostya. As far as I'm concerned, you can have the phylactery. *He* doesn't deserve it."

"I'm so glad to have your permission," Gabriel answered with a twinkle of humor in his eyes that quickly faded away.

"Why don't we take this opportunity of momentary calm to finish up before someone notices the lack of security?" I suggested.

Gabriel nodded, taking my hand as he led me toward the vault. "I take it that it's safe for us to go in there?"

"Yes, unless you have some sort of a phobia about singing and dancing imps."

He shot me an odd look as he opened the door. The others followed, Kostya bringing up the rear in a half-shuffling, half-crab-walking sort of gait.

Misha the attendant was waiting in his room when

we all piled in. His eyebrows shot up at the sight of us, but other than making a few sounds of disapproval at the sight of the bloody men, he said nothing. "Sign here," he said, holding out a clipboard and pen.

I scanned the paper quickly, but it was just a statement that I had received my property back in the state it had been taken from me. I signed and handed the clipboard back.

"Next time, please adhere to the stated hours," he said, handing me a small box.

"Gabriel?" I said, nodding toward it.

"That's mine!" Kostya said in a still somewhat strangled voice as he lurched forward.

Gabriel reached for the box but Misha held tight to it, backing up a couple of steps as he eyed us.

"You are who?" he asked.

"Konstantin Fekete, wyvern of the black dragons. The phylactery belongs to me."

"The black dragons," Misha said slowly. "Surely they all died centuries ago?"

"Not all. There are still a few of us. And we will regain what we once held—"

Everyone in the room except Cyrene chanted in unison, "—but was taken from us. We will face death to restore to the sept the pride, the glory, the true essence, of what it once was."

Kostya glared at us all.

"Don't get him going about that, please," Aisling said from where she stood behind us, leaning against Drake. "It's late, and once he starts, it can take hours."

"And this is your wyvern?" Misha asked me, nodding at Gabriel.

Gabriel bowed and introduced himself and his bodyguards.

Cyrene edged toward me, giving Kostya a glare as she did so. "Who's that?" she whispered.

"He's the vault keeper. I wish now we'd done a twin identity swap before we came in here," I whispered back.

"Why?" she asked, but I didn't have time to explain to her the importance of someone other than me taking the box.

Misha peered over Gabriel's shoulder. "Ah. Drake Vireo, is it not? I had no idea the committee rescinded its order concerning your presence in Suffrage House."

Drake looked momentarily taken aback as Aisling gave him a long look. "It is nothing, *kincsem*," he told her. "A little misunderstanding about some items which might have gone missing."

"Misunderstanding," Misha snorted, saying in an aside to me, "Caught him trying to break into the vault more than one time over the centuries. He succeeded once. But that was before we got the electronics, eh, Vireo?"

Drake adopted a haughty look. "I have no knowledge of what you speak."

Jim snickered.

"May I have the phylactery, please," Gabriel said, holding out his hand for the small box Misha held. "As you can see by the inventory, it belongs to my mate, not Kostya."

Misha shoved the box toward me. "That would appear in order, yes."

I held up my hands and took a step back. "Thanks. Just give it to Gabriel, please."

Misha frowned at me. So did everyone else. "I am trying to do just that. Please take it so that I may get back to my rehearsals."

"Rehearsals? Do I want to know?" Aisling asked softy.

"I don't think so," Drake answered.

"Just give it to Gabriel, please," I said, taking another step back.

Misha clicked his tongue in an exasperated manner. "I must return it to the owner. So far as the L'au-delà is concerned, you are the owner of this piece, and it is to your hands I must return it."

Kostya, standing mostly straight, started to move toward me, but Maata and Tipene blocked his way.

"I understand that, and as owner, I give you permission to give it to Gabriel," I said, moving back yet another step. I wondered briefly if I could get Misha to give it to Cyrene, instead of me, but suspected that even if he would, the dragons wouldn't accept that.

"I cannot do that," Misha said.

"What is the problem, Mayling?" Gabriel asked, his lovely brows pulled together.

"I can't take it," I told him, unwilling to say any more.

"Why not?"

"I just can't. You take it."

Gabriel looked at the box. "Does it contain something dangerous?"

"No, I just can't—"

"For the love of the sun and moon! I do not have time for this!" Misha shoved the box into my hands. The second it hit my flesh, the world shimmied for a few seconds. My fingers tightened around the box holding the phylactery as I gazed in absolute horror at Gabriel.

Before anyone could say anything, a demon opened up the fabric of being behind me, wrapped its hand around my upper arm, and yanked me with it through the gaping hole.

Chapter Twenty-five

Being summoned to Magoth is never a pleasant experience, but when he used a demon to do the summoning, it was downright sickening. The demon dropped me on the floor, where I lay fighting the urge to retch, unaware for a moment of everything but the horrible sickness caused by being yanked through a hole in reality.

The second I heard Magoth drawl, "Greetings, dragon. I assume I have the pleasure of addressing the wyvern of the silver sept," I realized two things: first, the tight feeling around my arm when the demon jerked me was due to Gabriel grabbing ahold of me (and thus being pulled along with me to Magoth's presence), and second, life as I knew it was about to cease.

"I am Gabriel Tauhou, yes. What business do you have with my mate that you must abuse her in this fashion?"

I used a chair next to me to drag myself to my feet. Gabriel looked even more battered than he had moments before, his nose bleeding again. "Don't talk to him," I begged, throwing myself toward Gabriel.

"Stop!" Magoth flicked his fingers toward me, capturing me in an invisible web that bound me where I stood. "I believe you have something of mine, sweet May. You will hand that over now."

Gabriel's eyes glittered with a burning light as he turned his gaze on the demon lord. "Release my mate."

"Don't talk to him. For the love of the gods, Gabriel, don't converse with him."

A slight frown appeared between his brows. "Are you well, mate? You seem overly distressed about a trivial matter."

"It's not trivial," I said, all but sobbing. "You have to leave, Gabriel. You have to leave now."

"I am not going to leave you by yourself," he said, a flash of disbelief in his eyes.

"You have to." I had a hard time catching my breath, but made an effort to calm my wildly beating heart. Gabriel would respond to reason—he had to. "This has nothing to do with you. Magoth cannot hold you prisoner without bringing down the wrath of the weyr upon his head. You must leave, now, before . . ." The words came to a stop. I couldn't tell him the truth, not while Magoth watched us with laughing black eyes.

"May," Gabriel said softly, taking my hands. "I thought you understood that there is nothing this demon lord can do to make you hurt me. You fear for my well-being unnecessarily. I told you that I'm incredibly difficult to kill. You really must learn to trust me."

I closed my eyes against the pain for a few seconds, my soul weeping tears of sheer agony. I wanted to scream to the heavens, to rail against the vault attendant and the pedantic rules that insisted he deliver my possessions into my hands. I wanted to destroy Magoth for the anguish he was about to wreak upon my life.

But most of all, I wanted to tell Gabriel how sorry I was, how deep into my being he had burrowed.

"Little bird, why do you cry?" he asked softly, the gentle brush of his thumb over my cheekbone so sweet, it broke down the last of my reserves, and I admitted the truth. I didn't just love him—I loved beyond all reason, with every atom of my being.

I stared at him, unable to speak the words before the abomination that was responsible for all my grief.

"As fascinating as this is, I do have an appointment in fifteen minutes," Magoth said, glancing at his watch. He stood and strolled over to where I was still bound to the floor, eyeing Gabriel curiously for a moment, clearly sizing him up. "This is what you spurned me for? Dreadlocks, sweet May? Or is it the beast within that holds such an attraction for you?"

I swallowed back a lump of hot, burning tears and met Magoth's gaze. "I will not discuss Gabriel with you."

"What is it you want of my mate?" Gabriel asked again, crossing his arms and moving a smidgen so he stood partially blocking me.

Magoth's stark black eyebrows rose at the protective gesture. "I wonder if it would be worth the trouble that would follow should I reprimand you for such insolence."

"You are welcome to try," Gabriel said pleasantly, but there was a clear warning in his eyes.

"Such temptation . . . but I believe I will be duly compensated despite refusing to give in to it. May, the phylactery." Magoth held out his hand for the box I still clutched.

Gabriel's gaze shot to me.

"Do I see a little crack in the relationship?" Magoth asked, smiling. "You look surprised, wyvern. Did you not know that your mate was charged with retrieving the phylactery for me? Ah, I see by that surprised look that you did not. How deliciously naughty of sweet May. I gather she also failed to inform you of the deal we made, whereby I would grant her a temporary cessation of her duties to the tune of a hundred years in return for the safe delivery of the phylactery."

I couldn't continue to look at Gabriel. The guilt was too much, my grief too overwhelming. My gaze dropped to my hands and stayed there until Gabriel put a finger under my chin and tilted my head back.

"Is this true?" he asked softly, hurt and confusion starkly evident in his face.

"Yes," I said without hesitation. "I told you that Magoth found out about the phylactery."

He was still for a moment, his eyes searching mine. "This release Magoth offers you—a hundred years may seem like a lot to you, but our life together will span many such centuries. To barter the phylactery for a brief moment of freedom—"

"I didn't barter it," I interrupted him. The lump was back in my throat. How could Gabriel believe I would trade temporary freedom for something that meant so much to him? "Magoth offered me that as a reward. I did not accept it."

Magoth sucked in a hissing breath, the room suddenly growing dark as if the corona of dark power that surrounded him leached all brightness from the overhead lights. "You would not dare," he said, little snakes of the power snapping around me.

Gabriel's fingers tightened around mine. "I do not understand what it is you intend to do, but I do not like this situation. We will leave now."

I nodded, suddenly wearied by the world. There was, of course, the quick way out of things, but that would leave me without Gabriel, and I wasn't willing to give him up. Not even for eternal peace. I just prayed that he felt the same way about me, because what I was about to ask him to do would go completely against the grain. "Yes. It is time to leave."

Magoth took a deep breath, his body growing in size until he stood a foot taller than Gabriel. "You would not dare!" he bellowed, and I knew that at that moment, he saw the true depth of feeling I had for Gabriel. "Think carefully, May Northcott. Do you know what the penalty is for a minion who goes dybbuk?"

"Dybbuk? What is this word? I am not familiar with it," Gabriel said, his frown growing blacker.

"I will lock you away in the darkest depths of Abaddon," Magoth warned, his voice taking on a pitch that was painful on the ears. "I will make you suffer every torment I can think of, and I assure you, minion, I have spent millennia devising tortures to bring even first-class demons to their knees begging for release."

My gut tightened, pain radiating outward from it.

"You will survive each day, living in perpetual torment, with no hope of reprieve, May Northcott. No hope whatsoever."

I nodded, my eyes on Gabriel. I wanted to drink in the sight of him until the last possible moment. Who knew when I would see him again—until then, I wanted to remember that strong jaw, the hint of indentation on his cheeks that I knew hid dimples, eyes so beautiful it almost hurt to look into them. I wanted to sear him into my memory so that no matter what happened, no matter what Magoth would do to me, I would always have the memory of Gabriel.

The man I loved more than my own life.

"Magoth, seventh principal spirit of Abaddon, lord of thirty legions, marquis of the order of dominations, I formally refute your bondage over me, and refuse your bidding. Take the phylactery," I said, turning the hand Gabriel held so that I could place the box on his palm. "It's yours. I give it to you freely."

Magoth screamed, a sound so horrible it blew out all of the windows in the room. "No! You will not do this!"

It was as if a tornado had been released around us. Magoth's fury manifested itself in the utter destruction of every nonliving thing in the room. Books exploded, furniture burst into a thousand pieces, glass and metal and wood all rained down upon us in a terrible downpour, the echoes of his scream gathering into him as he stalked toward me.

I released the box just as Gabriel understood what was happening. A look of panic filled his eyes as he tried to shove it back at me. "No, May—"

"It can't be undone," I said, wanting more than anything else to kiss him. Just one last time.

"One last—" Gabriel read my mind, his eyes going dark as the full repercussions of my act were driven home. "No. I will not allow this. Mate—"

"She is no longer your mate," Magoth snarled, jerking me out of Gabriel's reach. "She is dybbuk. She is mine to let live or destroy as I desire."

His hand was cold on my arm, an icy pain piercing my flesh and sinking deep into my soul.

Gabriel stood shaking his head for a few seconds, anger and pain and confusion taking turns on his face. "Why, little bird? Why would you do this?"

"I meant for things to be different. I meant for you to take the phylactery, so I could not be charged with an outright refusal to do Magoth's bidding. I thought there was a chance for us. I *wanted* to believe there was a chance." I let the full depth of my feelings show in my eyes, praying he could read beyond mere words to what was in my heart.

"Do you know, I've had a thought," Magoth said,

his voice suddenly normal. The hand that held me in such an icy grip relaxed, his fingers stroking an intricate path down my skin. "I originally thought to destroy you—slowly, over several centuries, so you would not be mistaken about the full depth of my wrath—but I do believe I have a better idea than even perpetual torment. I have long thought it was time to take a consort. And it would be a stupid act indeed to overlook the perfect candidate, which not so coincidentally has just dropped into my lap."

Magoth wrapped an arm around me, pulling me close to his body.

Gabriel gathered himself as if to spring, but I held up a hand to stop him, knowing without any doubt that Magoth would destroy him if he tried to free me. "Do not, Gabriel. It's not worth it."

He stopped, a stunned look of disbelief nearly bringing me to my knees. Pain unlike anything I've ever experienced lashed through me, the last fragments of my heart shattering completely. Did he not understand? Did he not see that this was the only way out for us? Did he not know just how much I was willing to give up in order to have a future together? "You wish to remain here?"

I nodded, unable to speak, searching his face for signs that he understood that this was the only way out of a very dangerous situation. I sent a mental plea to him to understand, to not take anything at face value, to know that my heart belonged to him, now and always.

"Tell me," Gabriel said, his lovely velvet voice now hoarse with emotion. "Say it, May. Say the words so that I may understand."

The effort to speak cost me more than I could have imagined. "I will stay here with Magoth. Take the phylactery. Use it to achieve your goals."

The image of him declaring that the phylactery was a treasure to be guarded, not used, was fresh in my memory, and with it, a light flashed in his eyes. I knew that at last, he understood that I had taken the only path available to save him and the dragons from Magoth's wrath. His eyes were bright with a promise, one that warmed me to the tips of my toes.

Magoth laughed, the sound causing a layer of plaster from the ceiling to crumble to our feet. "Oh, yes, this promises to be greatly amusing. A consort who was once the mate of a wyvern. Come, sweet May. We have many plans to make. Many, many plans."

I stumbled backward out of the room, my eyes on Gabriel as Magoth hauled me off. I wanted desperately to tell Gabriel that I loved him with every bit of my being, that nothing Magoth could do would ever change that, but I didn't dare. Magoth might suspect my feelings for Gabriel, but he would not act without assurance of them . . . and I would not give him the ability to destroy Gabriel.

"I will do as you ask, little bird," was all that he said as Magoth dragged me out of the doorway. Gabriel's eyes, his beautiful expressive eyes, glowed with emotion so brightly, it made my soul weep. "Just remember that I am a dragon, and I do *not* give up what is mine."

My heartache eased despite the finality of the door closing between us. I had faith in Gabriel. I had faith in us both. My life spent in the shadows was over; now it was time to step out into the light and take my place at Gabriel's side.

I took a deep breath and followed Magoth into the depths of Abaddon.

Author's Note

Fans of the dragons and Otherworld are welcome to visit both at www.dragonsepts.com, where you can play dragon games, read up on dragon history and lore, join a dragon sept or Guardians' Guild, visit with Katie and others in the message forum, listen to behind-the-scenes podcasts, consult the Otherworld Encyclopedia, and much more.

Read on for a peek at what's next
for Gabriel and May.

Up in Smoke

Coming in October 2008!

"Beautiful in is beautiful out—that's what they taught us at Carrie Fay, and I absolutely believe it's true. I mean, think about it—the sort of person you are doesn't just stay inside you, now, does it?"

Before I could sort through that odd bit of logic, a cold, wet blob smelling of earth and minerals was slathered across my mouth. "Mmmhmm," I contented myself with answering.

"I'll wipe off your lips, but no talking, sugar. We can't have you moving your mouth as the mask dries. Anyway, it's absolutely true. Just look at you, for instance!"

The petite, blond, perky woman in front of me, who had been applying an olive green clay mask to my face, stepped back to consider me. She had a small bowl in one hand, and her other hand was sheathed in a latex glove covered in the same gloop. She waved at me with the bowl. "You don't look evil in the least, and yet here you are about to wed a demon lord!"

"Sally, I'm not marrying Magoth—" I started to say, but she cut me off with a frown.

"No talking, sugar! I just told you that! Where were we? Oh, yes, how appearances can be deceiving." Her frown deepened somewhat as she eyeballed me. I squirmed in the chair, never comfortable to be the center of anyone's attention . . . with one notable exception.

My heart gave a little quiver as a familiar ache started within me at the vision that rose in my mind's eye—a man laughing with utter delight, dimples set in his beautiful latte-colored skin, his eyes flashing like quicksilver. Just the thought of him had my heart speeding up even as I mourned the fact that I hadn't seen Gabriel in more than a month.

"You look like a normal woman. I have to say that the 1920s flapper hairstyle you seem to enjoy is a bit less than mainstream—but other than that, you look perfectly normal, kind almost, not at all like you were to become Mrs. Demon Lord."

"I'm not marrying Magoth," I said without moving my lips.

"Oh, well, consort, marrying . . . it's all the same thing, isn't it? Just a smidgen more on your forehead, sugar. You need a lot of exfoliating there. Whatever have you been using on your face? No, don't answer—let the mask dry. Here, do you want to see yourself?" Sally put down her things and peeled off the glove, admiring her handiwork for a moment before offering me a mirror.

I kept my jaw clamped shut as I said slowly, moving my mouth as little as possible, "No, thanks."

She admired her own image in the mirror for a moment, fluffing up a strand of extremely styled blond hair before setting down the mirror, giving me a big sharky smile. "Well, still, you have to admit that all this is awfully romantic."

"Romantic?" I asked, my thoughts immediately turning to the dragon in human form who made my knees weak.

"Yes! Terribly so!" She must have seen the look of

confusion in my eyes, because she continued as she packed a good fifty pounds of cosmetics and accompanying items away into a small pink duffel bag. "Magoth making you his consort and giving you access to all that goes with such a position, I mean. It's so incredibly romantic that he wants you so much, he's willing to overlook the fact that you're not at all suited for the position. It just goes to show that even a demon lord has his soft side."

I rolled my eyes. "Magoth has no soft side, and he doesn't want me. Nor have I said I'd become his consort. I'm a wyvern's mate, and that is where my heart lies, not here in Abaddon with Magoth."

Sally's jaw sagged a little. "You're a wyvern's mate? The dragon kind of wyvern? The leader of—what do they call it? A dragon sept?"

"That's it," I answered, still trying not to move my mouth at all. The mask was drying, pulling my flesh taut, which didn't make it easy.

"A wyvern's mate!" She looked thoughtful for a moment. "Then what are you doing here?"

I sighed. "It's a long story, too long to tell you now, but the abridged version is that when my twin created me, I was bound to Magoth as his servant. Because I'm a doppelganger, he used me to steal items he wanted. One day I ran across Gabriel—he's the wyvern for the silver dragons—and we discovered I was his mate. Magoth found out about it and demanded I hand over a priceless dragon artifact, the Lindorm Phylactery. I refused and gave it to Gabriel instead."

Her eyes, kind of a muddy green, almost popped out of her head. "You *refused*? You went dybbuk?"

I nodded.

"Sins of Bael! But . . . you're still alive. And whole. Not to mention the fact that Magoth told me you

agreed to be his consort. Why would he say that, let
alone allow you to live *without* being in perpetual torment, if you went dybbuk?"

"Magoth is a bit . . . different," I said, only barely
stifling in time the wry smile that hovered on my lips.
"I guess he knows that being his consort is more of a
perpetual torment than anything he could do to me
physically."

"You find him unattractive?" she asked, shaking her
head in disbelief. "He's gorgeous!"

"I think he's very attractive physically. What woman
could resist those smoldering dark looks? Certainly
the women of the last century couldn't. And didn't.
You know he was a silent film star, yes?"

"Well, I know he looks kind of familiar." She
thought for a moment, then mentioned a name.

"That's him. The resemblance to his film self is
more noticeable when he wears his hair slicked back.
But regardless of his handsome exterior, the interior
gives me nightmares." I grabbed at her sleeve as she
wandered past, continuing to gather up her things.
"Sally, I know you're spending time in Abaddon as
part of your application for the empty demon lord
position, but I don't think you really understand what
things here are really like, what the demon lords are.
They may appear to be human, but they lost all shreds
of humanity long, long ago, and Magoth is no different
from any of the others . . . well, except he may be
slightly more airheaded than the rest."

"Not the biggest garbanzo in the three-bean salad?"
she asked with a smile.

I gave her a wary look. "Not even close to it, no."

"That's all right." She patted my hand for a moment,
then turned to preen in front of the black-draped mirror that sat in the room Magoth had (unwillingly) as-

signed to me. "I like my men a bit dim. Makes them easier to handle."

It was my turn to stare in disbelief, and stare I did. "It's true I don't know anything about your background other than the fact that you felt it important, for some reason completely beyond my comprehension, to try and obtain the currently vacant position of prince of Abaddon. But that aside, I think you are grossly underestimating Magoth's true nature. He's manipulative, greedy, self-centered, ruthless to the extreme, and brings new meaning to the word 'diabolical.' In short, he is everything evil you can possibly imagine . . . and so much more."

"Sweet, sweet May . . . singing my praises to the delicious Sally, are you? How thoughtful."

The voice that spoke held a note of amusement that didn't lull me into a sense of comfort. Magoth in a normal (read: evil) mood I could handle, but a playful, amused Magoth was especially dangerous.

"I'm simply telling her the truth about you," I said cautiously, turning to eye him. As a mortal, Magoth had been an incredibly handsome man, with sinfully black hair and eyes, and a seductive manner that had left women over the centuries sighing . . . those who survived his attentions, that is. Although demon lords could change their appearance to suit their whims, Magoth had never altered his, finding that his true form suited his purposes just fine.

He leaned with languid grace against the doorframe to my room, a wicked light dancing in his black eyes, his hair once again slicked back, making obvious the resemblance to his movie-star self from some ninety years before. "May I enter?" he asked now with a slightly raised eyebrow at my slowness.

"Sins of the saints, you make him ask to come into

your room?" Sally's little gasp of surprise drew Magoth's attention to her as he oiled his way in.

"It is a little game we play, my sweet May and me— she insists that I not enter her so-charming chamber without her express consent, and I pretend to go along with it. And speaking of games, shall we indulge in a threesome?" Magoth flung himself down on my bed and patted the mattress with a seductive look pointed at me. "I'll have to let May go first, since she will be my consort, but you may feel free to indulge in your wildest fantasies with me, Sally. I'm sure May won't protest if you ride me like a rented mule."

"Oh!" Sally said, shooting me a quick glace, but I was unsure whether she was startled by the thought of indulging in a threesome or by the fact that I would apparently not be bothered about my so-called lover's infidelities. "I don't . . . um . . ."

"She's not interested any more than I am," I said, coming to Sally's rescue. I would have added a frown at Magoth for lounging around on my bed, but the mask was now so tight that it prohibited movement . . . not to mention the fact that Magoth wasn't in the least concerned with whether I frowned at his actions. "Did you want something in particular?"

"If I said you, would you hold it against me?" he asked with a waggle of his eyebrows. "And by *it*, I mean your delectable self. Naked? And dabbed with just a light touch of that edible jasmine oil I had made for you?"

I crossed my arms over my chest. "Take a look at my face, Magoth. What do you see?"

"I see a woman who is trying desperately to make herself beautiful for me, and yet I already find you attractive. Did you want me to bed you wearing the facial mask? It's rather kinky, although not nearly so kinky as having you slathered in pig's grease and bound to that delightful little device I showed you in my playroom—"

I held back a shudder. "Your playroom could double as a torture museum, not that I'm going to enter it again."

"But, my sweetest of all sweet Mays, I assure you that a little tingle of electricity in clamps placed on well-oiled nipples can be stimulating in ways—"

"Will you stop?" I interrupted in a loud voice, not wanting to get him wound up again. "I am not going to sleep with you. Not now, not ever, and certainly not when there are pig's grease and nipple clamps around."

Sally sucked in another startled breath, no doubt in response to the manner in which I had addressed Magoth. "May, my dear, you must take a smidgen of advice from one who is wiser and very, very slightly older: An attitude of respect, tinged with a tiny little morsel of humility, can go a long way when dealing with those in authority."

Magoth laughed, and rose from the bed, waving a hand that had his clothing melting right off his body. "Perhaps you just need to be reminded of what it is you are so callously and ignorantly spurning, my queen?"

"I'm not your queen," I said evenly, holding back my temper.

"Oh, my!" Sally's eyes just about bugged out as she took in Magoth in all his glory. "You're . . . er . . . aroused."

He leered at her as I said, "He's *always* aroused."

"My sweet one speaks the truth," he said, glancing down with pride at his penis. "I have incredible sexual prowess and can give pleasure for hours on end."

"Hours?" Sally asked, sounding a little breathless. Her eyes went a bit misty as she gave him a very thorough visual once-over.

"His idea of pleasure isn't the same as yours and mine," I said softly, leaning in toward her.

"How do you know what I find pleasurable?" she shot back, and for a moment there was a glimpse of something in her eyes that might explain why a woman who appeared perfectly normal would suddenly decide she wanted to become a demon lord.

"I don't," I admitted. "But Magoth's form of pleasure usually holds a sting. Sometimes it's fatal."

"I haven't killed a woman with sex in days," he said with another leer, cocking a hip so his penis, tattooed with a curse put there by an unhappy lover, waved at me.

I shot him a horrified glance. He laughed again. "May, my adorable one, you're like putty in my hands. A silky-skinned, blue-eyed vixen sort of putty, but putty nonetheless. I take it my suggestion of a threesome is out?"

"Way out," I agreed.

"Ah." He glanced down at his penis in mock regret. "Perhaps the lady prefers a different color scheme? Maybe this would be more to your favor?"

His form shimmered for a moment, blurring slightly before settling down into that of a tall man with skin the color of my favorite latte, shoulder-length dreadlocks, and a close-cropped goatee and moustache framing lips that were firm, yet so very sensitive. My heart leaped in my chest, thudding madly as I beheld the vision of the man for whom I had sacrificed so much. I fisted my hands, fighting to control the urge to strike Magoth for his cruelty, knowing that he was fishing for just such a reaction from me. It took a moment, but at last I mastered my emotions and leveled him a gaze that by rights should have struck him down.

"You're not even a fraction the man Gabriel is," I told him.

"Ah, but he's not a man at all," Magoth answered, looking down at himself. He shuddered delicately and returned to his normal appearance, thankfully complete with clothing. "I tell myself that one day I will understand your preference for the silver wyvern over me, but I begin to wonder whether it is not just some perverse obstinacy on your part."

I took a deep breath, ignoring the need to lash out. My voice was as bland as I could make it as I asked, "Was there something you wanted, a threesome aside?"

"How about a threesome *astride*?" he asked hopefully.

I tightened my lips.

"That dragon has ruined you," he said with a sigh, shaking his head. "You used to be such fun. As it happens, I did have a bit of news about which I wish to inform you—"

I never heard the rest of the sentence. A faint tingling sensation swept over me for the space between seconds; then suddenly I was yanked out of the room, out of Magoth's house, clear out of Abaddon, and plopped down in the center of a familiar room.

My vision, which had blurred for a few seconds, resolved itself. A black woman with a white stripe in her shoulder-length hair leaned forward and peered at me through red glasses. "Are you all right?" she asked, concern evident in her warm brown eyes.

"I . . . yes. I think." As I was about to ask who the woman was—and, more important, how she'd gotten me out of Abaddon—a flicker of movement at the edge of my peripheral vision had me spinning around, my heart suddenly singing at the sight of the man who stood there.

"Gabriel!" I shouted, and flung myself into his arms as he ran forward to catch me.